A RICH TREASURY OF CONTEMPORARY SHORT FICTION

Gail Godwin's "Over the Mountain" offers a nostalgic and bittersweet evocation of a lonely young girl's special relationship with her mother . . . David Long's "The Last Photograph of Lyle Pettibone" takes a sharp look through a camera lens back to the Montana of 1917 and the violence of a miners' strike . . . Jayne Anne Phillips' "Bess" is a stirring, intense, coming-of-age tale about an adolescent's complex relationship with her worldly-wise younger brother . . . John Updike's "Made in Heaven" pointedly observes the path of an upwardly mobile marriage that has no room to move at the end . . . Ann Beattie's subtle, yet striking "In the White Night" explores the heartbreaking emptiness of a home after a young child has died. These are just a few of the brilliant stories that represent the very best of American fiction today.

GLORIA NORRIS has had her short stories selected for three recent *O. Henry Prize Stories* collections, as well as for *New Stories from the South: The Year's Best in 1986*. Her first novel, *Looking for Bobby*, was published in 1985. She is also co-author of *The Working Mother's Complete Handbook*, available in a Plume edition. She lives in New York.

NEW AMERICAN
SHORT STORIES

THE WRITERS SELECT THEIR OWN FAVORITES

EDITED BY GLORIA NORRIS

A PLUME BOOK
NEW AMERICAN LIBRARY
NEW YORK AND SCARBOROUGH, ONTARIO

NAL BOOKS ARE AVAILABLE AT QUANTITY DISCOUNTS WHEN USED TO PROMOTE PRODUCTS OR SERVICES. FOR INFORMATION PLEASE WRITE TO PREMIUM MARKETING DIVISION, NEW AMERICAN LIBRARY, 1633 BROADWAY, NEW YORK, NEW YORK 10019.

A hardcover edition of *New American Short Stories* has been published simultaneously by New American Library and, in Canada, The New American Library of Canada Limited.

ACKNOWLEDGMENTS

"Made in Heaven" by John Updike. This story first appeared in *The Atlantic Monthly.* Copyright © 1985 by John Updike. Reprinted by permission of the author.

"Boxes" by Raymond Carver. This story first appeared in *The New Yorker.* Copyright © 1986 by Raymond Carver. Reprinted by permission of the author.

"The Starlight Express" by Ellen Gilchrist. This story first appeared in *Cosmopolitan.* Copyright © 1986 by Ellen Gilchrist. Reprinted by permission of Don Congdon Associates, Inc.

"Sweethearts" by Richard Ford. This story first appeared in *Esquire.* Copyright © 1986 by Richard Ford. Reprinted by permission of the author.

"We are Norsemen" by T. Coraghessan Boyle. This story first appeared in *Harper's.* Copyright © 1978 by T. Coraghessan Boyle. Reprinted by permission of Georges Borchardt, Inc.

"Blight" by Stuart Dybek. This story first appeared in *Chicago Magazine.* Copyright © 1985 by Stuart Dybek. Reprinted by permission of the author.

"The Most Girl Part of You" by Amy Hempel. This story first appeared in *Vanity Fair.* Copyright © 1986 by Amy Hempel. Reprinted by permission of the author.

"Miles City, Montana" by Alice Munro. From *The Progress of Love* by Alice Munro. Copyright © 1985 by Alice Munro. Reprinted by permission of Alfred A. Knopf, Inc., and McClelland and Stewart Ltd.

"The Last Photograph of Lyle Pettibone" by David Long. This story first appeared in *Antaeus.* Copyright © 1985 by David Long. Reprinted by permission of the author.

"Escapes" by Joy Williams. Copyright © 1985 by Joy Williams. This story first appeared in *Chicago.* Reprinted by permission of the author.

"Solomon's Seal" by Mary Hood. From *How Far She Went* by Mary Hood. Copyright © 1984 by Mary Hood. Reprinted by permission of the University of Georgia Press.

(The following page constitutes an extension of this copyright page.)

PLUME TRADEMARK REG. U.S. PAT. OFF. AND FOREIGN COUNTRIES
REG. TRADEMARK—MARCA REGISTRADA
HECHO EN HARRISONBURG, VA., U.S.A.

SIGNET, SIGNET CLASSIC, MENTOR, ONYX, PLUME, MERIDIAN and NAL BOOKS are published *in the United State* by NAL PENGUIN INC., 1633 Broadway, New York, New York 10019, *in Canada* by The New American Library of Canada Limited, 81 Mack Avenue, Scarborough, Ontario M1L 1M8

Library of Congress Cataloging-in-Publication Data

New American short stories.

1. Short stories, American. 2. American fiction—20th century. I. Norris, Gloria.
PS648.S5N36 1986 813′.01′08 86-23447
ISBN 0-453-00518-7
ISBN 0-452-25879-0 (pbk.)

Designed by Fritz Metsch

First Printing, January, 1987

3 4 5 6 7 8 9 10 11

PRINTED IN THE UNITED STATES OF AMERICA

CONTENTS

NEW AMERICAN
SHORT STORIES

THE WRITERS SELECT THEIR OWN FAVORITES

INTRODUCTION

I have long observed that writers make perceptive critics, knowing as they do the machinery of writing from the inside. And as I read and enjoy a fine story, I often—as I believe other readers do—wonder about how it came to be created. When I was asked to assemble a collection of new American stories, I decided to make use of both beliefs and involve the writers themselves in the selection.

First I selected a number of writers whose work I admire and who span a range of sensibilities and styles. My choices include such gifted and recognized practitioners as Alice Adams, Alice Munro, and John Updike. They also include writers, such as Raymond Carver and Joy Williams, whose innovations have added new dimensions to the short story. And they additionally include writers like Robley Wilson, Jr., and Stuart Dybek, whose stories have not yet won the readership they deserve.

I asked these writers to select one or several stories of their own, published in the last three years, that they felt deeply attached to or that represented their best work. In some cases, I selected a story I greatly admired and solicited that particular story. Then I weeded out stories that had already been widely read, and I asked each writer to comment on the story chosen.

I'd expected that a writer's favorite story would be typical of his work—would be an especially successful rendering of the characters and conflicts he usually deals with. This did not prove to be the case. Instead I quickly saw that writers remain attached to a particular story primarily for two reasons. The first is that the story forced the writer to do something new: it enabled him to write about a new subject, spurred a technical innovation, or, for reasons that are still unclear, stimulated a new burst of writing. The second—and equally common—reason is that the story was extraordinarily hard to write and caused the writer a great deal of pain.

Though American writers are credited with developing the short story to its highest and most varied expression, many readers today complain that the form has been terribly narrowed in subject. Indeed, it does sometimes seem that the protagonist one keeps meeting in story after story is an upper-middle-class person residing in a major East or West Coast city and just undergoing a divorce or in the middle of a love affair. Happily the stories here do not merit such complaints.

The twenty stories in this collection are set in Georgia, Wyoming, Montana (three take place in that state), Iowa, the state of Washington, Maine, North Carolina, Tennessee, West Virginia, California, Boston, and Chicago. Not one is set in my own city of New York, and many are from the traditional American heartland of small town and farm.

The characters speak from variegated experiences, demonstrating the wonderful diversity of American life that is often obscured in our TV fare of homogenized sitcoms and commercials reducing us to genial Grandpop, bumbling Dad, and Mom-obsessed-with-oven-cleaning. The voices of these stories range from John Updike's successful Episcopal broker in Boston to Stuart Dybek's rowdy, restless teenagers in a seedy neighborhood in Chicago; from the isolated and dislocated mother of Raymond Carver's West to Gail Godwin's southern child growing up in a world dense with connections to the past.

These stories show that, far from fixating on a current contemporary type, these writers are energetically exploring both the traditional and the changing shapes of life in our times. And the skill and art with which they do that shows them to be among the most gifted short-story writers working today. Those who read with an eye to writing themselves will also find inspiration in the highly developed techniques and tools for telling a story that these writers employ.

This does not mean that each does everything according to prescribed form. Theorists of the short story generally agree that the form demands a compact action bound by a short time-span. Henry James warned that the short story is limited by its compression in how much it can show the passage of time and its complex effect on character. (Indeed he grumbled that if writers really *understood* how hard it is to condense time in art, they'd be more terrified of trying.) John Updike's "Made in Heaven" defies that notion and boldly covers nearly fifty years that gradually change the lives of a couple and their city of Boston around them. The husband and wife move up and up financially and out to Newton; FDR, Truman, Eisenhower, Kennedy, and Carter in turn become president; the city fills with skyscrapers. Meanwhile, their own deep conflict runs under the surface of their seemingly happy marriage and forms the tension of the story. Updike comments in his afterword to the story, "It is not easy, for a short story, to contain time and to display its abyss," and then, in a fascinating peek into the machinery of writing technique, reveals how his repetition and contrast of certain images help achieve a time span that the short story supposedly shouldn't reach for.

Coming next on Alice Adams's "Sintra," I was struck by how her story—also about the loss that time inevitably visits on us—is similar in theme to Updike's, but develops quite differently. "Sintra" mainly deals with only one day in the life of Arden, a San Francisco art critic who is on vacation in Portugal with her younger lover, Gregor. But the memories of her earlier love affair with a Portuguese painter, Luiz, steadily become more vivid and real than Gregor's presence. Instead of proceeding chronologically, as Updike does, this story allows the past to invade the present.

Gail Godwin's "Over the Mountain" also spans a long time in a life. Her "I," who introduces the story as a grown woman, provides a kind of long-shot opening view of the child who is the chief actor in the story, and this view of the mature "I" gives meaning and depth to the child's still ambiguous experiences. Alice Munro's narrator in "Miles City, Montana" does not speak to us as a separate person as does Godwin's, but it is clear that the narrator is telling the story with the insight of someone long past the experiences of childhood and young-motherhood, which have now become connected. Neither of these approaches is revolutionary, of course; rather, it is inspiring to see how these techniques, in the hands of talented writers, still work freshly and provide a credible means for the story to show us much in a short space.

Writers often say that a story only comes to life when they get the "voice" in which to tell it. In these stories there is an abundant variety of voices, showing the almost infinite shadings of tone, vision, and particularity that make a writer unique. I use "voice" to mean the unquantifiable amalgam of emotional tone, imagery, and diction that convey the feeling of an unique teller, just as we get it from meeting a stranger and hearing him talk. There may be only a limited number of basic human experiences and universal themes to write about; it is finally the voices of writers that makes reading each like entering a different world.

Raymond Carver's "Boxes," which deals with the fragility of love and human connection, depicts a man's efforts to remain close to his mother, whose perpetual sense of being abused and unloved drives him away. The story is all the more moving for being told in so level, exact, and undemonstrative a voice. The final image of a porch light briefly flickering on, and then going dark, beautifully sums up the story and holds great emotional power.

Mary Hood's "Solomon's Seal" traces the lifelong combat between a country wife and her husband, neither of whom will bend to the other's ways. (She gardens; he keeps dogs.) Hood's is a deadly accurate and clear voice; it is as though she possesses the ice-cold center of each character's self. I believe it is this voice of revelation that keeps the story from being grim, even through the couple's bitter estrangement—and the wife's final, terrible decision not to cry over his new happiness, which excludes her.

"Sweethearts," by Richard Ford, is told in the tightly controlled voice of a man who has been cruelly disappointed but is determined to start over. Yet this voice is capable of revealing the complicated emotions of a man and woman—lovers who are starting a new life—as they take her ex-husband to jail. They sympathize, but fear his failure will taint their tentative bond.

T. Coraghessan Boyle's Norse skald blithely but bitingly relates the raids of his murderous tribesmen on Atlantic shores in a voice that manages simultaneously to evoke his own time and ours. Yet Boyle makes this original combination work—and gives us a vision of history's tragic repetition.

There are three other historical stories in this collection, and how differently they each bring the past to life! Robert Taylor, Jr's., "The Tennessee War of the Roses" chronicles the 1886 Tennessee gubernatorial campaign, in which two of his great-great-uncles ran against each other, campaigning side by side from the same buggy and sometimes trading speeches. Taylor's male forebears were gifted fiddle players, and his style of evoking the past reminds us of fiddle music with its verses that hauntingly echo and repeat.

Jayne Anne Phillip's "Bess" creates a West Virginia girl and her intense, subliminally sexual relationship with her brother Warwick through lyrical language and a series of dreamlike scenes that include an accidentally witnessed act of adult sex and Warwick's walking naked on a wire.

David Long's "The Last Photograph of Lyle Pettibone" takes place in Montana in 1917 and uses the perfect witness to show a conflict between mine owners and Wobblies at the outbreak of World War I. Willy, a budding photographer with a new Brownie Autographic, is a young man with no fixed views of the political and patriotic conflicts going on and is thus more able than his townspeople in Stillwater, Montana, to understand the motives and ultimate tragedy of a Wobbly organizer. Moreover, Willy's craft as photographer makes him the only witness who can document a crime that is elaborately staged. But Willy, like witnesses in most good stories, turns out not to be just an observer, but the chief character of the story.

Young people face critical choices in several of these stories. In "Blight," Stuart Dybek's David, Zig Zilinsky, Pepper Rosado, and Deejo—the teenage peer group of a Mexican-Polish neighborhood—lust after women, music, and fame. Their slice of Chicago is invaded by Mayor Daley's politicians on the take, deafened by 1950s rock and roll, and peopled by paunchy Korean War vets still trying to act as neighborhood heroes in the local taverns. Still, Dybek's teenagers find joy and promise amid official blight, and the ending, which preserves a warm and safe place from youth for David, will not be forgotten.

In "The Most Girl Part of You," Amy Hempel uses a short short story (though, she says, it's long for her) to show a girl waiting breathlessly for her boyfriend to initiate her into love. The seduction may be bizarre, but Hempel's ability to combine convincingly the outlandish with adolescent vulnerability is remarkable.

Stephen Minot's Fern in "The Seawall" has at fifteen taken on the responsibility for the relationships among the disorderly and spoiled adults around her, including her parents, stepmother, stepfather, and stepbrother. To do that, Fern must grow up fast. Minot says, "It isn't easy to grow up fast. It's kind of a combat experience. With luck you survive—a veteran of sorts—but not without damage."

Not without damage. That is the message of Joy Williams' "Escapes," a story almost hypnotic in its tension. It tells of a girl and her unhappy, alcoholic mother, ending in a magically compressed line about time and its abyss.

Two stories might have been taken out of news headlines—something that fiction rarely does these days, probably because television uses up events and reduces their complexities by endless exposure and thirty-second analyses. At best, an event becomes a TV movie of the week, where child abuse, wife beating or abortion all become miraculously resolved into simple misunderstanding and liberal goodwill by the last commercial.

Robley Wilson, Jr.'s, "Payment in Kind" presents an Iowa farm wife struggling against her husband's anger and defeat over the collapse of their life's work. They are squeezed between a new U.S. farm program and the demands of environmentalists who consider they have as much right to the land as those who have worked it for generations. But Wilson raises this story above topical interest by creating a complex and fully realized woman at the heart of the action.

In "Nights and Days," Ernest J. Finney's young cashier at a convenience store could have stepped out of headlines about yesterday's holdup. But the story is really about his uneasy teetering between his pseudo-fatherly macho boss, his carping mother, and his dismal girl friend. We see here a person who can be pushed to violence or saved by his own inner values, uncertain and fragile though they are.

Ellen Gilchrist's "The Starlight Express" is unusual in that it carries forward a character Gilchrist has starred in four earlier stories. Nora Jane was first met in New Orleans at nineteen, but she's long since left the South and made a new life in California. She's a new kind of southern heroine, for she has kept no baggage from her past.

"In the White Night" by Ann Beattie has one of the best endings I've read. It conveys the grief of a couple whose daughter has died and does so in one great image in which their feelings and those of the reader coalesce.

John E. Wideman's "Surfiction" is an ironic story that pokes fun at the illusion of fiction. It begins as an earnest, professorial effort to dissect the lies of fiction. Wideman's professor dutifully analyzes the tricks: the seductive narrative voice that makes us believe *it* is real; the careful setting of scene with suspense, making us wait eagerly to know what will happen. But behind his pompous front, Wideman's professor shows slips of confidence. He solemnly (and comically) footnotes his own journal as written in "many hands." Before the story ends, the professor wins us just as the character of any conventional story does: by entertaining us so intriguingly and by showing himself as another human being caught in dilemma—in his case, an inability to write that finally resembles nothing so much as a man kicking a lawnmower that won't turn over.

In the excellent guide *Writing in General and the Short Story in Particular,* editor Rust Hills discusses the critical moment, as he calls it, when action, theme, language, and characterization must come together and convincingly show the heroine or hero in a moment of change. Or, as Hills points out, it may be the moment when the character *loses* his last chance to change. This moment, when the story's meaning is revealed, often causes the writer the most trouble. Will the change seem too pat? Too contrived? Will the mystery of behavior, of what makes us as we are, be revealed afresh? For me, the success of this moment is what makes a short story either ephemeral or lasting. To my mind, each of the stories that follows successfully brings this moment off.

All kinds of people confront their lives and make choices. And as they do, they enlarge our own experience and understanding of life.

—Gloria Norris
New York City

JOHN UPDIKE

MADE IN HEAVEN

Brad Schaeffer was attracted to Jeanette Henderson by her Christianity; at an office Christmas party, in Boston in the thirties, in one of those eddies of silence that occur amid gaiety like a swirl of backwater in a stream, he heard her crystal-clear voice saying, "Why, the salvation of my soul!"

He looked over. She was standing by the window, pinned between a hot radiator and Arthur Gleb, the office Romeo. Outside, behind the black window, it had begun to snow, and the lighted windows of the office building across Milk Street were blurring and fluttering. Jeanette had come to the brokerage house that fall, a tidy secretary in a pimento wool suit, with a prim ruffled blouse. For this evening's event she had essayed open-toed shoes and a dress of lavender gabardine, with zigzag pleats marked at their points by flattened bows. The flush the party punch had put in her cheeks and throat helped him see for the first time the something highly polished about her compact figure, an impression of an object finely made, down to the toenails that peeked through the tips of her shoes. Her profile showed pert and firm as she strained to look up into Arthur's overbearing, beetle-browed, darkly suffused face. Brad stepped over to them, into the steamy warmth near the radiator. The snow was intensifying; across the street the golden windows were softening like pats of butter.

Jeanette's face turned to her rescuer. She was lightly sweating. The excited blush of her cheeks made the blue of her eyes look icy. "Arthur was saying," she appealed, "that only money matters!"

"Then I asked this crazy little gal what mattered to her," Arthur said, giving off heat through his black serge suit. A sprig of mistletoe, pale and withering, had been pinned to his lapel.

"And I told him the first thing I could think of," Jeanette said. Her hair, waved and close to her head, was a soft brown that tonight did not look mousy. "Of course a lot of things matter to me," she hurried on, "more than money."

"Are you Catholic?" Brad asked her.

This was a question of a more serious order than Arthur's badinage. Her face composed itself; her voice became secretarial, factual. "Of course not. I'm a Methodist."

Brad felt relief. He was free to love her. In Boston, an aspiring man did not love Catholics, even if he came from Ohio with the name of Schaeffer.

"Did I sound so silly?" she asked, when Arthur had gone off in search of another cup of punch and another little gal.

"Unusual, but not silly." In his heart Brad did not expect capitalism to last another decade, and it would take with it what churches were left; he assumed religion was already as dead as Marx and Mencken claimed. There was a gloom in the December streets, and in the statistics that came to the office, that made the cheer of Christmas carols sound obscene. From the deep doorways of Boston's business buildings, ornamented like little Gothic chapels, people actually starving peered out, too bitter and numb to beg. Each morning the Common was combed for frozen bodies.

"I *do* believe," Jeanette told him. The contrast between her blue eyes and rosy, glazed skin had become almost garish. "Ever since I can remember, even before anything was explained to me. It seems so natural, so necessary. Do you think that's strange?"

"I think that's lovely," he told her.

By Lententide they were going together to church. It was his idea, to accompany her; he loved seeing her in new settings, in the new light each placed her in. At work she was drab and brisk, a bit aloof from the other "girls," with a dry way of pursing her lips into crinkles that made her look older than she was. At her ancestral home in Framingham, with her parents and brothers, she became girlish and slightly drunk on family atmosphere, as she had been on punch; he greedily inhaled the spicy air of this old house, with its worn Orientals and sofas of leather and horsehair, knowing that this was the aroma of her childhood. On the streets and in restaurants, Jeanette was perfectly the lady, like a figure etched on a city scene, making him, in their scenic anonymity, a gentleman, an escort, a gallant. Her smiling face gleamed, and the satin lapels of her blue wool coat, and the pointed tips of her shiny black boots. Involuntarily his arm encircled her waist at crossings, and he could not let go even when they had safely crossed the street. Her bearing was so nicely honed in every move—the pulling off, for instance, finger by finger, of her kid gloves in Locke-Ober's—that Brad would sometimes clown or feign clumsiness just to crack her composed expression with a blush or a grimace. He was afraid that otherwise he might slip from her mind. It did not occur to him, when, during a rapt *pianissimo* moment in Symphony Hall, he nudged her and whispered a joke, that he was rending something precious to her, invading a fragile feminine space. In church, he loved standing tall at her side and hearing her frail, crystalline voice lift up the words of the hymns. He basked in her gravity, which had something shy about it, and even uncertain, as if she feared an excess of feeling might leap from the musty old forms and overwhelm her. He knew the forms; he had been raised as a Presbyterian, though only his mother attended services, and then only on those Sundays when she wasn't needed in the fields or at the barn. Jeanette had resisted, at first, his accompanying her. It would be, she murmured, distracting. And it was true; her shy, uncertain reverence made him, perversely, want to turn and hug her and lift her up with a shout of pride and animal gladness.

He was twenty-eight, and she was twenty-five—old enough that marriage might have slipped her by. Her composure, the finished neatness of her figure, already seemed a touch old-maidenly. She shared rooms with another young woman on Marlborough Street; he lived on Joy, on the dark, Cambridge Street side of Beacon Hill. She had been going to church at the brick Copley Methodist over on Newbury Street, with its tall domed bell tower and its Byzantine gold-leaf ceiling. Brad found within an easy walk of his own apartment—down Chambers Street as it curved, and then up a little court opposite the Mayhew School—a precious oddity, a Greek Revival clapboard church tucked among the brick tenements of the West End. Built by the Unitarians in the 1830s and taken over by the Wesleyans during their post–Civil War resurgence, the little building had box pews, small leaded panes of gray glass, and an oak pulpit shaped somewhat like a bass viol. Brad was to remember with special fondness coming here with Jeanette for the Wednesday-night Lenten services, on raw spring nights when the east wind was bringing the smell of brine in from the harbor. The narrow dim streets bent and resounded as they imagined old quarters in Europe did; the young couple walked through the babble and the cooking odors of Jewish and Italian and Lithuanian families, and then came to this closet of Protestantism, this hushed vacant space—scarcely a dozen heads in the pews, and the church so chilly that overcoats were left on. There was no choir, and each shift of weight on a pew seat rang out like a cough. Perhaps Brad was still an unbeliever at that point, for he relished (as if he were whispering a joke to Jeanette) the emptiness, the chill, the pathos of the aged minister's trite and halting sermon as once again the old clergyman, set down to die in this dying parish, led his listeners along the worn path to the Crucifixion and the bafflement beyond. During these pathetic sermons Brad's mind would range wonderfully far, a falcon scouting his future, while Jeanette sat at his side, compact and still and exquisite. She would lift him up, he felt. In the virtual vacancy of this old meetinghouse she seemed most intimately his.

Roosevelt was newly president then, and Curley was still mayor; their boasts came true, the country survived. The precious little hollow church, with its wooden Ionic columns and viol-shaped pulpit, was swept away in the fifties with the tenements of the West End. By this time Brad and

Jeanette had moved with their children to Newton and become Episcopalians.

On their wedding night, hoping to please her, he had held her body in his arms and prayed aloud. He thanked God for bringing them together, and asked that they be allowed to live fruitful and useful lives together. The prayer in time was answered, though on this occasion it did little to relax Jeanette. Always his love of her, when distinctly professed, made her a little reserved and tense, as if a certain threat were being masked, and a trap might be sprung.

Their four children were all born healthy, and Brad's four years as a naval officer passed with no more injury to him than the devastating impression the black firmament of spattered stars made when seen from the flight deck of an aircraft carrier, in the middle of the Pacific. How little, little to the point of nothingness, he was under those stars! Even the great ship, the *Enterprise,* that held him a tall building's height above the silvery-black swells, was reduced to the size of a pinpoint in such a perspective. And yet, it was he who was witnessing the stars; they knew nothing of themselves, so in this dimension he was greater than they. As far as he could reason, religion begins with this strangeness, this standstill; faith tips the balance in favor of the pinpoint. So, though he had never had Jeanette's smiling intuitions or sensations of certainty, he became in his mind a believer.

Ten years later, in the mid-fifties, he suggested they become Episcopalians, because the church was handier to the Newton house—a shingled, many-dormered affair full of corridors for vanished servants and with even a cupola. Narrow stairs wound up to a small round room that became Jeanette's "retreat." She installed rugs and pillowed furniture, did crocheting and watercolors. From its curved windows one could see to the east the red warning light topping the spire of the John Hancock Building. Brad did not need to say that his associates and clients tended to be Episcopalians, and that this church held more of the sort of people they would like to get to know. Although he never quite grew accustomed to the droning wordiness of the service, and the awkward and repetitive kneeling, he did love the look of the congregation—the ruddy men with their blue blazers and ever-fresh haircuts, the sleek Episcopal women with their furs in winter and in summer their wide pastel garden hats that showed the backs of their necks when they bowed their heads. He loved Jeanette among them, in her black silk dress and the strand of real pearls, each costing as much as a refrigerator, with which he had paid tribute to their twentieth anniversary. Money gently glimmered on her fingers and ears. All capitalism had needed, it had turned out, was an infusion of war. The postwar stock market climbed; even plumbers and grocers needed a stockbroker now. Shares Brad had picked up for peanuts in the Depression doubled in value, and redoubled every few years.

Jeanette never took quite as active a role in the life of the church as he had expected. He himself taught Sunday school, passed the plate, sat on the vestry, read the lesson. It was like an extension of his business life; he felt at home in the committee room, in the linoleum-floored offices and robing rooms that mere worshipers never saw. There was always some practical reason for him to be at the church Sunday mornings, whereas in growing season Jeanette often stayed home to garden, much as Brad's mother had worked in the fields. Her body had added a sturdy plumpness to that polished, glossy quality that had first enchanted him. Her Christianity, as he imagined it, was, like water sealed into an underground cistern, unchangingly pure. Standing beside her in church, hearing her small true voice lifted in song, he still felt empowered by her fineness, so that in the jostle after the service his arm involuntarily crept around her waist, and he would let go only to shake the minister's overworked hand.

"I wish you wouldn't paw me in church," she said one Sunday as they drove home. "We're too middle-aged."

"I wasn't so much pawing you as steering you through the mob," he offered, embarrassed.

"I don't *need* to be steered," Jeanette said. She tried to

stamp her foot, but the gesture was ineffectual on the carpeted car floor.

Here we are, Brad thought, in our beige Mercedes coming home from church, having a quarrel; and he had no idea why. He saw them from afar, with the eyes of aspiration, like a handsome mature couple in a four-color ad, and there was no imperfection in the picture. "If I can't help touching you," he said, "it's because I still love you. Isn't that good?"

"It is," she said sulkily, then added, "Are you sure it's me you love or just some idea you have of me?"

This seemed to Brad a finicking distinction. She was positing a "real" her, a person apart from the one he was married to. But who would this be, unless it was the woman who took a cup of tea and went up the winding stairs to her cupola at odd hours? This woman disappeared. And no sooner did she disappear, when he was home, than two children began fighting, or the dry cleaner's delivery truck pulled into the driveway, and she had to be called down again.

"Did it ever occur to you," she asked now, "that you love me because it suits you? That for you it's an exercise in male power?"

"My God," he said indignantly, "who have you been reading? Would you rather I loved you because it *didn't* suit me?"

"That would be more romantic," she admitted, in her smallest, tidiest voice, and he knew this was a conciliatory joke, and their mysterious lapse of harmony would be smoothed away.

He became head of the vestry, and spent hours at the church, politicking, soothing ruffled feathers. After the last of the children had been confirmed and excused from faithful attendance, Jeanette began to go to the eight o'clock service, before Brad was fully awake. She would return, shiny-faced, just as he was settling, a bit foggy and hung over, to a second cup of coffee and the sheaves of the Sunday *Globe.* She loved the lack of a sermon, she said, and the absence of that oppressive choir with those Fred Waring–like arrangements. She did not say that she enjoyed being by herself in church, as she had been in Boston many years ago. At the ten o'clock service, he missed her, the thin sweet piping of her singing beside him. He felt naked, as when alone on the deck of the imperiled *Enterprise*. He explained to Jeanette that he would happily push himself out of bed and go with her to the eight o'clock, but the committee people he had to talk to expected him to be at the ten o'clock. She relented, gradually, and resumed her place at his side. But she complained at the length of the sermon, and winced when the choir came on too strong. Brad wondered if their sons, who had become more or less anti-establishment, and incidentally antichurch, had infected her with their rebellion.

Ike was president, and then JFK. Joseph Kennedy, when Brad was young, had been a man to gossip about in Boston financial circles—a cocky mick with the bad taste not only to make a pot of money but then to leave Boston and head up the SEC under Roosevelt and his raving liberals. The nuances of the regional Irish-Yankee feud escaped and amused Brad, since to his midwestern eyes the two hostile camps were very similar—thin-skinned, clubby men from damp green islands, fond of a nip and long, malicious stories. Though Brad eventually lived all his adult life in and around Boston, he never could catch the accent, never bring himself to force his *a*'s and to say "Cuber" and "idear" the way the young president did so ringingly on television.

With their own young, the Schaeffers were lucky—the boys were a bit too old to fall into the heart of the drugs craze, and the girls were safely married before just living together became fashionable. One boy didn't finish college and became a carpenter in Vermont; the other did finish, at Amherst, but then moved to the West Coast to live. The two girls, however, stayed in the area, and provided new grandchildren at regular intervals. Brad's wedding-night prayer was, to all appearances, still being answered.

As the sixties wore into the seventies, some misfortunes

befell the Schaeffers as well as the country. Both daughters went through messy divorces, involving countersuing husbands, scandalous depositions, and odd fits of nocturnal violence on the weedless lawns and in the neo-colonial bedrooms of Wellesley and Dover. Freddy, the son on the West Coast, never could seem to get what would be called a job; he was always "in" things—in real estate, in public relations, in investments—without ever drawing a salary or making, as far as Brad could figure, a profit. Like Brad, Freddy had turned gray early, and suddenly there he was, well over thirty, a gray-haired boy, sweet-natured and with gracious, expensive tastes, who had never found his way into the economy. It worried Jeanette that to keep him going out there they were robbing the other children, especially the carpenter son, who by now had become a condo contractor and part-owner of a ski resort. They were grieved but at some level not surprised when poor Freddy was found dead in Glendale, of what was called an accidental drug overdose. A cocaine habit had backed him, financially, to the wall. He was found neatly dressed in a blue blazer and linen slacks—to the end, a gentleman, something Brad, in his own mind, had never become.

The Newton house huge and empty around them, the couple talked of moving to an apartment, but it seemed easier to turn off the radiators in a few rooms and stay where they were. Amid the ramparts of familiar furniture were propped and hung photographs of the children at happy turning points—graduations, marriages, trips abroad. This grinning, tinted population extended now into the third generation, and was realer, more present, than the intermittent notes and phone calls from the children themselves. Brad knew in the abstract that he had changed diapers, driven boys to hockey and girls to ballet, supervised bedtime prayers, paternally stood by while tears were being shed and games were being played and the traumas of maturation endured; yet he could not muster much actual sensation of parenthood—those years were like a television sitcom during which he sat watching himself play the father.

More vivid, returning in such unexpected detail that his eyes stung and the utter lostness of it all made him gasp, were moments of his and Jeanette's Boston days in the L-shaped apartment on St. Botolph Street and then in the fifth-floor Commonwealth Avenue place with its leaky skylight and birdcage elevator, and of old times at the firm, before it moved from the walnut-paneled offices on Milk Street to a flimsy, flashy new skyscraper on State. Certain business epiphanies—workday afternoons when an educated guess paid off in spades, or a carefully cultivated friendship produced a big commission—could still put the taste of triumph into his mouth. Fun like that had fled in the business when the sixties bull market had collapsed. The people he had looked up to, the crusty Yankee money managers, had all retired. Brad himself retired at the age of sixty-eight, the same summer that Nixon resigned. In his loneliness those first months, in his guilty unease at being out of business uniform, he would visit Jeanette in her cupola.

She did not say she minded, but everything seemed to halt when he climbed the last, pie-slice-shaped steps, so the room had the burnished silence of a clock that has just stopped ticking. She sat surrounded by windows, lit from all sides, her soft brown hair scarcely touched by gray and the wrinkles of her face none of them deep, so that her head seemed her youthful head, softened by a webbed veil. The rug she had been hooking was set in its frame at the side of her armchair, and a magazine lay in her lap, but she did not seem to be doing anything—so deeply engaged in gazing out a window through the tops of the beeches that she did not even move her head at his entrance. Her motionlessness slightly frightened him. He stood a second, getting his breath. Where just the tip of the old Hancock Building had once showed above the treetops, now a silvery cluster of tall glass boxes reflected the sun. He had always been nervous in high places, and as his eyes plunged down, parallel with her gaze, through the bare winter branches toward the dead lawn three stories below, his bowels tightened and he shuffled self-protectively toward the center of the room.

Since she said nothing, he asked, "Do you feel all right?"

"Of course," Jeanette answered, firmly. "Why wouldn't I?"

"I don't know, my dear. You seem so quiet."

"I like being quiet. I always have. You know that."

"Oh yes." He felt challenged, and slightly dazed. "I know that."

"So let's think of something for you to do," she said, at last turning, with one of her usual neat motions, to give him her attention. And she would send him back down, down to the basement, say, to reglaze a storm window a neighbor child had broken with a golf ball. It was strange, Brad reflected, that in this room of her own Jeanette had hung no pictures of the children, or of him. But then, there was little wall space between the many windows, and the cushioned window seats, two-thirds of the way around the room, were littered with old paintings, crocheted cushions, and books whose cloth covers the circling sun had bleached. He thought of it as her meditation room, though he had no clear idea of what meditation was; in even the silent seconds inserted between rote petitions at church, his own brain skidded off into that exultant plotting which divine service stimulated in him.

Her illness came on imperceptibly at first, and then with cruel speed. They were watching television one night—the hostages had been taken in Iran, and every day it seemed something *had* to happen. Suddenly Jeanette put her hand on his wrist. They were sitting side by side on the red upholstered Hepplewhite-style settee, or love seat, that they had impulsively bought at Paine's in the late forties, during a blizzard, before the move to Newton. Because of the storm, the vast store was nearly empty, and it seemed they must do something to justify their presence, and to celebrate the weather. His love for her always returned full force when it snowed. "What?" he asked now, startled by her unaccustomed gesture.

"Nothing." She smiled. "A tiny pain."

"Where?" he asked, monosyllabic as if just awakened.

The news at that moment showed an interview with a young Iranian revolutionary who spoke fluent, midwestern-accented English, and Jeanette's exact answer escaped Brad. If in the course of their marriage there was one act for which he blamed himself, could identify as a sin for which he deserved to be punished, it was this moment of inattention, when Jeanette first, after weeks of hugging her discomforts to herself, began to confide, in her delicate voice, what she would rather have kept hidden.

The days that followed, full of doctors and their equipment, lifted all secrecy from the disease and its course. It was cancer, metastasizing from the liver, though she had never been a drinker. For Brad these days were busy ones; after the five years of retirement, of not knowing quite what to do with himself, he was suddenly housekeeper, cook, chauffeur, switchboard operator, nurse. Isolated in their big house, while their three children anxiously visited and then hurried back to their own problems, and their friends and neighbors tried to tread the thin line between kindness and interference, the couple that winter had a kind of honeymoon. An air of adventure, of the exotic, tinged their excursions to clinics and specialists tucked into sections of Boston they had never visited before. They spent all their hours together, and became more than ever one. His own scalp itched as her soft hair fell away under the barrage of chemotherapy; his own stomach ached when she would not eat. She would greet with a bright smile the warmth and aroma of the food he brought to the table or her bed, and she would take one forkful, so she could tell him how good it was; then, with a magical slowness meant to make the gesture invisible, Jeanette would let the fork slowly sink back to the plate, keeping her fingers on the silver handle as if at any moment she might decide to use it again. In this position she sometimes even dozed off, under the sway of medication. Brad learned to treat her not eating as a social lapse he must overlook. If he urged the food upon her, sternly or playfully, real anger, of the petulant sudden kind that a child harbors, would break through her stoical, drugged calm.

The other irritant, strangely, seemed to be the visits of the young Episcopal clergyman. He had come to the church this year, after the long reign of a hearty facetious man no one had had to take seriously. The new man possessed a self-conscious, honey-smooth voice, and curly blond hair already receding, young as he was, back from his temples. Brad, who of course knew of the infighting amid the search-committee members that had preceded his selection, admired his melodious sermons and his conservative demeanor; ten years ago a clergyman his age would have been trying to radicalize everybody. But Jeanette complained that his visits to the house tired her, though they rarely extended for more than fifteen minutes. When she became too frail, too emaciated and constantly drowsy, to leave her bedroom, and the young man offered to bring Communion to her, she asked Brad to tell him, "Another time."

The room at Mass. General Hospital to which she was eventually moved overlooked, across a great air well, a brick wall of windows identical with hers. The wing was modern, built on the rubble of the old West End. It was late March, the first spring of a new decade. Though on sunny days a few giggling nurses and hardy patients took their lunches on cardboard trays out to the patio at the base of the air well, the sky was usually an agitated gray and the hospital heat was turned way up. During his visits Brad often removed his suit coat, it was so hot in Jeanette's room.

Dressed in a white hospital johnny and a pink quilted bed jacket with ribbons, she looked pretty against her pillows, though on a smaller scale than the woman he had known so long. Her cheeks still had some plumpness, and her fine straight nose and clear eyes and narrow arched brows—old-fashioned eyebrows that looked plucked, though they weren't—still made the compact, highly finished impression that had always excited him, her tidy face like a kindling within him. Her hair was growing back, a cap of soft brown bristle, since chemotherapy had been abandoned. Only her hands, laid inert and fleshless on the blanket, betrayed that something terrible was happening to her.

One day she told him, with a touch of mischief, "Our young parson was in from Newton this morning, and I told him not to bother anymore."

"You sent the priest away?" Brad's aged voice seemed to rumble and crackle in his ears, in contrast to Jeanette's, crystalline and distant as wind chimes.

" 'Priest,' for heaven's sake," she said. "Why can't you just call him a minister?" It had been a joke of sorts between them, how High Church he had become. When on occasion they visited the Church of the Advent on Brimmer Street, she had ridiculed the incense, the robed teams of acolytes. "He makes me tired," she said.

"But don't you want to keep up with Communion?" It was his favorite sacrament; he harbored an inner image, a kind of religious fantasy, of the wafer and wine turning, with a muffled explosion, to pure light in the digestive system.

"Like 'keeping up' an insurance policy," she sighed, and did sound tired, tired to death. "It seems so pointless."

"But you *must*," Brad said, panicked.

"I must? Why must I? Who says I must?" The blue of her challenging eyes and the fevered flush of her cheeks made a garish contrast.

"Why, because . . . you know why. Because of the salvation of your soul. That's what you used to talk about when I first met you."

She looked toward the window with a faint smile. "When I used to go alone to Copley Methodist. I loved that church; it was so bizarre, with its minaret. Dear old Doctor Stidger, on and on. Now it's just a parking lot. Salvation of the soul." Her gaunt chest twitched—a laugh that didn't reach her lips.

He lowered his eyes, feeling mocked. His own hands, an old man's gnarled spotted claws, were folded together between his knees. "You mean you don't believe?" In his inner ear he felt all the height of space concealed beneath the floor, down and down.

"Oh, darling," she said. "Doesn't it just seem an awful lot of bother?"

"Not a bit?" he persisted.

Jeanette sighed again and didn't answer.

"Since when?"

"I don't know. No," she said, "that's not being honest. We should start being honest. I do know. Since you took it from me. You moved right in. It didn't seem necessary, for the *two* of us to keep it up."

"But . . . " He couldn't say, so late, how fondly he had intended it, enlisting at her side.

She offered to console him. "It doesn't matter, does it?" When he remained silent, feeling blackness all about him, to every point on the horizon, as on those nights in the Pacific, she shifted to a teasing note: "Honey, why does it matter?"

She knew. Because his death was also close. He lifted his eyes and saw her as enviably serene, having wrought this vengeance. A nurse rustled at the door, her syringe tingling in its aluminum tray, and across the air well in the blue spring twilight the lights had come on, rectangles of gold. It had begun, a few dry flakes, to spit snow.

Though she had asked that there be absolutely no religious service, Brad and the young minister arranged one, following the oldest-fashioned, impersonal rite. Jeanette would have been seventy-one in May, and he was three years older. He continued to go to the ten o'clock service, his erect figure carrying his white hair like a flag. But it was sheer inert motion, there were no falcon flights of his mind anymore, no small true voice at his side. There was nothing. He wished he could think otherwise, but he had believed in her all those years and could not stop now.

John Updike, asked to comment on his choice of this story, wrote: "I like it because in it I tried several things rather new for me: to locate a story firmly and circumstantially in my adopted terrain of Boston, and to show a marriage over the years, developing, as long marriages do, its secret and final revenge, its redressing of a long-sustained imbalance. It is not easy, for a short story, to contain time and to display its abyss; but in certain images here—the recurrence of snow as the motif of their love, and Brad's sudden realization, from within Jeanette's rarely visited cupola, that a whole glittering population of skyscrapers had grown up at the city's distant heart—I felt I had succeeded. I remember fondly, in connection with this story, an hour spent in the Boston Public Library, examining old city maps of the vanished West End, and another spent at the theological library of Boston University, discussing the fragile thread of Methodism in the city's historical fabric. Also, 'Made in Heaven' concerns one of my favorite subjects, the mystery of churchgoing."

Born in Shillington, Pennsylvania, Updike attended Harvard University and the Ruskin School of Drawing and Fine Arts in Oxford, England. His short-story collections include The Same Door, Pigeon Feathers, The Music School, Museums and Women, Too Far to Go: The Maple Stories, *and* Problems and Other Stories. *He is the author of seventeen other books—novels, collections of poetry, and essays. His novel* Rabbit Is Rich *won the 1982 Pulitzer Prize for fiction, the American Book Award for fiction, and the National Book Critics Circle Award.*

First published in 1985 in The Atlantic Monthly.

RAYMOND CARVER

BOXES

My mother is packed and ready to move. But Sunday afternoon, at the last minute, she calls and says for us to come eat with her. "My icebox is defrosting," she tells me. "I have to fry up this chicken before it rots." She says we should bring our own plates and some knives and forks. She's packed most of her dishes and kitchen things. "Come on and eat with me one last time," she says. "You and Jill."

I hang up the phone and stand at the window for a minute longer, wishing I could figure this thing out. But I can't. So finally I turn to Jill and say, "Let's go to my mother's for a good-bye meal."

Jill is at the table with a Sears catalogue in front of her, trying to find us some curtains. But she's been listening. She makes a face. "Do we have to?" she says. She bends down the corner of a page and closes the catalogue. She sighs. "God, we been over there to eat two or three times in this last month alone. Is she ever actually going to leave?"

Jill always says what's on her mind. She's thirty-five years old, wears her hair short, and grooms dogs for a living. Before she became a groomer, something she likes, she used to be a housewife and mother. Then all hell broke loose. Her two children were kidnapped by her first husband and taken to live in Australia. Her second husband, who drank, left her with a broken eardrum before he drove their car through a bridge into the Elwha River. He didn't have life insurance, not to mention property-damage insurance. Jill had to borrow money to bury him, and then—can you beat it?—she was presented with a bill for the bridge repair. Plus, she had her own medical bills. She can tell this story now. She's bounced back. But she has run out of patience with my mother. I've run out of patience, too. But I don't see my options.

"She's leaving day after tomorrow," I say. "Hey, Jill, don't do any favors. Do you want to come with me or not?" I tell her it doesn't matter to me one way or the other. I'll say she has a migraine. It's not like I've never told a lie before.

"I'm coming," she says. And like that she gets up and goes into the bathroom, where she likes to pout.

We've been together since last August, about the time my mother picked to move up here to Longview from California. Jill tried to make the best of it. But my mother pulling into town just when we were trying to get our act together was nothing either of us had bargained for. Jill said it reminded her of the situation with her first husband's mother. "She was a clinger," Jill said. "You know what I mean? I thought I was going to suffocate."

It's fair to say that my mother sees Jill as an intruder. As far as she's concerned, Jill is just another girl in a series of girls who have appeared in my life since my wife left me. Someone, to her mind, likely to take away affection, attention, maybe even some money that might otherwise come to her. But someone deserving of respect? No way. I remember—how can I forget it?—she called my wife a whore before we were married, and then called her a whore fifteen years later, after she left me for someone else.

Jill and my mother act friendly enough when they find themselves together. They hug each other when they say hello or good-bye. They talk about shopping specials. But Jill dreads the time she has to spend in my mother's company. She claims my mother bums her out. She says my mother is negative about everything and everybody and ought to find an outlet, like other people in her age bracket. Crocheting, maybe, or card games at the Senior Citizens Center, or else going to church. Something, anyway, so that she'll leave us in peace. But my mother had her own way of solving things. She announced she was moving back to California. The hell with everything and everybody in this town. What a place to live! She wouldn't continue to live in this town if they gave her the place and six more like it.

Within a day or two of deciding to move, she'd packed her things into boxes. That was last January. Or maybe it was February. Anyway, last winter sometime. Now it's the end of June. Boxes have been sitting around inside her house for months. You have to walk around them or step over them to get from one room to another. This is no way for anyone's mother to live.

After a while, ten minutes or so, Jill comes out of the bathroom. I've found a roach and am trying to smoke that and drink a bottle of ginger ale while I watch one of the neighbors change the oil in his car. Jill doesn't look at me. Instead, she goes into the kitchen and puts some plates and utensils into a paper sack. But when she comes back through the living room I stand up, and we hug each other. Jill says, "It's O.K." What's O.K. I wonder. As far as I can see, nothing's O.K. But she holds me and keeps patting my shoulder. I can smell the pet shampoo on her. She comes home from work wearing the stuff. It's everywhere. Even when we're in bed together. She gives me a final pat. Then we go out to the car and drive across town to my mother's.

I like where I live. I didn't when I first moved here. There was nothing to do at night, and I was lonely. Then I met Jill. Pretty soon, after a few weeks, she brought her things over and started living with me. We didn't set any long-term goals. We were happy and we had a life together. We told each other we'd finally got lucky. But my mother didn't have anything going in her life. So she wrote me and said she'd decided on moving here. I wrote her back and said I didn't think it was such a good idea. The weather's terrible in the winter, I said. They're building a prison a few miles from town, I told her. The place is bumper-to-bumper tourists all summer, I said. But she acted as if she never got my letters, and came anyway. Then, after she'd been in town a little less than a month, she told me she hated the place. She acted as if it were my fault she'd moved here and my fault she found everything so disagreeable. She started calling me up and telling me how crummy the place was. "Laying guilt trips," Jill called it. She told me the bus service was terrible and the drivers unfriendly. As for the people at the Senior Citizens—well, she didn't want to play casino. "They can go to hell," she said, "and take their card games with them." The clerks at the supermarket were surly, the guys in the service station didn't give a damn about her or her car. And she'd made up her mind about the man she rented from, Larry Hadlock. King Larry, she called him. "He thinks he's *superior* to everyone because he has some shacks for rent and a few dollars. I wish to God I'd never laid eyes on him."

It was too hot for her when she arrived, in August, and in September it started to rain. It rained almost every day for weeks. In October it turned cold. There was snow in November and December. But long before that she began to put the bad mouth on the place and the people to the extent that I didn't want to hear about it anymore, and I told her so finally. She cried, and I hugged her and thought that was the end of it. But a few days later she started in again, same stuff. Just before Christmas she called to see when I was coming by with her presents. She hadn't put up a tree and didn't intend to, she said. Then she said something else. She said if this weather didn't improve she was going to kill herself.

"Don't talk crazy," I said.

She said, "I mean it, honey. I don't want to see this place again except from my coffin. I hate this g.d. place. I don't know why I moved here. I wish I could just die and get it over with."

I remember hanging on to the phone and watching a man high up on a pole doing something to a power line. Snow whirled around his head. As I watched, he leaned out from the pole, supported only by his safety belt. Suppose he falls, I thought. I didn't have any idea what I was going to say next. I had to say something. But I was filled with unworthy feelings, thoughts no son should admit to. "You're my mother," I said finally. "What can I do to help?"

"Honey, you can't do anything," she said. "The time for doing anything has come and gone. It's too late to do anything. I wanted to like it here. I thought we'd go on picnics and take drives together. But none of that happened. You're always busy. You're off working, you and Jill. You're never at home. Or else if you are at home you have the phone off the hook all day. Anyway, I never see you," she said.

"That's not true," I said. And it wasn't. But she went on as if she hadn't heard me. Maybe she hadn't.

"Besides," she said, "this weather's killing me. It's too damned cold here. Why didn't you tell me this was the North Pole? If you had, I'd never have come. I want to go back to California, honey. I can get out and go places there. I don't know anywhere to go here. There are people back in California. I've got friends there who care what happens to me. Nobody gives a damn here. Well, I just pray I can get through to June. If I can make it that long, if I can last to June, I'm leaving this place forever. This is the worst place I've ever lived in."

What could I say? I didn't know what to say. I couldn't even say anything about the weather. Weather was a real sore point. We said good-bye and hung up.

Other people take vacations in the summer, but my mother moves. She started moving years ago, after my dad lost his job. When that happened, when he was laid off, they sold their home, as if this were what they should do, and went to where they thought things would be better. But things weren't any better there, either. They moved again. They kept on moving. They lived in rented houses, apartments, mobile homes, and motel units even. They kept moving, lightening their load with each move they made. A couple of times they landed in a town where I lived. They'd move in with my wife and me for a while and then they'd move on again. They were like migrating animals in this regard, except there was no pattern to their movement. They moved around for years, sometimes even leaving the state for what they thought would be greener pastures. But mostly they stayed in northern California and did their moving there.

Then my dad died, and I thought my mother would stop moving and stay in one place for a while. But she didn't. She kept moving. I suggested once that she go to a psychiatrist. I even said I'd pay for it. But she wouldn't hear of it. She packed and moved out of town instead. I was desperate about things or I wouldn't have said that about the psychiatrist.

She was always in the process of packing or else unpacking. Sometimes she'd move two or three times in the same year. She talked bitterly about the place she was leaving and optimistically about the place she was going to. Her mail got fouled up, her benefit checks went off somewhere else, and she spent hours writing letters, trying to get it all straightened out. Sometimes she'd move out of an apartment house, move to another one a few blocks away, and then, a month later, move back to the place she'd left, only to a different floor or a different side of the building. That's why when she moved here I rented a house for her and saw to it that it was furnished to her liking. "Moving around keeps her alive," Jill said. "It gives her something to do. She must get some kind of weird enjoyment out of it, I guess." But enjoyment or not, Jill thinks my mother must be losing her mind. I think so, too. But how do you tell your mother this? How do you deal with her if this is the case? Crazy doesn't stop her from planning and getting on with her next move.

She is waiting at the back door for us when we pull in. She's seventy years old, has gray hair, wears glasses with rhinestone frames, and has never been sick a day in her life. She hugs Jill, and then she hugs me. Her eyes are bright, as if she's been drinking. But she doesn't drink. She quit years ago, after my dad went on the wagon. We finish hugging and go inside. It's around five in the afternoon. I smell whatever it is drifting out of her kitchen and remember I haven't eaten since breakfast. My buzz has worn off.

"I'm starved," I say.

"Something smells good," Jill says.

"I hope it tastes good," my mother says. "I hope this

chicken's done." She raises the lid on a fry pan and pushes a fork into a chicken breast. "If there's anything I can't stand, it's raw chicken. I think it's done. Why don't you sit down? Sit anyplace. I still can't regulate my stove. The burners heat up too fast. I don't like electric stoves and never have. Move that junk off the chair, Jill. I'm living here like a damned gypsy. But not for much longer, I hope." She sees me looking around for the ashtray. "Behind you," she says. "On the windowsill, honey. Before you sit down, why don't you pour us some of that Pepsi? You'll have to use these paper cups. I should have told you to bring some glasses. Is the Pepsi cold? I don't have any ice. This icebox won't keep anything cold. It isn't worth a damn. My ice cream turns to soup. It's the worst icebox I've ever had."

She forks the chicken onto a plate and puts the plate on the table along with beans and coleslaw and white bread. Then she looks to see if there is anything she's forgetting. Salt and pepper! "Sit down," she says.

We draw our chairs up to the table, and Jill takes the plates out of the sack and hands them around the table to us. "Where are you going to live when you go back?" she says. "Do you have a place lined up?"

My mother passes the chicken to Jill and says, "I wrote that lady I rented from before. She wrote back and said she had a nice first-floor place I could have. It's close to the bus stop and there's lots of stores in the area. There's a bank and a Safeway. It's the nicest place. I don't know why I left there." She says that and helps herself to some coleslaw.

"Why'd you leave then?" Jill says. "If it was so nice and all." She picks up her drumstick, looks at it, and takes a bite of the meat.

"I'll tell you why. There was an old alcoholic woman who lived next door to me. She drank from morning to night. The walls were so thin I could hear her munching ice cubes all day. She had to use a walker to get around, but that still didn't stop her. I'd hear that walker *scrape, scrape* against the floor from morning to night. That and her icebox door closing." She shakes her head at all she had to put up with.

"I had to get out of there. *Scrape, scrape* all day. I couldn't stand it. I just couldn't live like that. This time I told the manager I didn't want to be next to any alcoholics. And I didn't want anything on the second floor. The second floor looks out on the parking lot. Nothing to see from there." She waits for Jill to say something more. But Jill doesn't comment. My mother looks over at me.

I'm eating like a wolf and don't say anything, either. In any case, there's nothing more to say on the subject. I keep chewing and look over at the boxes stacked against the fridge. Then I help myself to more coleslaw.

Pretty soon I finish and push my chair back. Larry Hadlock pulls up in back of the house, next to my car, and takes a lawnmower out of his pickup. I watch him through the window behind the table. He doesn't look in our direction.

"What's he want?" my mother says and stops eating.

"He's going to cut your grass, it looks like," I say.

"It doesn't need cutting," she says. "He cut it last week. What's there for him to cut?"

"It's for the new tenant," Jill says. "Whoever that turns out to be."

My mother takes this in and then goes back to eating.

Larry Hadlock starts his mower and begins to cut the grass. I know him a little. He lowered the rent twenty-five a month when I told him it was my mother. He is a widower—a big fellow, mid-sixties. An unhappy man with a good sense of humor. His arms are covered with white hair, and white hair stands out from under his cap. He looks like a magazine illustration of a farmer. But he isn't a farmer. He is a retired construction worker who's saved a little money. For a while, in the beginning, I let myself imagine that he and my mother might take some meals together and become friends.

"There's the king," my mother says. "King Larry. Not everyone has as much money as he does and can live in a big house and charge other people high rents. Well, I hope I never see his cheap old face again once I leave here. Eat the rest of this chicken," she says to me. But I shake my head and light a cigarette. Larry pushes his mower past the window.

"You won't have to look at it much longer," Jill says.

"I'm sure glad of that, Jill. But I know he won't give me my deposit back."

"How do you know that?" I say.

"I just know," she says. "I've had dealings with his kind before. They're out for all they can get."

Jill says, "It won't be long now and you won't have to have anything more to do with him."

"I'll be so glad."

"But it'll be somebody just like him," Jill says.

"I don't want to think that, Jill," my mother says.

She makes coffee while Jill clears the table. I rinse the cups. Then I pour coffee, and we step around a box marked "Knickknacks" and take our cups into the living room.

Larry Hadlock is at the side of the house. Traffic moves slowly on the street out in front, and the sun has started down over the trees. I can hear the commotion the mower makes. Some crows leave the phone line and settle onto the newly cut grass in the front yard.

"I'm going to miss you, honey," my mother says. Then she says, "I'll miss you, too, Jill. I'm going to miss both of you."

Jill sips from her coffee and nods. Then she says, "I hope you have a safe trip back and find the place you're looking for at the end of the road."

"When I get settled—and this is my last move, so help me—I hope you'll come and visit," my mother says. She looks at me and waits to be reassured.

"We will," I say. But even as I say it I know it isn't true. My life caved in on me down there, and I won't be going back.

"I wish you could have been happier here," Jill says. "I wish you'd been able to stick it out or something. You know what? Your son is worried sick about you."

"Jill," I say.

But she gives her head a little shake and goes on. "Sometimes he can't sleep over it. He wakes up sometimes in the night and says, 'I can't sleep. I'm thinking about my mother.' There," she says and looks at me. "I've said it. But it was on my mind."

"How do you think I must feel?" my mother says. Then she says, "Other women my age can be happy. Why can't I be like other women? All I want is a house and a town to live in that will make me happy. That isn't a crime, is it? I hope not. I hope I'm not asking too much out of life." She puts her cup on the floor next to her chair and waits for Jill to tell her she isn't asking for too much. But Jill doesn't say anything, and in a minute my mother begins to outline her plans to be happy.

After a time Jill lowers her eyes to her cup and has some more coffee. I can tell she's stopped listening. But my mother keeps talking anyway. The crows work their way through the grass in the front yard. I hear the mower howl and then thud as it picks up a clump of grass in the blade and comes to a stop. In a minute, after several tries, Larry gets it going again. The crows fly off, back to their wire. Jill picks at a fingernail. My mother is saying that the secondhand-furniture dealer is coming around the next morning to collect the things she isn't going to send on the bus or carry with her in the car. The table and chairs, TV, sofa, and bed are going with the dealer. But he's told her he doesn't have any use for the card table, so my mother is going to throw it out unless we want it.

"We'll take it," I say. Jill looks over. She starts to say something but changes her mind.

I will drive the boxes to the Greyhound station the next afternoon and start them on the way to California. My mother will spend the last night with us, as arranged. And then, early the next morning, two days from now, she'll be on her way.

She continues to talk. She talks on and on as she describes the trip she is about to make. She'll drive until four o'clock in the afternoon and then take a motel room for the night. She figures to make Eugene by dark. Eugene is a nice town—she stayed there once before, on the way up here. When she leaves the motel, she'll leave at sunrise and should, if God is looking out for her, be in California that afternoon. And God *is* looking out for her, she knows he is. How else explain her being kept around on the face of the earth? He has a plan for her. She's been praying a lot lately. She's been praying for me, too.

"Why are you praying for him?" Jill wants to know.

"Because I feel like it. Because he's my son," my mother says. "Is there anything the matter with that? Don't we all need praying for sometimes? Maybe some people don't. I don't know. What do I know anymore?" She brings a hand to her forehead and rearranges some hair that's come loose from a pin.

The mower sputters off, and pretty soon we see Larry go around the house pulling the hose. He sets the hose out and then goes slowly back around the house to turn the water on. The sprinkler begins to turn.

My mother starts listing the ways she imagines Larry has wronged her since she's been in the house. But now I'm not listening, either. I am thinking how she is about to go down the highway again, and nobody can reason with her or do anything to stop her. What can I do? I can't tie her up, or commit her, though it may come to that eventually. I worry for her, and she is a heartache to me. She is all the family I have left. I'm sorry she didn't like it here and wants to leave. But I'm never going back to California. And when that's clear to me I understand something else, too. I understand that after she leaves I'm probably never going to see her again.

I look over at my mother. She stops talking. Jill raises her eyes. Both of them look at me.

"What is it, honey?" my mother says.

"What's wrong?" Jill says.

I lean forward in the chair and cover my face with my hands. I sit like that for a minute, feeling bad and stupid for doing it. But I can't help it. And the woman who brought me into this life, and this other woman I picked up with less than a year ago, they exclaim together and rise and come over to where I sit with my head in my hands like a fool. I don't open my eyes. I listen to the sprinkler whipping the grass.

"What's wrong? What's the matter?" they say.

"It's O.K.," I say. And in a minute it is. I open my eyes and bring my head up. I reach for a cigarette.

"See what I mean?" Jill says. "You're driving him crazy. He's going crazy with worry over you." She is on one side of my chair, and my mother is on the other side. They could tear me apart in no time at all.

"I wish I could die and get out of everyone's way," my mother says quietly. "So help me Hannah, I can't take much more of this."

"How about some more coffee?" I say. "Maybe we ought to catch the news," I say. "Then I guess Jill and I better head for home."

Two days later, early in the morning, I say good-bye to my mother for what may be the last time. I've let Jill sleep. It won't hurt if she's late to work for a change. The dogs can wait for their baths and trimmings and such. My mother holds my arm as I walk her down the steps to the driveway and open the car door for her. She is wearing white slacks and a white blouse and white sandals. Her hair is pulled back and tied with a scarf. That's white, too. It's going to be a nice day, and the sky is clear and already blue.

On the front seat of the car I see maps and a thermos of coffee. My mother looks at these things as if she can't recall having come outside with them just a few minutes ago. She turns to me then and says, "Let me hug you once more. Let me love your neck. I know I won't see you for a long time." She puts an arm around my neck, draws me to her, and then begins to cry. But she stops almost at once and steps back, pushing the heel of her hand against her eyes. "I said I wouldn't do that, and I won't. But let me get a last look at you anyway. I'll miss you, honey," she says. "I'm just going to have to live through this. I've already lived through things I didn't think were possible. But I'll live through this, too, I guess." She gets into the car, starts it, and runs the engine for a minute. She rolls her window down.

"I'm going to miss you," I say. And I *am* going to miss her. She's my mother, after all, and why shouldn't I miss her? But, God forgive me, I'm glad, too, that it's finally time and that she is leaving.

"Good-bye," she says. "Tell Jill thanks for supper last night. Tell her I said good-bye."

"I will," I say. I stand there wanting to say something else. But I don't know what. We keep looking at each other, trying to smile and reassure each other. Then something comes into her eyes, and I believe she is thinking about the highway and how far she is going to have to drive that day. She takes her eyes off me and looks down the road. Then she rolls her window up, puts the car into gear, and drives to the intersection, where she has to wait for the light to change. When I see she's made it into traffic and headed toward the highway, I go back in the house and drink some coffee. I feel sad for a while, and then the sadness goes away and I start thinking about other things.

A few nights later my mother calls to say she is in her new place. She is busy fixing it up, the way she does when she has a new place. She tells me I'll be happy to know she likes it just fine to be back in sunny California. But she says there's something in the air where she is living, maybe it's pollen, that is causing her to sneeze a lot. And the traffic is heavier than she remembers from before. She doesn't recall there being so much traffic in her neighborhood. Naturally, everyone still drives like crazy down there. "California drivers," she says. "What else can you expect?" She says it's hot for this time of the year. She doesn't think the air-conditioning unit in her apartment is working right. I tell her she should talk to the manager. "She's never around when you need her," my mother says. She hopes she hasn't made a mistake in moving back to California. She waits before she says anything else.

I'm standing at the window with the phone pressed to my ear, looking out at the lights from town and at the lighted houses closer by. Jill is at the table with the catalogue, listening.

"Are you still there?" my mother asks. "I wish you'd say something."

I don't know why, but it's then I recall the affectionate name my dad used sometimes when he was talking nice to my mother—those times, that is, when he wasn't drunk. It was a long time ago, and I was a kid, but always, hearing it, I felt better, less afraid, more hopeful about the future. "*Dear*," he'd say. He called her "dear" sometimes—a sweet name. "Dear," he'd say, "if you're going to the store, will you bring me some cigarettes?" Or "Dear, is your cold any better?" "Dear, where is my coffee cup?"

The word issues from my lips before I can think what else I want to say to go along with it. "Dear." I say it again. I call her "dear." "Dear, try not to be afraid," I say. I tell my mother I love her and I'll write to her, yes. Then I say good-bye, and I hang up.

For a while I don't move from the window. I keep standing there, looking out at the lighted houses in our neighborhood. As I watch, a car turns off the road and pulls into a driveway. The porch light goes on. The door to the house opens and someone comes out on the porch and stands there waiting.

Jill turns the pages of her catalogue, and then she stops turning them. "This is what we want," she says. "This is more like what I had in mind. Look at this, will you." But I don't look. I don't care five cents for curtains. "What is it you see out there, honey?" Jill says. "Tell me."

What's there to tell? The people over there embrace for a minute, and then they go inside the house together. They leave the light burning. Then they remember, and it goes out.

Raymond Carver's short stories convey such concentrated feeling that it's no surprise that his published work includes as many books of poetry as stories. This story is a favorite with Carver because "it's the first story I had written in two years—I was busy writing the poems that went into the two books of poems, Where Water Comes Together with Other Water *and* Ultramarine." *Writing this story made him put aside poetry for awhile and begin work on a new short-story collection. "If I hadn't written* "Boxes"*—whatever prompted me to write it—I'm sure I wouldn't have written the half-dozen stories I've written since." He goes on: "Some stories that one writes seem rather removed from one after they're finished, and the writer tends not to think about them much ever again. But I like this story a good deal; it feels like a 'keeper' to me. It seems to have opened the door to many more stories."*

Carver is one of the most widely read short-story writers in America today; his stories have appeared in The New Yorker, Esquire, The Atlantic Monthly, Grand Street, Paris Review, Antaeus, The Iowa Review, The Ohio Review, Ploughshares, *and other publications, and they have been translated into twenty languages in Europe and Asia. His short-story collections include* Will You Please Be Quiet, Please?, What We Talk About When We Talk About Love, *and* Cathedral. Fires *is a collection of his essays, poetry, and stories. His story* "A Small Good Thing" *won first prize in the 1983* O. Henry Prize Stories, *and his work has been selected for* The Best American Short Stories *and* Pushcart Prize Anthology. *He is editor of* The Best American Short Stories 1986. *Carver lives in the state of Washington and, among many other prizes he has received, he was recently awarded the Strauss Living Award.*

First published in 1986 in The New Yorker.

ELLEN GILCHRIST

THE STARLIGHT EXPRESS

1

Nora Jane was seven months pregnant when Sandy disappeared again. Dear Baby, the note said. I can't take it. Here's all the money that is left. Don't get mad if you can help it. I love you, Sandy.

She folded up the note and put it in a drawer. Then she made up the bed. Then she went outside and walked along the water's edge. At least we are living on the water, she was thinking. I always get lucky about things like that. Well, I know one thing. I'm going to have these babies no matter what I have to do and I'm going to keep them alive. They won't die on me or get drunk or take cocaine. Freddy was right. A decent home is the best thing.

Nora Jane was on a beach fifty miles south of San Francisco, beside a little stucco house Sandy's old employer had been renting them for next to nothing. Nora Jane had never liked living in that house. Still, it was on the ocean.

The ocean spread out before her now, gray and dark, breaking against the boulders where it turned into a little cove. There were places where people had been making fires. Nora Jane began to pick up all the litter she could find and put it in a pile beside a firesite. She walked around for half an hour picking up cans and barrettes and half-burned pieces of cardboard and piled them up beside a boulder. Then she went back to the house and got some charcoal lighter fluid and a match and lit the mess and watched it burn. It was the middle of October. December the fifteenth was only two months away. I could go to Freddy, she was thinking. He will always love me and forgive me anything.

But what will it do to him? Do I have a right to get around him so he'll only love me more? This was a question Nora Jane was always asking herself about Freddy Harwood. Now she asked it once again.

A cold wind was blowing off the ocean. She picked up a piece of driftwood and added it to the fire. She sank down upon the sand. She was carrying ten pounds of babies, but she moved as gracefully as ever. She wiggled around until her back was against the boulder, sitting up very straight, not giving in to the cold or the wind. I'm one of those people that could go to the Himalayas, she decided. Because I never give in to cold. If you hunch over it will get you.

Freddy Harwood stood on the porch of his half-finished house deep in the woods outside of Willets, California, and thought about Nora Jane. He was thinking about her voice, trying to remember how it sounded when she said his name. If I could remember that sound, he decided. If I could remember what she said that first night it would be enough. If that's all I get it will have to do.

He looked deep into the woods past the madrona tree, where once he had seen a bobcat come walking out and stop at the place where the trees ended and the grass began. A huge yellow cat with a muff around its neck and brilliant eyes. The poet Gary Snyder had been visiting and they had made up a song about the afternoon called "The Great Bobcat Visit and Other Mysteries of Willets." If she was here I could teach it to her, Freddy thought. So, there I go again. Everything either reminds me of her or it doesn't remind me of her, so everything reminds me of her. What good does it do to have six million dollars and two houses and a bookstore if I'm in love with Nora Jane? Freddy left his bobcat lookout and walked around the side of the house toward the road. A man was hurrying up the path.

It was his neighbor, Sam Lyons, who lived a few miles away up an impassable road. Freddy waved and went to meet him. He's coming to tell me she's dead, he decided. She died in childbirth in the hands of a midwife in Chinatown and I'm supposed to go on living after that. "What's happening?" he called out. "What's going on?"

"You got a call," Sam said. "Your girl friend's coming on the train. I'm getting tired of this, Harwood. You get yourself a phone. That's twice this week. *Two calls in one week!*"

In a small neat room near the Berkeley campus a young Chinese geneticist named Lin Tan Sing packed a change of clothes and his toilet articles, left a note for himself about some things to do when he returned, and walked out into the beautiful fall day. He had been saving his money for a vacation and today was the day it began. As soon as he finished work that afternoon he would ride the subway to the train station and get on board The Starlight Express and travel all the way up the California coast to Puget Sound. He would see the world. My eyes have gone too far inside, Lin Tan told himself. Now I will go outside and see what's happening at other end. People will look at me and I will look at them. We will learn about each other. Perhaps train will fall off cliff into the ocean. There will be stories in the newspapers. Young Chinese scientist saves many lives in daring rescues. President of United States invites young Chinese scientist to live in White House and tutor children of politicians. Young Chinese scientist adopted by wealthy man whose life he saves in train wreck. I am only an humble scientist trying to unravel genetic code, young Chinese scientist tells reporters. Did not mean to be hero. Do not know what came over me. I pushed on fallen car and great strength came to me when it was least expected.

Lin entered the Berkeley campus and strolled along a sidewalk leading to the student union. Students were all around. A man in black was playing a piano beneath a tree. The sky was clear with only a few clouds to the west. The Starlight Express, Lin was thinking. All Plexiglas across the top. Stars rolling by while I am inside with something nice to drink. Who knows? Perhaps I will find a girl on the train who wishes to talk with me. I will tell her all things scientific and also of poetry. I will tell her the poetry of my country and also of England. Lin folded his hands before him as he walked, already he was on the train, speeding up the California coast telling some dazzling blonde the story of his life and all about his work. Lin worked at night in the lab of The Berkeley Women's Clinic. He did chemical analyses on the fluid removed during amniocentesis. So far he had only made one mistake in his work. One time a test had to be repeated because he knocked a petri dish off the table with his sleeve. Except for that his results had proved correct in every single instance. No one else in the lab had such a record. Because of this Lin always kept his head politely bowed in the halls and was always extra nice to the other technicians and generous with advice and help. He had a fellowship in the graduate program in biology and he had this easy part-time job and his sister, Jade Tan Lee, was coming in six months to join him. Only one thing was lacking in Lin's life and that was a girl friend. He had what he considered a flaw in his character and wished to be in love with a western girl with blond hair. It was only fate, the I Ching assured him. A fateful flaw that would cause disaster and ruin but not of his own doing and therefore nothing to worry about.

On this train, he was thinking, I will sit up straight and hold my head high. If she asks where I come from I will say Shanghai or Hong Kong as it is difficult for them to picture village life in China without thinking of rice paddies. I am businessman, I will say, and have only taken time off to learn science. No, I will say only the truth so she may gaze into my eyes and be at peace. I will buy you jewels and perfume, I will tell her. Robes with silken dragons eating the moon, many pearls. Shoes with flowers embroidered on them for every minute of the day. Look out the Plexiglas ceiling at the stars. They are whirling by and so are we even when we are off the train.

Nora Jane bought her ticket and went outside to get some air while she waited for the train. She was wearing a long gray sweatshirt with a black leather belt riding on top of the twins. On her legs were bright yellow tights and yellow ballet shoes. A yellow-and-white scarf was tied around her black curls. She looked just about as wonderful as someone carrying ten pounds of babies could ever look in the world. She was deserted and unwed and on her way to find a man whose heart she had broken only four months before and she should have been in a terrible mood but she couldn't work up much enthusiasm for despair. Whatever chemicals Tammili and Lydia were pumping into her bloodstream were working nicely to keep Nora Jane in a good mood. She stood outside the train station watching a line of cirrus clouds chugging along the horizon, thinking about the outfits she would buy for her babies as soon as they were born. Nora Jane loved clothes. She couldn't wait until she had three people to dress instead of only one. All her life she had wanted to be able to wear all her favorite colors at one time. Now she would have her chance. She could just see herself walking into a drugstore holding her little girls by the hand. Tammili would be wearing blue. Lydia would be wearing red or pink. Nora Jane would have on peach or mauve or her old standby, yellow. Unless that was too many primaries on one day. I'll start singing, she decided. That way I can work at night while they're asleep. I have to have some money of my own. I don't want anyone supporting us. When I go shopping and buy stuff I don't want anybody saying why did you get this stuff and you didn't need that shirt and so forth. No, the minute I get well I'll go to work and make some money. Nieman said I could sing anyplace in San Francisco. Nieman should know. After all, he writes for the newspaper. If they don't like it then I'll just get a job in a daycare center like I meant to last fall. I'll do whatever I have to do.

A whistle blew. Nora Jane walked back down the concrete stairs. "Starlight Express," a black voice was calling out. "Get on board for the long haul to Washington State. Don't go if you're scared of stars. Stars all the way to Marin, San Rafael, Petaluma, and Sebastopol. Stars all the way to Seattle, Washington, and Portland, Oregon. Stars to Alaska and points north. Stars to the North Pole. Get on board this train. . . ."

Nora Jane threw her backpack over her shoulder and ran for the train. Lin Tan Sing caught a glimpse of her yellow stockings and reminded himself not to completely rule out black hair in his search for happiness.

Freddy Harwood was straightening up his house. He moved the wooden table holding his jigsaw puzzle of the suspended whale from the Museum of Natural History. He watered his paper-white narcissus. He got a broom out of a closet and began to sweep the floor. He found a column Nieman did about *My Dinner With Andre* and leaned on the broom reading it. It was two o'clock in the afternoon and there was no reason to leave for the station before five. They aren't my babies, he reminded himself. She's having someone else's babies and they aren't mine and I don't want them anyway. Why do I want her at all? Because I like to talk to her, that's why. I like to talk to her more than anyone in the world. That's that. It's my business. Mine and only mine. I like to look at her and I like to talk to her. Jesus Christ! Could I have a maid? I mean would it violate every tenet if I just had a goddamn maid once a week?

He threw the broom into a closet and pulled on his boots and walked out into the yard to look for the bobcat.

The house he was stamping out of was a structure he had been building on and off for years. It was on a bluff overlooking the Sanhedrin Range in Mendocino County, California, and could only be reached by a stone-covered dirt road that was impassable during the rainy season. The land was covered with Douglas fir and spruce and northern pine. Freddy had bought the land with the first money he had ever earned. That was years ago, before his grandmother died, during the time when he stopped speaking to his family and smoked dope all day and worked as a chimney sweep. He had lived in a van and saved twelve thousand dollars. Then he had driven up the California coast until he found Douglas fir on land with no roads leading to it. He bought as much as twelve thousand dollars would buy. Two acres, almost three. Then he set up a tent and started building. He built a cistern to catch water and laid pipes to carry it to where the kitchen would later be. He leveled the land and poured a concrete foundation and marked off rooms and began to haul stones for a fireplace. He planted fruit trees and a small vineyard and put in root plants and an herb garden for medical emergencies. He had been working on the house off and on for twenty-three years. The house was as much a part of Freddy Harwood as his skin. When he was away from Willets for long stretches of time he thought about the house every day, the red sun of early morning and the redder sun of sundown. The eyes of the bobcat in the woods, the endless lines of mountains in the distance. The taste of the air and the taste of the water. His body sleeping in peace in his own invention.

Now she's ruined my house for me, he was thinking, leaning against the madrona tree while he waited for the bobcat. She's slept in all the rooms and sat on the chairs and touched the furniture. She's used all the forks and spoons and moved that table. I'm putting it back where it goes today. Well, let her come up here and beg for mercy. I don't care. I'll give it to her. Let her cry her dumb little Roman Catholic heart out. I guess she looks like hell. I bet she's as big as a house.

He had turned toward the house. A redbird was throwing itself against the windows. Bird in the house means bad luck. Well, don't let it get in. I'll have to put some screens on those windows. Ruin the light.

The house was very tall with many windows. It was a house a child might draw, tall and thin. Inside were six rooms, or areas, filled with books and mattresses and lamps and tables. Everything was white or black or brown or gray. Freddy had made all the furniture himself except for two chairs by Mies Van Der Rohe. A closet held all of Buiji Dalton's pottery in case she should come to visit. A shelf held Nieman's books. On a peg behind the bathroom door was Nora Jane's yellow silk kimono.

When she comes, Freddy was saying to himself as he trudged back up the hill to do something about the bird, I won't say a word about anything. I'll just act like everything is normal. Sam came over and said you'd be on the train and it was getting into Fort Bragg at eight and would I meet you. Well, great. I mean, what brought you here? I thought you and the robber baron had settled down for the duration. I mean, I thought I'd never see you again. I mean, it's okay with me. It's not your fault I am an extremely passionate and uncontrollably sensitive personality. I can tell you one thing. It's not easy being this sensitive. Oh, shit, he concluded. I'll just go on and get drunk. I'm a match for her when I'm drunk. Drunk I'm a match for anyone, even Nora Jane. He opened the closet and reached in behind one of Buiji Dalton's handpainted Egyptian funeral urns and took out a bottle of Red Ausbruch his brother had sent from somewhere. He found a corkscrew and opened it. He passed the cork before his nose, then lifted the bottle and began to drink. There ain't no little bottle, he was thinking. Like that old bottle of mine.

At about the same time that Freddy Harwood was resorting to this time-honored method of acquiring courage, Lin Tan Sing was using a similar approach aboard The Starlight Express. He was drinking gin and trying not to stare at the yellow stockings, which were all he could see of Nora Jane. She was in a highbacked swivel chair turned around to look out the glassed-in back of the train. She was thinking about whales, how they had their babies in the water, and also about Sandra Draine, who had a baby in a tub of salt water in Sausalito while her husband videotaped the birth. They had shown the tape at the gallery when Sandra had her fall show. It won't be like that for me, Nora Jane was thinking. I'm not letting anyone take any pictures or even come in the room except the doctor and maybe Freddy, but no cameras.

I know he'll want to bring a camera if he's there. He's the silliest man I have ever known.

But I love him anyway. And I hate to do this to him but I have to do what I have to do. I can't be alone now. I have to go somewhere. The train rounded a curve. The wheels screeched. Nora Jane's chair swiveled around. Her feet flew out and she hit Lin Sing in the knee with a ballet shoe.

"Oh, my God," she said. "Did I hurt you?"

"Is nothing."

"We hit a curve. I'm really sorry. I thought the chair was fastened down."

"You are going to have a baby?" His face was very close to her face. It was the biggest Oriental face Nora Jane had ever seen. The bluest eyes. She had not known there were blue eyes in China. She lowered her own.

"Yes," she said. "I am."

"I am geneticist. This interests me very much."

"It does me too."

"Would you like to talk with me?"

"Sure. I'd like to have someone to talk to. I was just thinking about the whales. I guess they don't even know it's cold, do they?"

"I have gone out in kayak to be near them. Is very mysterious. Was the best experience I have had in California. A friend of mine in lab at Berkeley Women's Clinic took me with him. He heads team of volunteers to collect money for whales. Next summer I will go again."

"Oh, my God. That's where I go. I mean, that's the doctor I used to have. Then we moved to San Jose." She looked at his hands. They were very still. Like Tam and Li Suyin's. "I'm going to have twin baby girls," she added. "I had an amnio at your clinic. That's how I know."

"Oh, this is very strange. You are Miss Whittington of 1512 Arch Street, is it not so? Oh, this is very strange meeting. I am technician in lab. Head technician for night lab. Yes. I am the one that did the test for you. I was very excited to have these twin girls show up. It was important day for me. I had just been given big honor at university.

Oh, this is chance meeting like in books." He stood up and took her hand. "I am Lin Tan Sing, of the province of Süchow, near Beijing, in central China. I am honored to make your acquaintance. Please accept unworthy offer of friendship." He stood above her waiting.

"I am Nora Jane Whittington, of New Orleans, Louisiana, and San Jose, California. And Berkeley. I am glad to know you also. What all did the test show? Do you remember anything else about it?"

"Oh, it was not in lab I learned things of substance. Only chip away at physical world in lab. Very humble. I took great liberty and cast I Ching for your daughters. I saw great honors for them and gifts of music brought to the world."

"Oh, my God," Nora Jane said. She leaned toward him. "I can't believe I met you on this train." Snowy mountains, Lin was thinking. Peony and butterfly. Two birds in the shade of willows.

Later a waiter came through the club car and Lin advised Nora Jane to have an egg-salad sandwich and a carton of milk. "I am surprised they allow you to travel so far along in pregnancy. Are you going far?"

"Oh, no one said I could go. I mean, I didn't ask anyone. They said I could travel until two months before they came. I guess I should have asked someone. But I was real upset about something and I need to come up here. I need to see this friend of mine."

"Be sure and get plenty of rest tonight. Very heavy burden for small body."

"My body's not so small. I have big bones. See my wrists." She held out her wrists and he pretended to be amazed at their size. "All the same, be sure and rest tomorrow. Don't take chances. Many very small babies at clinic now. I am worrying very much about so many months in machine for tiny babies. Still, it is United States and they will not allow anything to die. Is the modern age."

"I want my babies no matter what size they are." She folded her hands across her lap. "I guess I shouldn't have come up here. Well, it's too late now. Anyway, where did you learn to speak English so well? Did you have it in school?"

"I studied your writers. I studied Ernest Hemingway and William Faulkner and John Dos Passos. Also, many American poets. Then since I am here I am learning all the time with my ears."

"I like poetry a lot. I'm crazy about it to tell the truth."

"I am going to translate poetry of women in my country for women of America. I have noticed there is much sadness in poetry of women here. But is not sadness in life here. In my country poetry is to overcome sadness, help people to understand how things are and see beauty and order and not give in to despair."

"Oh, like what? Tell me some."

"Here is poem by famous poet of Nanchin Province, near my village.

> "A *shoot is cut from the bamboo plant*
> *the bamboo does not grieve*
> *And goes on growing.*"

"Oh, that's wonderful."

"This poet is called The White Poppy. She is very old woman now but her poems will always be new. This is how it is with the making of beautiful things, don't you find it so?"

"Whenever I think of being on this train I'll remember you telling me that poem." She was embarrassed and lowered her eyes to be talking of such important things with a stranger.

"Poem very light," Lin laughed, to save the moment. "Not like babies. Easy to transport or carry." Nora Jane laughed too. The train sped through the night. The whales gave birth in the water. The stars stayed on course. The waiter appeared with the tray and they began to eat their sandwiches.

Freddy was waiting on the platform when the train arrived at the Noyo—Point Cabrillo Station. He was wearing his old green stadium coat and carrying a blanket. Nora Jane stepped down from the train and kissed him on the cheek. Lin pressed his face against the window and smiled and waved. Nora Jane waved back. "That's my new friend," she said. "He gave me his address in Berkeley. He's a scientist. Get this. He did the amnio on Lydia and Tammili. Can you believe it? Can anybody believe the stuff that happens?"

Freddy wrapped the blanket around her shoulders. "I thought you might like to see a movie before we go back. *The Night of the Shooting Stars* is playing at the Courthouse in Willets."

"He ran off and left me," she said. "I knew he would. I don't think I even care."

"You met the guy on the train that did the amnio. I don't believe it."

"He knew my name. I almost fainted when he said it."

"Look, we don't have to go to a movie unless you feel like it. I just noticed it was playing. It's got a pregnant woman in it."

"I've seen it three times. We went last year, don't you remember? But I'll go again if you want to."

"We could eat instead. Have you eaten anything?"

"I had a sandwich on the train. I guess we better go on to the house. I'm supposed to take it easy. I don't have any luggage. I just brought this duffel bag. I was too mad to pack."

"We'll get something to eat." He took her arm and pulled her close to him. Her skin beneath her sleeve was the same as the last time he had touched her. They began to move in the direction of the car. "I love the way you smell," she said. "You always smell just like you are. Listen, Freddy, I don't know exactly what I'm doing right now. I'm just doing the best I can and playing it by ear. But I'm okay. I really am okay. Do you believe everything that's happened?"

"You want to buy anything. Is there anything you need? You want to see a doctor or anything like that?"

"No, let's just go up to the house. I've been thinking about the house a lot. About the windows. Did you get the rest of them put in?"

"Yeah, and now the goddamn birds are going crazy crashing into them. Five dead birds this week. They fight their reflections. How's that for a metaphor." He helped her into the car. "Wear your seat belt, okay. So, what's going on inside there?"

"They just move around all the time. If I need to I can sell the car. I don't want anybody supporting us, even you. I'm really doing great. I don't know all the details yet but I'm figuring things out." He started the motor and began to drive. She reached over and touched his knee. They drove through the town and turned onto the road to Willets. Nora Jane moved her hand and fell asleep curled up on the seat. She didn't wake again until they were past Willets and had started up the long hill leading to the gravel road that led to the dirt road that led to the broken path to Freddy's house. "He said they were going to give great gifts to the world out of great hunger," she said when she woke. "What do you think that meant? I want to call Li Suyin and tell her about it. I forgot you didn't have a phone. I need to tell her where I am."

"You can call tomorrow. Look, how about putting your hand back on my leg. That way I'll believe you're here." He turned and looked at her. "I want to believe you're here."

"You're crazy to even talk to me."

"No, I'm not. I'm the sane one, remember? I'm the control." She was laughing now so he could afford to look right at her. She looked okay. Tired and not much color in her face, but okay. Perfect as always from Freddy Harwood's point of view.

2

"I want to take them on the grand tour as soon as they're old enough," Freddy was saying. They were lying on a futon on top of a mattress in the smallest of the upstairs rooms. "My grandmother took me when I was twelve. She took my cousin, Sally, and hired a gigolo to dance with her in Vienna.

I had this navy blue raincoat with a zip-in lining. God, I wish I still had that coat." Nora Jane snuggled down beside him, smelling his chest. It smelled like a wild animal. There were many things about Freddy Harwood that excited her almost as much as love. She patted him on the arm. "So, anyway," he continued. "I have this uncle in New Orleans and he's married two women with three children. He's raised six children that didn't belong to him and he's getting along all right. He says at least his subconscious isn't involved. There's a lot to be said for that. . . . What I'm saying is, I haven't lived in Berkeley all my life to give in to some kind of old worn-out masculine pride. Not with all the books I've read."

"All I've ever done is make you sad. I always end up doing something mean to you."

"Maybe I like it. Anyway, you're here and that's how it is. But we ought to go back to town in a few days. You can stay with me there, can't you?" He pulled her closer, as close as he dared. She was so soft. The babies only made her softer. "I ought to call Stuart and tell him you're here."

"He's a heart doctor. He doesn't know anything about babies."

"Wait a minute. One of them did something. Oh, shit, did you feel that."

"I know. They're in there. Sometimes I forget it but not very often. Tell me some more about when you went to Europe. Tell me everything you can remember just the way it happened. Like what you had to eat and what everyone was wearing."

"Okay. Sally had a navy blue skirt and a jacket and she had some white blouses and in Paris we got some scarves. She had this scarf with the Visigoth crowns on it and she had it tied in a loop so a whole crown showed. She fixed it all the time she wore it. She couldn't leave it alone. Then they went somewhere and got some dresses made out of velvet but they only wore them at night."

"What did you wear?" She had a vision of him alone in a hotel room putting on his clothes when he was twelve. "I bet you were a wonderful-looking boy," she said out loud. "I bet you were the smartest boy in Europe."

"We met Jung. We talked to him. So, what else did you talk about to this Chinese research biologist?"

"A genetic-research biologist. He's still studying it. He has to finish school before he can do his real work. He wants to do things to DNA and find out how much we remember. He thinks we remember everything that ever happened to anyone from the beginning of time because there wouldn't be any reason to forget it, and if you can make computer chips so small, then the brain is much larger than that. We talked all the way from Sausalito. His father was a painter. When his sister gets here they might move to Sweden. He believes in the global village."

"He says they're musicians, huh?"

"Well, it wasn't that simple. It was very complicated. He had the biggest face of any Oriental I've met. I just love him. I'm going to talk to him a lot more when we both get back to San Francisco." Her voice was getting softer, blurring the words. "Go to sleep," Freddy said. "Don't talk anymore." He felt a baby move, then move again. They were moving quite a bit.

-'I'm cold," she said. "Also, he said the birth process was the worst thing we ever go through in our life. He told me about this boy in England that's a genius, his parents are both doctors and they let him stay in the womb for eighteen months for an experiment and he can remember being born and tells about it. He said it was like someone tore a hole in the universe and jerked you out. Get closer, will you. God, I'm tired."

"We ought to go downstairs and sleep in front of the fire. I'm going to make a bed down there and come get you." Freddy went downstairs and pulled a mattress up before the fireplace and built up the fire and brought two futons in and laid them on top of the mattress and added a stack of wool blankets and some pillows. When he had everything arranged just like he wanted it he went back upstairs and carried her down and tucked her in. Then he rubbed her back and told her stories about Vienna and wondered what time it was. I am an hour from town, he told himself, and Sam is twenty minutes away and probably drunk besides. It's at least three o'clock in the morning and the water's half frozen in the cistern and I let her come up here because I was too goddamn selfish to think of a way to stop it. So, tomorrow we go to town.

"Freddy?"

"Yes."

"I had a dream a moment ago . . . a dream of a meadow. All full of light and this dark tree. I had to go around it."

"Go to sleep, honey. Please go to sleep."

When she fell asleep he got up and sat on the hearth. We are here as on a darkling plain, he thought. We forget who we are. Branching plants, at the mercy of water. But tough. Tough and violent, some of us anyway. Oh, shit, if anything happened to her I couldn't live. Well, I've got to get some air. This day is one too many.

He pulled on a long black cashmere coat that had belonged to his father and went outside and took a sack of dog food out of the car and walked down into the hollow to feed the bobcat. He spread part of the food on the ground and left the open sack beside it. "I know you're in there," he said out loud. "Well, here's some food. Come and get it. Nora Jane's here. I guess you know that by now. Don't kill anything until she leaves." He listened. The only sound was the wind in the distance. It was very cold. The stars were very clear. Then there was a rustle, about forty yards away. Then nothing. "Good-night then," Freddy said. "I guess this dog food was grown in Iowa. The global village. Well, why not." He started back up the hill, liking thinking the bobcat could jump on him from behind at any minute. It took his mind off Nora Jane for almost half a second.

At that moment The Starlight Express came to a stop in Seattle, Washington, and Lin Tan Sing climbed down from the train and started off in search of adventure. Before the week was over he would fall in love with the daughter of a politician. His life would be shadowed for five years by the events of the next few hours but he didn't know that yet. He was in a great mood. All his philosophical and mystical beliefs were coming together like ducks on a pond. How could anything go wrong when fate had put him on a train with a girl whose amnio he had done only four months before? Twin baby girls with A-B positive, the luckiest of all blood. Not many scientists have also great feeling for mystical properties, he decided, and see genetic structure when they gaze at stars. Very lucky Father taught me to recognize beauty. Moss on Pond, Light on Water, Smoke Rising Beneath Wheels of Locomotive. Yes, Lin concluded. He was the most fortunate of men in a universe that really knows what it is doing.

Freddy let himself back into the house. He built up the fire and covered Nora Jane and lay down beside her to try to sleep. I am not paranoid, he told himself. I am hyperaware, which is a different thing. If it wasn't for people like me the race would have disappeared years ago. Who tends the lines at night? Who watches for the big cats with their night vision? Who stays outside the circle and guards the tribe?

He snuggled closer, smelling her hair. In the quiver on Paris' back the arrow for Achilles' heel smiled in its sleep. Adonai, Elohainou, Praised be thou, Lord our God, King of the Universe, who has brought forth bread from the earth. Praised be thou, Lord our God, King of the Universe, who has sanctified us by thy commandments. Now by this moon, before this moon shall wane, I shall be dead or I shall be with you.

It was five-thirty when she woke him. "I'm wet," she said. "I think my water broke. I guess that's it. You'd better go and get someone."

"Oh, no, you didn't do this to me." He was bolt upright, pulling on his boots. "You're joking. There isn't even a phone."

"Go use one somewhere. Freddy, this is serious. I'm in a lot of pain I think. I can't tell. Please go on. Go right now."

"Nora Jane. This isn't happening to us." He was pulling on his boots.

"Go on. It'll be okay. This Chinese guy said they were going to be great so they can't die. But hurry up. How far is it to Sam's?"

"Twenty minutes. Oh, shit. Okay, I'm going. Don't do anything until I get back. If you have to go to the bathroom do it right there." He leaned fiercely down over her. His hands were on her shoulders. "I'll be right back here. Don't move until I come." He ran from the house, jumped into his car, and began driving down the rocky drive. It was impossible to do more than five miles an hour over the rocks. The whole thing was impossible. The sun was lighting up the sky behind the mountains to the east. The sky was silver. Brilliant clouds covered the south and west. Freddy came to the communal gate he shared with the other people on the mountain and drove right through it, leaving it torn off the post. He drove as fast as he dared down the rocky incline and turned onto gravel and saw the smoke coming from the chimney of Sam Lyons's house.

Nora Jane was in great pain. "I'm your mother," she was pleading. "Don't hurt me. I wouldn't hurt you. Please don't do it. Don't come now. Just wait awhile, go back to sleep. Oh, my God. Oh, Jesus Christ. It's too cold. I'm freezing. I have to stop this. Pray for us sinners." The bed filled with water. She looked down. It wasn't water. It was blood. So much blood. What's going on, she thought. Why is this happening to me? I don't want it. Holy Mary, Mother of God, pray for us sinners now and at the hour of our death, Amen. Hail Mary, Mother of God, blessed art thou among women and blessed is the fruit of your womb, Jesus. Oh, Christ. Oh, shit. Oh, god damn it all to hell. I don't know what's so cold. I don't know what I'm going to do. Someone should be here. I want to see somebody. The blood continued to pour out upon the bed.

Sam came to the door. "A woman's up there having babies," Freddy said. "Get on the phone and call an ambulance and the nearest helicopter service. Try Ukiah but call the hospital in Willets first. Do it now. Sam, a woman's in my house having babies. Please." Sam turned and ran back through the house to the phone. Freddy followed him. "I'm going back. Get everyone you can get. Then come and help me. Make sure they understand the way. Or wait here for them if they don't seem to understand. Be very specific about the way. Then come. No, wait here for them. Get Selby and tell him to come to my house. I'm leaving." He ran back out the door and got back into his car and turned it around and started driving. His hands were burning into the wheel. He had never known anything in his life like this. Worse than the earthquake that ruined the store. He was alone with this. "No," he said out loud as he drove. "I couldn't love them enough to let them call me on the phone. No, I had to have this goddamn fucking house a million miles from nowhere. She'll die. I know it. I have known it from the first moment I set eyes on her. Every time I ever touched her I knew she would die and leave me. Now it's coming true." The car hit a boulder and the wheel was wrenched from his hand but he straightened it with another wrench and went on driving. The sky was lighter now. The clouds were blowing away. He parked the car a hundred yards from the house and got out and started running.

Lydia came out into the place between Nora Jane's legs and she reached for the child and held her, struggling to remember what you did with the cord. Then Freddy was there and took the baby from her and bit the cord in two and wrapped the baby in his coat and handed it to her and Tammili's head moved down into the space where Lydia's had been. Nora Jane screamed a long scream that filled all the spaces of the house and then Nora Jane didn't care anymore. Tammili's body moved out into Freddy's hands and he wrapped her in a pillowcase and laid her beside her sister, picking up one and then the other, then turning to Nora Jane. Blood was everywhere and more was coming. There was nothing to do, and there was too much to do. There wasn't any way to hold them and help her too. "It's all right," she said. "Wipe them off. I don't want blood all over them. You can't do anything for me."

"I want you to drink something." He ran into the kitchen and pulled open the refrigerator door. He found a bottle of Coke and a bottle of red wine and held them in his hands trying to decide. He took the wine and went back to where she lay. "Drink this. I want you to drink this. You're bleeding, honey. You have to drink something. They'll be here in a minute. It won't be a minute from now."

She shook her head. "I'm going to die, Freddy. It's all right. It looks real good. You wouldn't believe how it looks. Get them some good-looking clothes . . . get them a red raincoat with a hood. And yellow. Get them a lot of yellow." He pulled her body into his. It felt like it weighed a thousand pounds. Then there was nothing. Nothing, nothing, nothing. "Wake up," he screamed. "Wake up. Don't die on me. Don't you dare die on me." Still, there was nothing. He turned to the babies. He must take care of them. No, he must revive Nora Jane. He lay his head down beside hers. She was breathing. He picked up the bottle of wine and drank from it. Then he turned to the baby girls and picked them up, one at a time, then one in each arm. Then he began to count. One, two, three, four, five, six, seven, eight. He laid Lydia down beside Nora Jane and holding Tammili he began to throw logs on the fire. Then he went into the kitchen and lit the stove and put water on to boil. He dipped a kitchen towel in cold water, then threw that away and took a bottle of cooking oil and soaked a rag in it and carried Tammili back to the fire and began to wipe the blood and mucus from the child's hair. Then he put Tammili down and picked up Lydia and cleaned her for a while. They were both crying, very small yelps like no sound he had ever heard and Nora Jane lay on the floor covered with a red wool blanket soaked in blood and Freddy kept on counting. Seven hundred and seventeen. Seven hundred and eighteen. Seven hundred and nineteen. He found more towels and made a nest for the babies in the chair and knelt beside them, patting and stirring them with his hands until he heard the cars drive up and the helicopter blades descending to the cleared place beside the cistern. Adonai, Elohainu, he was saying now. Praised be thou, Lord our God, King of the Universe, who has brought forth bread from the earth. Praise be thou, inventor of helicopters, miner of steel, King of applied science. Oh, shit, they're here.

When Nora Jane came to, the helicopter pilot was on top of her, Freddy was doing something with her arms, and people were moving around the room. A man in a leather jacket was holding the twins. "They're going to freeze," she said. "I want to see them. I think I died. I died, didn't I?" The pilot moved away and Freddy propped her body up with his own and Sam tucked a blanket around her legs. "The ambulance is coming," he said. "It's okay. Everyone's okay."

"I died and it was light, like walking through a field of light. A fog made out of light. Do you think it's really like that or only shock?"

"Oh, honey," Freddy crooned into her hair. "It was the end of light. Listen, they're so cute. Wait till you see them. They're like little kittens or mice, like baby mice. They have black hair. Listen, they imprinted on my black cashmere coat. God knows what will happen now."

"I want to see them if nobody minds too much," she said. The man in the leather jacket brought them to her. She tried to reach out for them but her arms were too tired to move. "You just be still," the pilot said. "I'm Doctor Windom from the Sausalito Air Emergency Service. We were in the neighborhood. I'm sorry it took so long. We had to make three passes to find the clearing. Well, a ground crew is coming up the hill. We'll take you out in a ground vehicle. Just hold on. Everything's okay."

"I'm holding on. Freddy?"

"Yes."

"Are we safe?"

"For now." He knelt beside her and buried his face in her shoulder. He began to tremble. "Don't do that," she whispered. "Not in front of people. It's okay."

Lydia began to cry. It was the first really loud cry either of the babies had uttered. Tammili was astonished at the sound and began to cry even louder than her sister. Help, help, help, she cried. This is me. Give me something. Do something, say something, make something happen. This is me, Tammili Louise Whittington, laying my first guilt trip on my people.

"This is not the first time I have written about Nora Jane Whittington," writes Ellen Gilchrist. "In 1978 I wrote a story about her called 'The Famous Poll at Jody's Bar.' Here is how I introduced her in that story: 'Nora Jane was nineteen years old, a self-taught anarchist and a quick-change artist. She owned six Dynel wigs in different hair colors, a makeup kit she stole from Le Petit Théâtre du Vieux Carré while working as a volunteer stagehand and a small but versatile wardrobe. She could turn her graceful body into any character she saw in a movie or on TV. . . . She could also do wonderful tricks with her voice, which had a range of almost two octaves.'

"All these attributes came in handy later in the story when Nora Jane, disguised as a Dominican nun, set out to rob a bar in the Irish Channel section of New Orleans. It was the quickest way she could think of to get enough money to go to California to join her young lover, Sandy Halter."

Since that story Gilchrist's Nora Jane has returned in two stories in Victory Over Japan *(the short-story collection that won the 1984 American Book Award for Fiction) and in another in* Drunk With Love.

For many years a poet, Gilchrist turned to short fiction in the late 1970s when she wrote "Rich," which became the leading story for her first collection, In the Land of Dreamy

Dreams. *She now lives in Jackson, Mississippi, and is at work on a novel about the Peloponnesian Wars. She is a commentator for National Public Radio.*

First published in 1986 in Cosmopolitan.

RICHARD FORD

SWEETHEARTS

I was standing in the kitchen while Arlene was in the living room saying good-bye to her ex-husband Danny. I had already been out to the store for groceries and come back and made coffee, and was standing drinking it and staring out the window while the two of them said whatever they had to say. It was a quarter to six in the morning.

This was not going to be a good day in Danny's life, that was clear, because he was headed to jail. He had written several bad checks, and before he could be sentenced for that he had robbed a convenience store with a pistol—completely gone off his mind. And everything had gone to hell, as you might expect. Arlene had put up the money for his bail, and there was some expensive talk about an appeal. But there wasn't any use to that. He was guilty. It would cost money and then he would go to jail anyway.

Arlene had said she would drive him to the sheriff's department this morning if I would fix him breakfast, so he could surrender on a full stomach. And that had seemed all right. Early in the morning Danny had brought his motorcycle around to the backyard and tied up his dog to the handlebars. I had watched him from the window. He hugged the dog and kissed it on the head and whispered something in its ear, then came inside. The dog was a black Lab, and it sat beside the motorcycle now and stared with blank interest across the river at the buildings of town, where the sky was beginning to turn pinkish, and the day was opening up. It was going to be our dog for a while now, I guessed.

Arlene and I had been together almost a year. She had divorced Danny long before and had gone back to school and gotten real-estate training and bought the house we lived in, then quit that and taught high school a year, and finally quit that and just went to work in a bar in town, which is where I came upon her. She and Danny had been childhood sweethearts and run crazy for fifteen years. But when I came into the picture things with Danny were settled, more or less. No one had hard feelings left, and when he came around I didn't have any trouble with him. We had things we talked about—our pasts, our past troubles. It was not the worst you could hope for.

From the living room I heard Danny say, "So how am I going to keep up my self-respect. Answer me that. That's my big problem."

"You have to get centered," Arlene said in an upbeat voice. "Be within yourself if you can."

"I feel like I'm catching a cold right now," Danny said. "On the day I enter prison I catch cold."

"Take Contac," Arlene said. "I've got some somewhere." I heard a chair scrape. She was going to get it for him.

"I already took that," Danny said. "I had some at home."

"You'll feel better then," Arlene said. "They'll have Contac in prison."

"I put all my faith in women," Danny said softly. "I see now that was wrong."

"I couldn't say," Arlene said. And then no one spoke.

I looked out the window at Danny's dog. It was still staring across the river at town as if it knew about something there.

The door to the back bedroom opened then and my daughter Cheryl came out wearing her little white nightgown with red valentines on it. "Be Mine" was on all the valentines. She was still asleep, though she was up. Danny's voice had waked her up.

"Did you feed my fish?" she said and stared at me. She was barefoot and holding a doll, and looked pretty as a doll herself.

"You were asleep already," I said.

She shook her head and looked at the open living-room door. "Who's that?" she said.

"Danny's here," I said. "He's talking to Arlene."

Cheryl came over to the window where I was and looked out at Danny's dog. She liked Danny, but she liked his dog better. "There's Buck," she said. Buck was the dog's name. A tube of sausage was lying on the sink top and I wanted to cook it, for Danny to eat, and then have him get out. I wanted Cheryl to go to school and for the day to flatten out and hold fewer people in it. Just Arlene and me would be enough.

"You know, Danny, sweetheart," Arlene said now in the other room, "in our own lifetime we'll see the last of the people who were born in the nineteenth century. They'll all be gone soon. Every one of them."

"We should've stayed together, I think," Danny whispered. I was not supposed to hear that, I knew. "I wouldn't be going to prison if we'd loved each other."

"I wanted to get divorced, though," Arlene said.

"That was a stupid idea."

"Not for me it wasn't," Arlene said. I heard her stand up.

"It's water over the bridge now, I guess, isn't it?" I heard Danny's hands hit his knees three times in a row.

"Let's watch TV," Cheryl said to me and went and turned on the little set on the kitchen table. There was a man talking on a news show.

"Not loud," I said. "Keep it soft."

"Let's let Buck in," she said. "Buck's lonely."

"Leave Buck outside," I said.

Cheryl looked at me without any interest. She left her doll on top of the TV. "Poor Buck," she said. "Buck's crying. Do you hear him?"

"No," I said. "I can't hear him."

Danny ate his eggs and stared out the window as if he was having a hard time concentrating on what he was doing. Danny is a handsome small man with thick black hair and pale eyes. He is likable, and it is easy to see why women would like him. This morning he was dressed in jeans and a red T-shirt and boots. He looked like somebody on his way to jail.

He stared out the back window for a long time and then he sniffed and nodded. "You have to face that empty moment, Russ." He cut his eyes at me. "How often have you done that?"

"Russ's done that, Dan," Arlene said. "We've all done that now. We're adults."

"Well that's where I am right now," Danny said. "I'm at the empty moment here. I've lost everything."

"You're among friends, though, sweetheart." Arlene smiled. She was smoking a cigarette.

"I'm calling you up. Guess who I am," Cheryl said to Danny. She had her eyes squeezed tight and her nose and mouth pinched up together. She was moving her head back and forth.

"Who are you?" Danny said and smiled.

"I'm the bumblebee."

"Can't you fly?" Arlene said.

"No. My wings are much too short and I'm too fat." Cheryl opened her eyes at us suddenly.

"Well you're in big trouble then," Arlene said.

"A turkey can go forty-five miles an hour," Cheryl said and looked shocked.

"Go change your clothes," I said.

"Go ahead now, sweetheart," Arlene said and smiled at her. "I'll come help you."

Cheryl squinted at Danny, then went back to her room. When she opened her door I could see her aquarium in the dark against the wall, a pale green light with pink rocks and tiny dots of fish.

Danny ran his hands back through his hair then and stared up at the ceiling. "Well here's the awful criminal now, ready for jail," he said. And he looked at us and he looked wild suddenly, as wild and desperate as I have ever seen a man look. And it was not for no reason, I knew that.

"That's off the wall," Arlene said. "That's just completely boring. I'd never be married to a man who was a fucking criminal." She looked at me, but Danny looked at me too.

"Somebody ought to come take her away," Danny said.

"You know that, Russell? Just put her in a truck and take her away. She always has such a wonderful fucking outlook. You wonder how she got in this fix here." He looked around the little kitchen which was shabby and white. At one time Arlene's house had been a jewelry store, and there was a black security camera above the kitchen door, though it wasn't connected now.

"Just try to be nice, Danny," Arlene said.

"I just oughta slap you," Danny said. I could see his jaw muscles tighten, and I thought he might slap her then. In the bedroom I saw Cheryl standing naked in the dark, sprinkling food in her aquarium. The light made her skin look the color of water.

"Try to calm down, Dan," I said and stayed put in my chair. "We're all your friends."

"I don't know why people came out here," Danny said. "The West is fucked up. It's ruined. I wish somebody would take me away from here."

"Somebody's going to, I guess," Arlene said, and I knew she was mad at him and I didn't blame her, though I wished she hadn't said that.

Danny's blue eyes got small and he smiled at her in a hateful way. I could see Cheryl looking in at us. She had not heard this kind of talk yet. Jail talk. Mean talk. The kind you don't forget. "Do you think I'm jealous of you two?" Danny said. "Is that it?"

"I don't know what you are," Arlene said.

"Well I'm not. I'm not jealous of you two. I don't want a kid. I don't want a house. I don't want anything you got. I'd rather go to Deer Lodge." His eyes flashed out at us.

"That's lucky, then," Arlene said. She stubbed out her cigarette on her plate, blew smoke, then stood up to go help Cheryl. "Here I am now, hon," she said and closed the bedroom door.

Danny sat at the kitchen table for a while then and did not say anything. I knew he was mad but that he was not mad at me; probably, in fact, he couldn't even think why I was the one here with him now—some man he hardly knew, who slept with a woman he had loved all his life, and at that moment thought he still loved, but who—among his other troubles—didn't love him anymore. I knew he wanted to say that and a hundred things more then. But words can seem weak. And I felt sorry for him, and wanted to be as sympathetic as I could be.

"I don't like to tell people I'm divorced, Russell," Danny said very clearly and blinked his eyes. "Does that make any sense to you?" He looked at me as if he thought I was going to lie to him, which I wasn't.

"That makes plenty of sense," I said.

"You've been married, haven't you? You have your daughter."

"That's right," I said.

"You're divorced, aren't you?"

"Yes," I said.

Danny looked up at the security camera above the kitchen door, and with his finger and thumb made a gun that he pointed at the camera, and made a soft popping with his lips, then he looked at me and smiled. It seemed to make him calmer. It was a strange thing.

"Before my mother died, okay?" Danny said, "I used to call her on the phone. And it took her a long time to get out of bed. And I used to wait and wait and wait while it rang. And sometimes I knew she just wouldn't answer it, because she couldn't get up. Right? And it would ring forever because it was me, and I was willing to wait. Sometimes I'd just let it ring, and so would she, and I wouldn't know what the fuck was going on. Maybe she was dead, right?" He shook his head.

"I'll bet she knew it was you," I said. "I bet it made her feel better."

"You think?" Danny said.

"It's possible. It seems possible," I said.

"What would you do though," Danny said. He bit his lower lip and thought about the subject. "When would you let it stop ringing? Would you let it go twenty-five or fifty?

I wanted her to have time to decide. But I didn't want to drive her crazy. Okay?"

"Twenty-five seems right," I said.

Danny nodded. "That's interesting. I guess we all do things different. I always did fifty."

"That's fine."

"Fifty's way too many, I think."

"It's what you think now," I said. "But then was different."

"There's a familiar story," Danny said.

"It's everybody's story," I said. "The then-and-now story."

"We're just short of paradise, aren't we, Russell?"

"Yes we are," I said.

Danny smiled at me then in a sweet way, a way to let anyone know he wasn't a bad man, no matter what he'd robbed.

"What would you do if you were me," Danny said. "If you were on your way to Deer Lodge for a year?"

I said, "I'd think about when I was going to get out, and what kind of day that was going to be, and that it wasn't very far in the future."

"I'm just afraid it'll be too noisy to sleep in there," he said and looked concerned about that.

"It'll be all right," I said. "A year can go by quick."

"Not if you never sleep," he said. "That worries me."

"You'll sleep," I said. "You'll sleep fine."

And Danny looked at me then, across the kitchen table, like a man who knows half of something and who is supposed to know everything, who sees exactly what trouble he's in and is scared to death by it.

"I feel like a dead man, you know?" And tears suddenly came into his pale eyes. "I'm really sorry," he said. "I know you're mad at me. I'm sorry." He put his head in his hands then and cried. And I thought: What else could he do? He couldn't avoid this now. It was all right.

"It's okay, bud," I said.

"I'm happy for you and Arlene, Russ," Danny said, his face still in tears. "You have my word on that. I just wish she and I had stayed together, and I wasn't such an asshole. You know what I mean?"

"I know exactly," I said. I did not move to touch him, though maybe I should have. But Danny was not my brother, and for a moment I wished I wasn't tied to all this. I was sorry I had to see any of it, sorry that each of us would have to remember it.

On the drive to town Danny was in better spirits. He and Cheryl sat in the back, and Arlene in the front. I drove. Cheryl held Danny's hand and giggled and Danny let her put on his black silk Cam Ran Bay jacket that he had won playing cards, and Cheryl said that she had been a soldier in some war.

The morning had started out sunny, but now it had begun to be foggy, though there was sun high up, and you could see the blue Bitterroots to the south. The river was cool and in a mist, and from the bridge you could not see the pulp yard or the motels a half mile away.

"Let's just drive, Russ," Danny said from the backseat. "Head to Idaho. We'll all become Mormons and act right."

"That'd be good, wouldn't it?" Arlene turned and smiled at him. She was not mad now. It was her nicest trait not to stay mad at anybody long.

"Good day," Cheryl said.

"Who's that talking?" Danny asked.

"I'm Paul Harvey," Cheryl said.

"He always says that, doesn't he?" Arlene said.

"Good day," Cheryl said again.

"That's all Cheryl's going to say all day now, daddy," Arlene said to me.

"You've got a honeybunch back here," Danny said and tickled Cheryl's ribs. "She's her daddy's girl all the way."

"Good day," Cheryl said again and giggled.

"Children pick up your life, don't they, Russ," Danny said. "I can tell that."

"Yes they do," I said. "They can."

"I'm not so sure about that one back there, though,"

Arlene said. She was dressed in a red cowboy shirt and jeans, and she looked tired to me. But I knew she didn't want Danny to go to jail by himself.

"I am. I'm sure of it," Danny said and then didn't say anything else.

We were on a wide avenue where it was foggy, and there were shopping centers and drive-ins and car lots. A few cars had their headlights on, and Arlene stared out the window at the fog. "You know what I used to want to be?" she said.

"What?" I said, when no one else said anything.

Arlene stared a moment out the window and touched the corner of her mouth with her fingernail and smoothed something away. "A Tri-Delt," she said and smiled. "I didn't really know what they were, but I wanted to be one. I was already married to him, then, of course. And they wouldn't take married girls in."

"That's a joke," Danny said, and Cheryl laughed.

"No. It's not a joke," Arlene said. "It's just something you don't understand and that I missed out on in life." She took my hand on the seat, and kept looking out the window. And it was as if Danny wasn't there then, as if he had already gone to jail.

"What I miss is seafood," Danny said in an ironic way. "Maybe they'll have it in prison. You think they will?"

"I hope so, if you miss it," Arlene said.

"I bet they will," I said. "I bet they have fish of some kind in there."

"Fish and seafood aren't the same," Danny said.

We turned onto the street where the jail was. It was an older part of town, and there were some old white two-story residences that had been turned into lawyers' offices and bail bondsmen's rooms. Some bars were farther on, and the bus station. At the end of the street was the courthouse. I slowed so we wouldn't get there too fast.

"You're going to jail right now," Cheryl said to Danny.

"Isn't that something?" Danny said. I watched him up in

the rearview. He looked down at Cheryl and shook his head as if it amazed him.

"I'm going to school soon as that's over," Cheryl said.

"Why don't I just go to school with you?" Danny said. "I think I'd rather do that."

"No sir," Cheryl said.

"Oh Cheryl, please don't make me go to jail. I'm innocent," Danny said. "I don't want to go."

"Too bad," Cheryl said and crossed her arms.

"Be nice," Arlene said. Though I knew Cheryl thought she was being nice. She liked Danny.

"She's teasing, mama. Aren't we, Cheryl baby? We understand each other."

"I'm not her mama," Arlene said.

"That's right, I forgot," Danny said. And he widened his eyes at her. "What's your hurry, Russ?" Danny said, and I saw I had almost come to a stop in the street. The jail was a half block ahead of us. It was a tall modern building built on the back of the old stone courthouse. Two people were standing in the little front yard looking up at a window. A stationwagon was parked on the street in front. The fog had begun to burn away now.

"I didn't want to rush you," I said.

"Cheryl's already dying for me to go in there, aren't you baby?"

"No she's not. She doesn't know anything about that," Arlene said.

"You go to hell," Danny said. And he grabbed Arlene's shoulder with his hand and squeezed it back hard. "This is not your business, it's not your business at all. Look, Russ," Danny said, and he reached in the black plastic bag he was taking with him and pulled a pistol out of it and threw it over onto the front seat between Arlene and me. "I thought I might kill Arlene, but I changed my mind." He grinned at me, and I could tell he was crazy and afraid and at the end of all he could do to help himself anymore.

"Jesus Christ," Arlene said. "Jesus, Jesus Christ."

"Take it, God damn it. It's for you," Danny said, with a

crazy look. "It's what you wanted. Boom," Danny said. "Boom-boom-boom."

"I'll take it," I said and pulled the gun under my leg. I wanted to get it out of sight.

"What is it?" Cheryl said. "Lemme see." She pushed up to see.

"It's nothing, honey," I said. "Just something of Danny's."

"Is it a gun?" Cheryl said.

"No, sweetheart," I said, "it's not." And I pushed the gun down on the floor under my foot. I did not know if it was loaded, and I hoped it wasn't. I wanted Danny out of the car then. I have had my troubles, but I am not a person who likes violence or guns. I pulled over to the curb in front of the jail, behind the gray stationwagon. "You better make a move now," I said to Danny. I looked at Arlene but she was staring straight ahead. I knew she wanted Danny gone now, too.

"I didn't plan this. This just happened," Danny said. "Okay? You understand that? Nothing's planned."

"Get out," Arlene said and did not turn to look at him.

"Give Danny back his jacket," I said to Cheryl.

"Forget it, it's yours," Danny said. And he grabbed his plastic string bag.

"She doesn't want it," Arlene said.

"Yes I do," Cheryl said. "I want it."

"Okay," I said. "That's nice, sweetheart."

Danny sat in the seat and did not move then. None of us moved in the car. I could see out the window into the little jail yard. Two Indians were sitting in plastic chairs outside the double doors. A man in a gray uniform stepped out the door and said something to them, and one got up and went inside. There was a large, red-faced woman standing on the grass now, staring at our car. The fog was almost gone.

I got out and walked around the car to Danny's door and opened it. It was cool out, and I could smell the sour pulp-mill smell being held in the fog, and I could hear a car laying rubber on another street.

"Bye-bye Danny," Cheryl said in the car. She reached over and kissed him.

"Bye-bye," Danny said. "Bye-bye."

The man in the gray uniform had come down off the steps and stopped halfway to the car, watching us. He was waiting for Danny, I was sure of that.

Danny got out and stood up on the curb. He looked around and shivered from the chill in the air. He looked cold, and I felt bad for him. But I would be glad when he was gone and I could live a normal life again.

"What do we do now?" Danny said. He saw the man in the gray uniform, but would not look at him. Cheryl was saying something to Arlene in the car, but Arlene didn't say anything. "Maybe I oughta run for it," Danny said, and I could see his pale eyes were jumping as if he was eager for something now, eager for things to happen to him. Suddenly he grabbed both my arms and pushed me back against the door and pushed his face right up to my face. "Fight me," he whispered and smiled a wild smile. "Knock the shit out of me. See what they do." I pushed against him, and for a moment he held me there, and I held him, and it was as if we were dancing without moving. And I smelled his breath and felt his cold thin arms and his body struggling against me, and I knew what he wanted was for me not to let him go, and for all this to be a dream he would forget about.

"What're you doing?" Arlene said, and she turned around and glared at us. She was mad, and she wanted Danny to be in jail now. "Are you kissing each other?" she said. "Is that what you're doing? Kissing good-bye?"

"We're kissing each other, that's right," Danny said. "That's what we're doing. I always wanted to kiss Russell. We're queers." He looked at her then, and I knew he wanted to say something more to her, to tell her that he hated her or that he loved her or wanted to kill her or that he was sorry. But he couldn't come to the words for that. And I felt him go rigid and shiver, and I didn't know what he would do. Though I knew that in the end he would give in to things and go along without a struggle. He was not a man to struggle against odds. That was his character, and it is the character of many people.

"Isn't this the height of something, Russell?" Danny said, and I knew he was going to be calm now. He let go my arms and shook his head. "You and me out here like trash fighting over a woman."

And there was nothing I could say then that would save him or make life better for him at that bad moment or change the way he saw things. And I went and got back in the car while Danny turned himself in to the uniformed man who was waiting.

I drove Cheryl to school then, and when I came back outside Arlene had risen to a better mood and suggested that we take a drive. She didn't start work until noon, and I had the whole day to wait until Cheryl came home. "We should open up some emotional distance," she said. And that seemed right to me.

We drove up onto the Interstate and went toward Spokane, where I had lived once and Arlene had, too, though we didn't know each other then—the old days, before marriage and children and divorce, before we met the lives we would eventually lead, and that we would be happy with or not.

We drove along the Clark Fork for a while above the fog that stayed with the river, until the river turned north and there seemed less reason to be driving anywhere. For a time I thought we should just drive to Spokane and put up in a motel. But that, even I knew, was not a good idea. And when we had driven on far enough for each of us to think about things besides Danny, Arlene said, "Let's throw that gun away, Russ." I had forgotten all about it, and I moved it on the floor with my foot to where I could see it—the gun Danny had used, I guessed, to commit crimes and steal people's money for some crazy reason. "Let's throw it in the river," Arlene said. And I turned the car around.

We drove back to where the river turned down even with the highway again, and went off on a dirt and gravel road for a mile. I stopped under some pine trees and picked up the gun and looked at it to see if it was loaded and found it wasn't. Then Arlene took it by the barrel and flung it out the window without even leaving the car, spun it not very far from the bank, but into deep water where it hit with no splash and was gone in an instant. "Maybe that'll change his luck," I said. And I felt better about Danny for having the gun out of the car, as if he was safer now, in less danger of ruining his life and other people's, too.

When we had sat there for a minute or two, Arlene said, "Did he ever cry? When you two were sitting in the kitchen? I wondered about that."

"No," I said. "He was scared. But I don't blame him for that."

"What did he say?" And she looked as if the subject interested her now, whereas before it hadn't.

"He didn't say too much. He said he loved you, which I knew anyway."

Arlene looked out the side window at the river. There were still traces of fog that had not burned off in the sun. Maybe it was eight o'clock in the morning. You could hear the Interstate back behind us, trucks going east at high speed.

"I'm not real unhappy that Danny's out of the picture now. I have to say that," Arlene said. "I should be more, I guess, sympathetic. It's hard to love pain if you're me, though."

"It's not really my business," I said. And I truly did not think it was or ever would be. It was not where my life was leading me, I hoped.

"Maybe if I'm drunk enough someday I'll tell you about how we got apart," Arlene said. She opened the glove box and got out a package of cigarettes and closed the latch with her foot. "Nothing should surprise anyone, though, when the sun goes down. I'll just say that. It's all melodrama." She thumped the pack against the heel of her hand and put her feet up on the dash. And I thought about poor Danny then, being frisked and handcuffed out in the yard of the jail and being led away to become a prisoner, like a piece of useless machinery. I didn't think anyone could blame him for anything he ever thought or said or became after that. He could die in jail and we would still be outside and free. "Would you tell me something if I asked you?" Arlene said, opening her package of cigarettes. "Your word's worth something isn't it?"

"To me it is," I said.

She looked over at me and smiled because that was a question she had asked me before, and an answer I had said. She reached her hand across the car seat and squeezed my hand, then looked down the gravel road to where the Clark Fork went north and the receding fog had changed the colors of the trees and made them greener and the moving water a darker shade of blue-black.

"What do you think when you get in bed with me every night? I don't know why I want to know that. I just do," Arlene said. "It seems important to me."

And in truth I did not have to think about that at all, because I knew the answer, and had thought about it already, had wondered, in fact, if it was in my mind because of the time in my life it was, or because a former husband was involved, or because I had a daughter to raise alone, and no one else I could be absolutely sure of.

"I just think," I said, "here's another day that's gone. A day I've had with you. And now it's over."

"There's some loss in that, isn't there?" Arlene nodded at me and smiled.

"I guess so," I said.

"It's not so all-bad though, is it? There can be a next day."

"That's true," I said.

"We don't know where any of this is going, do we?" she said, and she squeezed my hand tight again.

"No," I said. And I knew that was not a bad thing at all, not for anyone, in any life.

"You're not going to leave me for some other woman, now, are you? You're still my sweetheart. I'm not crazy am I?"

"I never thought that," I said.

"It's your hole card, you know," Arlene said. "You can't leave twice. Danny proved that." She smiled at me again.

And I knew she was right about that, though I did not want to hear about Danny anymore for a while. He and I were not alike. Arlene and I had nothing to do with him. Though I knew, then, how you became a criminal in the world and lost it all. Somehow and for no apparent reason, your decisions got tipped over and you lost your hold. And one day you woke up and you found yourself in the very situation you said you would never ever be in, and you did not know what was most important to you anymore. And after *that* it was all over. I did not want that to happen to me, did not in fact think it ever would. I knew what love was about. It was about not giving trouble or inviting it. It was about not leaving a woman for the thought of another one. It was about never being in that place you said you'd never be in. And it was not about being alone. Never that. Never that.

"I suppose I don't write a story and finish it without its being my favorite," says Richard Ford. "It's my best effort with the particular things I have to work with at that time. I don't work at two stories at once, not usually, and so there is no competition.

"I wrote 'Sweethearts' partly because when I was living in Montana, in Missoula, there was a story in the local paper about a man who was scheduled to surrender himself to jail one morning, but who disappeared the night before. He had spent the early evening with friends and then just didn't show up the next morning. His crime was not a violent one, as I remember, and he wasn't considered dangerous. For a long time no one knew where he'd gone, and most people believed he'd left the country. But his friends thought some foul play had befallen him. And after a while, a period of months, he was found dead along the banks of the Clark Fork River, and

it was learned that he had killed himself. This is where 'Sweethearts' began, with the memory of that man—whose name I don't know now—and my own feelings for him on that night he died. I suppose I felt some tenderness for him and for his plight. And what I most like about the story I wrote are its circumstances—its dire setting and action—and a tenderness which might have come to that poor suicide, a tenderness that might not even have consoled him, but that he could at least have known had he only lived."

Richard Ford was born in Mississippi and attended college at Michigan State University and the University of California. He has lived in New York, Chicago, Princeton, New Orleans, Los Angeles, Vermont, and Montana. His first novel, A Piece of My Heart, *is largely set in Mississippi. His second novel,* The Ultimate Good Luck, *is set in Oaxaca, Mexico, and his novel* The Sportswriter *takes place in the Northeast. His first collection of stories will appear soon. He and his wife live in Mississippi.*

First published in 1986 in Esquire.

T. CORAGHESSAN BOYLE

WE ARE NORSEMEN

We are Norsemen, hardy and bold. We mount the black waves in our doughty sleek ships and go a-raiding. We are Norsemen, tough as stone. At least some of us are. Myself, I'm a skald—a poet, that is. I go along with Thorkell Son of Thorkell the Misaligned and Kolbein Snub when they sack the Irish coast and violate the Irish children, women, dogs and cattle and burn the Irish houses and pitch the ancient priceless Irish manuscripts into the sea. Then I sing about it. Doggerel like this:

Fell I not nor failed at
Fierce words, but my piercing
Blade mouth gave forth bloody
Bane speech, its harsh teaching.

Catch the kennings? That's the secret of this skaldic verse—make it esoteric and shoot it full of kennings. Anyway, it's a living.

But I'm not here to carp about a skald's life, I'm here to make art. Spin a tale for posterity. Weave a web of mystery.

That year the winter ran at us like a sword, October to May. You know the sort of thing: permafrosting winds, record cold. The hot springs crusted over, birds stiffened on the wing and dropped to the earth like stones, Thorkell the Old froze to the crossbar in the privy. Even worse: thin-ribbed wolves yabbered on our doorstep, chewed up our coats and boots, and then—one snowy night—made off with Thorkell the Young. It was impossible. We crouched round the fire, thatch leaking, and froze our norns off. The days were short, the mead barrel deep. We drank, shivered, roasted a joint, told tales. The fire played off our faces, red-gold and amber, and we fastened on the narrator's voice like a log on a dark sea, entranced, falling in on ourselves, the soft cadences pulling us through the waves, illuminating shorelines, battlefields, mountains of plunder. Unfortunately, the voice was most often mine. Believe me, a winter like that a skald really earns his keep—six months, seven days a week, and an audience of hard-bitten critics with frost in their beards. The nights dragged on.

One bleak morning we saw that yellow shoots had begun to stab through the cattle droppings in the yard—we stretched, yawned, and began to fill our boats with harrying matériel. We took our battle-axes, our throwing axes, our hewing axes, our massive stroke-dealing swords, our disemboweling spears, a couple of strips of jerky and a jug of water. As I said, we were tough. Some of us wore our twin-horned battle helmets, the sight of which interrupts the vital functions of our victims and enemies and inspires high-keyed vibrato. Others of us, in view of fifteen-degree temperatures and a stiff breeze whitening the peaks of the waves, felt that the virtue of toughness had its limits. I decided on a lynx hat that gave elaborate consideration to the ears.

We fought over the gravel brake to launch our terrible swift ship. The wind shrieked of graves robbed, the sky was a hearth gone cold. An icy froth soaked us to the waist. Then we were off, manning the oars in smooth Nordic sync, the ship lurching through rocky breakers, heaving up, slapping down. The spray shot needles in our eyes, the oars lifted and dipped. An hour later the mainland winked into oblivion behind the dark lids of sea and sky.

There were thirteen of us: Thorkell Son of Thorkell the Misaligned, Thorkell the Short, Thorkell Thorkellsson, Thorkell Cat, Thorkell Flat-Nose, Thorkell-neb, Thorkell Ale-Lover, Thorkell the Old, Thorkell the Deep-minded, Ofeig, Skeggi, Grim and me. We were tough. We were hardy. We were bold.

Nonetheless the voyage was a disaster. A northeaster roared down on us like a herd of drunken whales and swept us far off course. We missed our landfall—Ireland—by at least two hundred miles and carried past into the open Atlantic. Eight weeks we sailed, looking for land. Thorkell the Old was bailing one gray afternoon and found three menhaden in his bucket. We ate them raw. I speared an albatross and hung it round my neck. It was no picnic.

Then one night we heard the cries of gulls like souls stricken in the dark. Thorkell Ale-Lover, keen of smell, snuffed the breeze. "Landfall near," he said. In the morning the sun threw our shadows on a new land—buff and green, slabs of gray, it swallowed the horizon.

"Balder be praised!" said Thorkell the Old.

"Thank Frigg," I said.

We skirted the coast, looking for habitations to sack. There were none. We'd discovered a wasteland. The Thorkells were for putting ashore to replenish our provisions and make sacrifice to the gods (in those days we hadn't yet learned to swallow unleavened bread and dab our foreheads with ashes. We were real primitives.) We ran our doughty sleek warship up a sandy spit and leaped ashore, fierce as flayed demons. It was an unnecessary show of force, as the countryside was desolate, but it did our hearts good.

The instant my feet touched earth the poetic fit came on me and I composed this verse:

New land, new-found beyond
The mickle waves by fell
Men-fish, their stark battle
Valor failèd them not.

No *Edda,* I grant you—but what can you expect after six weeks of bailing? I turned to Thorkell Son of Thorkell the Misaligned, my brain charged with creative fever. "Hey!" I shouted, "let's name this new-found land!" The others crowded round. Thorkell Son of Thorkell the Misaligned looked down at me (he was six four, his red beard hung to his waist). "We'll call it—Newfoundland!" I roared. There was silence. The twin horns of Thorkell's helmet pierced the sky, his eyes were like stones. "Thorkell-land," he said.

We voted. The Thorkells had it, 9 to 4.

For two and a half weeks we plumbed the coast, catching conies, shooting deer, pitching camp on islands or guarded promontories. I'd like to tell you it was glorious—golden sunsets, virgin forests, the thrill of discovery and all that—but when your business is sacking and looting, a virgin forest is the last thing you want to see. We grumbled bitterly. But Thorkell Son of Thorkell the Misaligned was loath to admit that the land to which he'd given his name was uninhabited—and consequently of no use whatever. We forged on. Then one morning he called out from his place at the tiller: "Hah!" he said, and pointed toward a rocky abutment a hundred yards ahead. The mist lay on the water like flocks of sheep. I craned my neck, squinted, saw nothing. And then suddenly, like a revelation, I saw them: three tall posts set into the earth and carved with the figures of men and beasts. The sight brought water to my eyes and verse to my lips (but no sense in troubling you with any dilatory stanzas now—this is a climactic moment).

We landed. Crept up on the carvings, sly and wary, silent as stones. As it turned out, our caution was superfluous: the place was deserted. Besides the carvings (fanged monsters, stags, serpents, the grinning faces of a new race) there was no evidence of human presence whatever. Not even a footprint. We hung our heads: another bootyless day. Ofeig—the berserker—was seized with his berserker's rage and wound up hacking the three columns to splinters with his massive stroke-dealing sword.

The Thorkells were of the opinion that we should foray inland in search of a village to pillage. Who was I to argue? Inland we went, ever hardy and bold, up hill and down dale, through brakes and brambles and bogs and clouds of insects that rushed up our nostrils and down our throats. We found nothing. On the way back to the ship we were luckier. Thorkell-neb stumbled over a shadow in the path, and when the shadow leaped up and shot through the trees, we gave chase. After a good rib-heaving run we caught what proved to be a boy, eleven or twelve, his skin the color of copper, the feathers of birds in his hair. Like the Irish, he spoke gibberish.

Thorkell Son of Thorkell the Misaligned drew pictures in the sand and punched the boy in the chest until the boy agreed to lead us to his people, the carvers of wood. We were Norsemen, and we always got our way. All of us warmed to the prospect of spoils, and off we went on another trek. We brought along our short-swords and disemboweling spears—just in case—though judging from the boy's condition (he was bony and naked, his eyes deep and black as the spaces between the stars) we had nothing to fear from his kindred.

We were right. After tramping through the under- and overgrowth for half an hour we came to a village: smoking cook pots, skinny dogs, short and ugly savages, their hair the color of excrement. I counted six huts of branches and mud, the sort of thing that might excite a beaver. When we stepped into the clearing—tall, hardy and bold—the savages set up a fiendish caterwauling and rushed for their weapons. But what a joke their weapons were! Ofeig caught an arrow in the air, looked at the head on it, and collapsed laughing: it was made of flint. Flint. Can you believe it? Here we'd come Frigg knows how many miles for plunder and the best we could do was a bunch of Stone Age aborigines who thought that a necklace of dogs' teeth was the height of fashion. Oh how we longed for those clever Irish and their gold brooches and silver-inlaid bowls. Anyway, we subdued these screechers as we called them, sacrificed the whole lot of them to the gods (the way I saw it we were doing them a favor), and headed back to our terrible swift ship, heavy of heart. There was no longer any room for debate: Ireland, look out!

As we pointed the prow east the westering sun threw the shadow of the new land over us. Thorkell the Old looked back over his shoulder and shook his head in disgust. "That place'll never amount to a hill of beans," he said.

And then it was gone.

Days rose up out of the water and sank behind us. Intrepid Norsemen, we rode the currents, the salt breeze tickling our nostrils and bellying the sail. Thorkell Flat-Nose was our navigator. He kept two ravens on a cord. After five and a half weeks at sea he released one of them and it shot off into the sky and vanished—but in less than an hour the bird was spotted off starboard, winging toward us, growing larger by turns until finally it flapped down on the prow and allowed its leg to be looped to the cord. Three days later Flat-Nose released the second raven. The bird mounted high, winging to the southeast until it became a black rune carved into the horizon. We followed it into a night of full moon, the stars like milk splattered in the cauldron of the sky. The sea whispered at the prow, the tiller hissed behind us. Suddenly Thorkell Ale-Lover cried, "Land-ho!" We were fell and grim and ravenous. We looked up at the black ribbon of the Irish coast and grinned like wolves. Our shoulders dug at the oars, the sea sliced by. An hour later we landed.

Ofeig was for sniffing out habitations, freebooting, and laying waste. But dawn crept on apace, and Thorkell Son of Thorkell the Misaligned reminded him that we Norsemen attack only under cover of darkness, swift and silent as a nightmare. Ofeig did not take it well: the berserker's rage came on him and he began to froth and chew at his tongue and howl like a skinned beast. It was a tense moment. We backed off as he grabbed for his battle-ax and whirred it about his head. Fortunately he stumbled over a root and began to attack the earth, gibbering and slavering, sparks slashing out from buried stones as if the ground had suddenly caught fire. (Admittedly, berserkers can be tough to live with—but you can't beat them when it comes to seizing hearts with terror or battling trolls, demons or demiurges.)

Our reaction to all this was swift and uncomplicated: we moved up the beach about two hundred yards and settled down to get some rest. I stretched out in a patch of wild flowers and watched the sky, Ofeig's howls riding the breeze like a celestial aria, waves washing the shore. The Thorkells slept on their feet. It was nearly light when we finally dozed off, visions of plunder dancing in our heads.

I woke to the sound of whetstone on ax: we were polishing the blade edges of our fearsome battle weapons. It was late afternoon. We hadn't eaten in days. Thorkell-neb and Skeggi stood naked on the beach, basting one another with black mud scooped from a nearby marsh. I joined them. We darkened our flaxen hair, drew grim black lines under our eyes, chanted fight songs. The sun hit the water like a halved fruit, then vanished. A horned owl shot out across the dunes. Crickets kreeked in the bushes. The time had come. We drummed one another about the neck and shoulders for a while ("Yeah!" we yelled, "yeah!"), fastened our helmets, and then raced our serpent-headed ship into the waves.

A few miles up the coast we came on a light flickering out over the dark corrugations of the sea. As we drew closer it became apparent that the source of light was detached from the coast itself—could it be an island? Our blood quickened, our lips drew back in anticipation. Ravin and rapine at last! And an island no less—what could be more ideal? There would be no escape from our pure silent fury, no chance of secreting treasures, no hope of reinforcements hastily roused from bumpkin beds in the surrounding countryside. Ha!

An island it was—a tiny point of land, slick with ghostly cliffs and crowned with the walls of a monastery. We circled it, shadows on the dark swell. The light seemed to emanate from a stone structure atop the highest crag—some bookish monk with his nose to the paper no doubt, copying by the last of the firelight. He was in for a surprise. We rode the bosom of the sea and waited for the light to fail. Suddenly Thorkell the Old began to cackle. "That'll be Inishmurray," he wheezed. "Fattest monastery on the west coast." Our eyes glowed. He spat into the spume. "Thought it looked familiar," he said. "I helped Thorir Paunch sack it back in '75." Then the light died and the world became night.

We watched the bookish monk in our minds' eyes: kissing the text and laying it on a shelf, scattering the fire, plodding wearily to his cell and the cold gray pallet. I recited an incendiary verse while we waited for the old ecclesiast to tumble into sleep:

Eye-bleed monk,
Night his bane.
Darkness masks
The sea-wound,
Mickle fell,
Mickle stark.

I finished the recitation with a flourish, rolling the mickles like thunder. Then we struck.

It was child's play. The slick ghostly cliffs were like rolling meadows, the outer wall a branch in our path. There was no sentry, no watchdog, no alarm. We dropped down into the courtyard, naked, our bodies basted black, our doughty death-dealing weapons in hand. We were shadows, fears, fragments of a bad dream.

Thorkell Son of Thorkell the Misaligned stole into one of the little stone churches and emerged with a glowing brand. Then he set fire to two or three of the wickerwork cells and a pile of driftwood. From that point on it was pandemonium—Ofeig tumbling stone crosses, the Thorkells murdering monks in their beds, Skeggi and Thorkell the Old chasing women, Thorkell Ale-Lover waving joints of mutton and horns of beer. The Irish defended themselves as best they could, two or three monks coming at us with barbed spears and pilgrim's staffs, but we made short work of them. We were Norsemen, after all.

For my own part, I darted here and there through the smoke and rubble, seized with a destructive frenzy, frightening women and sheep with my hideous blackened features, cursing like a jay. I even cut down a doddering crone for the sake of a gold brooch, my sweetheart Thorkella in mind. Still, despite the lust and chaos and the sweet smell of anarchy, I kept my head and my poet's eye. I observed each of the principal Thorkells with a reporter's acuity, noting each valorous swipe and thrust, the hot skaldic verses already forming on my lips. But then suddenly I was distracted: the light had reappeared in the little chapel atop the crag. I counted Thorkells (no mean feat when you consider the congeries of legs and arms, sounds and odors, the panicked flocks of sheep, pigs and chickens, the jagged flames, the furious womanizing, gormandizing and sodomizing of the crew). As I say, I counted Thorkells. We were all in sight. Up above, the light grew in intensity, flaming like a planet against the night sky. I thought of the bookish monk and started up the hill.

The night susurrated around me: crickets, katydids, cicadas, and far below the rush of waves on the rocks. The glare from the fires behind me gave way to blackness, rich and star-filled. I hurried up to the chapel, lashed by malice aforethought and evil intent—bookish monk, bookish monk—and burst through the door. I was black and terrible, right down to the tip of my foreskin. "Arrrrr!" I growled. The monk sat at a table, his hands clenched, head bent over a massive tome. He was just as I'd pictured him: pale as milk, a fringe of dark pubic hair around his tonsure, puny and frail. He did not look up. I growled again, and when I got no response I began to slash at candles and pitchers and icons and all the other superstitious trappings of the place. Pottery splashed to the floor, shelves tumbled. Still he bent over the book.

The book. What in Frigg's name was a book anyway? Scratchings on a sheet of cowhide. Could you fasten a cloak with it, carry mead in it, impress women with it, wear it in your hair? There was gold and silver scattered round the room, and yet he sat over the book as if it could glow or talk or something. The idiot. The pale, puny, unhardy, unbold idiot. A rage came over me at the thought of it—I shoved him aside and snatched up the book, thick pages, dark characters, the mystery and magic. Snatched it up, me, a poet, a Norseman, an annihilator, an illiterate. Snatched it up and watched the old monk's suffering features as I fed it, page by filthy page, into the fire. Ha!

We are Norsemen, hardy and bold. We mount the black waves in our doughty sleek ships and go a-raiding. We are Norsemen, tough as stone. We are Norsemen.

"We Are Norsemen" grew out of a course in Norse sagas that Boyle took and has remained a favorite because "I like the way it blends the colloquial and a modern sensibility with the classic Norse references." The tale of this skald has the same high energy-level as its conquering Norsemen and is characteristic of Boyle's style of satire—which has produced stories ranging from an imagined romance between President Eisenhower and Nina Khrushchev to a reworking of Gogol's "The Overcoat" in contemporary Russia.

Boyle suggested several of his favorite stories, but since this one had had the least previous exposure, I decided to make an exception this once and use a story published earlier than within the past three years.

Boyle's short stories have been collected in Greasy Lake and Other Stories *and* The Descent of Man. *His novels include* Budding Prospects *and* Water Music. *Born in Peekskill, New York, Boyle is currently at work on a novel about the intertwined destinies of three families over three hundred years of life in the Hudson Valley. He lives in Los Angeles.*

First published in 1972 in Harper's.

STUART DYBEK

BLIGHT

During those years between Korea and Vietnam, when rock and roll was being perfected, our neighborhood was proclaimed an Official Blight Area.

Richard J. Daley was mayor then. It seemed as if he had always been, and would always be, the mayor. Ziggy Zilinsky claimed to have seen the mayor himself riding down 23rd Place in a black limousine flying one of those little purple pennants from funerals, except his said WHITE SOX on it. The mayor sat in the backseat sorrowfully shaking his head as if to say "Jeez!" as he stared out the bulletproof window at the winos drinking on the corner by the boarded-up grocery.

Of course, nobody believed that Zig had actually seen the mayor. Ziggy had been unreliable even before Pepper Rosado had accidentally beaned him during a game of It with the Bat. People still remembered as far back as third grade when Ziggy had jumped up in the middle of mass yelling, "Didja see her? She nodded! I asked the Blessed Virgin would my cat come home and she nodded yes!"

All through grade school the statues of saints winked at Ziggy. He was in constant communication with angels and the dead. And Ziggy sleepwalked. The cops had picked him up once in the middle of the night for running around the bases in Washtenaw Playground while still asleep.

When he'd wake up, Ziggy would recount his dreams as if they were prophecies. He had a terrible recurring nightmare in which atomic bombs dropped on the city the night the White Sox won the pennant. But he had wonderful dreams, too. My favorite was the one in which he and I and Little Richard were in a band playing in the center of St. Sabina's roller rink.

After Pepper brained him out on the boulevard with a bat—a fungo bat that Pepper whipped like a tomahawk across a twenty-yard width of tulip garden that Ziggy was trying to hide behind—Zig stopped seeing visions of the saints. Instead, he began catching glimpses of famous people, not movie stars so much as big shots in the news. Every once in a while Zig would spot somebody like Bo Diddley going by on a bus. Mainly, though, it would be some guy in a homburg who looked an awful lot like Eisenhower, or he'd notice a reappearing little gray-haired fat guy who could turn out to be either Nikita Khrushchev or Mayor Daley. It didn't surprise us. Zig was the kind of kid who read newspapers. We'd all go to Potok's to buy comics and Zig would walk out with the *Daily News.* Zig had always worried about things no one else cared about, like the population explosion, people starving in India, the world blowing up. We'd be walking along down 22nd and pass an alley and Ziggy would say, "See that?"

"See what?"

"Mayor Daley scrounging through garbage."

We'd all turn back and look, but only see a bag lady picking through cans.

Still, in a way, I could see it from Ziggy's point of view. Mayor Daley *was* everywhere. The city was tearing down buildings for urban renewal and tearing up streets for a new expressway, and everywhere one looked there were signs in front of the rubble reading:

SORRY FOR THE INCONVENIENCE
ANOTHER IMPROVEMENT
FOR A GREATER CHICAGO
RICHARD J. DALEY, MAYOR

Not only were there signs everywhere, but a few blocks away a steady stream of fat, older, bossy-looking guys emanated from the courthouse on 26th. They looked like a corps of Mayor Daley doubles and sometimes, especially on election days, they'd march into the neighborhood chewing cigars and position themselves in front of the flag-draped barbershops that served as polling places.

But back to blight.

That was an expression we used a lot. We'd say it after going downtown, or after spending the day at the Oak Street Beach, which we regarded as the beach of choice for sophisticates. We'd pack our towels and, wearing our swimsuits under our jeans, take the subway north.

"North to freedom," one of us would always say.

Those were days of longing without cares, of nothing to do but lie out on the sand inspecting the world from behind our sunglasses. At the Oak Street Beach the city seemed to realize our dreams of it. We gazed out nonchalantly at the white-sailed yachts on the watercolor-blue horizon, or back across the Outer Drive at the lake-reflecting glass walls of high-rises as if we took it all for granted. The blue, absorbing shadow would deepen to azure, and a fiery orange sun would dip behind the glittering buildings. The crowded beach would gradually empty, and a pitted moon would hover over sand scalloped with a million footprints. It would be time to go.

"Back to blight," one of us would always joke.

I remember a day shortly after blight first became official. We were walking down Rockwell, cutting through the truck docks, Zig, Pepper, and I, on our way to the viaduct near Douglas Park. Pepper was doing his Fats Domino impression, complete with opening piano riff: *Bum-pah-da bum-pah-da dummmmm . . .*

Ah foun' mah thrill
Ahn Blueberry Hill . . .

It was the route we usually walked to the viaduct, but since blight had been declared we were trying to see our surroundings from a new perspective, to determine if anything had been changed, or at least appeared different. Blight sounded serious, Biblical in a way, like something locusts might be responsible for.

"Or a plague of gigantic, radioactive cockroaches," Zig said, "climbing out of the sewers."

"Blight, my kabotch," Pepper said, grabbing his kabotch and shaking it at the world. "They call this blight? Hey, man, there's weeds and trees and everything, man. You shoulda seen it on Eighteenth Street."

We passed a Buick somebody had dumped near the railroad tracks. It had been sitting there for months and was still crusted with salt-streaked winter grime. Someone had scraped WASH ME across its dirty trunk, and someone else had scrawled WHIP ME across its hood. Pepper snapped off the aerial and whipped it back and forth so that the air whined, then slammed it down on a fender and began rapping out a Latin beat. We watched him smacking the hell out of it, then Zig and I picked up sticks and broken hunks of bricks and started clanking the headlights and bumpers as if they were bongos and congas, all of us chanting out the melody to "Tequila." Each time we grunted out the word *tequila*, Pepper, who was dancing on the hood, stomped out more windshield.

We were revving up for the viaduct, a natural echo chamber where we'd been going for blues-shout contests ever since we'd become infatuated with Screamin' Jay Hawkins's "I Put a Spell on You." In fact, it was practicing blues shouts together that had led to the formation of our band, the No Names. We practiced in the basement of the apartment building I lived in: Zig on bass, me on sax, Pepper on drums, and a guy named Deejo who played accordion, though he promised us he was saving up to buy an electric guitar.

Pepper could play. He was a natural.

"I go crazy," was how he described it.

His real name was Stanley Rosado. His mother sometimes called him Stashu, which he hated. She was Polish and his father was Mexican—the two main nationalities in the neighborhood together in one house. It wasn't always an easy alliance, especially inside Pepper. When he got pissed he was a wild man. Things suffered, sometimes people, but always things. Smashing stuff seemed to fill him with peace.

Sometimes he didn't even realize he was doing it, like the time he took flowers to Linda Molina, a girl he'd been nuts about since grade school. Linda lived in one of the well-kept two-flats along Marshall Boulevard, right across from Assumption Church. Maybe it was just that proximity to the church, but there had always been a special aura about her. Pepper referred to her as "the unadulterated one." He finally worked up the nerve to call her, and when she actually invited him over, he walked down the boulevard to her house in a trance. It was late spring, almost summer, and the green boulevard stretched like an enormous lawn before Linda Molina's house. At its center was a blazing garden of tulips. The city had planted them. Their stalks sprouted tall, more like corn than flowers, and their colors seemed to vibrate in the air. The tulips were the most beautiful thing in the neighborhood. Mothers wheeled babies by them; old folks hobbled for blocks and stood before them as if they were sacred.

Linda answered the door and Pepper stood there holding a huge bouquet.

"For you," Pepper said.

Linda, smiling with astonishment, accepted the flowers; then her eyes suddenly widened in horror. "You didn't—?" she asked.

Pepper shrugged.

"*¡Lechón!*" the Unadulterated One screamed, pitching a shower of tulips into his face and slamming the door.

That had happened over a year before and Linda still refused to talk to him. It had given Pepper's blues shouts a particularly soulful quality, especially since he continued to preface them, in the style of Screamin' Jay Hawkins, with the words "I love you." *I love you! Aiiiyyaaaaaaa!!!*

Pepper even had Screamin' Jay's blues snork down.

We'd stand at the shadowy mouth of the viaduct, peering at the greenish gleam of light at the other end of the tunnel. The green was the grass and trees of Douglas Park. Pepper would begin slamming an aerial or board or chain off the girders, making the echoes collide and ring, while Ziggy and

I clonked empty bottles and beer cans, and all three of us would be shouting and screaming like Screamin' Jay or Howlin' Wolf, like those choirs of unleashed voices we'd hear on *Jam with Sam's* late-night blues show. Sometimes a train streamed by, booming overhead like part of the song, and we'd shout louder yet, and I'd remember my father telling me how he could have been an opera singer if he hadn't ruined his voice as a kid imitating trains. Once, a gang of black kids appeared on the Douglas Park end of the viaduct and stood harmonizing from bass through falsetto just like the Coasters, so sweetly that though at first we tried outshouting them, we finally shut up and listened, except for Pepper keeping the beat.

We applauded from our side, but stayed where we were, and they stayed on theirs. Douglas Park had become the new boundary after the riots the summer before.

"How can a place with such good viaducts have blight, man?" Pepper asked, still rapping his aerial as we walked back.

"Frankly, man," Ziggy said, "I always suspected it was a little fucked up around here."

"Well, that's different," Pepper said. "Then let them call it an Official Fucked-Up Neighborhood."

Nobody pointed out that you'd never hear a term like that from a public official, at least not in public, and especially not from the office of the mayor who had once promised, "We shall reach new platitudes of success."

Nor did anyone need to explain that Official Blight was the language of revenue, forms in quintuplet, grants, and Federal aid channeled through the Machine and processed with the help of grafters, skimmers, wheeler-dealers, an army of aldermen, precinct captains, patronage workers, their relatives and friends. No one said it, but instinctively we knew we'd never see a nickel.

Not that we cared. They couldn't touch us if we didn't. Besides, we weren't blamers. Blight was just something that happened, like acne or old age. Maybe declaring it official mattered in that mystical world of property values, but it wasn't radical, like condemning buildings or labeling a place a slum. Slums were on the other side of the viaduct.

Blight, in fact, could be considered a kind of official recognition, a grudging admission that among blocks of factories, railroad tracks, truck docks, industrial dumps, scrapyards, expressways, and the drainage canal, people had managed to wedge in their everyday lives.

Deep down we believed what Pepper had been getting at: Blight had nothing to do with ecstasy. They could send in the building inspectors and social workers, the mayor could drive through in his black limo, but they'd never know about the music of viaducts, or churches where saints winked and nodded, or how right next door to me our guitar player, Joey "Deejo" DeCampo, had finally found his title, and inspired by it had begun the Great American Novel, *Blight*, which opened: "The dawn rises like sick old men playing on the rooftops in their underwear."

We had him read that to us again and again.

Ecstatic, Deejo rushed home and wrote all night. I could always tell when he was writing. It wasn't just the wild, dreamy look that overcame him. Deejo wrote to music, usually the *1812 Overture,* and since only a narrow gangway between buildings separated his window from mine, when I heard bells and cannon blasts at two in the morning I knew he was creating.

Next morning, bleary-eyed, sucking a pinched Lucky, Deejo read us the second sentence. It ran twenty ball-point scribbled loose-leaf pages and had nothing to do with the old men on the rooftops in their underwear. It seemed as though Deejo had launched into a digression before the novel had even begun. His second sentence described an epic battle between a spider and a caterpillar. The battle took place in the gangway between our apartment buildings and that's where Deej insisted on reading it to us. The gangway lent his voice an echoey ring. He read with his eyes glued to the page, his free hand gesticulating wildly, pouncing spiderlike, fingers jabbing like a beak tearing into green caterpillar guts, fist opening like a jaw emitting shrieks. His voice rose as the caterpillar reared, howling like a damned soul, its poisonous hairs bristling. Pepper, Ziggy, and I listened, occasionally exchanging looks.

It wasn't Deejo's digressing that bothered us. That was how we all told stories. But we could see that Deejo's inordinate fascination with bugs was surfacing again. Not that he was alone in that, either. Of all our indigenous wildlife—sparrows, pigeons, mice, rats, dogs, cats—it was only bugs that suggested the grotesque richness of nature. A lot of kids had, at one time or another, expressed their wonder by torturing them a little. But Deejo had been obsessed. He'd become diabolically adept as a destroyer, the kind of kid who would observe an ant hole for hours, even bait it with a Holloway Bar, before blowing it up with a cherry bomb. Then one day his grandpa Tony said, "Hey, Joey, pretty soon they're gonna invent little microphones and you'll be able to hear them screaming."

He was kidding, but the remark altered Deejo's entire way of looking at things. The world suddenly became one of an infinite number of infinitesimal voices, and Deejo equated voices with souls. If one only listened, it was possible to hear tiny choirs that hummed at all hours as on a summer night, voices speaking a language of terror and beauty that, for the first time, Deejo understood.

It was that vision that turned him into a poet, and it was really for his poetry, more than his guitar playing, that we'd recruited him for the No Names. None of us could write lyrics, though I'd tried a few takeoffs, like the one on Jerry Lee Lewis's "Great Balls of Fire":

My BVDs were made of thatch,
You came along and lit the match,
I screamed in pain, my screams grew higher,
Goodness gracious! My balls were on fire!

We were looking for a little more soul, words that would suggest Pepper's rages, Ziggy's prophetic dreams. And we might have had that if Deejo could have written a bridge. He'd get in a groove like "Lonely Is the Falling Rain":

Lonely is the falling rain,
Every taste
Seems the same,

Lonely is the willow tree,
Green dress draped
Across her knee,

Lonely is the boat at sea . . .

Deejo could go on listing lonely things for pages, but he'd never arrive at a bridge. His songs refused to circle back on themselves. They'd just go on and were impossible to memorize.

He couldn't spell, either, which never bothered us but created a real problem when Pepper asked him to write something that Pepper could send to Linda Molina. Deejo came up with "I Dream," which ended with the lines:

I dream of my arms
Around your waste.

Linda mailed it back to Pepper with those lines circled and in angry slashes of eyebrow pencil the exclamations: *¡LECHON! ¡¡ESTUPIDO!!* PERVERT!!!

Pepper kept it folded in his wallet like a love letter.

But back to *Blight.*

We stood in the gangway listening to Deejo read. His seemingly nonstop sentence was reaching a climax. Just when the spider and caterpillar realized their battle was futile, that neither could win, a sparrow swooped down and gobbled them both up.

It was a parable. Who knows how many insect lives had been sacrificed in order for Deejo to have finally scribbled those pages?

We hung our heads and muttered, "Yeah, great stuff, Deej, that was good, man, no shit, keep it up, be a best seller."

He folded his loose-leaf papers, stuffed them into his back pocket, and walked away without saying anything.

Later, whenever someone would bring up his novel, *Blight,* and its great opening line, Deejo would always say, "Yeah, and it's been all downhill from there."

As long as it didn't look like Deejo would be using his title in the near future we decided to appropriate it for the band. We considered several variations—Boys from Blight, Blights Out, The Blight Brigade. We wanted to call ourselves Pepper and the Blighters, but Pepper said no way, so we settled on just plain Blighters. That had a lot better ring to it than calling ourselves the No Names. We had liked being the No Names at first, but it had started to seem like an advertisement for an identity crisis. The No Names sounded too much like one of the tavern-sponsored softball teams the guys back from Korea had formed. Those guys had been our heroes when we were little kids. They had seemed like legends to us as they gunned around the block on Indians and Harleys while we walked home from grade school. Now they hung out at corner taverns, working on beer bellies, and played softball a couple of nights a week on teams that lacked both uniforms and names. Some of their teams had jerseys with the name of the bar that sponsored them across the back, but the bars themselves were mainly named after beers—the Fox Head 500 on 25th Street, or the Edelweiss Tap on 26th, or down from that the Carta Blanca. Sometimes, in the evenings, we'd walk over to Lawndale Park and watch one of the tavern teams play softball under the lights. Invariably some team calling itself the Damon Demons or the Latin Cobras, decked out in gold-and-black uniforms, would beat their butts.

There seemed to be some unspoken relationship between being nameless and being a loser. Watching the guys from Korea after their ball games as they hung around under the buzzing neon signs of their taverns, guzzling beers and flipping the softball, I got the strange feeling that they had actually chosen anonymity and the loserhood that went with it. It was something they looked for in one another, that held them together. It was as if Korea had confirmed the choice in them, but it had been there before they'd been drafted. I could still remember how they once organized a motorcycle club. They called it the Motorcycle Club. Actually, nobody even called it that. It was the only nameless motorcycle gang I'd ever heard of.

A lot of those guys had grown up in the housing project that Pepper and Ziggy lived in, sprawling blocks of row houses known simply as "the projects," rather than something ominous-sounding like Cabrini-Green. Generations of nameless gangs had roamed the projects, then disappeared, leaving behind odd, anonymous graffiti—unsigned warnings, threats, and imprecations without the authority of a gang name behind them.

It wasn't until we became Blighters that we began to recognize the obscurity that surrounded us. Other neighborhoods at least had identities, like Back of the Yards, Marquette Park, Logan Square, Greektown. There were places named after famous intersections like Halsted and Taylor. Everyone knew the mayor still lived in Bridgeport, the neighborhood he was born in. We heard our area referred to sometimes as Zone 8, after its postal code, but that never caught on. Nobody said, "Back to Zone 8." For a while Deejo had considered *Zone 8* as a possible title for his novel, but he finally rejected it as sounding too much like science fiction.

As Blighters, just walking the streets we became suddenly aware of familiar things we didn't have names for, like the trees we'd grown up walking past, or the flowers we'd always admired that bloomed around the blue plastic shrine of the Virgin in the front yard of the Old Widow. Even the street names were mainly numbers, something I'd never have noticed if Debbie Weiss, a girl I'd met downtown, hadn't pointed it out.

Debbie played sax, too, in the band at her all-girls high school. I met her in the sheet-music department of Lyon & Healy's music store. We were both flipping through the same Little Richard songbooks. His songs had great sax breaks, the kind where you roll onto your back and kick your feet in the air while playing.

"Tenor or alto?" she asked without looking up from the music.

I glanced around to make sure she was talking to me. She was humming "Tutti Frutti" under her breath.

"Tenor," I answered, amazed we were talking.

"That's what I want for my birthday. I've got an alto, an old Martin. It was my Uncle Seymour's. He played with Chick Webb."

"Oh, yeah," I said, impressed, though I didn't know exactly who Chick Webb was. "How'd you know I played sax?" I asked her, secretly pleased that I obviously looked like someone who did.

"It was either that or you've got weird taste in ties. You always walk around wearing your neck strap?"

"No, I just forgot to take it off after practicing," I explained, effortlessly slipping into my first lie to her. Actually, I had taken to wearing the neck strap for my saxophone sort of in the same way that the Mexican guys in the neighborhood wore gold chains dangling outside their T-shirts, except that instead of a cross at the end of my strap I had a little hook from which the horn was meant to hang.

We went to a juice bar Debbie knew around the corner from the music store. I had a Coco-Nana and she had something with mango, papaya, and passion fruit.

"So how'd you think I knew you played sax? By your thumb callus?" she laughed.

We compared the thumb calluses we had from holding our horns. She was funny. I'd never met a girl so easy to talk to. We talked about music and saxophone reeds and school. The only thing wrong was that I kept telling her lies. I told her that I played in a band in Cicero in a club that was run by the Mafia. She said she'd never been to Cicero, but it sounded like really the pits. "Really the pits" was one of her favorite phrases. She lived on the North Side and invited me to visit. When she wrote her address down on a napkin and asked if I knew how to get there I said, "Sure, I know where that is."

North to Freedom, I kept thinking on my way to her house the first time, trying to remember all the bull I'd told her. It took over an hour and two transfers to get there. I ended up totally lost. I was used to streets that were numbers, streets that told you exactly where you were and what was coming up next. "Like knowing the latitude," I told her.

She argued that the North Side had more class because the streets had names.

"A number lacks character, David. How can you have a feeling for a street called Twenty-second?" she asked.

She'd never been on the South Side except for a trip to the museum.

I'd ride the Douglas Park B train home from her house and pretend she was sitting next to me, and as my stop approached I'd look down at the tar-paper roofs, back porches, alleys, and backyards crammed between factories, and try to imagine how it would look to someone seeing it for the first time.

At night, 22nd was a streak of colored lights, electric winks of neon glancing off plate glass and sidewalks as headlights surged by. The air smelled of restaurants—frying burgers, pizza parlors, the cornmeal and hot-oil blast of *taquerías.* Music collided out of open bars. And when it rained and the lights on the oily street shimmered, Deejo would start whistling "Harlem Nocturne" in the backseat.

I'd inherited a '53 Chevy from my father. He hadn't died, but he figured the car had. It was a real Blightmobile, a kind of mustardy, baby-shit yellow where it wasn't rusting out, but built like a tank, and rumbling like one, too. That car would not lay rubber, not even when I'd floor it in neutral, then throw it into drive.

Some nights there would be drag races on 25th Place, a dead-end street lined with abandoned factories and junkers that winos dumped along the curb. It was suggested to me more than once that my Chevy should take its rightful place along the curb with the junkers. The dragsters would line up, their machines gleaming, customized, bullnosed, raked, and chopped, oversize engines revving through chrome pipes; then someone would wave a shirt and they'd explode off, burning rubber down an aisle of wrecks. We'd hang around watching till the cops showed up, then scrape together some gas money and go riding ourselves, me behind the wheel, and Ziggy fiddling with the radio, tuning in on the White Sox while everyone else shouted for music.

The Chevy had one customized feature: a wooden bumper. It was something I was forced to add after I almost ruined my life forever on Canal Street. When I first inherited the car all I had was my driver's permit, so Ziggy, who already had his license, rode with me to take the driving test. On the way there, wheeling a corner for practice, I jumped the curb on Canal Street and rumbled down the sidewalk until I hit a No Parking sign and sent it flying over the bridge. Shattered headlights showered the windshield and Ziggy was choking on a scream caught in his throat. I swung a U and fled back to the neighborhood. It took blocks before Ziggy was able to breathe again. I felt shaky, too, and started to laugh. Zig stared at me as if I were crazy and had purposely driven down the sidewalk in order to knock off a No Parking sign.

"Holy Christ! Dave, you could have ruined your life back there forever," Zig told me. It sounded like something my father would have said. Worries were making Ziggy more nervous that summer than ever before. The Sox had come from nowhere to lead the league, triggering Zig's old nightmare about atom bombs falling on the night the White Sox won the pennant.

Besides the busted headlights, the sign pole had left a perfect indentation in my bumper. It was Pepper's idea to wind chains around the bumper at the point of indentation, attach the chains to the bars of a basement window, and floor the car in reverse to pull out the dent. When we tried it the bumper tore off. So Pepper, who saw himself as mechanically inclined, wired on a massive wooden bumper.

He'd developed a weird affection for the Chevy. I'd let him drive and he'd tool down alleys clipping garbage cans with the wooden front end in a kind of steady bass-drum beat: *boom boom boom.*

Pepper reached the point where he wanted to drive all the time. I understood why. There's a certain feeling of freedom you can get only with a beater, that comes from being able to wreck it without remorse. In a way it's like being indestructible, impervious to pain. We'd cruise the neighborhood on Saturdays, and everywhere we looked guys would be waxing their cars or tinkering under the hoods.

I'd honk at them out the window on my sax and yell, "You're wasting a beautiful day on that hunk of scrap."

They'd glance up from their swirls of Simonize and flip me the finger.

"Poor, foolish assholes," Pepper would scoff.

He'd drive with one hand on the wheel and the other smacking the roof in time to whatever was blaring on the radio. The Chevy was like a drum-set accessory to him. He'd jump out at lights and start bopping on the hood. Since he was driving, I started toting along my sax. We'd pull up to a bus stop where people stood waiting in a trance and Pepper would beat on a fender while I wailed a chorus of "Hand Jive"; then we'd jump back in the Chevy and grind off, as if making our getaway.

Finally, I sold Pepper the Chevy for twenty-five dollars. He said he wanted to fix it up. Instead, he used it as a battering ram. He drove it at night around the construction sites of the new expressway, mowing down the blinking yellow barricades and signs that read: SORRY FOR THE INCONVENIENCE . . .

Ziggy, who had developed an eye twitch and had started to stutter, refused to ride with him anymore.

The Sox kept winning.

One night, as Pepper gunned the engine at a red light on 39th, the entire transmission dropped out into the street. He, Deejo, and I pushed the car for blocks and never saw a cop. There was a slight decline to the street and once we got it moving the Chevy rolled along on its own momentum. Pepper sat inside steering. With the key in the ignition the radio still played.

"Anybody have any idea where we're rolling to?" Deejo wanted to know.

"To the end of the line," Pepper said.

We rattled across a bridge that spanned the drainage canal, and just beyond it Pepper cut the wheel and we turned off onto an oiled, unlighted cinder road that ran past a foundry and continued along the river. The road angled downhill, but it was potholed and rutted and it took all three of us grunting and struggling to keep the car moving.

"It would have been a lot easier to just dump it on Twenty-fifth Place," Deejo panted.

"No way, man," Pepper said, "we ain't winos."

"We got class," I said.

The road was intersected by railroad tracks. After half an hour of rocking and heaving we got the Chevy onto the tracks and from there it was downhill again to the railroad bridge. We stopped halfway across the bridge. Pepper climbed onto the roof of the car and looked out over the black river. The moon shined on the oily surface like a single, intense spotlight. Frankie Avalon was singing on the radio.

"Turn that simp off. I hate him," Pepper yelled. He was peeing down onto the hood in a final benediction.

I switched the radio dial over the late-night mush music station—Sinatra singing "These Foolish Things"—and turned the volume on full. Pepper jumped down, flicked the headlights on, and we shoved the car over the bridge.

The splash shook the girders. Pigeons crashed out from under the bridge and swept around confusedly in the dark. We stared over the side half expecting to see the Chevy bob back up through the heavy grease of the river and float off in the moonlight. But except for the bubbles on the surface, it was gone. Then I remembered that my sax had been in the trunk.

A week later, Pepper had a new car, a red Fury convertible. His older cousin Carmen had cosigned. Pepper had made the first payment, the only one he figured on making, by selling his massive red sparkle drum set—bass, snare, tom-tom, cymbals, high-hat, bongos, conga, cowbell, wood block, tambourine, gong—pieces he'd been accumulating on birthdays, Christmases, confirmation, graduation, since fourth grade, the way girls add pearls to a necklace. When he climbed behind those drums he looked like a mad king beating his throne, and at first we refused to believe he had sold it all, or that he was dropping out of school to join the marines.

He drove the Fury as gently as a chauffeur. It was as if some of the craziness had drained out of him when the Chevy went over the bridge. Ziggy even started riding with us again, though every time he'd see a car pass with a Go Go Sox sign he'd get twitchy and depressed.

Pennant fever was in the air. The city long accustomed to losers was poised for a celebration. Driving with the top down brought the excitement of the streets closer. We were part of it. From Pepper's Fury the pace of life around us seemed different, slower than it had from the Chevy. It was as if we were in a speedboat gliding through.

Pepper would glide repeatedly past Linda Molina's house, but she was never out as she'd been the summer before, sunning on a towel on the boulevard grass. There was a rumor that she'd gotten knocked up and had gone to stay with relatives in Texas. Pepper refused to believe it, but the rest of us got the feeling that he had joined the marines for the same reason Frenchmen supposedly joined the Foreign Legion.

"Dave, man, you wanna go by that broad you know's house on the North Side, man?" he would always offer.

"Nah," I'd say, as if that would be boring.

We'd just drive, usually farther south, sometimes almost to Indiana, where the air smelled singed, and towering foundry smokestacks erupted shooting sparks like gigantic Roman candles. Then, skirting the worst slums, we'd head back through dark neighborhoods broken by strips of neon, the shops grated and padlocked, but bands of kids still out splashing in open hydrants, and guys standing in the light of bar signs, staring hard as we passed.

We toured places we'd always heard about—the Fulton produce mart with its tailgate-high sidewalks, Midway Airport, skid row—stopped for carry-out ribs, or at shrimp houses along the river, and always ended up speeding down the Outer Drive, along the skyline-glazed lake, as if some force had spun us to the inner rim of the city. That was the summer Deejo let his hair get long. He was growing a beard, too, a Vandyke, he called it, though Pepper insisted it was really trimmings from other parts of Deejo's body pasted on with Elmer's glue.

Wind raking his shaggy hair, Deejo would shout passages from his dog-eared copy of *On the Road*, which he walked around reading like a breviary ever since seeing Jack Kerouac on *The Steve Allen Show*. I retaliated in a spooky Vincent Price voice, reciting poems off an album called *Word Jazz* that Deej and I had nearly memorized. My favorite was "The Junkman," which began:

In a dream I dreamt that was no dream,
In a sleep I slept that was no sleep,
I saw the junkman in his scattered yard . . .

Ziggy dug that one, too.

By the time we hit downtown and passed Buckingham Fountain with its spraying, multicolored plumes of light, Deejo would be rhapsodic. One night, standing up in the backseat and extending his arms toward the skyscraper we called God's House because of its glowing blue dome—a blue the romantic, lonely shade of runway lights—Deejo blurted out, "I dig beauty!"

Even at the time, it sounded a little extreme. All we'd had were a couple of six-packs. Pepper started swerving, he was laughing so hard, and beating the side of the car with his fist, and for a while it was like he was back behind the wheel of the Chevy. It even brought Ziggy out of his despair. We rode around the rest of the night gaping and pointing and yelling, "Beauty ahead! Dig it!"

"Beauty to the starboard!"

"Coming up on it fast!"

"Can you dig it?"

"Oh, wow! I am digging it! I'm digging beauty!"

Deejo got pimped pretty bad about it in the neighborhood. A long time after that night, guys would still be asking him, "Digging any beauty lately?" Or introducing him: "This is Deejo. He digs beauty." Or he'd be walking down the street and from a passing car someone would wave, and yell, "Hey, Beauty-Digger!"

The last week before the Fury was repoed, when Pepper would come by to pick us up, he'd always say, "Hey, man, let's go dig some beauty."

A couple of weeks later, on a warm Wednesday night in Cleveland, Gerry Staley came on in relief with the bases loaded in the bottom of the ninth, threw one pitch, a double-play ball, Aparicio to Kluszewski, and the White Sox clinched their first pennant in forty years. Pepper had already left on the bus for Parris Island. He would have liked the celebration. Around 11:00 P.M. the air-raid sirens all over the city began to howl. People ran out into the streets in their bathrobes crying and praying, staring up past the roofs as if trying to catch a glimpse of the mushroom cloud before it blew the neighborhood to smithereens. It turned out that Mayor Daley, a lifelong Sox fan, had ordered the sirens as part of the festivities.

Ziggy wasn't the same after that. He could hardly get a word out without stammering. He said he didn't feel reprieved, but as if he had died. When the sirens started to wail, he had climbed into bed clutching his rosary which he still had from grade-school days, when the Blessed Mother used to smile at him. He'd wet the bed that night and had continued having accidents every night since. Deej and I tried to cheer him up, but what kept him going was a book by Thomas Merton called *Seven Storey Mountain*, which one of the priests at the parish church had given him. It meant more to Zig than *On the Road* did to Deejo. Finally, Ziggy decided that since he could hardly talk anyway, he might be better off in the Trappists like Thomas Merton. He figured if he just showed up with the book at the monastery in Gethsemane, Kentucky, they'd have to take him in.

"I'll be taking the vow of silence," he stammered, "so don't worry if you don't hear much from me."

"Silence isn't the vow I'd be worrying about," I said, still trying to joke him out of it, but he was past laughing and I was sorry I'd kidded him.

He, Deejo, and I walked past the truck docks and railroad tracks, over to the river. We stopped on the California Avenue Bridge, from which we could see a succession of bridges spanning the river, including the black railroad bridge we had pushed the Chevy over. We'd been walking most of the night, past churches, under viaducts, along the boulevard, as if visiting the landmarks of our childhoods. Without a car to ride around in, I felt like a little kid again. It was Zig's last night and he wanted to walk. In the morning he intended to leave home and hitchhike to Kentucky. I had an image of him standing along the shoulder holding up a sign that read GETHSEMANE to the oncoming traffic. I didn't want him to go. I kept remembering things as we walked along and then not mentioning them, like that dream he'd had about him and me and Little Richard. Little Richard had found religion and been ordained a preacher, I'd read, but I didn't think he had taken the vow of silence. I had a fantasy of all the monks with their hoods up, meditating in total silence, and suddenly Ziggy letting go with an ear-splitting, wild, howling banshee blues shout.

The next morning he really was gone.

Deejo and I waited for a letter, but neither of us heard anything.

"He must have taken the vow of silence as far as writing, too," Deejo figured.

I did get a postcard from Pepper sometime during the winter, a scene of a tropical sunset over the ocean, and scrawled on the back the message "Not digging much beauty lately." There was no return address, and since Pepper's parents had divorced and moved out of the projects I couldn't track him down.

There was a lot of moving going on. Deejo moved out after a huge fight with his old man. Deej's father had lined up a production-line job for Deejo at the factory where he'd worked for twenty-three years. When Deej didn't show up for work the first day his father came home in a rage and tried to tear Deejo's beard off. So Deejo moved in with his older brother, Sal, who'd just gotten out of the navy and had a bachelor pad near Old Town. The only trouble for Deejo was that he had to move back home on weekends, when Sal needed more privacy.

Deejo was the last of the Blighters still playing. He actually bought a guitar, though not an electric one. He spent a lot of time listening to scratchy old 78s of black singers whose first names all seemed to begin with either Blind or Sonny. Deejo even cut his own record, a paper-thin 45 smelling of acetate, with one side blank. He took copies of it around to all the bars that the guys from Korea used to rule, and talked the bartenders into putting his record on the jukebox. Those bars had quieted down. There weren't enough guys from the Korean days still drinking to field the corner softball teams anymore. The guys who had become regulars were in pretty sad shape. They sat around, endlessly discussing baseball and throwing dice for drinks. The jukeboxes that had once blasted The Platters and Buddy Holly had filled up with polkas again and with Mexican songs that sounded suspiciously like polkas. Deejo's record was usually stuck between Frank Sinatra and Ray Charles. Deej would insert a little card hand printed in ball-point pen: HARD HEARTED WOMAN BY JOEY DECAMPO.

It was a song he'd written. Deejo's hair was longer than ever, his Vandyke had filled in, and he'd taken to wearing sunglasses and huaraches. Sometimes he would show up with one of the girls from Loop Junior College, which was where he was going to school. He'd bring her into the

Edelweiss or the Carta Blanca, usually a wispy blonde with scared eyes, and order a couple of drafts. The bartender or one of us at the bar would pick up Deejo's cue and say, "Hey, how about playing that R5?" and feed the juke box. "Hard Hearted Woman" would come thumping out as loud as the "She's Too Fat Polka" scratchy as an old 78, Deejo whining through his nose, strumming his three chords.

Hard hearted woman,
Oh yeah, Lord,
She's a hard hearted woman,
Uuuhhh . . .

Suddenly, despite the Delta accent, it would dawn on the girl that it was Deejo's voice. He'd kind of grin, shyly admitting that it was, his fingers on the bar tapping along in time with the song, and I wondered what she would think if she could have heard the one I wished he had recorded, the one that opened:

The dawn rises,
Uuuhhh,
Like sick old men,
Oh Lord,
Playing on the rooftops in their underwear,
Yeah . . .

Back to blight.

It was a saying that faded from my vocabulary, especially after my parents moved to Berwyn. Then, some years later, after I quit my job at UPS in order to hide out from the draft in college, the word resurfaced in an English-lit survey class. Maybe I was just more attuned to it than most people ordinarily would be. There seemed to be blight all through Dickens and Blake. The class was taught by a professor nicknamed "the Spitter." He loved to read aloud and after the first time, nobody sat in the front rows. He had acquired an Oxford accent, but the more excitedly he read and spit, the more I could detect the South Side of Chicago underneath the veneer, as if his *th*'s had been worked over with a drill press. When he read us Shelley's "Hail to thee, blithe spirit," I thought he was talking about blight again until I looked it up.

One afternoon in spring I cut class and rode the Douglas Park B back. It wasn't anything I planned. I just wanted to go somewhere and think. The draft board was getting ready to reclassify me and I needed to figure out why I felt like telling them to get rammed rather than just saying the hell with it and doing what they told me to do. But instead of thinking, I ended up remembering my early trips back from the North Side, when I used to pretend that Debbie Weiss was riding with me, and when I came to my stop this time it was easier to imagine how it would have looked to her—small, surprisingly small in the way one is surprised returning to an old grade-school classroom.

I hadn't been back for a couple of years. The neighborhood was mostly Mexican now, with many of the signs over the stores in Spanish, but the bars were still called the Edelweiss Tap and the Budweiser Lounge. Deejo and I had lost touch, but I heard that he'd been drafted. I made the rounds of some of the bars looking for his song on the jukeboxes, but when I couldn't find it even in the Carta Blanca, where nothing else had changed, I gave up. I was sitting in the Carta Blanca having a last, cold *cerveza* before heading back, listening to "CuCuRuCuCu Paloma" on the jukebox and watching the sunlight streak in through the dusty wooden blinds. Then the jukebox stopped playing, and through the open door I could hear the bells from three different churches tolling the hour. They didn't quite agree on the precise moment. Their rings overlapped and echoed one another. The streets were empty, no one home from work or school yet, and something about the overlapping of those bells made me remember how many times I'd had dreams, not prophetic ones like Ziggy's but terrifying all the same, in which I was back in my neighborhood, but lost, everything at once familiar and strange, and I knew if I tried to run, my feet would be like lead, and if I stepped off a curb, I'd drop through space, and then in the dream I would come to a corner that would feel so timeless and peaceful, like the Carta Blanca with the bells fading and the sunlight streaking through, that for a moment it would feel as if I'd wandered into an Official Blithe Area.

Stuart Dybek grew up in Chicago in the Eastern European neighborhood around Eighteenth Street and Blue Island Avenue, a place he strenuously resisted leaving in the summer. "Who wanted to go to camp when you could burn up junk cars, hitch rides on freight trains, and climb around the girders on the bridges across the drainage canal?"

"Blight" started as a poem, but bloomed into a story when Dybek found in an old trunk the fragment of a novel by a teenage friend along with "my own first scribblings." "Blight," which won the 1985 Nelson Algren Award, remains a favorite because it helps "defeat time and capture the past. I felt that urge very strongly in this particular story."

Dybek's stories have appeared in Antaeus, The Atlantic Monthly, The Iowa Review, The New Yorker, The North American Review, The Paris Review, *and* TriQuarterly. *"Hot Ice" won first prize in the 1985 O. Henry Prize Stories. His poetry has been collected in* Brass Knuckles *and his short stories in* Childhood and Other Neighborhoods. *He teaches at Western Michigan University of Kalamazoo.*

First published in 1985 in Chicago.

AMY HEMPEL

THE MOST GIRL PART OF YOU

Jack "Big Guy" Fitch is trying to crack his teeth. He swishes a mouthful of ice water, then straightaway throws back slugs of hot coffee.

"Like in Antarctica," he says, where, if you believe what Big Guy tells you, the people are forever cracking their teeth when they come in from the cold and gulp their coffee down.

I believe what Big Guy tells you. I'm his partner in crime, so I'm chewing on the shaved ice, too. I mean, someone that good-looking tells you what to do, you pretty much do what he says.

Big Guy (he is so damn big!) can make you do anything. He made us become blood brothers—brothers, even though I am a girl—back when we were clumsy little dopes playing with jacks. He got a sewing needle and was going to stick our fingers until I chickened out. I pointed to the sore on his elbow and the abrasions on my knee, and, in fact, what we became was scab brothers.

But this business with the teeth—I say Big Guy is asking for it. He hasn't done something like this since the seventh grade when he ate a cigarette for a dollar. Now when he brushes his teeth at night, he says he treats the gums like the cuticle of a nail. He says he pushes them back with the hard bristles of the brush, laying the enamel clear.

This is a new Big Guy, a bafflement to us all. The old one trimmed the perforated margins from sheets of stamps. He kept a chart posted beside his bed that showed how his water intake varied from day to day. The old Big Guy ate sandwiches with a knife and fork. He wore short-sleeved shirts!

That was before his mother died. She died eight days ago. She did it herself. Big Guy showed me the rope burns in the beam of the ceiling. He said, "Anyplace I hang myself is home." In the movie version, that is where his father would have slapped him.

But of course his father did not—didn't slap him, didn't even hear him. Although Big Guy's father has probably heard the other. It's what Big Guy says about the Cubs. It's the funniest thing he can imagine; it's what he doesn't have to imagine because his father really said it when he had to tell his son what the boy's mother had done.

"And what's more—" his father had said.

It may have been the sheer momentum of bad news, because in the vast thrilling silence after Big Guy heard the news, his father had added, "And what's more, the Cubs lost."

"So you see," Big Guy says these days about matters large and small, "it's not as if the Cubs lost."

Any minute now he could say it again. Here, between the swishing and gulping, in the round red booth of the airport coffee shop, with his tired, traveling grandparents sitting across the table. They flew in for the services, and they are flying home today. Big Guy drove so fast that now we have time to kill. He thinks the posted speed limit is what you can't go *below*. He has just earned a learner's permit so he drives every chance he gets (I have six months on Big Guy; this makes me the adult in the eyes of the DMV). The grandfather orders breakfast from the plastic menu. He says he will have "the ranch-fresh eggs, crisp bacon, and fresh-squeezed orange juice." Big Guy finds this excruciating. More so when his grandmother reads from the menu aloud.

"What about the golden French toast with maple syrup?" she says. "Jack, honey, how about the Belgian waffle?"

Before his grandmother can say "flapjacks" instead of "pancakes," Big Guy signals the waitress and points to what he wants on the menu.

The rest of us order. Then the grandfather addresses his grandson. "So," he says. He says, "So, what do you say?"

"What?" says Big Guy. "Oh. I don't know. I don't know what I say."

The past few days have seen us in many a bistro. It hasn't been easy for Big Guy. His grandfather is always trying to take waitresses into his confidence, believing they will tell him the truth about what is good that day. Big Guy finds this excruciating. He says, "Gramps, have some dignity—snub them."

But his grandfather goes on, asking, with equal gravity, for more coffee and what Big Guy plans to do after high school.

Big Guy heads for a glass of water. *Ice* water. Then his hand moves in slow motion (this for my benefit) toward the refilled cup of coffee.

"Like in Egypt," he says, an aside, a reference to my telling him how Egyptians used to split stone—how they tunneled under a boulder and chipped a narrow fissure in the underside of the rock. How they lit a fire there, let it slow-burn for several days. How, when they poured cold water on top of the rock, the thing cracked clean as lightning.

We will have to eat quickly if the grandparents are going to make their flight. While we wait for the return of the grandfather's new best friend, he teases his grandson about something that happened yesterday, something that Big Guy found excruciating. The grandfather says, "Come on, Jack, what's wrong with talking in elevators?"

For that matter, *I* could say it. I could catch my friend's eye, and *I* could be the one to say, "He's right. Look here, it's not as if the Cubs lost."

Big Guy is the person I tell everything to. In exchange for my confessions, Big Guy tells me secrets which I can't say what they are or else they wouldn't be our secrets.

Sewing is one of the secrets between us. Only Big Guy knows how considerably I had to cheat to earn the Girl Scout merit badge in sewing. It's a fact that my Seamstress badge is glued to the green cotton sash.

So it had to be a joke when Big Guy asked me to teach him to sew. I cannot baste a facing or tailor-tack a dart, but I can thread the goddamn needle and achieve a fairly even running stitch. It was the running stitch I taught Big Guy; he picked it up faster than I ever did. He practiced on a square of stiff blue denim, and by "practiced," I mean that Big Guy did it once.

That was a week ago today, or, to put it another way, it was the day after Mrs. Fitch did it. Now I am witness to her son's seamsmanship, to the use that he has put his skill to.

He met me at the door to his room with one hand held behind his back. I had to close my eyes to create suspense before he brought his left hand forward. I opened my eyes, and that's when my stomach grabbed.

Where I think he has sewn two fingers together, I see that it is both worse than that and not as bad. On the outer edge of his left thumb, stitched into the very skin, my name is spelled out in small block print. It is spelled out in tight blue thread. My name is sewn into the skin of his hand!

Big Guy shows me that he still holds the threaded needle. In my presence, he completes the final stitch, guiding the needle slowly. I watch the blue thread that trails like a vein and turns milky as it tunnels through the bloodless calloused skin.

I can't sew, but my mother you would swear had majored in Home Ec. She favors a shirtwaist dress for at-home, and she calls clothes "garments." She makes desserts with names like Apple Brown Betty, and when she serves them, usually with a whipped topping product, she says, "M.I.K.," which abbreviation means, "More in Kitchen."

Big Guy is in thrall to her, to her tunafish sandwiches on soft white bread, to her pink lemonade from frozen concentrate cans. He likes to horrify my mother by telling her what he would otherwise be eating: salt sandwiches, for example, or Fizzies and Space Food Sticks.

Big Guy is a welcome guest. At my house, he is the man of the house—the phrase my mother uses. My father's been dead for most of my life. We are more of a family at these lunches and dinners where, once again, the man of the house is at the head of the table.

Big Guy cooks corn by placing the opened can on the burner. For breakfast, he tells my mother, he pours milk into the cardboard boxes of Kellogg's miniature assortment. Since his mother died, I have seen him steam a cucumber, thinking it was zucchini. That's the kind of thing that turns my heart right over.

One thing he *can* make is a melted cheese sandwich, open-faced and melted under the broiler. It's what he brought to his mother for lunch when she was sick. He brought her two months' worth of melted cheese.

Big Guy says he brought her one that day.

"The last thing I said to her," Big Guy remembers, "was, 'Mom, guess what kids at school have.' He told her, 'Sunglasses,' and she said, 'Save your money.' "

Big Guy wanted to know, What about me?

"You were there," I remind him. "Remember about her hair?"

The last thing I had said to Mrs. Fitch was that I liked her hair. Big Guy had accused me of trying to get in good, but it was true—I did like her hair.

Later, it's a long story how, Big Guy got a copy of the coroner's report. The coroner described Mrs. Fitch's auburn hair as being "worn in a female fashion."

I'm doing my homework in bed, drinking ginger ale, feeling a little woopsy. I'm taking a look at a book on French grammar because is there anything cooler than talking in a foreign language? ("*Dites-moi,*" Big Guy says to me whenever I have a problem.)

I turn the page and see that Big Guy has been there first. In addition to reading my mail, he writes in the margins of my books, usually the number of shopping days left until his birthday.

Here in the French grammar, there is no telling why, Big

Guy has written, "Dots is spots up close. Spots is dots far away."

I read this, and then there he is in my room. Big Guy can do that—walk into my bedroom when I am in the bed. Years ago, at school, the girls were forced to watch a film called *The Most Girl Part of You.* I had gone home and told my mother that Jack and I weren't doing anything. My mother, who hadn't asked if we *were*, had said, "More's the pity."

In other words, it is all my mother can do to keep from dimming the lights for us.

The truth is—it does something to me, seeing him in my bedroom.

Big Guy does the female thing in a mood—goes shopping, or changes the part in his hair. So when I see his hair is puffed and no doubt painful at the roots for being brushed in another direction, I am tipped off.

I don't have to ask.

"No need to go to Antarctica," he says, and smiles a phony smile so I can see where his front tooth has been broken off on the diagonal.

"From *ice* water?" I say.

Big Guy says his bike collided with a garbage truck. "Actually," he says, "it wasn't an accident.

"And speaking of Antarctica," he says, to change the subject, "did you know that no matter how hungry an Eskimo gets, he will never eat a penguin?"

"Why is that?"

Big Guy, triumphant: "Because Eskimos live at the North Pole, and penguins live at the *South* Pole!"

And then he is gone, gone downstairs to eat more funny food, to fix himself a glass of Fizzies, or, if they have stopped *making* Fizzies, powdered dry Kool-Aid on a wet licked finger.

I see his schoolbooks where he left them on my dresser; I see my chance.

I skip the texts and make for his spiral notebook, there to leave searing commentary in the margins. I find handwriting which only after a moment becomes the words that I am reading.

Big Guy has written: "If we had trimmed the cat's claws before she snagged the bedspread? If we'd had French toast for breakfast instead of eggs? If we had gone to the movies instead of Dad being tired?"

The bottom half of the page is filled with inky abstract drawings. On the next page he continues: "Am I thinking the wrong things? Should I wonder, instead, what took you so long? Is the reason because—why not? Would you say, if you could, why not?"

I reason that if he left it here, he wanted me to see it.

Big Guy takes me to a party the same day he goes to the dentist. There are refreshments for an hour, then the lights go out in the basement and the records start to play.

Big Guy says, "May I challenge you to a dance?"

I move into his arms—it is the first time we have danced—and the hand that is at the small of my back catches as it slides across the silk of my good new dress. I don't have to look to know what it is. It's the dry, jagged skin from where he pulled my threaded name out of the place where he had sewn it.

Big Guy leads me to the side of the room where a black light turns our white clothes purple. The black light does something else, I notice. When Big Guy talks, it turns the capped tooth dingy gray. Another girl notices; she says that is why you never see a black light used in Hollywood.

"Get it?" she says.

This is the birth of vanity for Jack. He says it's time to go, and if I want to go with him, I can. Of course I do—it's so cheap to leave with someone who is not the person you came with!

To show that I can give it as well as I can take it, I say, "Big Guy, come on, it's not as if the Cubs lost."

He says, "Cut me some slack," and we get into Mr. Fitch's car. I tune in the oldies station and mouth a Motown hit, the words of which clash ridiculously with Jack's and my frame of reference. When I stop knowing enough of the words, I hum along with the radio.

"We hum," Big Guy informs, "because people are evolved from insects. Humming, buzzing—you see what I mean?"

This is something he probably heard the same place he learned about the cracking teeth of Antarctica.

Big Guy drives me home. Nobody is there, not that it would matter if anybody was. I sit on the couch in the family room, in the dark. Big Guy finds the oldies station on my mother's antique Zenith. The music comes in faintly; you would have to strain to hear the words if, unlike myself, you did not know the words already.

Then it's both of us sitting in the humid dark, Big Guy buzzing along with the radio, me scratching the mosquito bites I always get. A few minutes of this and Big Guy is off to the bathroom. He comes back with a small pink bottle. He sings, "You're gonna need an ocean / of calamine lotion," as he dabs it on the hot white bites.

I tell him he ought to chill it first, so he takes the bottle into the kitchen. He opens the refrigerator, and calls me in to look.

He shows me where a moth has been drawn by the single light. Its wings beat madly in the cold air; they drag across the uncovered butter, dust the chocolate pudding, graze the lipstick smear on the open end of a milk carton.

We try to get the thing out, but it flaps behind a jar of wheat germ, and from there into the vegetable Humidrawer. At that point, Big Guy shuts the door (once, in the library, he dropped a dead worm in the card file under W).

"I've got another idea," he says. "Wait for me on the couch."

He comes back with a razor blade. He says, "This will take the itch out." He drags the blade twice across a bite on the back of my wrist; the tiny X turns red as blood comes up to the cut surface.

I am too amazed to say anything, so Big Guy continues, razoring X's into bites on my legs and arms.

Now, I think—*now* we could become blood brothers.

But that is not what Big Guy is thinking, and finally I come to know it. I submit to his crude doctoring until he cuts an X into a bite on my shoulder. Suddenly he lowers his head until it isn't the blade, but his mouth on my skin.

I had only been kissed once before. The fellow had made me think of those kids whose mouths cover the spigot when they drink from a fountain. When I had pulled away from him, this fellow had said, "B-plus."

Big Guy is going to kiss me.

And here is the thrill of my short life: he does.

And I see that not touching for so long was a drive to the beach with the windows rolled up so the waves feel that much colder.

When I can get my bearings, I make light of what could happen. I say the cool thing I've been saving up to say; I say, "Stop it, Big Guy. Stop it some more."

And then he says the cool thing *he* has been saving, or, being Big Guy, has made up on the spot. He says, "I always give a woman what she wants—whether she wants it or not."

And that is the end of the joking around; we get it out of our systems. We take the length of the couch, squirming like maggots in ashes.

I'm not ready for this, but here is what I come up with: he's a boy without a mother. I look beyond my own hesitation; I find my mother, Big Guy's father. We are on this couch for our newly and lastingly widowed parents, as well.

Big Guy and I are still dressed. I am bleeding through my clothes from the razored bites when Big Guy pushes his knee up between my legs.

"If you have to get up," he says, "don't."

I play back everything that has happened to me before this. I want to ask Big Guy if he is doing this, too. I want him to know what it clearly seems to me: that if it's true your life flashes past your eyes before you die, then it is also the truth that your life rushes forth when you are ready to start to truly be alive.

Amy Hempel has a special fondness for "The Most Girl Part of You" because the story ended a year in which she wrote no fiction. After the publication of her first collection, Reasons to Live, *she spent some time writing only nonfiction. This story, which is marked by a mixture of what she describes as "humor and horror," led her back to writing stories.*

Hempel's story "Today Will Be a Quiet Day" appears in both The Best Short Stories 1986, *and the* Pushcart Prize Anthology. *Born in Chicago, she was raised in Chicago, Denver, and San Francisco. She has been writing fiction for only about four years and credits her quick publication both in many magazines and in collections to her work in Gordon Lish's writing workshop at Columbia, which, she says, "cuts years off the time it takes for a writer to learn her craft." She is a contributing editor at* Vanity Fair *and now lives in New York.*

First published in 1986 in Vanity Fair.

ALICE MUNRO

MILES CITY, MONTANA

My father came across the field, carrying the body of the boy who had been drowned. There were several men together, returning from the search, but he was the one carrying the body. The men were muddy and exhausted, and walked with their heads down, as if they were ashamed. Even the dogs were dispirited, dripping from the cold river. When they all set out, hours before, the dogs were nervy and yelping, the men tense and determined, and there was a constrained, unspeakable excitement about the whole scene. It was understood that they might find something horrible.

The boy's name was Steve Gauley. He was eight years old. His hair and clothes were mud-colored now and carried some bits of dead leaves, twigs, and grass. He was like a heap of refuse that had been left out all winter. His face was turned in to my father's chest, but I could see a nostril, an ear, plugged up with greenish mud.

I don't think I really saw all this. Perhaps I saw my father carrying him, and the other men coming with him, and the dogs, but I would not have been allowed to get close enough to see something like mud in his nostril. I must have heard someone talking about that and imagined that I saw it. I see his face unaltered except for the mud—Steve Gauley's familiar, sharp-honed, sneaky-looking face—and it wouldn't have been like that; it would have been bloated and changed and perhaps muddied all over after so many hours in the water.

To have to bring back such news, such evidence, to a waiting family, particularly a mother, would have made searchers move heavily, but what was happening here was worse. It seemed a worse shame (to hear people talk) that there was no mother, no woman at all—no grandmother or aunt, or even a sister—to receive Steve Gauley and give him his due of grief. His father was a hired man, a drinker but not a drunk, an erratic man without being entertaining, not friendly but not exactly a troublemaker. His fatherhood seemed accidental, and the fact that the child had been left with him when the mother went away, and that they continued living together, seemed accidental. They lived in a steep-roofed, gray-shingled hillbilly sort of house that was just a bit better than a shack—the father fixed the roof and put supports under the porch, just enough and just in time—and their life was held together in a similar manner; that is, just well enough to keep the Children's Aid at bay. They didn't eat meals together or cook for each other, but there was food. Sometimes the father would give Steve money to buy food at the store, and Steve was seen to buy quite sensible things, such as pancake mix and macaroni dinner.

I had known Steve Gauley fairly well. I had not liked him more often than I had liked him. He was two years older than I was. He would hang around our place on Saturdays, scornful of whatever I was doing but unable to leave me alone. I couldn't be on the swing without him wanting to try it, and if I wouldn't give it up he came and pushed me so that I went crooked. He teased the dog. He got me into trouble—deliberately and maliciously, it seemed to me afterward—by daring me to do things I wouldn't have thought of on my own: digging up the potatoes to see how big they were, when they were still only the size of marbles, and pushing over the stacked firewood to make a pile we could jump off. At school we never spoke to each other. He was solitary, though not tormented. But on Saturday mornings when I saw his thin, self-possessed figure sliding through the cedar hedge I knew I was in for something, and he would decide what. Sometimes it was all right. We pretended we were cowboys who had to tame wild horses. We played in the pasture by the river, not far from the place where Steve drowned. We were horses and riders both, screaming and neighing and bucking and waving whips of tree branches beside a little nameless river that flows into the Saugeen, in southern Ontario.

The funeral was held in our house. There was not enough room at Steve's father's place for the large crowd that was expected, because of the circumstances. I have a memory of the crowded room but no picture of Steve in his coffin, or of the minister, or of wreaths of flowers. I remember that I was holding one flower, a white narcissus, which must have come from a pot somebody forced indoors, because it was too early for even the forsythia bush or the trilliums and marsh marigolds in the woods. I stood in a row of children, each of us holding a narcissus. We sang a children's hymn, which somebody played on our piano: "When He Cometh, When He Cometh, to Make Up His Jewels." I was wearing white ribbed stockings, which were disgustingly itchy and which wrinkled at the knees and ankles. The feeling of these stockings on my legs is mixed up with another feeling in my memory. It is hard to describe. It had to do with my parents. Adults in general but my parents in particular. My father, who had carried Steve's body from the river, and my mother, who must have done most of the arranging of this funeral. My father in his dark-blue suit and my mother in her brown velvet dress with the creamy satin collar. They stood side by side opening and closing their mouths for the hymn, and I stood removed from them, in the row of children, watching. I felt a furious, and sickening, disgust. Children sometimes have an access of disgust concerning adults. The size, the lumpy shapes, the bloated power. The breath, the coarseness, the hairiness, the horrid secretions. But this was more. And the accompanying anger had nothing sharp and self-respecting about it. There was no release, as when I would finally bend and pick up a stone and throw it at Steve Gauley. It could not be understood or expressed, though it died down after a while into a heaviness, then just a taste, an occasional taste—a thin, familiar misgiving.

Twenty years or so later, in 1961, my husband, Andrew, and I got a brand-new car, our first—that is, our first brand-new.

It was a Morris Oxford, oyster-colored (the dealer had some fancier name for the color)—a big small car, with plenty of room for us and our two children. Cynthia was six and Meg three and a half.

Andrew took a picture of me standing beside the car. I was wearing white pants, a black turtleneck, and sunglasses. I lounged against the car door, canting my hips to make myself look slim.

"Wonderful," Andrew said. "Great. You look like Jackie Kennedy." All over this continent probably, dark-haired, reasonably slender young women were told, when they were stylishly dressed or getting their pictures taken, that they looked like Jackie Kennedy.

Andrew took a lot of pictures of me, and of the children, our house, our garden, our excursions and possessions. He got copies made, labeled them carefully, and sent them back to his mother and his aunt and uncle, in Ontario. He got copies for me to send to my father, who also lived in Ontario, and I did so, but less regularly than he sent his. When he saw pictures he thought I had already sent lying around the house, Andrew was perplexed and annoyed. He liked to have this record go forth.

That summer we were presenting ourselves, not pictures. We were driving back from Vancouver, where we lived, to Ontario, which we still called "home," in our new car. Five days to get there, ten days there, five days back. For the first time, Andrew had three weeks' holiday. He worked in the legal department at B.C. Hydro.

On a Saturday morning we loaded suitcases, two thermos bottles—one filled with coffee and one with lemonade—some fruit and sandwiches, picture books and coloring books, crayons, drawing pads, insect repellent, sweaters (in case it got cold in the mountains), and our two children into the car. Andrew locked the house and Cynthia said ceremoniously, "Good-bye, house."

Meg said, "Good-bye, house." Then she said, "Where will we live now?"

"It's not good-bye forever," said Cynthia. "We're coming back. Mother! Meg thought we weren't ever coming back!"

"I did not," said Meg, kicking the back of my seat.

Andrew and I put on our sunglasses and we drove away, over the Lions Gate Bridge and through the main part of Vancouver. We shed our house, the neighborhood, the city, and—at the crossing point between Blaine, Washington, and British Columbia—our country. We were driving east across the United States, taking the most northerly route, and would cross into Canada again at Sarnia, Ontario. I don't know if we chose this route because the Trans-Canada Highway was not completely finished at the time or if we just wanted the feeling of driving through a foreign, a very slightly foreign, country—that extra bit of interest and adventure.

We were both in high spirits. Andrew congratulated the car several times. He said he felt so much better driving it than our old car, a 1951 Austin that slowed down dismally on the hills and had a fussy-old-lady image. So Andrew said now.

"What kind of image does this one have?" said Cynthia. She listened to us carefully and liked to try out new words such as "image." Usually she got them right.

"Lively," I said. "Slightly sporty. It's not show-off."

"It's sensible, but it has class," Andrew said. "Like my image."

Cynthia thought that over and said with a cautious pride, "That means like you think you want to be, Daddy?"

As for me, I was happy because of the shedding. I loved taking off. In my own house, I seemed to be often looking for a place to hide—sometimes from the children but more often from the jobs to be done and the phone ringing and the sociability of the neighborhood. I wanted to hide so that I could get busy at my real work, which was a sort of wooing of distant parts of myself. I lived in a state of siege, always losing just what I wanted to hold on to. But on trips there was no difficulty. I could be talking to Andrew, talking to the children and looking at whatever they wanted me to look at—a pig on a sign, a pony in a field, a Volkswagen on a revolving stand—and pouring lemonade into plastic cups, and all the time those bits and pieces would be flying together inside me. The essential composition would be achieved. This made me hopeful and lighthearted. It was being a watcher that did it. A watcher, not a keeper.

We turned east at Everett and climbed into the Cascades. I showed Cynthia our route on the map. First I showed her the map of the whole United States, which showed also the bottom part of Canada. Then I turned to the separate maps of each of the states we were going to pass through. Washington, Idaho, Montana, North Dakota, Minnesota, Wisconsin. I showed her the dotted line across Lake Michigan, which was the route of the ferry we would take. Then we would drive across Michigan to the bridge that linked the United States and Canada, at Sarnia. Ontario. Home.

Meg wanted to see, too.

"You won't understand," said Cynthia. But she took the road atlas into the backseat.

"Sit back," she said to Meg. "Sit still. I'll show you."

I could hear her tracing the route for Meg, very accurately, just as I had done it for her. She looked up all the states' maps, knowing how to find them in alphabetical order.

"You know what that line is?" she said. "It's the road. That line is the road we're driving on. We're going right along this line."

Meg did not say anything.

"Mother, show me where we are right this minute," said Cynthia.

I took the atlas and pointed out the road through the mountains, and she took it back and showed it to Meg. "See where the road is all wiggly?" she said. "It's wiggly because there are so many turns in it. The wiggles are the turns." She flipped some pages and waited a moment. "Now," she said, "show me where we are." Then she called to me, "Mother, she understands! She pointed to it! Meg understands maps!"

It seems to me now that we invented characters for our children. We had them firmly set to play their parts. Cynthia was bright and diligent, sensitive, courteous, watchful. Sometimes we teased her for being too conscientious, too eager to be what we in fact depended on her to be. Any reproach or failure, any rebuff, went terribly deep with her. She was fair-haired, fair-skinned, easily showing the effects of the sun, raw winds, pride, or humiliation. Meg was more solidly built, more reticent—not rebellious but stubborn sometimes, mysterious. Her silences seemed to us to show her strength of character, and her negatives were taken as signs of an imperturbable independence. Her hair was brown, and we cut it in straight bangs. Her eyes were a light hazel, clear and dazzling.

We were entirely pleased with these characters, enjoying the contradictions as well as the confirmations of them. We disliked the heavy, the uninventive, approach to being parents. I had a dread of turning into a certain kind of mother—the kind whose body sagged and ripened, who moved in a woolly-smelling, milky-smelling fog, solemn with trivial burdens. I believed that all the attention these mothers paid, their need to be burdened, was the cause of colic, bedwetting, asthma. I favored another approach—the mock desperation, the inflated irony of the professional mothers who wrote for magazines. In those magazine pieces the children were splendidly self-willed, hard-edged, perverse, indomitable. So were the mothers, through their wit, indomitable. The other mothers I warmed to were the sort who would phone up and say, "Is my embryo Hitler by any chance over at your house?" They cackled clear above the milky fog.

We saw a dead deer strapped across the front of a pickup truck.

"Somebody shot it," Cynthia said. "Hunters shoot the deer."

"It's not hunting season yet," Andrew said. "They may have hit it on the road. See the sign for deer crossing?"

"I would cry if we hit one," Cynthia said sternly.

I had made peanut-butter-and-marmalade sandwiches for the children and salmon-and-mayonnaise for us. But I had not put any lettuce in, and Andrew was disappointed.

"I didn't have any," I said.

"Couldn't you have got some?"

"I'd have had to buy a whole head of lettuce just to get enough for sandwiches, and I decided it wasn't worth it."

This was a lie. I had forgotten.

"They're a lot better with lettuce."

"I didn't think it made that much difference." After a silence I said, "Don't be mad."

"I'm not mad. I like lettuce on sandwiches."

"I just didn't think it mattered that much."

"How would it be if I didn't bother to fill up the gas tank?"

"That's not the same thing."

"Sing a song," said Cynthia. She started to sing:

Five little ducks went out one day,
Over the hills and far away.
One little duck went
"Quack-quack-quack."
Four little ducks came swimming back.

Andrew squeezed my hand and said, "Let's not fight."

"You're right. I should have got lettuce."

"It doesn't matter that much."

I wished that I could get my feelings about Andrew to come together into serviceable and dependable feeling. I had even tried writing two lists, one of things I liked about him, one of things I disliked—in the cauldron of intimate life, things I loved and things I hated—as if I hoped by this to prove something, to come to a conclusion one way or the other. But I gave it up when I saw that all it proved was what I already knew—that I had violent contradictions. Sometimes the very sound of his footsteps seemed to me tyrannical, the set of his mouth smug and mean, his hard, straight body a barrier interposed—quite consciously, even dutifully, and with a nasty pleasure in its masculine authority—between me and whatever joy or lightness I could get in life. Then, with not much warning, he became my good friend and most essential companion. I felt the sweetness of his light bones and serious ideas, the vulnerability of his love, which I imagined to be much purer and more straightforward than my own. I could be greatly moved by an inflexibility, a harsh propriety, that at other times I scorned. I would think how humble he was, really, taking on such a ready-made role of husband, father, breadwinner, and how I myself in comparison was really a secret monster of egotism. Not so secret, either—not from him.

At the bottom of our fights we served up what we thought were the ugliest truths. "I know there is something basically selfish and basically untrustworthy about you," Andrew once said. "I've always known it. I also know that that is why I fell in love with you."

"Yes," I said, feeling sorrowful but complacent.

"I know that I'd be better off without you."

"Yes. You would."

"You'd be happier without me."

"Yes."

And finally—finally—racked and purged, we clasped hands and laughed, laughed at those two benighted people, ourselves. Their grudges, their grievances, their self-justification. We leapfrogged over them. We declared them liars. We would have wine for dinner, or decide to give a party.

I haven't seen Andrew for years, don't know if he is still thin, has gone completely gray, insists on lettuce, tells the truth, or is hearty and disappointed.

We stayed the night in Wenatchee, Washington, where it hadn't rained for weeks. We ate dinner in a restaurant built about a tree—not a sapling in a tub but a tall, sturdy cottonwood. In the early-morning light we climbed out of the irrigated valley, up dry, rocky, very steep hillsides that would seem to lead to more hills, and there on the top was a wide plateau, cut by the great Spokane and Columbia rivers. Grainland and grassland, mile after mile. There were straight roads here, and little farming towns with grain elevators. In fact, there was a sign announcing that this county we were going through, Douglas County, had one of the highest wheat yields of any county in the United States. The towns had planted shade trees. At least, I thought they had been planted, because there were no such big trees in the countryside.

All this was marvelously welcome to me. "Why do I love it so much?" I said to Andrew. "Is it because it isn't scenery?"

"It reminds you of home," said Andrew. "A bout of severe nostalgia." But he said this kindly.

When we said "home" and meant Ontario, we had very different places in mind. My home was a turkey farm, where my father lived as a widower, and though it was the same house my mother had lived in, had papered, painted, cleaned, furnished, it showed the effects now of neglect and of some wild sociability. A life went on in it that my mother could not have predicted or condoned. There were parties for the turkey crew, the gutters and pluckers, and sometimes one or two of the young men would be living there temporarily, inviting their own friends and having their own impromptu parties. This life, I thought, was better for my father than being lonely, and I did not disapprove, had certainly no right to disapprove. Andrew did not like to go there, naturally enough, because he was not the sort who could sit around the kitchen table with the turkey crew, telling jokes. They were intimidated by him and contemptuous of him, and it seemed to me that my father, when they were around, had to be on their side. And it wasn't only Andrew who had trouble. I could manage those jokes, but it was an effort.

I wished for the days when I was little, before we had the turkeys. We had cows, and sold the milk to the cheese factory. A turkey farm is nothing like as pretty as a dairy farm or a sheep farm. You can see that the turkeys are on a straight path to becoming frozen carcasses and table meat. They don't have the pretense of a life of their own, a browsing idyll, that cattle have, or pigs in the dappled orchard. Turkey barns are long, efficient buildings—tin sheds. No beams or hay or warm stables. Even the smell of guano seems thinner and more offensive than the usual smell of stable manure. No hints of hay coils and rail fences and songbirds and the flowering hawthorn. The turkeys were all let out into one long field, which they picked clean. They didn't look like great birds there but like fluttering laundry.

Once, shortly after my mother died and I was married—in fact, I was packing to join Andrew in Vancouver—I was at home alone for a couple of days with my father. There was a freakishly heavy rain all night. In the early light we saw that the turkey field was flooded. At least, the low-lying parts of it were flooded—it was like a lake with many islands. The turkeys were huddled on these islands. Turkeys are very stupid. (My father would say, "You know a chicken? You know how stupid a chicken is? Well, a chicken is an Einstein compared with a turkey.") But they had managed to crowd to higher ground and avoid drowning. Now they might push each other off, suffocate each other, get cold and die. We couldn't wait for the water to go down. We went out in an old rowboat we had. I rowed and my father pulled the heavy, wet turkeys into the boat and we took them to the barn. It was still raining a little. The job was difficult and absurd and very uncomfortable. We were laughing. I was happy to be working with my father. I felt close to all hard, repetitive, appalling work, in which the body is finally worn out, the mind sunk (though sometimes the spirit can stay marvelously light), and I was homesick in advance for this life and this place. I thought that if Andrew could see me there in the rain, redhanded, muddy, trying to hold on to turkey legs and row the boat at the same time, he would only want to get me out of there and make me forget about it. This raw life angered him. My attachment to it angered him. I thought that I shouldn't have married him. But who else? One of the turkey crew?

And I didn't want to stay there. I might feel bad about leaving, but I would feel worse if somebody made me stay.

Andrew's mother lived in Toronto, in an apartment building looking out on Muir Park. When Andrew and his sister were both at home, his mother slept in the living room. Her husband, a doctor, had died when the children were still too young to go to school. She took a secretarial course and sold her house at Depression prices, moved to this apartment, managed to raise her children, with some help from relatives—her sister Caroline, her brother-in-law Roger. Andrew and his sister went to private schools and to camp in the summer.

"I suppose that was courtesy of the Fresh Air Fund?" I said once, scornful of his claim that he had been poor. To my mind, Andrew's urban life had been sheltered and fussy. His mother came home with a headache from working all day in the noise, the harsh light of a department-store office, but it did not occur to me that hers was a hard or admirable life. I don't think she herself believed that she was admirable—only unlucky. She worried about her work in the office, her clothes, her cooking, her children. She worried most of all about what Roger and Caroline would think.

Caroline and Roger lived on the east side of the park, in a handsome stone house. Roger was a tall man with a bald, freckled head, a fat, firm stomach. Some operation on his throat had deprived him of his voice—he spoke in a rough whisper. But everybody paid attention. At dinner once in the stone house—where all the dining-room furniture was enormous, darkly glowing, palatial—I asked him a question. I think it had to do with Whittaker Chambers, whose story was then appearing in *The Saturday Evening Post.* The question was mild in tone, but he guessed its subversive intent and took to calling me Mrs. Gromyko, referring to what he alleged to be my "sympathies." Perhaps he really craved an adversary, and could not find one. At that dinner I saw Andrew's hand tremble as he lit his mother's cigarette. His Uncle Roger had paid for Andrew's education, and was on the board of directors of several companies.

"He is just an opinionated old man," Andrew said to me later. "What is the point of arguing with him?"

Before we left Vancouver, Andrew's mother had written, "Roger seems quite intrigued by the idea of your buying a small car!" Her exclamation mark showed apprehension. At that time, particularly in Ontario, the choice of a small, European car over a large, American car could be seen as some sort of declaration—a declaration of tendencies Roger had been sniffing after all along.

"It isn't that small a car," said Andrew huffily.

"That's not the point," I said. "The point is, it isn't any of his business!"

"He's bored."

We spent the second night in Missoula. We had been told in Spokane, at a gas station, that there was a lot of repair work going on along Highway 2, and that we were in for a very hot, dusty drive, with long waits, so we turned onto the interstate, and drove through Cur d'Alene and Kellogg into Montana. After Missoula we turned south, toward Butte, but detoured to see Helena, the state capital. In the car we played Who Am I?

Cynthia was somebody dead, and an American, and a girl. Possibly a lady. She was not in a story. She had not been seen on television. Cynthia had not read about her in a book. She was not anybody who had come to the kindergarten, or a relative of any of Cynthia's friends.

"Is she human?" said Andrew, with a sudden shrewdness.

"No! That's what you forgot to ask!"

"An animal," I said reflectively.

"Is that a question? Sixteen questions!"

"No, it is not a question. I'm thinking. A dead animal."

"It's the deer," said Meg, who hadn't been playing.

"That's not fair!" said Cynthia. "She's not playing!"

"What deer?" said Andrew.

I said, "Yesterday."

"The day before," said Cynthia. "Meg wasn't playing. Nobody got it."

"The deer on the truck," said Andrew.

"It was a lady deer, because it didn't have antlers, and it was an American and it was dead," Cynthia said.

Andrew said, "I think it's kind of morbid, being a dead deer."

"I got it," said Meg.

Cynthia said, "I think I know what morbid is. It's depressing."

Helena, an old silver-mining town, looked forlorn to us even in the morning sunlight. Then Bozeman and Billings, not forlorn in the slightest—energetic, strung-out towns, with miles of blinding tinsel fluttering over used-car lots. We got too tired and hot even to play Who Am I? These busy, prosaic cities reminded me of similar places in Ontario, and I thought about what was really waiting there—the great tombstone furniture of Roger and Caroline's dining room, the dinners for which I must iron the children's dresses and warn them about forks, and then the other table a hundred miles away, the jokes of my father's crew. The pleasures I had been thinking of—looking at the countryside or drinking a Coke in an old-fashioned drugstore with fans and a high, pressed-tin ceiling—would have to be snatched in between.

"Meg's asleep," Cynthia said. "She's so hot. She makes me hot in the same seat with her."

"I hope she isn't feverish," I said, not turning around.

What are we doing this for, I thought, and the answer came—to show off. To give Andrew's mother and my father the pleasure of seeing their grandchildren. That was our duty. But beyond that we wanted to show them something. What strenuous children we were, Andrew and I, what relentless seekers of approbation. It was as if at some point we had received an unforgettable, indigestible message—that we were far from satisfactory, and that the most commonplace success in life was probably beyond us. Roger dealt out such messages, of course—that was his style—but Andrew's mother, my own mother and father couldn't have meant to do so. All they meant to tell us was "Watch out. Get along." When I was in high school my father teased me that I was getting to think I was so smart I would never find a boyfriend. He would have forgotten that in a week. I never forgot it. Andrew and I didn't forget things. We took umbrage.

"I wish there was a beach," said Cynthia.

"There probably is one," Andrew said. "Right around the next curve."

"There isn't any curve," she said, sounding insulted.

"That's what I mean."

"I wish there was some more lemonade."

"I will just wave my magic wand and produce some," I said. "O.K., Cynthia? Would you rather have grape juice? Will I do a beach while I'm at it?"

She was silent, and soon I felt repentant. "Maybe in the next town there might be a pool," I said. I looked at the map. "In Miles City. Anyway, there'll be something cool to drink."

"How far is it?" Andrew said.

"Not so far," I said. "Thirty miles, about."

"In Miles City," said Cynthia, in the tones of an incantation, "there is a beautiful blue swimming pool for children, and a park with lovely trees."

Andrew said to me, "You could have started something."

But there was a pool. There was a park, too, though not quite the oasis of Cynthia's fantasy. Prairie trees—cottonwoods and poplars—worn grass, and a high wire fence around the pool. Within this fence, a wall, not yet completed, of cement blocks. Nobody was around. There were no shouts or splashes. Over the entrance I saw a sign that said the pool was closed every day from noon until two o'clock. It was then twenty-five after twelve.

Nevertheless I called out, "Is anybody there?" I thought somebody must be around, because there was a small truck parked near the entrance. On the side of the truck were these words: "We have Brains, to fix your Drains. (We have Roto-Rooter too.)"

A girl came out, wearing a red lifeguard's shirt over her bathing suit. "Sorry, we're closed."

"We were just driving through," I said.

"We close every day from twelve until two. It's on the sign." She was eating a sandwich.

"I saw the sign," I said. "But this is the first water we've seen for so long, and the children are awfully hot, and I wondered if they could just dip in and out—just five minutes. We'd watch them."

A boy came into sight behind her. He was wearing jeans and a T-shirt with the words "Roto-Rooter" on it.

I was going to say that we were driving from British Columbia to Ontario, but I remembered that Canadian place names usually meant nothing to Americans. "We're driving right across the country," I said. "We haven't time to wait for the pool to open. We were just hoping the children could get cooled off."

Cynthia came running up barefoot behind me. "Mother. Mother, where is my bathing suit?" Then she stopped, sensing the serious adult negotiations. Meg was climbing out of the car—just wakened, with her top pulled up and her shorts pulled down, showing her pink stomach.

"Is it just those two?" the girl said.

"Just the two. We'll watch them."

"I can't let any adults in. If it's just the two, I guess I could watch them. I'm having my lunch." She said to Cynthia, "Do you want to come in the pool?"

"Yes, please," said Cynthia firmly.

Meg looked at the ground.

"Just a short time, because the pool is really closed," I said. "We appreciate this very much," I said to the girl.

"Well, I can eat my lunch out there, if it's just the two of them." She looked toward the car as if she thought I might try to spring some more children on her.

When I found Cynthia's bathing suit, she took it into the changing room. She would not permit anybody, even Meg, to see her naked. I changed Meg, who stood on the front seat of the car. She had a pink cotton bathing suit with straps that crossed and buttoned. There were ruffles across the seat.

"She *is* hot," I said. "But I don't think she's feverish."

I loved helping Meg to dress or undress, because her body still had the solid unself-consciousness, the sweet indifference, something of the milky smell, of a baby's body. Cynthia's body had long ago been pared down, shaped and altered, into Cynthia. We all liked to hug Meg, press and nuzzle her. Sometimes she would scowl and beat us off, and this forthright independence, this ferocious bashfulness, simply made her more appealing, more apt to be teased and tickled in the way of family love.

Andrew and I sat in the car with the windows open. I could hear a radio playing, and thought it must belong to the girl or her boyfriend. I was thirsty, and got out of the car to look for a concession stand, or perhaps a softdrink machine, somewhere in the park. I was wearing shorts, and the backs of my legs were slick with sweat. I saw a drinking fountain at the other side of the park and was walking toward it in a roundabout way, keeping to the shade of the trees. No place became real till you got out of the car. Dazed with the heat, with the sun on the blistered houses, the pavement, the burned grass, I walked slowly. I paid attention to a poor thin leaf, ground a Popsicle stick under the heel of my sandal, squinted at a trash can strapped to a tree that I would never see again.

Where are the children?

I turned around and moved quickly, not quite running, to a part of the fence beyond which the cement wall was not completed. I could see some of the pool. I saw Cynthia, standing about waist-deep in the water, fluttering her hands on the surface and discreetly watching something at the end of the pool, which I could not see. I thought by her pose, her discretion, the look on her face that she must be watching some byplay between the lifeguard and her boyfriend. I couldn't see Meg, but I thought she must be playing in the shallower water—both the shallow and the deep ends of the pool were out of my sight.

"Cynthia!" I had to call twice before she knew where my voice was coming from. "Cynthia! Where's Meg?"

It always seems to me, when I recall this scene, that Cynthia turns very gracefully toward me, then turns all around in the water—making me think of a ballerina on point—then spreads her arms in a gesture of the stage. "Dis-ap-peared!"

Cynthia was naturally graceful, and she did take dancing lessons, so these movements may have been as I have described. She did say "Disappeared," after looking all around the pool, but the strangely artificial style of speech and gesture, the lack of urgency, is more likely my invention. The fear I felt instantly when I couldn't see Meg—even while I was telling myself she must be in the shallower water—must have made Cynthia's movements seem unbearably slow and inappropriate to me, and the tone in which she could say "Disappeared" before the implications struck her (or was she covering, at once, some ever-ready guilt?) was heard by me as quite exquisitely, monstrously self-possessed.

I cried out for Andrew, and the lifeguard came into view. She was pointing toward the deep end of the pool, saying, "What's that?"

There, just within my view, a cluster of pink ruffles appeared, a bouquet, beneath the surface of the water. Why would a lifeguard stop and point, why would she ask what that was, why didn't she just dive into the water and swim to it? She didn't swim, she ran all the way around the edge of the pool. But by this time Andrew was over the fence. So many things seemed not quite plausible—Cynthia's behavior, then the lifeguard's—and now I had the impression that Andrew jumped with one bound over this fence, which seemed about seven feet high. He must have climbed it very quickly, getting a grip on the wire.

I could not jump or climb it, so I ran to the entrance, where there was a sort of latticed gate, locked. It was not very high, and I did pull myself over it. I ran through the cement corridors, through the disinfectant pool for your feet, and came out on the edge of the pool.

The drama was over.

Andrew had got to Meg first, and had pulled her out of the water. He just had to reach over and grab her, because she was swimming somehow, with her head underwater—she was moving toward the edge of the pool. He was carrying her now, and the lifeguard was trotting along behind. Cynthia had climbed out of the water and was running to meet them. The only person aloof from the situation was the boyfriend, who had stayed on the bench at the shallow end, drinking a milkshake. He smiled at me, and I thought that unfeeling of him, even though the danger was past. He may have meant it kindly. I noticed that he had not turned the radio off, just down.

Meg had not swallowed any water. She hadn't even scared herself. Her hair was plastered to her head and her eyes were wide open, golden with amazement.

"I was getting the comb," she said. "I didn't know it was deep."

Andrew said, "She was swimming! She was swimming by herself. I saw her bathing suit in the water and then I saw her swimming."

"She nearly drowned," Cynthia said. "Didn't she? Meg nearly drowned."

"I don't know how it could have happened," said the lifeguard. "One moment she was there, and the next she wasn't."

What had happened was that Meg had climbed out of the water at the shallow end and run along the edge of the pool toward the deep end. She saw a comb that somebody had dropped lying on the bottom. She crouched down and reached in to pick it up, quite deceived as to the depth of the water. She went over the edge and slipped into the pool, making such a light splash that nobody heard—not the lifeguard, who was kissing her boyfriend, nor Cynthia, who was watching them. That must have been the moment under the trees when I thought, Where are the children? It must have been the same moment. At that moment Meg was slipping, surprised, into the treacherously clear blue water.

"It's O.K.," I said to the lifeguard, who was nearly crying. "She can move pretty fast." (Though that wasn't what we usually said about Meg at all. We said she thought everything over and took her time.)

"You swam, Meg," said Cynthia, in a congratulatory way. (She told us about the kissing later.)

"I didn't know it was deep," Meg said. "I didn't drown."

We had lunch at a takeout place, eating hamburgers and fries at a picnic table not far from the highway. In my excitement I forgot to get Meg a plain hamburger, and had to scrape off the relish and mustard with plastic spoons, then wipe the meat with a paper napkin, before she would eat it. I took advantage of the trash can there to clean out the car. Then we resumed driving east, with the car windows open in front. Cynthia and Meg fell asleep in the backseat.

Andrew and I now talked quietly about what had happened. Suppose I hadn't had the impulse just at that moment to check on the children? Suppose we had gone uptown to get drinks, as we had thought of doing? How had Andrew got over the fence? Did he jump or climb? (He couldn't remember.) How had he reached Meg so quickly? And think of the lifeguard not watching. And Cynthia, taken up with the kissing. Not seeing anything else. Not seeing Meg drop over the edge.

Disappeared.

But she swam. She held her breath and came up swimming.

What a chain of lucky links.

That was all we spoke about—luck. But I was compelled to picture the opposite. At this moment we could have been filling out forms. Meg removed from us, Meg's body being prepared for shipment. To Vancouver—where we had never noticed such a thing as a graveyard—or to Ontario? The scribbled drawings she had made this morning would be still in the backseat of the car. How could this be borne all at once, how did people bear it? The plump, sweet shoulders and hands and feet, the fine brown hair, the rather satisfied, secretive expression—all exactly the same as when she had been alive. The most ordinary tragedy. A child drowned in a swimming pool at noon on a sunny day. Things tidied up quickly. The pool open as usual at two o'clock. The lifeguard is a bit shaken up and gets the afternoon off. She drives away with her boyfriend in the Roto-Rooter truck. The body sealed away in some kind of shipping coffin. Sedatives, phone calls, arrangements. Such a sudden vacancy, a blind sinking and shifting. Waking up groggy from the pills, thinking for a moment it wasn't true. Thinking if only we hadn't stopped, if only we hadn't taken this route, if only they hadn't let us use the pool. Probably no one would ever have known about the comb.

There's something trashy about this kind of imagining, isn't there? Something shameful. Laying your finger on the wire to get the safe shock, feeling a bit of what it's like, then pulling back. I believed that Andrew was more scrupulous than I about such things, and that at this moment he was really trying to think about something else.

When I stood apart from my parents at Steve Gauley's funeral and watched them, and had this new, unpleasant feeling about them, I thought that I was understanding something about them for the first time. It was a deadly serious thing. I was understanding that they were implicated. Their big, stiff, dressed-up bodies did not stand between me and sudden death, or any kind of death. They gave consent. So it seemed. They gave consent to the death of children and to my death not by anything they said or thought but by the very fact that they had made children—they had made me. They had made me, and for that reason my death—however grieved they were, however they carried on—would seem to them anything but impossible or unnatural. This was a fact, and even then I knew they were not to blame.

But I did blame them. I charged them with effrontery, hypocrisy. And not just on my own behalf. On Steve Gauley's behalf, and on behalf of all children, who knew that by rights they should have sprung up free, to live a new, superior kind of life, not to be caught in the snares of grownups, with their sex and funerals.

Steve Gauley drowned, people said, because he was next thing to an orphan and was let run free. If he had been warned enough and given chores to do and kept in check, he wouldn't have fallen from an untrustworthy tree branch into a spring pond, a full gravel pit near the river—he wouldn't have drowned. He was neglected, he was free, so he drowned. And his father took it as an accident, such as might happen to a dog. He didn't have a good suit for the funeral, and he didn't bow his head for the prayers. But he was the only grownup that I let off the hook. He was the only one I didn't see giving consent. He couldn't prevent anything, but he wasn't implicated in anything, either—not like the others, saying the Lord's Prayer in their unnaturally weighted voices, oozing religion and dishonor.

At Glendive, not far from the North Dakota border, we had a choice—either to continue on the Interstate or head northeast, toward Williston, taking Route 16, then some secondary roads that would get us back to Highway 2.

We agreed that the Interstate would be faster, and that it was important for us not to spend too much time—that is, money—on the road. Nevertheless, we decided to cut back to Highway 2.

"I just like the idea of it better," I said.

Andrew said, "That's because it's what we planned to do in the beginning."

"We missed seeing Kalispell and Havre. And Wolf Point. I like the names."

"We'll see them on the way back."

Andrew's saying "on the way back" in such an easy tone was a surprising pleasure to me. Of course, I had believed that we would be coming back, with our car and our lives and our family intact, having covered all that distance, having dealt somehow with those loyalties and problems, held ourselves up for inspection in such a foolhardy way. But it was a relief to hear him say it.

"What I can't get over," said Andrew, "is how you got the signal. It's got to be some kind of extra sense that mothers have."

Partly I wanted to believe that, to bask in my extra sense. Partly I wanted to warn him—to warn everybody—never to count on it.

"What I can't understand," I said, "is how you got over that fence."

"Neither can I."

So we went on, with the two in the backseat trusting us, because of no choice, and we ourselves trusting to be forgiven in time what first had to be seen and condemned by those children: whatever was flippant, arbitrary, careless, callous—all our natural, and particular, mistakes.

This story remains a favorite with Alice Munro because "it was tremendously difficult for me to write. I was trying to do something that would have a simple surface, and I had to struggle a long time until I found the right framework. I think that's the first time I ever used a time jump like that. What I try to do is get my stories to the point where they seem to have an uncomplicated surface—so much so that the reader thinks, Oh, this must be autobiographical. When I get to that point, then they're finished. When I finally got to that point with this story, it pleased me."

Alice Munro grew up in a small town in Ontario and now lives in Victoria. Her short-story collections include Dance of the Happy Shades, Something I've Been Meaning to Tell You, The Beggar Maid, The Moons of Jupiter, *and* The Progress of Love. *She has published one novel,* Lives of Girls and Women.

First published in 1985 in The New Yorker.

DAVID LONG

THE LAST PHOTOGRAPH OF LYLE PETTIBONE

I took this early on a Sunday morning, the twenty-sixth of August, that blistering summer of 1917. I was using a Brownie Autographic, bought for eighteen dollars at the Stillwater Mercantile—you can see where I scratched the date and hour along the bottom of the negative. The people who'd been up all night were gone. Others would soon be rising and dressing for church, and stories would crackle through the streets, but I was alone then, or nearly so, crouched on the rails at the west edge of Stillwater, shivering. I could still smell the fire on my clothes, and the first light, when it finally arrived, came thickened with smoke. I made the picture, folded in the bellows of the camera, and walked back along the tracks toward home.

You asked me how I got started . . . it was then.

I was twenty-one that summer, caught between working as my father's factotum at the Dupree Hotel and being conscripted for the war. Some boys I knew had already left their jobs and shipped out; some others had fashioned hasty marriages . . . I'd see them walking through Depot Park with their pregnant wives after supper, heads bent to the grass. I wasn't so gung ho on the war myself. When the *Clarion* ran the first cull of Sperry County names, three hundred to the man, I was mortally relieved to skim to the end of it without seeing mine. But the relief wore thin before long. Flanders was falling, Russia was going to hell, American recruits were funneling into Pershing's army by the thousands. . . . As for matrimony, the only girl in Stillwater I'd cared for had gone east that May to study piano in earnest. Her name was Marcelle, and she wore a French braid that hung down her back like a bullwhip. Her picture shone at me mornings from the bevel of my shaving mirror. In her last letter, she told of going to the Opera House in Chicago to hear Irma Kincaid perform Chopin. *I know you'll think I'm just being dramatic, Willy, but Irma Kincaid has changed my life.*

I spent my free time staring at the town through the Brownie's viewfinder, developing what I saw in a room off the cold storage under the Dupree. I had a picture of the mayor with his foot planted ceremoniously on the running board of his new Saxon roadster . . . schoolchildren poling their raft down McAfferty's Slough . . . drifters sleeping under a wagon behind the Pastime. "What do you want to take pictures of old bums for?" my sister Ellen would scold me mildly. "There's enough unpleasantness in life without going out and *scrounging* for it." "That's not what I'm doing," I'd tell her, "I'm just keeping my eyes open."

One afternoon I sweet-talked Ellen into sitting for me with her clothes off. We went up to an empty room on the top floor and I made dozens of pictures of her lolling on her quilt pretending she was one of the women on Calhoun Street. She was never a beauty, but her skin was white as bar soap, freckled pleasantly across the bosom, and she was capable of a wicked droopy-eyed smile. "How's this, Willy?" she'd ask, draping herself in a new travesty of wantonness. "You're one to reckon with, all right," I said, and we had a high time, the two of us, there under our father's roof. But when I mentioned the developing and printing, Ellen suddenly glazed with worry and told me she wouldn't allow it. "You have to promise me you won't print them," she said.

"You looked awfully good," I said. "Trust me."

"I'll trust you to never *ever* print those pictures," she said, and threw her robe around herself. "I'm not fooling."

And so I left her glaring out over the roofs of Stillwater, on the edge of tears. Later, I made the negatives and looked at them by myself against the light bulb, then put them away in a drawer and never printed them up, more's the pity.

Of course, I took my father as well: a florid, girth-heavy widower of Scotch-French-Canadian stock, a man burdened by an ungenerous nature and nagging social aspirations, burdened, too, by a daughter who drank and a son he called a runt and a dreamer. . . .

But here's the first picture of Lyle Pettibone. He's down in front of the Montana Cafe, around the corner from where the IWW headquarters had been till that June, when the troopers had come after hours and shut it down. He's just endured another set-to with Wilbur Embree, who was on the town council, and E. C. Doyle, the banker, one of that high-minded crew that came to the hotel at noon every day to pack away one of Ellen's heavy lunches and smoke Cuban cigars with my father. By the time I got across the street, the shoving was done and Pettibone's copies of *Solidarity* were strewn down the boardwalk. Winded, hat aslant, he collected the papers in silence, waiting for the other men to get on with their rightful business. Men like Doyle and Embree thought harassment of unionists *was* their rightful business.

Pettibone was a tall man for those days, sober-looking as the Lutheran pastor, but it wasn't God on Pettibone's mind that summer, or not as yet. You can see his sawtooth of a nose, those chiseled-out cheeks . . . his voice was the same, sharp as a sickle, rife with a union spiel that either sickened and terrified you or sliced through all the built-up half-dead parts of you to a place that was still tender and ripe for such radical encouragement—depending on how you fell in the scheme of things. I'd heard where Helena had whistled through an ordinance to ban Wobbly organizers from public declamation, but Pettibone had spoken on our streets for weeks, and up in Depot Park as well. I'd watched him with his long arms thrown open to the sky, and I'd watched the people watching him, people of all kinds, in all kinds of costume, but mostly men I didn't recognize, shading their eyes, listening hard, and a few at the back I did know, taking notes.

They blamed the fire on him. Of course they did.

They'd been expecting something like it and then it happened and there was no question who was behind it and what it meant. All summer the *Clarion* had wailed and prophesied against the Wobbly Menace. Back in July, when trouble broke out down in Arizona, when they loaded Wobbly miners onto cattle cars and rode them out to the Mexican border and dumped them without so much as a tin cup full of water, Will McKinnon wrote that it wouldn't surprise him if citizens all through the West declared an open season on IWWs. He said we'd have a reign of terror. He wasn't personally in any position to advocate such a perversion of justice, but the deaf could've heard him pardon it. He worked that vein so hard, none of the *Clarion*'s right-thinking readers could've harbored any doubt that the IWWs were enemies of the flag, a plague on the country's war effort worse than slackers or pacifists or the few outright cowards dodging conscription. Of course, the Anaconda Company owned McKinnon, owned him outright, as they did damn near every other editor in Montana, then and for a long time after . . . but that distinction was lost on me at twenty-one. The town was afraid, you could feel that for certain. Myself, I was restless, and some afraid too; though not of Pettibone or what he said; not yet.

Well, I made that picture of Pettibone on the boardwalk and it wasn't until I started to thank him that he came to his senses and glowered at me.

"What're you doing?" he wanted to know.

It was so obvious I didn't know what to say. Nobody'd ever cared one way or the other if I took their picture, except that time with Ellen.

"Who's this for?" he said.

"It's not for anyone," I said. "I mean, it's for me."

He gave the street a sidelong check, but commerce had resumed around us.

"I liked hearing you talk the other day," I added suddenly . . . unaware until right then that I'd even listened. An illicit pleasure came crushing over me, so palpable Pettibone couldn't fail to witness it. He laid a hand on my shoulder and bent to squint me in the eye.

"You did," he said, solemn and testing, both. "What did you like about it?"

"I don't know," I said. "Sounded fair, what you were saying."

"We should live so long, you and I," Pettibone said.

Then he asked who I was. And I told him, leaving my father and his well-regarded name out of it.

"Willy the photographer . . . " Pettibone said. "You know there's going to be a strike . . . at the mill, here in Stillwater."

All I'd heard so far was the wary grumbling talk of the lunch crowd at the hotel, and McKinnon's. . . .

"I want you to come out to the mill and take some pictures," he said. "I think it would be very good if you would help us this way. You think you're up to that?"

I told him I was.

I told him he could count on me.

But a week later, when the strike came, I was back at the hotel reshaking the back roof with my father. He could've paid to have it done—there were plenty who wanted a day or two's wage—but he was deviled to do for himself. He hauled his prosperity up the ladder, puffing and swearing at me. You'd think these would've been prime days for an innkeeper, Stillwater swelled out with newcomers as it was. A generation earlier there was woods here, and people still called it Stumptown sometimes, but no one worried anymore that Stillwater would prove another flash in the pan. Even so, these were not peaceable days for my father. Too many of the passers-through couldn't afford the Dupree. Some were family men who'd lost homesteads east of the mountains . . . honyockers they were called, immigrants lured west by the Great Northern to farm 320-acre parcels of dust. Many were single, though, with no change of clothes and—to my father's mind—unhealthy ambitions, or no ambitions at all. Anyone with a whisper of an accent, or a complexion darker than his own, he suspected of being an agitator. He rented rooms to strangers who could pay, but kept his eye on them, using spies like my sister and the hired girls who served them dinner. What he did with such intelligence as he came by, I didn't know.

We worked side by side on the roof all morning, and I itched to be out at the mill where I didn't belong, but I kept my tongue. I watched the traffic on Main and around the corner on First Street, and it passed for an ordinary day of high summer, though it was hard to pin down what was ordinary anymore. Just before lunch, my father pounded his thumb and cursed the Lord and flung the hammer across the alley, end over end . . . shattering the back window of the Mercantile. He stood on the ladder glaring down into the jagged hole, slack-jawed, as if now he'd surprised even himself.

We'd had strikes before, but nothing since 1909, and the tension was sharper now. What Pettibone was talking about was a general strike Big Bill Haywood and the Wobbly brass had called for the whole Northwest: pickers and harvest hands, miners, mill workers, and bindle stiffs who worked out of logging camps. They wanted five dollars for an eight-hour day and respectable living conditions in the camps. They wanted to run their union without being harassed and shot at and picked up for every kind of petty charge from vagrancy to suspicion of sedition. And they wanted the ones already in jail let go.

They were perfect fodder for the Wobblies. Nobody else was going to stand up for them, that was for damn sure. Timber beasts, people around here called them, illiterate footloose rabble. The mills and camps went through men like cans of beans. The Wobbly talk about One Big Union struck home. *An injury to one is an injury to all,* Pettibone and men like Pettibone said. *Live to be an old man or woman and hear the whistle blow for the bosses to go to work.* It sounded glorious, this talk, but the rest of it, the politics, the trashing of capitalism itself, that was only a farfetched dream. They'd slept forty or fifty or sixty to a bunkhouse, doubled on straw-covered slabs, their clothes still rank and wet in the morning and no match for the ferocious cold. To a man they'd had lice and dysentery, and plenty had bronchitis they couldn't shake even when the summers finally came. And there weren't any over thirty with two hands full of fingers.

The Wobblies said you can forget about the sweet by-and-by, strike now, and they did.

For a few days, the *Clarion* ignored the strike, except for McKinnon's mighty editorializing, calling for federal troops to root out the IWWs. Then on the twentieth of August he announced that the strike had proved a grand failure. But it hadn't . . . or it hadn't yet. For a time, it tied up three-quarters of the mills in the Northwest. But the strikers were isolated . . . nobody but the Lumbermen's Association and men like McKinnon knew for a fact how far it had gotten.

Now something let loose in McKinnon, and when it let loose in him it let loose all over the county. Other IWWs before Pettibone had stood up and said this wasn't their war, but this was Pettibone's favorite string to harp on. "Stay home," he preached to his people. "Fight your real enemy, fight the bosses." It was too much for McKinnon. *My friends,* he wrote, *treason is treason.* Nothing short of rounding up every last one of them would do, but authority was dragging its heels.

It was a dry summer, as I said. The streams ran low and the sloughs caked over and the grain heads shriveled before harvest. Out east of the mountains it was worse, of course, because the land was infinitely drier there to begin with, but even here in the valley the long afternoons of sun and the promise of a poor crop added to the strain. Early in August, a timber fire started up in Idaho near the Canadian line and burned eastward for eight days. It was far away, but you could smell it every morning and see the haze backed up against the mountains to the east. Someone called it sabotage, and a few probably believed it, though surely lightning had touched it off. The forest was government-owned up there, and the Wobs had no kick against that.

Anyway, sabotage was on people's minds. I never heard

Pettibone favor it, for his thoughts were on the strike by then, and on the problem of keeping Wobblies out of the conscription. But others had. They called it soldiering on the job. Grain sacks would come unsewn. Shovel handles would break soon as they were passed around. Spikes would appear in logs bound for the headsaw. Whole shipments of cut timber would turn up four inches short. And nobody to blame. Hit the boss in the pocketbook and play dumb, that was the idea. But by that August sabotage had come to explain *anything* going haywire, from polluted wells to derailings of the Great Northern. There were some who'd swear the drought itself was a Wobbly trick.

That Saturday, a week into the strike, the town was stuffed with people. Common sense said it was too hot to sit in the movie house, but some were braving it to watch Myrtle Stedman in a five-reeler called *Prison Without Walls.* There was a benefit for the Red Cross out at the Pavillion. At the hotel, we had a wedding party in progress—the Upshaws, important friends of my father, had married their oldest girl to a fellow from Spokane. The groom's mother was a disciple of Temperance, so the cut-glass bowls on the buffet held a strawberry punch, but the men excused themselves now and again to work on flasks or bottles of ale my father'd stowed in crushed ice under a tarp on the back-porch landing.

Earlier he'd called for pictures, and I'd lined the celebrants up and frozen them for posterity, still fresh. But now it was stifling inside. Even the cut flowers were droopy on their stems. The dining room was cleared of tables and Mort Pickerell's string band played and the guests danced. My sister Ellen looped freely about the room in the grasp of the groom's brother, her shoes off and her eyes half shut. My father and Matthew Upshaw and the groom's father presided over it all, smiling heavily and dabbing at their foreheads with handkerchiefs.

I'd had enough of noise and pleasantry, and I thought I'd expire without some air. I headed out toward the kitchen and slipped up the back hall to my quarters on the third floor where I could sit in the window with my feet out on the peak of the porch roof. It was nine-thirty by my watch, just growing dark. The sky west of town was still aglow and overhead was a smear of deepening blues. Some of the mill workers had taken their last roll of wages over to Calhoun Street, I imagined, but most were down below, drinking. Men were spilling out the doorways of the Pastime, the Grandee, the Silver Dollar, and already there was yelling.

From up here, the town didn't look like so much, a few streets of commerce, a grid of frame houses stretching north to the Great Northern yard, south to the elevators, a little cluster of lights on the valley floor you could imagine snuffed out by the Lord's little finger. In a while, the evening wind came across the roofs. I stretched and breathed it in, expecting the smell of hay . . . not creosote and burning pitch. I jerked my head up and caught sight of the train yard. All up one siding, boxcars and flatbeds loaded with lumber were shooting out flames, full-blown at the western end, just getting going down by the station. For an instant, it seemed I was the only witness . . . then a few figures broke into running, and the head lamps of a few cars veered into Depot Square . . . then, all at once, the people on Main Street began to know.

I hustled back inside and bolted into the hallway and down through the back wing . . . but a door opened in front of me and a man backed out, latching the door gingerly, as if he'd left someone sleeping. He straightened and saw me and stopped short.

It was Pettibone. What was he doing here? *My God!*

"William," he said. He looked enormously tired. His shoulders drooped and his hands hung from his sleeves like skinned rabbits.

"The train's on fire," I said.

The words didn't reach him at first.

"The train," I said. "The whole . . . all the lumber's burning."

There's no picture of Pettibone in the hallway, gazing down at me in bewilderment . . . except as I've called it to mind so many times. They say action was Pettibone's long suit, action and oratory. Still, with such a picture in hand, you'd see how the real man was given more to brooding and intellection. You'd see the incomprehension letting down into understanding and disappointment and weariness.

Then, standing opposite, we heard the fire bell. Pettibone returned a wayward suspender to his shoulder and peered over me at the empty hallway.

"I thought we were going to have pictures of the strike," he said.

"Well, I didn't make it," I started in, but Pettibone wouldn't have any use for cowardice, so I shut up. *I'll make it up to you,* I was thinking.

Pettibone shook his head. He turned and went back into the room and threw the bolt.

By the time I got to the fire, things were already out of hand. Not only were the cars burning, but a storage shed had caught, and the fire had leapt from it to a snarl of weeds and torn across them like a dam burst to a garage on Railroad Street. From the platform I could hear the popping glass and the whoosh of air, and from all sides commands and argument flaring and jumping from man to man. They'd managed to get some of the cars unhitched, but by the time they could get an engine jockeyed to the right track it was pointless to try and pull them all apart.

Some councilmen had arrived, and volunteer firemen, and men who worked the yard for the Great Northern, but for all this authority, nobody was in charge. A couple of hundred others pressed around, many come straight from the dance, the women in summer linen with flowers or hair ribbons worked loose, the men holding their jackets and staring. Through this crowd soon pushed some stalwarts of the Lumbermen's Association, including two of the mill owners, brothers named Kavanaugh, who'd made it in from a lodge on the lake with remarkable haste.

One boxcar was wheat, and two flatbeds were ties soaked in tar and creosote, but the other twenty-four were stacked full of contract lumber. The two Kavanaughs halted on the platform, observably angrier—and more stupefied—than the rest of us. They searched the line of fires, then turned and searched the line of flickering faces. In a moment they set off down the spur for a closer inspection, but the heat and the down-swooping coils of black smoke stopped them short, and they stood silhouetted in the cinders finally, gawking with the rest of us.

The firemen had now turned to that tongue of blaze threatening Railroad Street. The pumper and the chemical truck were pulled up at the edge of the heat. The south wall of Kramer's car barn was eaten away and smoke came chuffing through the roof shakes. If the firemen knew that railroad bums sometimes slept off bad weather or liquor in Kramer's loft, it didn't figure in their attentions. They sprayed down the sides of the next building up the line, some of the water turning instantly to steam. For a handful of minutes, the rest of that scraggly block—and who could tell what else—hung on the whim of the wind.

Then the crowd's first amazement burned off. The men in front got tired of standing around. Helplessness offended them. Shoving broke out by the depot doors. By the time I could worm myself near, one man had been wrestled to the pavement and another was being restrained by a beefy Sperry County deputy. They held the man down with a knee at his neck, like a calf for branding. In no time they'd been through his pockets and found his red card and showed it around for everyone, and the same with his friend's.

"No law against being in the union," the friend said, but he was a small man and surrounded.

"Don't give me law, mister," the deputy said.

Someone reached in and kicked at the down man's ribs, and the struggling started up again. A third man, who'd been standing by, was shoved forward.

"Here's another one," somebody yelled.

The depot door opened and the county sheriff stood illuminated by the fire, a man tall as Pettibone but solid as a steer. He eyed the boxcars, then popped open his watch and had a look at that, closed it with a patient click, then came striding down through the people to where the trouble was, one hand on his holster. Out the door behind him came the two preened heads of the Kavanaughs, but they slipped away into the commotion, and that was all I saw of them that night.

Maybe it was the sheriff who said it, or maybe the word was spat from some other mouth, but I heard it clear enough.

Pettibone.

I won't say I fit this all together right then, for I was a slow blossomer in most all things, matters of deceit included. But I worked my way out from the people and the rising clamor at the station and headed down through the alleys toward the Dupree.

I ran up through the shadows onto the back porch and my boot sent an empty bottle ringing across the landing, but no one was left to hear. The party had gone astray. Some of the guests had dashed off to the station, not being able to stand not going any longer, and some had come back and were loitering in the big room wondering what kind of mood to take up now. The bride and groom had departed. There was no sign of my father. Even the band had left their instruments on top of the piano and were gone.

I ran up the two flights of back stairs and down to the door where I'd had my sudden audience with Pettibone. No one answered my knocking. I put my ear to the door, but was breathing too hard to hear. Next thing, without a thought, I had my third-floor key out.

The curtains flapped into the room indifferently, those strips of cheap poplin my father assigned to his dollar-fifty rooms. The bed was stirred up, cigarettes were snuffed out in a water glass on the windowsill . . . that was it. I tried to fix Pettibone there in the room, that dark lankiness and agitation. And who it was *with* him . . . and what would possess him to trespass under my father's roof, so near the authorized gaiety downstairs? It occurred to me with a cold rush that I didn't know the first blessed thing about men like

Pettibone . . . where they could find their respite in a town like ours, where they could turn when they had to.

When you thought of Stillwater, you thought of the railroad. You saw the depot in your mind's eye, looming at the end of Main, huge, white-painted, monument to the wheeling and dealing that secured us the GN's northern route, when everyone expected it to dip south to Sperry. It'd been my duty, since the age of fourteen, to loiter there, outside on a baggage cart by summer, inside on the curved walnut benches by winter, waiting for the train to disgorge guests for the Dupree.

But tonight, by the time I'd returned, the depot was ringed by men with guns.

Some were police and some were National Guard, and some were just men from town. They'd started rounding up Wobblies. The jail was too puny for such a job, so they were herded into the depot's generous waiting room. I climbed up on the back railing and stole a look through the stationmaster's window. Fifty or more of them were in there, packed together under the lights. They looked like they were waiting for a train, but where they were going they didn't need bags.

I tried to wiggle the window up enough to stick the Brownie through . . . but someone suckered me back of the knees and I fell from the railing and my head careened back against the concrete. The noise and the lights went dead for a moment, then came pounding back with the bang of my heart. I got up on all fours, but crumpled again with an awful pain and dizziness, and was a moment later hauled up by the back of the shirt and marched around into the light on spidery legs, then searched. The man was in uniform, no one I knew or who knew me. He stood me against the depot wall while he composed himself. I could feel the fires on my face. Burning like that, it seemed like they could burn forever. Nothing in focus, I strayed a few feet toward the tracks, but he had me again and prodded me past the windows and thrust me in.

The smoke was worse inside, trapped under shafts of heavy electric light. One guardsman had the door and there was one in each corner and one more perched in the ticket window with a shotgun cocked over his forearm, five in all, against a roomful of herded-up men.

"What you waiting for, bohunk?" the one at the door said.

I stumbled out into the middle. The nearest men looked me up and down and saw they didn't know me and turned back to themselves. I found space and collapsed to the bench and held my head. Slowly, the pounding lightened and my thoughts began to clear. I looked at the faces around me . . . and remembered the camera, felt it dropping from my hand again, falling away into the trampled shadows.

The door snapped open in a while and another man was driven inside. A languid wave rolled through the hanging smoke and broke against the far wall, then the air settled again. He was middle-aged, this one, with a dazed, swollen face and the tails of his shirt blood-soaked. He was as lost in here as I was . . . and I realized then that I knew him, or recognized him, from the photo I'd taken behind the Pastime, when he was sleeping under Von Ebersole's wagon. He was no Wobbly, this one.

For a time it was quiet. The heat grew and pressed in on us and the room took on a mean smell. Some of the men wouldn't sit down anymore.

"You," one was saying, up staring the nearest guardsman in the face. "How old you supposed to be?"

The guardsman was hardly older than me, a moon-faced boy in a clean uniform that didn't fit. He jockeyed the gun around in his arms and squinted off above our heads at the other guards, but the haze isolated him.

"Look at what they get to point guns at good union men," the man said, louder, narrowing in on the boy and his gun. Another two steps and he could wrap his hand around the muzzle. I couldn't tell how people would act anymore, what they'd give the most weight to any particular moment. I could see how the first shot would be touched off in panic and self-regard maybe, or would just expel itself like matter in a boil, then the others would have their reason and they'd lace us in a crossfire, and we'd be in no shape to say boo about it afterwards, though the guards would say plenty enough and McKinnon would write it up in a high style and people would believe it gladly and completely.

"Sit down, Blue," somebody called out.

This Blue rocked back on his heels and turned to us. He was drunk, or he'd been started that way when they'd caught up with him. His mouth was chapped with tobacco, his eyes flat and watery as he tried to light on the one who'd yelled at him.

"Shut him the hell up," someone farther back shouted.

Blue shook his head, stranded between us and the guard. "You pukes," he said. "You ain't worth boot grease."

There was nothing of Pettibone in him, nothing of entitlement or pride, I understood then, and got a sick feeling for us all.

Pettibone could've told us what they were doing: penning us up until morning when they could march us out in the daylight past the stench and ruin of the lumber train and load us onto cattle cars just readied for the purpose, the idea not even fresh, stolen from the Bisbee, Arizona, copper mines, or over at Everett, Washington . . . and haul us out of the valley and the county and the state on the suspicion of sabotage.

Pettibone could've stood up and told them—*us*—it wasn't his fire, and engendered a silence around him, in which every one of us at the station—Wobbly or no—would get clearheaded and remember that we weren't individually or in concert stupid enough to bolt up the line of train cars with gallon bottles of kerosene and punks, with the sun barely down and the town crawling with people and no realizable good to come from it, only trouble, which had materialized in force. It's true, Pettibone, by himself, or with the rest of us solidified around him, wouldn't have been able to *stop* the deportation, any more than he, or any of the others, right up to Big Bill Haywood himself, could stop the War Department from shipping IWWs off to army camps, but with him there the men could've known the extent of what was going on and not gone at each other, empty-handed and down in their hearts. But, of course, Pettibone could not have risked being there himself.

The filigreed hands of the station clock said one-forty. The door to the tracks cracked open then and the sheriff pushed his way in, a gang of deputies in tow.

The room got quiet again, man by man.

The sheriff looked around for something to stand on, then just raised his voice. "Listen like this mattered," he said. "You're going to line up against that wall for me, that one with the bulletin board on it," he said. "Fast and orderly would be a good way."

After a decent interval, the nearest bunch rose as if their bones hurt and moved grudgingly toward the wall. A few more straggled over and I joined them and then most of the rest came, leaving Blue alone, slouched on the last bench, talked out. The boy guard moved in on him, happily, and pointed the gun at his face.

The sheriff drifted over to the two of them.

"Where's Pettibone?" he asked Blue.

Blue didn't say anything. He looked from the sheriff's face to the snout of the gun and down to his shoes.

The sheriff nodded. He picked his watch out again, opened it, and turned to compare it with the clock on the wall.

"All right," he said. He motioned to the boy to get Blue up and standing like the rest of us. Blue swung his arm out to bat the gun barrel away from his face, but the boy swiveled the butt around and cracked him in the temple and he went down across the bench and lay there, derelict.

The sheriff walked back over to us. "Where's Pettibone?" he said to the first man.

The man said he didn't know.

The sheriff watched him impassively. "If you knew, you'd tell me, wouldn't you," he said.

The man didn't say anything.

"I know what kind you are," the sheriff said, still eyeing him. "I know what you'd do."

He moved down the line, one deputy following along with a note pad, taking names. When he got to me he stopped and scowled.

It wasn't Pettibone, I thought, the sheriff hulking over me. *It could not have been Pettibone, even carried out by someone else's hand, could not have been.*

"Well, Mr. Dupree," the sheriff said. "Looks to me like it's time for you to get on home."

And like that, like sleight of hand, or worse, I was outside again, where it was cooler and the air was less concentrated and the crowd had been broken into factions and dispersed. The fires were still going but I didn't want to look at them anymore. I started back to the Dupree, despite myself. Where else was I going to go?

It occurred to me that I might walk up to that third-floor room and find the door open and the bed clean-made, and no vestige of Pettibone except in my imagination . . . my father's tremulous baritone reiterating in my mind's ear how untrustworthy I was, how weak to give myself over time and again to the made-up instead of the certifiably real and necessary. But if all that milled lumber was burning and the depot was full of men to be locked inside cattle cars, then anything else could, or could've happened, I was thinking. Salmon could come raining down out of the sky. I was halfway down Dakota Street near the Chinese laundry before I remembered the camera.

I knew I'd find it ruined, the lens shattered and the bellows ripped like a rag, but I had a sudden fierce desire to secure it and carry it home. I snuck back through the elms to the dark side of the depot and pawed through the heavy shadows beneath the railing, and down in the gap between some packing crates and the wall, then out on the grass, though that was too far for it to have flown. I was kneeling there, stupefied, my hands wet with dew, when a flurry of raised voices from up on the platform drove me back behind the boxes. In a moment, three men came past, one in uniform, the others decently dressed, men I knew I'd seen before but didn't know. They couldn't decide whether to run or walk fast. They crossed to a car waiting along the park and two got in. The other leaned down and kept talking, his free hand flitting like a huge bug against the streetlight.

Finally the head lamps came on and the two men drove off and the third stood looking after them, then did an about-face and peered back at the train yard and up at the putrid orange halo above it. Then he was gone too. I pulled myself up by the lid of the packing box and it came free in my hands, and there, swaddled in shavings, was the Brownie.

Try these other pictures: Pettibone and the woman—for it was now, in my mind, surely a woman, hard-faced comrade and lover under the guise of a traveling widow, whose room he had visited in the hotel—hurtling in a car away from Sperry County toward shelter and counsel at the Wobbly cabal in Spokane. Or Pettibone alone—just as likely—striding west on the GN tracks toward that skinny part of Idaho that should still have been Montana, satchels in either hand swinging like ballast, long legs hitting every second tie in perfect cadence. I could see him halting every little while to listen—for what, for dogs? They didn't have dogs, these officers or citizens who were after him, or have need of them apparently. Pettibone, his head cocked east, just the dimmest smudge of sky-reflected firelight glancing off his face, would hear only the yap and howl of a coyote, most of the timber wolves having retreated to British Columbia by our time, and the clamor of the town not carrying much beyond its boundaries, and the worst of *that* just spoken and confirmed between men in voices not meant to carry. . . .

Or picture any of the others I dreamed up, still hidden in the lee of the depot, the camera folded against my shirt, not twenty feet from where the sweating-out of Pettibone's actual whereabouts continued, the sheriff's shadow obliterating each man's night-beaten face in turn. What they'd have in common, these pictures, would be Pettibone in flight . . . for I couldn't shake the image of him in the upstairs hallway, face abruptly unleavened by the news I'd delivered and all the implication he wrung from it in a few consecutive instants. *Battles are won by the remnants of armies*, that was a Pettibone refrain, lifted maybe from an Old Testament litany of suffering and endurance. *Outnumber, outsmart, outlast them.* . . . I could only imagine him using his head start like a weapon.

And as for the Wobblies inside, it wouldn't matter if they knew or didn't know, if they broke ranks or not . . . whatever any of them said, it could be taken as more sabotage, more red-inspired trickery. These thoughts in mind, I tried out a new idea: that I might be forgiven for not telling what I knew, the truth about Pettibone and the fire . . . that my silence might even be strategic, the better part of valor. All of which was consoling . . . but missed the point entirely. For I'd managed all night not to ask myself the question that counted.

If it wasn't Pettibone's fire, whose was it?

McKinnon was right: it was the end of the Wobblies in Sperry County, beginning of the end even in Butte, union town above all others. "The expected has happened," he wrote in Monday's paper, the rest of the state and the Northwest looking on, meaning not the fire itself, which he decried separately, but the work of the twenty or so free-lance men who located Pettibone and took him into their collective custody, at roughly the same late hour of the night that the sheriff finally concluded that not one of those miserable Wobblies in the depot actually knew where Pettibone was.

Deportation by boxcar, that must've been the heart of the plan, as conceived, for the cars were too readily at hand, paid for by the sacrifice of a *portion* of the lumber train—but not the whole of it, certainly, and not those car barns down Railroad Street, and not the railroad bum charred to futility inside one of them. Nor the combustion of anger—most of all that—in no time surpassing their design. McKinnon played it straight. He passed the buck to Congress for not protecting industry, then turned his vitriol on Pettibone for a last time. "Hysterical," McKinnon said of Lyle Pettibone, "mentally unbalanced, preying on uneducated, unsophisticated laborers. . . . "

I left Stillwater.

The rest I know you're familiar enough with: the staff work I did those years for the *Post-Dispatch*, then my great fortune at meeting Roy Stryker who added me to the group he had at the Farm Security Administration, Dorothea Lange and Russ Lee and Walker Evans and those others making pictures of the tenants and croppers blown out of the Dustbowl . . . all of it, I can see now, fitting together, aiming me toward that day in 1941, outside General Tire in Akron, when some union men swarmed and beat down a strikebreaker, which was the shot they gave the Pulitzer for.

It's luck who gets the prize, that's an article of faith. But I took it as an honor, regardless . . . because even then, forty-four years old, older even than Pettibone had been, I would still sometimes hear my father's grinding deprecations of me and was tempted, despite the evidence, to believe in them . . . and because luck's not enough to explain what I was doing at General Tire that day, that change of shift. The tire workers, ganging in union regalia, with balled fists and nightsticks, and smiles burning into frantic bloom on their faces . . . and the scabs, this one here cut from the pack, bent double under one thickness of overcoat, nothing showing but a bony hand aimed at the sky like half a prayer . . . they knew what they were doing, all of them. And I knew my business by then as well, for it's a man's duty to find what he's good for, if he finds nothing else worth the cost of learning it. In all his days, in all his dogged sucking up to men of property and office my father never found this out.

That Sunday morning in Stillwater, after I'd talked myself home along the tracks, holding the folded Brownie inside my shirt, I slipped down into the cellar of the Dupree where it was cool and no one ever came—except my sister, in search of potatoes for the kitchen, or communion with her private store of red wine hidden among the Ball jars of Sperry County cherries. In a few minutes I had the film stripped, developed, and hanging by a clothespin to dry. I sat down in the dark and touched the clotted lump at the back of my head. I heard the morning commencing above me, the wince of guests reaching the bottom tread of the front staircase, one after another, pausing on the foyer carpet struck lavender by sunlight spewing through the transom, then crossing onto the bare floor of the dining room where the tables had been restored. I heard the hired girl's feet clipping back and forth to the kitchen, Ellen's dragging by the stove. I heard the waste water come coursing down the pipes and in a while I heard the church bells start in. Gradually, the dining room grew quiet. I got up and turned on the light and passed the negative before it. There they all were . . . the bride and her earnest groom, the mothers, Matthew Upshaw and my father and their friends, everyone shoulder to shoulder, dignified before the camera . . . and there at the end of the roll, Lyle Pettibone, uninvited, hanging from a trestle just west of town.

David Long, a native of Massachusetts, moved to Montana in the early 1970s to study writing at the University of Montana and has since written many stories set in Montana. He is fond of this particular story because "I became comfortable inhabiting this time period." Writing the story prompted him to go on and write a number of stories imagined in Montana's past, including "The Flood of '64," the title story of his new collection.

Home Fires, *Long's first collection of short fiction, won the 1983 St. Lawrence Award for fiction. His poetry has been collected in* Early Returns. *He lives in Kalispell with his wife and two sons, Montana and Jackson.*

First published in 1985 in Antaeus.

JOY WILLIAMS

ESCAPES

When I was very small, my father said,

"Lizzie, I want to tell you something about your grandfather. Just before he died, he was alive. Fifteen minutes before."

I had never known my grandfather. This was the most extraordinary thing I had ever heard about him.

Still, I said, No.

"No!" my father said. "What do you mean, 'No.' " He laughed.

I shook my head.

"All right," my father said, "it was one minute before. I thought you were too little to know such things, but I see you're not. It was even less than a minute. It was one *moment* before."

"Oh stop teasing her," my mother said to my father.

"He's just teasing you, Lizzie," my mother said.

In warm weather once we drove up into the mountains, my mother, my father and I, and stayed for several days at a resort lodge on a lake. In the afternoons, horse races took place in the lodge. The horses were blocks of wood with numbers painted on them, moved from one end of the room to the other by ladies in ball gowns. There was a long pier that led out into the lake and at the end of the pier was a nightclub that had a twenty-foot-tall champagne glass on the roof. At night, someone would pull a switch and neon bubbles would spring out from the lit glass into the black air. I very much wanted such a glass on the roof of our own house and I wanted to be the one who, every night, would turn on the switch. My mother always said about this, "We'll see."

I saw an odd thing once, there in the mountains. I saw my

father, pretending to be lame. This was in the midst of strangers in the gift shop of the lodge. The shop sold hand-carved canes, among many other things, and when I came in to buy bubble gum in the shape of cigarettes, to which I was devoted, I saw my father, hobbling painfully down the aisle, leaning heavily on a dully gleaming, yellow cane, his shoulders hunched, one leg turned out at a curious angle. My handsome, healthy father, his face drawn in dreams. He looked at me. And then he looked away as though he did not know me.

My mother was a drinker. Because my father left us, I assumed he was not a drinker, but this may not have been the case. My mother loved me and was always kind to me. We spent a great deal of time together, my mother and I. This was before I knew how to read. I suspected there was a trick to reading, but I did not know the trick. Written words were something between me and a place I could not go. My mother went back and forth to that place all the time, but couldn't explain to me exactly what it was like there. I imagined it to be a different place.

As a very young child, my mother had seen the magician Houdini. Houdini had made an elephant disappear. He had also made an orange tree grow from a seed right on the stage. Bright oranges hung from the tree and he had picked them and thrown them out into the audience. People could eat the oranges or take them home, whatever they wanted.

How did he make the elephant disappear, I asked.

"He disappeared in a puff of smoke," my mother said. "Houdini said that even the elephant didn't know how it was done."

Was it a baby elephant, I asked.

My mother sipped her drink. She said that Houdini was more than a magician, he was an escape artist. She said that he could escape from handcuffs and chains and ropes.

"They put him in straitjackets and locked him in trunks and threw him in swimming pools and rivers and oceans and he escaped," my mother said. "He escaped from water-filled vaults. He escaped from coffins."

I said that I wanted to see Houdini.

"Oh, Houdini's dead, Lizzie," my mother said. "He died a long time ago. A man punched him in the stomach three times and he died."

Dead. I asked if he couldn't get out of being dead.

"He met his match there," my mother said.

She said that he turned a bowl of flowers into a pony who cantered around the stage.

"He sawed a lady in half too, Lizzie." Oh, how I wanted to be that lady, sawed in half and then made whole again!

My mother spoke happily, laughing. We sat at the kitchen table and my mother was drinking from a small glass which rested snugly in her hand. It was my favorite glass too but she never let me drink from it. There were all kinds of glasses in our cupboard but this was the one we both liked. This was in Maine. Outside, in the yard, was our car which was an old blue convertible.

Was there blood, I asked.

"No, Lizzie, no. He was a magician!"

Did she cry that lady, I wanted to know.

"I don't think so," my mother said. "Maybe he hypnotized her first."

It was winter. My father had never ridden in the blue convertible which my mother had bought after he had gone. The car was old then, and was rusted here and there. Beneath the rubber mat on my side, the passenger side, part of the floor had rusted through completely. When we went anywhere in the car, I would sometimes lift up the mat so I could see the road rushing past beneath us and feel the cold round air as it came up through the hole. I would pretend that the coldness was trying to speak to me, in the same way that words written down tried to speak. The air wanted to tell me something, but I didn't care about it, that's what I thought. Outside, the car stood in the snow.

I had a dream about the car. My mother and I were alone together as we always were, linked in our hopeless and incomprehending love of one another, and we were driving to a house. It seemed to be our destination but we only arrived to move on. We drove again, always returning to the house which we would circle and leave, only to arrive at it again. As we drove, the inside of the car grew hair. The hair was gray and it grew and grew. I never told my mother about this dream just as I had never told her about my father leaning on the cane. I was a secretive person. In that way, I was like my mother.

I wanted to know more about Houdini. Was Houdini in love, did Houdini love someone, I asked.

"Rosabelle," my mother said. "He loved his wife, Rosabelle."

I went and got a glass and poured some ginger ale in it and I sipped my ginger ale slowly in the way that I had seen my mother sip her drink many, many times. Even then, I had the gestures down. I sat opposite her, very still and quiet, pretending.

But then I wanted to know was there magic in the way he loved her. Could he make her disappear. Could he make both of them disappear was the way I put my question.

"Rosabelle," my mother said. "No one knew anything about Rosabelle except that Houdini loved her. He never turned their love into loneliness which would have been beneath him of course."

We ate our supper and after supper my mother would have another little bit to drink. Then she would read articles from the newspaper aloud to me.

"My goodness," she said, "what a strange story. A hunter shot a bear who was carrying a woman's pocketbook in its mouth."

Oh, oh, I cried. I looked at the newspaper and struck it with my fingers. My mother read on, a little oblivious to me. The woman had lost her purse years before on a camping trip. Everything was still inside it, her wallet and her compact and her keys.

Oh, I cried. I thought this was terrible. I was frightened, thinking of my mother's pocketbook, the way she carried it always, and the poor bear too.

Why did the bear want to carry a pocketbook, I asked.

My mother looked up from the words in the newspaper. It was as though she had come back into the room I was in.

"Why, Lizzie," she said.

The poor bear, I said.

"Oh, the bear is all right," my mother said. "The bear got away."

I did not believe this was the case. She herself said the bear had been shot.

"The bear escaped," my mother said. "It says so right here," and she ran her finger along a line of words. "It ran back into the woods to its home." She stood up and came around the table and kissed me. She smelled then like the glass that was always in the sink in the morning, and the smell reminds me still of daring and deception, hopes and little lies.

I shut my eyes and in that way I felt I could not hear my mother. I saw the bear holding the pocketbook, walking through the woods with it, feeling fine in a different way and pretty too, then stopping to find something in it, wanting something, moving its big paw through the pocketbook's small things.

"Lizzie," my mother called to me. My mother did not know where I was which alarmed me. I opened my eyes.

"Don't cry, Lizzie," my mother said. She looked as though she were about to cry too. This was the way it often was at night, late in the kitchen with my mother.

My mother returned to the newspaper and began to turn the pages. She called my attention to the drawing of a man holding a hat with stars sprinkling out of it. It was an advertisement for a magician who would be performing not far away. We decided we would see him. My mother knew just the seats she wanted for us, good seats, on the aisle close to the stage. We might be called up on the stage, she said, to be part of the performance. Magicians often used people from the audience, particularly children. I might even be given a rabbit.

I wanted a rabbit.

I put my hands on the table and I could see the rabbit

between them. He was solid white in the front and solid black in the back as though he were made up of two rabbits. There are rabbits like that. I saw him there, before me on the table, a nice rabbit.

My mother went to the phone and ordered two tickets, and not many days after that, we were in our car driving to Portland for the matinee performance. I very much liked the word matinee. Matinee, matinee, I said. There was a broad hump on the floor between our seats and it was here where my mother put her little glass, the glass often full, never, it seemed, more than half empty. We chatted together and I thought we must have appeared interesting to others as we passed by in our convertible in winter. My mother spoke about happiness. She told me that the happiness that comes out of nowhere, out of nothing, is the very best kind. We paid no attention to the coldness which was speaking in the way that it had, but enjoyed the sun which beat through the windshield upon our pale hands.

My mother said that Houdini had black eyes and that white doves flew from his fingertips. She said that he escaped from a block of ice.

Did he look like my father, Houdini, I asked. Did he have a moustache.

"Your father didn't have a moustache," my mother said, laughing. "Oh, I wish I could be more like you."

Later, she said, "Maybe he didn't escape from a block of ice, I'm not sure about that. Maybe he wanted to, but he never did."

We stopped for lunch somewhere, a dark little restaurant along the road. My mother had cocktails and I myself drank something cold and sweet. The restaurant was not very nice. It smelled of smoke and dampness as though once it had burned down, and it was so noisy that I could not hear my mother very well. My mother looked like a woman in a bar, pretty and disturbed, hunched forward saying, who do you think I look like, will you remember me? She was saying all matter of things. We lingered there, and then my mother asked the time of someone and seemed surprised. My mother was always surprised by time. Outside, there were woods of green fir trees whose lowest branches swept the ground, and as we were getting back into the car, I believed I saw something moving far back in the darkness of the woods beyond the slick, snowy square of the parking lot. It was the bear, I thought. Hurry, hurry, I thought. The hunter is playing with his children. He is making them something to play in as my father had once made a small playhouse for me. He is not the hunter yet. But in my heart I knew the bear was gone and the shape was just the shadow of something else in the afternoon.

My mother drove very fast but the performance had already begun when we arrived. My mother's face was damp and her good blouse had a spot on it. She went into the ladies' room and when she returned the spot was larger, but it was water now and not what it had been before. The usher assured us that we had not missed much. The usher said that the magician was not very good, that he talked and talked, he told a lot of jokes and then when you were bored and distracted, something would happen, something would have changed. The usher smiled at my mother. He seemed to like her, even know her in some way. He was a small man, like an old boy, balding. I did not care for him. He led us to our seats, but there were people sitting in them and there was a small disturbance as the strangers rearranged themselves. We were both expectant, my mother and I, and we watched the magician intently. My mother's lips were parted, and her eyes were bright. On the stage were a group of children about my age, each with a hand on a small cage the magician was holding. In the cage was a tiny bird. The magician would ask the children to jostle the cage occasionally and the bird would flutter against the bars so that everyone would see it was a real thing with bones and breath and feelings too. Each child announced that they had a firm grip on the bars. Then the magician put a cloth over the cage, gave a quick tug and cage and bird vanished. I was not surprised. It seemed just the kind of thing that was going to happen. I decided to withhold my applause when I saw that my mother's hands too were in her lap. There were several more tricks of the magician's invention, certainly nothing I would have asked him to do. Large constructions of many parts and colors were wheeled onto the stage. There were doors everywhere which the magician opened and slammed shut. Things came and went, all to the accompaniment of loud music. I was confused and grew hot. My mother too moved restlessly in the next seat. Then there was an intermission and we returned to the lobby.

"This man is a far, far cry from the great Houdini," my mother said.

What were his intentions exactly, I asked.

He had taken a watch from a man in the audience and smashed it for all to see with a hammer. Then the watch, unharmed, had reappeared behind the man's ear.

"A happy memory can be a very misleading thing," my mother said. "Would you like to go home?"

I did not want to leave really. I wanted to see it through. I held the glossy program in my hand and turned the pages. I stared hard at the print beneath the pictures and imagined all sorts of promises being made.

"Yes, we want to see how it's done, don't we, you and I," my mother said. "We want to get to the bottom of it."

I guessed we did.

"All right, Lizzie," my mother said, "but I have to get something out of the car. I'll be right back."

I waited for her in a corner of the lobby. Some children looked at me and I looked back. I had a package of gum cigarettes in my pocket and I extracted one carefully and placed the end in my mouth. I held the elbow of my right arm with my left hand and smoked the cigarette for a long time and then I folded it up in my mouth and I chewed it for a while. My mother had not yet returned when the performance began again. She was having a little drink, I knew, and she was where she went when she drank without me, somewhere in herself. It was not the place where words could take you but another place even. I stood alone in the lobby for a while, looking out into the street. On the sidewalk outside the theater, sand had been scattered and the sand ate through the ice in ugly holes. I saw no one like my mother who passed by. She was wearing a red coat. Once she had said to me, You've fallen out of love with me, haven't you, and I knew she was thinking I was someone else, but this had happened only once.

I heard the music from the stage and I finally returned to our seats. There were not as many people in the audience as before. On stage with the magician was a woman in a bathing suit and high-heeled shoes holding a chain saw. The magician demonstrated that the saw was real by cutting up several pieces of wood with it. There was the smell of torn wood for everyone to smell and sawdust on the floor for all to see. Then a table was wheeled out and the lady lay down on it in her bathing suit which was in two pieces. Her stomach was very white. The magician talked and waved the saw around. I suspected he was planning to cut the woman in half and I was eager to see this. I hadn't the slightest fear about this at all. I did wonder if he would be able to put her together again or if he would cut her in half only. The magician said that what was about to happen was too dreadful to be seen directly, that he did not want anyone to faint from the sight, so he brought out a small screen and placed it in front of the lady so that we could no longer see her white stomach, although everyone could still see her face and her shoes. The screen seemed unnecessary to me and I would have preferred to have been seated on the other side of it. Several people in the audience screamed. The lady who was about to be sawed in half began to chew on her lip and her face looked worried.

It was then that my mother appeared on the stage. She was crouched over a little, for she didn't have her balance back from having climbed up there. She looked large and strange in her red coat. The coat, which I knew very well, seemed the strangest thing. Someone screamed again, but more uncertainly. My mother moved toward the magician, smiling and speaking and gesturing with her hands, and the magician said, No, I can't of course, you should know better than this, this is a performance, you can't just appear like this, please sit down. . . .

My mother said, But you don't understand I'm willing, though I know the hazards and it's not that I believe you, no one would believe you for a moment but you can trust me, that's right, your faith in me would be perfectly placed because I'm not part of this, that's why I can be trusted because I don't know how it's done. . . .

Someone near me said, Is she kidding, that woman, what's her plan, she comes out of nowhere and wants to be cut in half. . . .

Lady . . . the magician said, and I thought a dog might appear for I knew a dog named Lady who had a collection of colored balls.

My mother said, Most of us don't understand I know and it's just as well because the things we understand that's it for them, that's just the way we are. . . .

She probably thought she was still in that place in herself, but everything she said were the words coming from her mouth. Her lipstick was gone. Did she think she was in disguise, I wondered.

But why not, my mother said, to go and come back, that's what we want, that's why we're here and why can't we expect something to be done you can't expect us every day we get tired of showing up every day you can't get away with this forever then it was different but you should be thinking about the children. . . . She moved a little in a crooked fashion, speaking.

My God, said a voice, that woman's drunk. Sit down, please! someone said loudly.

My mother started to cry then and she stumbled and pushed her arms out before her as though she were pushing away someone who was trying to hold her, but no one was trying to hold her. The orchestra began to play and people began to clap. The usher ran out onto the stage and took my mother's hand. All this happened in an instant. He said something to her, he held her hand and she did not resist his holding it, then slowly the two of them moved down the few steps that led to the stage and up the aisle until they stopped beside me for the usher knew I was my mother's child. I followed them, of course, although in my mind I continued to sit in my seat. Everyone watched us leave. They did not notice that I remained there among them, watching too.

We went directly out of the theater and into the streets, my mother weeping on the little usher's arm. The shoulders of his jacket were of cardboard and there was gold braid looped around it. We were being taken away to be murdered which seemed reasonable to me. The usher's ears were large and he had a bump on his neck above the collar of his shirt. As we walked he said little soft things to my mother which gradually seemed to be comforting her. I hated him. It was not easy to walk together along the frozen sidewalks of the city. There was a belt on my mother's coat and I hung onto that as we moved unevenly along.

Look, I've pulled myself through, he said. You can pull yourself through. He was speaking to my mother.

We went into a coffee shop and sat down in a booth. You can collect yourself in here, he said. You can sit here as long as you want and drink coffee and no one will make you leave. He asked me if I wanted a donut. I would not speak to him. If he addressed me again, I thought, I would bite him. On the wall over the counter were pictures of sandwiches and pies. I did not want to be there and I did not take off either my mittens or my coat. The little usher went up to the counter and brought back coffee for my mother and a donut on a plate for me. Oh, my mother said, what have I done, and she swung her head from side to side.

I could tell right away about you, the usher said. You've got to pull yourself together. It took jumping off a bridge for me and breaking both legs before I got turned around. You don't want to let it go that far.

My mother looked at him. I can't imagine, my mother said.

Outside, a child passed by, walking with her sled. She

looked behind her often and you could tell she was admiring the way the sled followed her so quickly on its runners.

You're a mother, the usher said to my mother, you've got to pull yourself through.

His kindness made me feel he had tied us up with rope. At last he left us and my mother lay her head down upon the table and fell asleep. I had never seen my mother sleeping and I watched her as she must once have watched me, the same way everyone watches a sleeping thing, not knowing how it would turn out or when. Then slowly I began to eat the donut with my mittened hands. The sour hair of the wool mingled with the tasteless crumbs and this utterly absorbed my attention. I pretended someone was feeding me.

As it happened, my mother was not able to pull herself through, but this was later. At the time, it was not so near the end and when my mother woke we found the car and left Portland, my mother saying my name. Lizzie, she said. Lizzie. I felt as though I must be with her somewhere and that she knew that too, but not in that old blue convertible traveling home in the dark, the soft, stained roof ballooning up in the way I knew it looked from the outside. I got out of it, but it took me years.

"I began this," writes Joy Williams, "when I was teaching a semester at Iowa. I wanted to write a story about drinking and love, and I thought, because I am teaching, I am really going to keep track of the writing of this story, where the needs and images come from, and record the things dropped or how they came to be transmuted and I will be able to tell how at least this one story came to be. I will be able to come back from the other side of the story and tell. I began with the last sentence. I got out of it, but it took me years. Then I couldn't write the story at all thinking in this manner. It's not

lucky to think of your story in such a cold-hearted fashion. I wrote the story later and it all came slowly like a glass filling slowly. I had a picture from a book of Houdini strapped to a wagon wheel. I had a memory of Maine's cold. I had a child's voice, a good child, doomed in love. With such a voice came the moment and the moment always is the story."

Joy Williams's short stories have appeared in The Paris Review, Esquire, Grand Sheet, *and* The New Yorker, *and other publications and anthologies, and have been collected in* Taking Care. *She is also the author of two novels,* The Changeling *and* State of Grace, *and has recently finished a third,* Willie and Liberty, *and another collection of stories. She lives in Florida.*

First published in 1986 in Chicago.

MARY HOOD

SOLOMON'S SEAL

When they were courting, her people warned her, but she knew better. Who had kept them in meat through the Hoover years? With his rabbit boxes and early mornings, he was a man already, guarding a man's politics and notions, and like a mountain, wearing his own moody climate, one she prospered in. He brought the rabbits to her mother's kitchen window and held them up by the hind legs, swinging them like bells. When he skinned them and dressed them, she watched his quick knife as though learning. But she never did.

How they started out, that was how they wound up: on the same half acre, in the same patched cabin. He was no farmer. Anything that grew on that red clay was *her* doing. After a few years she had cleared the stones from the sunny higher ground, piling them in a terrace, backfilling with woods dirt she gathered in flour sacks on her walks. She planted strawberries there. In the red clay of the garden she grew beans in the corn, peas, tomatoes, and bunching onions an uncle had given her as a wedding present. Some years, when the rains favored, she grew squash and mushmelons, the sweet little ones like baby heads.

They never had children. They never lacked dogs. He kept a pen full of coon dogs and spent the nights with them in the moonlight, running them, drinking with his friends, unmending the darns she had applied to his overalls. He was a careless man. He had a way of waiting out her angers, a way of postponing things by doing something else just as necessary. So she postponed a few things too. She didn't even unpack her trunk filled with linens and good dishes her mama and aunts had assembled for her. They had practically blinded themselves sewing white on white, making that coverlet, but it was yellowed now, in its original folds, deep in the naphthaed heart of her hope chest. What was the use of being house-proud in a house like that? She decided it was good enough for him to eat off oilcloth. She decided he didn't care if his cup matched his saucer, and if he didn't care, why should she? She decided after a time to give as good as she got, which wasn't much. The scarcity of it, and her continuous mental bookkeeping, set her face in a mask and left her lips narrowed. She used to sing to him, before they could afford a radio. Now he had the TV on, to any program, it didn't matter which, and watched it like a baby watches the rustling leaves of a tree, to kill a little time between feedings. She didn't sing to him anymore. She didn't sing at all. But she talked to her plants like they were people.

Sometimes he thought maybe there was company in the yard, and he'd move to the window to see if a man had come to buy one of his dogs. But it was only her. He'd give the wall a knock with the side of his fist, just to let her know he was listening.

"I'm praying," she'd say, without looking up from where she was pouring well water from a lard pail onto the newest seedlings.

"Witch," he'd mutter, and go back to his TV.

She had the whole place covered by now; she was always bringing in new plants, little bothersome herbs she warned him against stepping on in his splayed boots as he stumbled along the trails she had outlined in fieldstones. The paths narrowed as she took more and more room for her pretties. It was like a child's game, where he could or could not step. And what were they anyway but weeds? Not real flowers, like his mama had grown. He told her that often enough. He'd been all over that lot and had never seen one rose. Sometimes he stopped at the hardware store and lifted a flat of petunias to his nose, but they weren't like the ones he remembered, they didn't smell like anything. He asked her about it, asked if she reckoned it was the rockets and satellites. She knew better. She blamed it on the dogs.

She blamed his dogs for stinking so you couldn't smell cabbage cooking. The health department ought to run him in, she said. He said if she called them she'd wind up in hell faster than corn popping. She said if he cut across the lower terrace one more time he'd be eating through a vein in his arm till his jaw healed, if ever. When he asked what she was so mad about, she couldn't for the life of her remember, it was a rage so old.

The madder she got, the greener everything grew, helped along, in the later years, by the rabbit manure. He was too old now to run rabbits in the field. And the land had changed, built up all around, not like it used to be. So he rigged up cages at home and raised rabbits right there. Then it was rabbits and dogs and TV and his meals and that was his whole life. That and not stepping on her plants.

He removed the spare tire from the trunk of the Dodge and fastened it to the roof of the car. In the extra space, and after taking off the trunk lid, he built a dog box. He started carrying his better hounds to the field trials and she went along too, for the ride. Everywhere they went she managed to find a new plant or two. She kept a shovel in the backseat, and potato-chip bags or cutoff milk jugs to bring the loot home in. They'd ride along, not speaking, or speaking both at once, her about the trees, him about the dogs, not hearing the one thing they were each listening their whole life for.

Sometimes she drank too. Sometimes, bottle-mellowed, they turned to each other in that shored-up bed, but afterward things were worse somehow, and he'd go off the whole next day to visit with other cooners, and she'd walk for miles in the woods, seeking wake-robin or Solomon's seal. She always dug at the wrong time, or too shallow, or something. For a few hours it would stand tall as it had grown, but the color would slowly fade, and with it her hopes. She'd be out there beside it, kneeling, talking to it softly, when he'd drive in, red-faced, beery. He'd see her turned back and head on up to the kennel to stand a few minutes, dangling his hands over the fence at the leaping dogs.

Forty years like that. It surprised her very much when he told her he wanted a divorce. He had been in the hospital a week and was home again. While he was in the hospital they told her not to upset him, so she held back the news. When he got home he found out that three of his whelps were sick and two more had already died. It was Parvo virus, locally epidemic, but the vet couldn't persuade him it wasn't somehow *her* fault. He spent the nights, sick as he still was, sitting up with the dogs, feeding them chicken soup from one of her saucepans. That was how the final argument started, her resenting that. If she really wanted to help him, he said, she'd just leave him alone. We'll see how you like that, she said, and took some clothes and went to her sister's. While she was there, a man came and served her with papers. He's crazy, is what he is, she said to the ferns; consider the source, she said to the laurel. He didn't want her? She knew better.

She used the rabbit's foot to rouge her cheeks, to add a little color. It surprised her, tying on her scarf to go to court, how much her face looked like his. The likeness was so sudden it startled her into a shiver. "Rabbit running over your grave," she said, thinking she was saying it to him.

There wasn't anything to the divorce. Uncontested, it was all over with very soon. But there was some heat over the division of property. He wound up with the house and she got the lot. He had custody of the dogs. He had six months to remove them and anything he wanted from the property, and after that he must stay away forever. He had the house moved in one piece. He hired a mover to come and load it onto a truck and haul it away. He set it up on a lot north of the river, among the pines, and in a few months he had pens for the dogs built alongside so he didn't have to walk far.

She bought a secondhand mobile home and moved it onto her lot when his six months were up. He had left things pretty well torn up; the housemovers had crushed and toppled her trellises and walls. She had weeks of work to right that. Even though it was all final, she was still afraid. She painted pieces of board with KEEP OUT and DO NOT DIG and nailed them to the trees. She tied scraps of rag to wires she ran from tree to tree, setting apart the not-to-be-trod-upon areas. She listened sharp, kept her radio tuned low, in case he was out there, coming back, like he used to, knocking over trash cans, beating on the door, crying, "It's me . . . Carl . . . let me in?"

But he didn't come back. She had no word of him at all, though she knew well enough where he was living, like some wild thing, deep in the woods with his hounds. Sometimes she saw his car going down the main road, it couldn't be missed, with that funny dog crate nailed in the trunk and the spare tire on the roof. She could watch the road from the hilltop as she stood at her clothesline. He drove as slow as always. It maddened her to see him go by so slow, as though he were waiting for her to fling herself down the hill headlong, to run after him crying, "Carl! Come back!" She wouldn't. She went on with her laundry. The old towel she picked up from the basket next was so bleach-burned it split in two when she snapped it. She hung the pieces on the line between her and the road, turned her back, picked up her basket, and headed for her trailer, down the hill, where he couldn't see her, though she knew how he drove, never looking left or right, even when she rode along with him, not turning his head one inch in her direction as he went on and on about the dogs. No more neck than a whale.

She was at the post office buying a money order when she heard he had remarried. She knew that couldn't be true. It wasn't a reliable source. She asked around. Nobody knew. She let it get to her, she couldn't rest just thinking of it. She didn't care; if she just knew *for sure,* that was it. "He's seventy-two years old," she said. Meaning: who could stand him but his dogs? She was out raking leaves from the main path when she decided to go see for herself. She finished up in her garden and changed to a clean shirt. She walked out to the store and phoned Yubo to come take her. Yubo was planting Miss Hamilton's garden, always did plant beans on

Good Friday, and he wouldn't be there right away. She said as soon as possible, and stood at the store waiting. It gave her time to think over what she was going to say when she got there. She knew where it was; she'd been by there once, just to see how it looked, had held her pocketbook up to shield her face in case he happened to be there and noticing anybody going by. Not that he was a noticer. She drank Coca-Cola while she waited, and when Yubo came she almost said take me home, because the long wait and the walk in the sun and the whole project was making her dizzy. But she had come this far, and so had Yubo.

The house looked about the same as when it had been hers, except it stood on concrete blocks now instead of those shimmed-up rocks from the river. She told Yubo to wait. She walked down the drive to the door, which was open, unscreened, and she called, before she could think better, "I'm home," but of course she meant, "I'm here." Confused, she didn't say anything when the woman came out to see who it was. An old woman as big and solid as Carl, bare-armed, bright-eyed. One of the dogs was out of the pen, two of the dogs, and they were following right at her heels. They had the run of the house! The old woman sat on the steps and the dogs lay beside her, close enough so she could pet them as they panted against her bare feet. "Carl's not here," the old woman said.

"I was just passing by," she said, and turned to go to Yubo, who had the taxi backed around and waiting. It wasn't a real taxi, not a proper taxi, and it was considerably run down. Still, she slammed the door harder than necessary. The wind of its closing made the just-set-out petunias in the circle around the mailbox post shiver and nod.

At home, among her borders and beds, she worked all afternoon carrying buckets of water up the hill to slop onto her tomato seedlings, her pepper sets, her potato slips. She worked till she was so weary she whimpered, on her sofa, unable to rest. She fell asleep and had a bad dream. Someone had come and taken things. She woke herself up to go check. She locked the door and moved the piled papers and canned goods off her hope chest and raised the lid. Everything she had held out against him all those years was there. She took the coverlet out and looked it over, as though someone might have stolen the French knots off it. Then she unwrapped the dishes, fine gold-rimmed plates. They weren't china, but they were good. She thought she heard someone. Startled, she turned quickly, knocking the plate against the trunk. The dish broke in two, exactly in two. She took up a piece in each hand and knelt there a long time, but the tears never came. Finally she said, "That's one he won't get," and the thought gave her peace. She broke all the others, one by one, and laid them back on the trunk. She kept the coverlet out. It would do to spread over her tomato plants; the almanac said there would be no more frost, but she knew better. There was always one last frost.

After staking the coverlet above her young plants, weighting it at the corners with rocks, she stooped to see how the Solomon's seal was doing. She had located it by its first furled shoots, like green straws, sticking up through the oak-leaf duff on one of her walks; had marked the place, going home for a bucket and pail, digging deep, replanting so it faced the same way to the sun. It had not dried out. It had good soil. But already it was dying. There was some little trick to it. "You'd think I could learn," she said. But she never did.

"Solomon's seal, an herb, is supposed to heal breaks—all kinds," writes Mary Hood. But just as the woman in this story never learns from her husband-to-be (in the story's first paragraph) how to skin rabbits, so she never learns (by the last paragraph) the healing arts of Solomon's seal.

Mary Hood lives in Cherokee County, Georgia, and writes "about the very county I live in; I simply visit my own stories—or plots—upon the scenery." This story draws "on conversations I had with country people about 'Hoover' days—the depression—and lore and legends in my own family as well as events from my community. I had been saving things for this story all my life, since I was a girl listening to my aunts talk."

Hood has an unusual writing method in that she tries not to begin writing until she's composed the story in her head: "I find it first, then the words. This saves me reams of paper and also allows me to go on with ordinary daily life, without being chained to the desk." This method enabled her, when she sat down, to write this story in only three hours.

Her two collections of stories are And Venus Is Blue *and* How Far She Went, *which received the Flannery O'Connor Prize for Short Fiction.*

First published in 1984 in How Far She Went *(University Press of Georgia).*

STEPHEN MINOT

THE SEAWALL

When Fern answered the phone it was Wesley. Poor Wesley was in the village and needed a ride. It had been a miserable day—the air conditioning on the train was broken and when he got to his car the battery was dead and it was going to be hours before they could get a new one and someone should come down and pick him up. Right away.

"That's kind of a problem."

"Of course it's a problem."

"I mean no one's here."

"You're there."

"Yuh, but . . . "

"Look, it was a hundred and ten in the club car and I'm stuck here with a dead car. Take Gloria's. Key's over the visor."

Fern closed her eyes for a moment, seeing Wesley standing there in the phone booth outside the station, his white seersucker suit all wrinkled, one hand gripping the receiver and the other probably holding an Amtrak gin-and-tonic, his enormous bulk dripping like a walrus just come up on the beach. Wesley had been her stepfather for over a year, and just because she was so tall he refused to believe she was only fifteen and didn't have a license.

"Look, Wesley, I don't have a license yet. Remember?"

"Well, get someone down here. Anyone. I don't care."

Fern stood there with the phone humming. He'd hung up. Not really angry. Just gruff. That must be the way he was in town. As a senior partner talking about retirement, he took the last train to Boston in the morning and the first one back, and she imagined that when he was there they all took care of him, harried secretaries and earnest young lawyers with horn-rimmed glasses, all jumping whenever he gave orders. But it sure got a little tiresome at home.

"Gloria!" she called. But she knew her mother wasn't home. Fern hung the phone up and looked out across the patio to the bay. The water was flat. The sun made her squint. Yes, poor Wesley would indeed expire if she didn't get someone down there.

She called Bibbo. Bibbo was her father and lived in the next house, just down the beach. Like all the houses along that section, it had once been just for summers. But now it was for year-round. It was wonderful, everyone said, that Fern could live with her mother and Wesley or over with Bibbo and his wife, Betty, or even up the hill with Bibbo's mother, moving about not by any legal arrangement but just as she wished. It was, as Gloria often said, very civilized.

Bibbo wasn't there, of course. Bibbo worked long hours redesigning and restoring historic homes and usually took the very last train from Boston. But surprisingly Betty wasn't there either. Betty was almost always there.

Fern left the house and walked along the seawall, enjoying the warmth of the concrete on her bare feet. Whenever she walked the wall she kept her eyes on the bay and the open sea beyond. It was always soothing. Winter or summer and even in storms, somehow, it was always soothing.

She thought of going up the hill to her grandmother, but she'd be no help now that she'd given up her car. The only other member of the family was Luke. He lived in a tent next to the beach.

"Hey Luke!"

He was not in his tent but was sitting on the seawall with a can of beer. He spent most of his days there with a can of beer. Sometimes he shot sea gulls from there and ate them. Luke made everyone nervous.

"Hey Luke," she said, "You've got to help."

She knew at once that was the wrong tack. It just didn't work to say "got to" to Luke. Sure enough, he grinned and shook his head. A great start.

"O.K., O.K., so you don't *have* to. But your father's down at the station and his car's got a dead battery. He's very hot."

"He's very hot?" Luke said, looking up at her. Somehow that struck him as funny. "*Real* hot?"

"You know what it's like in the village when there's no wind."

"Hot? Look, Sweet Pea, let me tell you about *hot.*"

She shook her head. She'd been through that one. Hot meant Vietnam and no one knew about hot if they hadn't been in Vietnam. Same for rainy weather, high winds. It didn't pay to let Luke get off on that. "Why not just go down and pick him up? You could take Gloria's car. The key's over the visor."

"Why not? Let me count the ways, Sweet Pea." He offered her his beer but she shook her head. "Let's put it this way, why *should* I?"

"Because there's going to be a big fuss if you don't, that's why. He'll come back real angry and that will get Gloria pissed and they'll all be shouting and no one will get any sleep, that's why."

"Why doesn't he take a cab?"

"He hates them. You weren't here then, but he did take the cab once and the guy said something nasty about the tip Wesley gave him and—well you know how he is at the end of the day—and he bellowed at the driver and then at us all evening and even the next day. He wouldn't call them if they had the last car on earth."

Luke leaned back on his elbows and laughed. His long hair fell back and she saw his Adam's apple under the beard where the skin wasn't tanned and she also noticed that he was getting a potbelly. He wore dirty white pants and no shirt and his stomach was bronzed but getting pudgy. She found that disappointing.

"Look," she said, "he's *your* father."

He stopped laughing. "You think? Listen, Sweet Pea, I'm thirty-five this summer and no one my age has a father."

So Luke didn't go to pick up his father, and Fern went

out on the sailfish, paddling on her stomach for lack of wind, just to get beyond earshot. There were times when she considered staying out there on her sailfish for the rest of her life, listening to nothing but gulls and the sound of the water. But of course she'd get hungry. You had to come back for that. And besides, they'd call her back. Wesley had a bullhorn which carried for miles.

She wondered if she were angry with Luke. Yes, she was. He just wouldn't do a damn thing to smooth things out. It wouldn't have taken him more than twenty minutes. *She* would have. But somehow she'd never expected him to go. That was sort of the way he was and it would be too bad to see him change. Was he fooling when he said he was thirty-five? When was that war anyway?

"Fern dear, it's time you kept track of things." Gloria was flipping through Fern's dresses, trying to decide which Fern should wear. "I mean, you're not a kid anymore. You're almost as tall as me, right? When you're a kid, you just tag along and no one expects you to remember where we're going or when. But you're—what, fifteen? Fifteen. Your father's been planning this for weeks. At the dock, and the bar's going to be on board. A little cutesie, if you ask me, but you know Dad."

"He's not *your* dad, Gloria."

"Honey, don't you think this first-name business is kind of a—what, affectation? I mean he *is* your father, and you may not be thrilled but I *am* your mother and most people don't mind using words like *mother* and *father*. Jesus, I call Bibbo's mother *Mumsie* as you well know, and no one thinks that's strange."

"I do."

"How about this little white thing?"

"That's a *dress*, Mumsie."

Gloria sat down on the bed, hauled out a cigarette, and lit it. "Fern honey, let's not get nasty tonight." Silence. "Look, it's not altogether easy for Wesley. His car broke down in the village. Did you know that? He had to wait there until

Bibbo came in on the 6:02 and get a ride from him and Bibbo's not always the most sensitive type as you well know and somehow the thought of Wesley sitting there without a drink for an hour and a half in that cruddy little station—well, it made your father start laughing and he couldn't stop and I think if Wesley were a younger man he would have punched your father in the nose but Wesley's not that type as you well know and besides he needed the ride. But Bibbo couldn't stop razzing him. You know how he is. So Wesley ended up telling your father that we weren't going over there tonight, any of us, and, Jesus, you know what it's going to be like around here if we don't show up and Betty gets her little hen feathers all ruffled and it turns into another dreary little feud and there goes the peace and quiet of the whole summer and frankly, Fern, frankly, I just can't stand . . . I just can't stand having *you* get nasty too."

She inhaled very deeply and held it the way younger people smoke dope and then blew it out. Her eyes were welling up and Fern decided to be real nice.

"You pick out a dress for me," she said.

It seemed odd to Fern at first that she and Gloria should both be getting dressed for the party if Wesley had decided that none of them would go, but then she realized that she was expected to straighten things out with Wesley; so she put on the long Indian print skirt her mother had picked out and a white blouse and pulled her hair back tight with a barrette. Wesley took a dark view of uncombed hair and jeans.

He was on the patio out front, somewhere between his second and third martini. Another good reason for taking time to change first. He was still in his rumpled seersucker, white shirt wrinkled and tie loosened. She sat down opposite him and pulled the metal chair up so her knees almost touched his.

"One more year and I'll have my license," she said.

"Never mind that." He brushed it off with a wave. She thought for a moment he was going into one of his sulks and that would be hard because once he was dug in he wouldn't talk to anyone for hours. He'd just stare into his martini as if it were a crystal ball and everyone would have to tiptoe around him. But no, she could see that he was not sulking—he was building up a head of steam.

"Can you imagine committing the integrity of a 100-year-old firm to a stockholders' class-action suit *pro bono*, mind you, with the promise of lengthy litigation involving successive appeals in three states and an outcome which is guaranteed, *guaranteed* to be a high dive into a wet sponge? Can you imagine it?"

"I sure can't."

"Of course you can't. Even you know what kind of risk is involved. Loring told me in no uncertain terms this would be a twenty-eight percent time commitment and not even a contingent fee for the first three years so of course we got a negative vote from the advisory board and a recommendation for arbitration but . . . "

She kept nodding and studying his face. His fleshy cheeks were getting red and also his neck, veins bulging, and beads of sweat on his brow, white hair getting all fuzzed up. He was really rather impressive once he got into one of these and she could see how juries and judges would be held by him; and she could even see how Gloria could admire him, though she once said he wasn't as *active* as she'd thought he would be, and what should she do about it—but luckily she never waited for an answer, going on about how famous Wesley had been years ago, but when he was like this he sure looked active enough for anyone and probably very bright too but how come he thought she knew all these terms and all these names and how did anyone hold all that in their head anyhow? Oh he was sure into it now but it made him sweat terribly and she must remember to ask Gloria if his heart is O.K. because that vein looks terrible and he has so much trouble getting his breath.

"So. . . . What do *you* think?"

"I think they must be crazy."

He threw his great bulk back in the chair and shouted, "Gloria, Gloria! This kid of yours is a thundering genius!"

But Gloria was in the Jacuzzi, so Fern leaned forward, putting her hands on his knees. "Wesley, how about putting on your blazer so we can go to Bibbo's?"

The house that Bibbo and Betty had was smaller but closer to the seawall and the bay. His yawl was kept at dockside rather than at a mooring, a kind of extension of the house. People said it was a classic. It had a wooden hull painted black with varnished spars and brass fittings which had to be polished. It leaked a lot but it was beautiful. Whenever they went cruising, people in port would row out just to stare and sometimes took photographs. Bibbo was very fond of it but Betty was not. Betty came from somewhere in Kentucky where no one sailed, not even on lakes. She didn't like day sailing and she refused to go cruising. "Some other time," she would say, smiling as she always did, but after a while it was clear to everyone that she meant *never.* She didn't like parties either. She was a bit dumpy and said all those hors d'oeuvres were a temptation. And she didn't like loud people. She said once, smiling, that people at New England parties shrieked a lot. Fern hadn't quite figured out what Betty did like.

There were already a number of cars parked in the circle, but most people had walked. It was that kind of area. "Laid back and natural," Gloria often said. You could see through from the open front door out the glass doors on the sea side, across the lawn to the pier where everyone was. It was twilight and everyone looked ruddy and healthy in the light of the setting sun and the Japanese lanterns strung between the masts and along the pier.

Bibbo had set up the bar in the cockpit so at least half the guests were on board and the rest on the pier. He'd done that before. The nice thing about the arrangement for Fern was that she could go up to the bow and sit on the deck with her feet dangling down the forward hatchway. Women in spiky heels didn't dare leave the cockpit but sometimes college boys would seek her out. Gloria said that with Fern's height all she needed now was to fill out a bit and as soon as she had something to show she would attract boys like flies, but Fern wasn't sure whether that was good or bad. In any case she liked sitting up near the bow and getting a view of things without having to talk with people.

But this time she got waylaid. They were passing through the deserted living room when Betty appeared from nowhere, smiling, greeting them with a big silver tray of hors d'oeuvres which she immediately gave to Fern. "Be a dear," she said to Fern. And to Wesley, "I'm so glad you decided to come after all, I really am."

Somehow she made it seem as if she wasn't all that pleased. Betty often made things come out wrong.

"Why wouldn't I?" Wesley said.

Betty, flustered, tried to kiss Gloria, which was a mistake because Gloria hated to get smudges of lipstick on her and did her best just to touch the cheek of would-be kissers.

"So good to see you," Betty said.

"It's been hours," Gloria said.

"Everyone's down by the pier."

"I was wondering."

"Do you want me to pass these around?" Fern asked. Anything to get Gloria safely into the crowd. After that she was no longer Fern's responsibility.

Passing a tea tray loaded with pigs-in-blankets was not Fern's idea of fun. Half the time she was taken as a maid. "Hey miss," the men would say and sometimes she would feel a hand on her thigh. Those who did know her were apt to say things about how she'd grown, by which they meant height, not figure, and express surprise and she'd explain that she'd been away at school in Connecticut and they hadn't seen her since the previous summer and then they would say something about how she wasn't a child anymore and what could she say to that? Luke was probably right. He said they weren't all that bright and couldn't think of anything else to say.

Bibbo was in the cockpit talking with two women and helping the bartender mix drinks at the same time. He did it with a flourish and without looking, keeping his eyes on his guests. People used to ask her how he stayed so young-looking and she was never sure how to respond. But they were right. He did manage to make other men seem kind of dull. She went over to him and he grinned, shaking his head in mock dismay at her being asked to perform as a maid. He relieved her of the tray, which was getting heavy, and set it on the gunwale saying "Fern, Lover-girl," hugging her enthusiastically and then, still holding her, continuing his conversation with the two women behind Fern's back. "What I mean is I always believed him when he said it was absolutely reliable until I stepped off the train and found him stranded there like a refugee with a dead battery."

Everyone laughed except Fern. He let go of her. "Wesley," he said, explaining.

"I know. Look, anything you want me to do?"

"Everything's taken care of. Don't you worry your little head over a thing. Look, when I get things organized, they just run like clockwork."

"I wouldn't razz Wesley anymore. He's . . . "

"He bounces like a rubber ball. A regular teddy bear." And to the two women, "People think we don't get along, but we're bosom pals. Really. I gave him a ride, didn't I?"

Fern saw out of a corner of her eye someone step back and knock the silver tray into the water but it was too late to do anything about it. No one even heard the splash. The last of the pigs-in-blankets bobbed in the dark water between the hull and the pier.

"Look," he said, speaking close to Fern but holding one of the women by the elbow to keep her from drifting off, "relax and have a good time. Find some guy and tell him you go to Barnard. That's what your Aunt Tillie did when she was your age and no one can accuse her of not having a good time." Fern remembered visiting her Aunt Tillie in a hospital but probably that had nothing to do with pretending she went to Barnard, but why would anyone do that anyway? "Oh, and do me a big favor, will you? Mumsie has a hard time at these things because she can't hear well. She's over on the bench. . . ."

He gave Fern a little nudge the way they do when you play Pin the Tail on the Donkey and asked his two friends if they had heard about Wesley and the plumber. They shook their heads but started giggling in anticipation, and Fern wondered how she was going to keep Wesley out of range up on the dock. She'd have to get drinks to him pretty fast.

She asked the bartender for two gin-and-tonics—doubles with no lime (garbage, Wesley called it)—and tried to worm her way from the cockpit back to the pier. She couldn't find him, though, so she went over to where she knew Mumsie would be, her hands growing a little numb with the two drinks.

The trouble with Mumsie was that she was too nice. She was forever inviting Fern to come up for a meal or tea and then suggesting that Fern move up there, live with her at least for the summer. She told Fern she could have friends in any time but there weren't many people Fern's age around there. Most of her friends were from school and lived in Connecticut or Long Island or California and besides she couldn't imagine taking someone her age up there.

"Fern dearest you are a sight for sore eyes. Did you bring that for me? I hope it doesn't have gin in it. . . . No, I can tell it doesn't. I don't touch it anymore except late in the evening and then just for sleep or maybe before lunch and of course just a dash of cognac in my tea to free the phlegm but you don't have to worry about phlegm yet and if I were you I wouldn't touch alcohol until you're my age. I keep telling that father of yours that active as he is he really needs a clear head and the best way to clear his head is to avoid this sort of thing." She gestured to the party with her glass, spilling some of it. "You might find life simpler and quieter if you moved up to my place and goodness knows I have enough room there. We used to have seven children in that house—summers only, of course—plus staff and I've watched them go off one by one. All but your father, of course. Franklin's in London now." Fern had heard he'd been transferred to Brussels but it wasn't worth mentioning. "And Jamison's down in South America now, did you know that?" Fern shook her head. "He's doing something in real estate in . . . in . . . "

"Brazil," Fern said. "Wood pulp in the Amazon."

"Argentina? That's it. Real estate in Argentina. For the life of me I can't imagine someone willingly moving from an ideal spot like this with friends and relatives all around . . . "

Later that night Fern found herself walking Mumsie up the winding road to her house on the hill. She held one elbow and the nurse, Miss Klauss, held on to the other. Miss Klauss had an odd way of clearing her throat about once every minute and because she never smiled or said anything except for that little "ar-umpf" every minute, she gave the appearance of disapproving of everyone and everything.

Most of the time Mumsie kept on a straight course, but occasionally she had to be nudged. Miss Klauss would shake Mumsie needlessly and Fern would say, "You're doing fine"—more to keep Miss Klauss from being so rough than an assurance to Mumsie who had the hiccups and couldn't hear anyhow.

It seemed like a long way, Mumsie taking all those tiny steps. When they finally got to the house and were standing on that great veranda which overlooked the bay, Mumsie started in on the invitations, but Fern was used to that. No, she would rather not stay and have a cup of Ovaltine; no, she didn't think she'd be able to come over first thing in the morning; no, she really was happy where she was but, yes, maybe some summer she would stay with Mumsie and Miss Klauss, the three of them like a little family, and Miss Klauss would teach Fern how to play Mah-Jongg because that's what they did every evening as soon as the meal was over and it wasn't a game designed for just two people. Yes, that sounded like a wonderful summer.

Miss Klauss suddenly spoke for the first time that evening. She said to Mumsie: "Enough of that. You come along right now."

Mumsie clutched Fern's wrist, looking up at her with watery blue eyes. Fern almost stayed. But no, she had to get Wesley back before there was real trouble.

Fern wished she didn't have to go back to Bibbo's party—it was so cool and hushed up there on the hill, and the distant cries of all those people down there on the dock sounded a little weird, but she realized she was still carrying the remaining double gin-and-tonic with no fruit and although it was warm and useless it reminded her that if Wesley and Bibbo got at it they would probably keep it up all summer and she really should get Wesley home even if Gloria wanted to stay real late as she usually did.

"Fern!" She jumped, slopping the drink on her hand. "Hey, Sweet Pea!"

"Where are you?"

It was Luke sitting on the hood of a car. "You sure took your time."

"I was walking Mumsie . . . "

"I know that. They told me. I've been waiting."

"For what?"

"You."

"Why?"

"I'm taking off."

"At this hour?"

"Ever hear about taking off under a cloud?" He took the drink from her hand, drained it, and tossed the glass over someone's garden wall. She hopped up on the hood with him. It didn't seem right, his leaving. But then she'd never understood why he'd come in the first place. It had been early spring when he arrived from nowhere and pitched that tent as far from the house as he could and still be on the property and dropped by for food from time to time like a stray cat. It must have been cold some of those spring nights; and it sure was hot in the day later on, the tent having no shade. He'd sit there and watch the house or stare out to sea for hours, sipping beers all day without getting drunk. Sometimes when they had guests over he would move to the edge of the patio for the evening, squatting there in the dark just far enough away so no one could talk with him easily. It bothered everyone when he did that and sometimes people went home early.

Wesley finally told Fern one night that he was fed up with the whole business and he was going to tell Luke to clear out and if he didn't go he'd call the sheriff and charge Luke with trespassing. And, besides, shooting sea gulls was a misdemeanor and crazy to boot and Luke ought to be locked up for his own good, shouldn't he? Fern said she was sorry about the sea gulls but that Luke was writing a novel and that it was taking him a long time to get everything straight in his head but that Wesley could help by just letting things be until cold weather set in. Actually Luke had never thought of any such thing. He didn't even have a typewriter.

"Luke, there's no trains or buses at this hour."

"I'm taking Gloria's car. Key's over the visor, I hear."

"They'll put you in jail. They really will."

"No they won't. I'm Wesley's son, didn't you tell me that?"

"You can put a son in jail."

"That a fact? Hey, how about coming along? Big adventure. Head west. No sweat, we could be just buddies if you want. Just old wartime buddies. How about it?"

Fern took in a deep breath. How come tears were coming to her eyes? It didn't make sense.

"Look, get going if you're going." She had her arms around him in the dark there and began patting his back the way people try to give other people courage. "Leave the car at Howard Johnson's next to the Interstate ramp. Hitch from there, O.K.? I'll tell them tomorrow before they call the police."

She hurried back to the party hoping that she would find Wesley at that stage when he couldn't complete sentences, ending each with a kind of rumble. Most people took that to be anger ("What was Wesley so worked up over last night?") when in fact he was at his most pliable and would let her lead him away, lead him home again, keeping him clear of Bibbo, and if she could include Gloria too that would keep Gloria from getting a second wind and teaming up with Bibbo, the two of them doing their soft-shoe routine together for old time's sake and singing "You Are My Sunshine" in harmony which everyone loved but was also about the only thing which could cause Betty to lose that smile of hers and lock herself in her bedroom for the whole of the next day with Bibbo saying to Fern, "Talk to her through the door, will you? Tell her nothing went on, nothing, will you?"

She started across the lawn toward the pier when she was intercepted by Betty coming the other way.

"Fern dear," she said, smiling, "wherever have you been? We needed you." Fern thought of the silver tray but decided to keep quiet. She could dive for it in the morning. "Fern dear," still smiling, "I seem to have this headache and I know it's just terrible of me but I've got to get my beauty rest and I was wondering if you wouldn't like to stay over. I mean on the boat."

Normally Fern liked to sleep on board, but it was clear that the party wouldn't be breaking up for hours and it smelled after a party. Someone always managed to throw up in the cabin. Always. "Tonight?"

"Well, it would save you walking back." (Was she serious?) "And everyone's about to go."

"Maybe tomorrow."

"No *tonight.*" No smile this time. Uh-oh. "Fern, I don't mean to burden you, but I'm asking you to stay on board. I mean I try, I really do. No one knows how I try. I made all those lovely things to eat and I talked to just about everyone there and I'm taking aerobics every afternoon until I ache all over but no matter what I do that boat turns into—excuse my language—into a broth-el. So if you just stayed there, you see, they . . . " She was clinging to Fern and swaying. Her perfume smelled of musty lilac. "It's not right, Fern, it's not moral—what your parents do with each other."

Back at the party she couldn't find Wesley. She hoped he

hadn't left early because then he'd see Luke taking the car and that would make things complicated. But then she couldn't find Bibbo either and then she wondered if the two of them had gone off together. Bibbo had an odd way of pretending Wesley was his very best friend and walking along the beach with him, arm around his shoulder, sort of kidding him, giving him little pokes in the stomach and laughing until Wesley, who did have his limits, finally punched him in the face. No one ever got hurt, but it wasn't a good way to end the party.

Bibbo wasn't anywhere on the pier or in the cockpit. And no one was up forward on the deck. Oh boy, the cabin. Right when everyone was still here? That would be just like him.

She went down the companionway cautiously, figuring the best approach would be to cough and ask something stupid like whether Betty was there and then back out quick enough so they wouldn't think she'd seen anything.

But the jolt wasn't what she expected. She stepped right into black water. It was surprisingly cold. The cabin lights were dim, but she could make out the rear end of a man bent over in the head. Why would anyone kneel in all that water to throw up in the bowl?

"Bibbo, is that you? Are you all right?"

"No problem."

She looked at the cushions and cracker boxes floating in the water and without thinking clearly said, "Did you know that there's a lot of water here?"

Bibbo snorted. "You noticed?" But when he pulled himself out of there, his white pants clinging to him, his shirt stained, he wasn't smiling. "Jesus, girl, where have you been? I need you. Someone's smashed the bowl here. Smashed it right down to the valve. Get me something to plug it."

"Shouldn't we warn the others?"

"Keep your voice down. You want to ruin the party? Get me something to stuff in here. Every time I let go, it really spurts."

They were interrupted by a woman calling down from the companionway. "Wesley? Is that you?" It was Betty.

"Wesley's up at the bar getting sloshed."

"But I just saw him go down there."

"You *what?*" Bibbo ran for the companionway, stumbling through water. "That son of a bitch!"

"Water!" Betty shrieked. "We're sinking!"

So Fern didn't have to sleep on board that night. She found it impossible to plug the leak and the electric pumps wouldn't work—the batteries drained from the Japanese lanterns. Bibbo and Wesley had one awful fight on the beach and neither of them saw that lovely yawl go down at the pier.

The crowd responded with late-night enthusiasm. After the initial shrieks of mock panic and cries of "Women and children first," they stood on the pier, watching and chattering, cracking jokes. There was absolutely nothing that could be done. As the waters finally closed over the cabin with a kind of sucking noise, a great cheer went up. Fern closed her eyes tight and shouted, "Shut up! Shut up! *Shut up!*"

Running back along the seawall, she reached her mother's house. It was dark and quiet. Then she continued to where she knew the tent would be.

"Luke?"

There was no answer. He'd made it. He'd taken his sleeping bag and pack but he'd left her an old army blanket neatly folded. Inside it there was a big candy bar. She curled up in the blanket and munched the chocolate. The feel of the wool and the sound of the water lapping just the other side of the seawall were as soothing as anything that had come her way in a long time. How'd he know she'd be staying here anyhow?

"Some stories are composed like a flute solo—one note at a time," says Stephen Minot. "When done well, they are deli-

cate, often haunting. More often the genre resembles a quartet—greater intricacies, more resonances. Only a novelist can employ a full orchestra, but there are stories which move in that direction. I have worked with all these approaches, but the one which concerns me the most is short fiction, which pushes toward the upper end of this continuum. Most of my novels began as stories which later called out for more complex treatment."

Fern is not only a survivor in this story but a survivor in her creator's head, and she will also appear in a novel he is writing. Thus "The Seawall" is written in the mode that Minot finds most rewarding.

His short stories have been published in The Atlantic, Harper's, The Kenyon Review, The Virginia Quarterly Review, Redbook, Playboy, The Sewanee Review, Paris Review, The North American Review, Missouri Review, *and other publications. His work has been selected for the* O. Henry Prize Stories *and* The Best American Short Stories *numerous times. Minot's novels include* Chill of Dusk, Ghost Images, *and* Surviving the Flood, *and his short stories have been collected in* Crossings. *He and his wife live in Connecticut and Maine.*

First published in 1983 in The Sewanee Review.

JAYNE ANNE PHILLIPS

BESS

You have to imagine: this was sixty, seventy, eighty years ago, more than the lifetimes allotted most persons. We could see no other farms from our house, not a habitation or the smoke of someone's chimney; we could not see the borders of the road anymore but only the cover of snow, the white fields, and mountains beyond. Winters frightened me, but it was summers I should have feared. Summers, when the house was large and full, the work out-of-doors so it seemed no work at all, everything done in company—summers all the men were home, the farm was crowded, lively; it seemed nothing could go wrong then.

Our parents joked about their two families, first the six sons, one after the other; then a few years later the four daughters, Warwick, and me. Another daughter after the boy was a bad sign, Pa said; there were enough children. I was the last, youngest of twelve Hampsons, and just thirteen months younger than Warwick. Since we were born on each other's heels, Mam said, we would have to raise each other.

The six elder brothers had all left home at sixteen to homestead somewhere on the land, each going first to live with the brother established before him. They worked mines or cut timber for money to start farms and had an eye for women who were not delicate. Once each spring they were all back to plant, garden with Pa, and the sisters talked amongst themselves about each one.

By late June the brothers had brought their families, each a wife and several children. All the rooms in the big house were used, the guesthouse as well, swept and cleaned. There was always enough space because each family lived in two big rooms, one given to parents and youngest baby and the other left for older children to sleep together, all fallen uncovered across a wide cob-stuffed mattress. Within those houses were many children, fifteen, twenty, more. I am speaking now of the summer I was twelve, the summer Warwick got sick and everything changed.

He was nearly thirteen. We slept in the big house in our same room, which was bay-windowed, very large and directly above the parlor, the huge oak tree lifting so close to our window it was possible to climb out at night and sit hidden on the branches. Adults on the porch were different from high up, the porch lit in the dark and chairs creaking as the men leaned and rocked, murmuring, drinking homemade beer kept cool in cellar crocks.

Late one night that summer, Warwick woke me, pinched my arms inside my cotton shift, and held his hand across my mouth. He walked like a shadow in his white nightclothes, motioning I should follow him to the window. Warwick was quickly through and I was slower, my weight still on the sill as he settled himself, then lifted me over when I grabbed a higher branch, my feet on his chest and shoulders. We climbed into the top branches that grew next the third floor of the house and sat cradled where three branches sloped; Warwick whispered not to move, stay behind the leaves in case they look. We were outside Claude's window, seeing into the dim room.

Claude was youngest of the older brothers and his wife was hugely with child, standing like a white column in the middle of the floor. Her white chemise hung wide round her like a tent and her sleeves were long and belled; she stood, both hands pressed to the small of her back, leaning as though to help the weight at her front. Then I saw Claude kneeling, darker than she because he wasn't wearing clothes. He touched her feet and I thought at first he was helping her take off her shoes, as I helped the young children in the evenings. But he had nothing in his hands and was lifting the thin chemise above her knees, higher to her thighs, then above her hips as she was twisting away but stopped and moved toward him, only holding the cloth bunched to conceal her belly. She pressed his head away from her, the chemise pulled to her waist in back and his one hand there trying to hold her. Then he backed her three steps to the foot of the bed and she half leaned, knees just bent; he knelt down again, his face almost at her feet and his mouth moving like he was biting her along her legs. She held him just away with her hands and he touched over and over the big globed belly, stroking it long and deeply like you would stroke a scared animal. Suddenly he stood quickly and turned her so her belly was against the heaped sheets. She grasped the bed frame with both hands so when he pulled her hips close she was bent prone forward from the waist; now her hands were occupied and he uncovered all of her, pushing the chemise to her shoulders and past her breasts in front; the filmy cloth hid her head and face, falling even off her shoulders so it hung halfway down her arms. She was all naked globes and curves, headless and wide-hipped with the swollen belly big and pale beneath her like a moon; standing that way she looked all dumb and animal like our white mare before she foaled. All this time she was whimpering, Claude looking at her. We saw him, he started to prod himself inside her very slow, tilting his head and listening. . . . I put my cool hands over my eyes then, hearing their sounds until Warwick pulled my arms down and made me look. Claude was tight behind her, pushing in and flinching like he couldn't get out of her, she bawled once. He let her go, stumbling; they staggered onto the bed, she lying on her back away from him with the bunched chemise in her mouth. He pulled her to him and took the cloth from her lips and wiped her face.

This was perhaps twenty minutes of a night in July 1900. I looked at Warwick as though for the first time. When he talked he was so close I could feel the words on my skin distinct from night breeze. "Are you glad you saw," he whispered, his face frightened.

He had been watching them from the tree for several weeks.

In old photographs of Coalton that July 4, the town looks scruffy and blurred. The blue of the sky is not shown in those black-and-white studies. Wooden sidewalks on the two main streets were broad and raised; that day people sat along them as on low benches, their feet in the road, waiting for the parade. We were all asked to stay still as a photographer took pictures of the whole scene from a nearby hillside. There was a prayer blessing the new century and the cornet band assembled. The parade was forming out of sight, by the river; Warwick and Pa had already driven out in the wagon to watch. It would be a big parade; we had word that local merchants had hired part of a circus traveling through Bellington. I ran up the hill to see if I could get a glimpse of them; Mam was calling me to come back and my shoes were blond to the ankles with dust. Below me the crowd began to cheer. The ribboned horses danced with fright and kicked, jerking reins looped over low branches of trees and shivering the leaves. From up the hill I saw dust raised in the woods and heard the crackling of what was crushed. There were five elephants; they came out from the trees along the road and the trainer sat on the massive harnessed head of the first. He sat in a sort of purple chair, swaying side to side with the lumbering swivel of the head. The trainer wore a red cap and jacket; he was dark and smooth on his face and held a boy close his waist. The boy was moving his arms at me and it was Warwick; I was running closer and the trainer beat with his staff on the shoulders of the elephant while the animal's snaky trunk, all alive, ripped small bushes. Warwick waved; I could see him and ran dodging the men until I was alongside. The earth was pounding and the animal was big like a breathing wall, its rough side crusted with dirt and straw. The skin hung loose, draped on the limbs like sacking crossed with many creases. The enormous creature worked, wheezing, and the motion of the lurching walk was like the swing of a colossal gate. Far, far up, I saw Warwick's face; I was yelling, yelling for them to stop, stop and take me up, but they kept on going. Just as the elephants passed, wind lifted the dust and ribbons and hats, the white of the summer skirts swung and billowed. The cheering was a great noise under the trees and birds flew up wild. Coalton was a sea of yellow dust, the flags snapping in that wind and banners strung between the buildings broken, flying.

Warwick got it in his head to walk a wire. Our Pa would not hear of such foolishness, so Warwick took out secretly to the creek every morning and practiced on the sly. He constructed a thickness of barn boards lengthwise on the ground, propped with nailed supports so he could walk along an edge. First three boards, then two, then one. He walked barefoot tensing his long toes and cradled a bamboo fishing pole in his arms for balance. I followed along silently when I saw him light out for the woods. Standing back a hundred feet from the creek bed, I saw through dense summer leaves my brother totter magically just above the groundline; thick ivy concealed the edges of the boards and made him appear a jerky magician. He still walked naked since the heat was fierce and his trousers too-large hand-me-downs that obstructed careful movement. He walked parallel to the creek and slipped often. Periodically he grew frustrated and jumped cursing into the muddy water. Creek bottom at that spot was soft mud and the water perhaps five feet deep; he floated belly-up like a seal and then crawled up the bank mud-streaked to start again. I stood in the leaves. He was tall and coltish then, dark from the sun on most of his body, long-muscled; his legs looked firm and strong and a bit too long for him, his buttocks were tight and white. It was not his nakedness that moved me to stay hidden, barely breathing lest he hear the snap of a twig and discover me—it was the way he touched the long yellow pole, first holding it close, then opening his arms gently as the pole rolled across his flat still wrists to his hands; another movement, higher, and the pole balanced like a visible thin line on the tips of his fingers. It vibrated as though quivering with a sound. Then he clasped it lightly and the pole turned horizontally with a half rotation; six, seven, eight quick flashes, turning hard and quick, whistle of air, snap of the light wood against his palms. Now the pole lifted, airborne a split second and suddenly standing, earthward end walking Warwick's palm. He moved, watching the sky and a wavering six feet of yellow needle. The earth stopped in just that moment, the trees still, Warwick moving, and then as the pole toppled in a smooth arc to water he followed in a sideways dive. While he was under, out of earshot and rapturous in the olive water, I ran quick and silent back to the house, through forest and vines to the clearing, the meadow, the fenced boundaries of the high-grown yard and the house, the barn where it was shady and cool and I could sit in the mow to remember his face and the yellow pole come to life. You had to look straight into the sun to see its airborne end and the sun was a blind white burn the pole could touch. Like Warwick was prodding the sun in secret, his whole body a prayer partly evil.

One day of course he saw me watching him, and knew in an instant I had watched him all along; by then he was actually walking a thick rope strung about six feet off the ground between two trees. For a week he'd walked only to a midpoint, as he could not rig the rope so it didn't sag and walking all the way across required balance on the upward slant. That day he did it; I believe he did it only that once, straight across. I made no sound but as he stood there poised above me his eyes fell upon my face; I had knelt in the forest cover and was watching as he himself had taught me to watch. Perhaps this explains his anger—I see still, again and again, Warwick jumping down from the rope, bending his knees to an impact as dust clouds his feet but losing no balance, no stride, leaping toward me at a run. His arms are still spread, hands palm-down as though for support in the air and then I hear rather than see him because I'm running, terrified—shouting his name in supplication through the woods as he follows, still coming after me wild with rage as I'd never seen anyone. Then I was nearly out of breath and just screaming, stumbling—

It's true I led him to the thicket, but I had no idea where I was going. We never went there, as it was near a rocky outcropping where copperheads bred, and not really a thicket at all but a small apple orchard gone diseased and long dead. The trees were oddly dwarfed and broken, and the ground cover thick with vines. Just as Warwick caught me I looked to see those rows of small dead trees; then we were fighting on the ground, rolling. I fought with him in earnest and scratched his eyes; already he was covered all over with small cuts from running through the briars. This partially explains how quickly he was poisoned but the acute nature of the infection was in his blood itself. Now he would be diagnosed severely allergic and given antibiotics; then we knew nothing of such medicines. The sick were still bled. In the week he was most ill, Warwick was bled twice daily, into a bowl. The doctor theorized, correctly, that the poison had worsened so as to render the patient's blood toxic.

Later Warwick told me, if only I'd stopped yelling—now that chase seems a comical as well as nightmarish picture; he was only a naked enraged boy. But the change I saw in his face, that moment he realized my presence, foretold everything. Whatever we did from then on was attempted escape from the fact of the future.

"Warwick? Warwick?"

In the narrow sun porch, which is all windows but for the house wall, he sleeps like a pupa, larva wrapped in a woven spit of gauze and never turning. His legs weeping in the loose bandages, he smells of clear fluid seeped from wounds. The seepage clear as tears, clear as sweat, but sticky on my hands when my own sweat never sticks but drips from my forehead onto his flat stomach where he says it stings like salt.

"Warwick. Mam says to turn you now."

Touching the wide gauze strips in the dark. His ankles propped on rolls of cloth so his legs air and the blisters scab after they break and weep. The loose gauze strips are damp when I unwrap them, just faintly damp; now we don't think he is going to die.

He says, "Are they all asleep inside?"

"Yes. Except Mam woke me."

"Can't you open the windows. Don't flies stop when there's dew?"

"Yes, but the mosquitoes. I can put the netting down but you'll have that dream again."

"Put it down but come inside, then I'll stay awake."

"You shouldn't, you should sleep."

Above him the net is a canopy strung on line, rolled up all the way round now and tied with cord like a bedroll. It floats above him in the dark like a cloud the shape of the bed. We keep it rolled up all the time now since the bandages are off his eyes; he says looking through it makes everyone a ghost and fools him into thinking he's still blind.

Now I stand on a chair to reach the knotted cords, find them by feel, then the netting falls all around him like a skirt.

"All right, Warwick, see me? I just have to unlatch the windows."

Throw the hooks and windows swing outward all along the sun-porch walls. The cool comes in, the lilac scent, and now I have to move everywhere in the dark because Mam says I can't use the lamp, have kerosene near the netting—

"I can see you better now," he says, from the bed.

I can tell the shadows, shapes of the bed, the medicine table, the chair beside him where I slept the first nights we moved him to the sun porch. Doctor said he'd never seen such a poison, Warwick's eyes swollen shut, his legs too big for pants, soles of his feet oozing in one straight seam like someone cut them with scissors. Mam with him day and night until her hands broke out and swelled; then it was only me, because I don't catch poison, wrapping him in bandages she cut and rolled wearing gloves.

"Let me get the rose water," I whisper.

Inside the tent he sits up to make room. I hold the bowl of rose water and the cloth, crawl in and it's like sitting low in high fields hidden away, except there isn't even sky, no opening at all.

"It's like a coffin, that's what," he'd said when he could talk.

"A coffin is long and thin," I told him, "with a lid."

"Mine has a ceiling," Warwick said.

Inside everything is clean and white and dry; every day we change the white bottom sheet and he isn't allowed any covers. He's sitting up—I still can't see him in the dark, even the netting looks black, so I find him, hand forehead nose throat.

"Can't you see me. There's a moon. I see you fine."

"Then you've turned into a bat. I'll see in a moment, it was light in the kitchen."

"Mam?"

"Mam and three lamps. She's rolling bandages this hour of the night. She doesn't sleep when you don't."

"I can't sleep."

"I know."

He only sleeps in daytime when he can hear people making noise. At night he wakes up in silence, in the narrow black room, in bandages in the tent. For a while when the doctor bled him he was too weak to yell for someone.

He says, "I won't need bandages much longer."

"A little longer," I tell him.

"I should be up walking. I wonder if I can walk, like before I wondered if I could see."

"Of course you can walk, you've only been in bed two weeks, and a few days before upstairs—"

"I don't remember when they moved me here, so don't it seem like I always been here."

Pa and two brothers and Mam moved him, all wearing gloves and their forearms wrapped in gauze I took off them later and burned in the wood stove.

"Isn't always. You had deep sleeps in the fever, you remember wrong." I start at his feet, which are nearly healed, with the sponge and the cool water. Water we took from the rain barrel and scented with torn roses, the petals pounded with a pestle and strained, since the doctor said not to use soap.

The worst week I bathed him at night so he wouldn't get terrified alone. He was delirious and didn't know when he slept or woke. When I touched him with the cloth he made such whispers, such inside sounds; they weren't even words but had a cadence like sentences. If he could feel this heat and the heat of his fever, blind as he was then in bandages, and tied, if he could still think, he'd think he was in hell. I poured the alcohol over him, and the water from the basin, I was bent close his face just when he stopped raving and I thought he had died. He said a word.

"Bessie," he said.

Bless me, I heard. I knelt with my mouth at his ear, in the sweat, in the horrible smell of the poison. "Warwick," I said. He was there, tentative and weak, a boy waking up after sleeping in the blackness three days. "Stay here, Warwick. Warwick."

I heard him say the word again, and it was my name, clearly.

"Bessie," he said.

So I answered him. "Yes, I'm here. Stay here."

Later he told me he slept a hundred years, swallowed in a vast black belly like Jonah, no time anymore, no sense but strange dreams without pictures. He thought he was dead, he said, and the moment he came back he spoke the only word he'd remembered in the dark.

Sixteen years later, when he did die, in the mine—did he say a word again, did he say that word? Trying to come back. The second time, I think he went like a streak. I had the color silver in my mind. A man from Coalton told us about the cave-in. The man rode out on a horse, a bay mare, and he galloped the mare straight across the fields to the porch instead of taking the road. I was sitting on the porch and saw him coming from a ways off. I stood up as he came closer; I knew the news was Warwick, and that whatever had happened was over. I had no words in my mind, just the color silver, everywhere. The fields looked silver too just then, the way the sun slanted. The grass was tall and the mare moved through it up to her chest, like a powerful swimmer. I did not call anyone else until the man arrived and told me, breathless, that Warwick and two others were trapped, probably suffocated, given up for dead. The man, a Mr. Forbes, was surprised at my composure. I simply nodded; the news came to me like an echo. I had not thought of that moment in years—the moment Warwick's fever broke and I heard him speak—but the moment returned in an instant. Having felt it once, that disappearance, even so long before, I was prepared. Memory does not work according to time. I was twelve years old, perceptive, impressionable, in love with Warwick as a brother and sister can be in love. I loved him then as one might love one's twin, without a thought. After that summer I understood too much. I don't mean I was ashamed; I was not. But no love is innocent once it has recognized its own existence.

At eighteen I went away to a finishing school in Lynchburg. The summer I came back, foolishly, I ran away west. I eloped partially because Warwick found fault with anyone who courted me, and made a case against him to Mam. The name of the man I left with is unimportant. I do not really remember his face. He was blond but otherwise he did resemble Warwick—in his movements, his walk, his way of speaking. All told, I was in his company eight weeks. We were traveling, staying in hotels. He'd told me he was in textiles but it seemed actually he gambled at cards and roulette. He had a sickness for the roulette wheel, and other sicknesses. I could not bear to stand beside him in the gambling parlors; I hated the noise and the smoke, the perfumes mingling, the clackings of the wheels like speeded-up clocks and everyone's eyes following numbers. Often I sat in a hotel room with a blur of noise coming through the floor, and imagined the vast space of the barn around me: dark air filling a gold oval, the tall beams, the bird sounds ghostly, like echoes. The hay, ragged heaps that spilled from the mow in pieces and fell apart.

The man who was briefly my husband left me in St. Louis.

Warwick came for me; he made a long journey in order to take me home. A baby boy was born the following September. It was decided to keep my elopement and divorce, and the pregnancy itself, secret. Our doctor, a country man and friend of the family, helped us forge a birth certificate stating that Warwick was the baby's father. We invented a name for his mother, a name unknown in those parts, and told that she'd abandoned the baby to us. People lived so far from one another, in isolation, that such deceit was possible. My boy grew up believing I was his aunt and Warwick his father, but Warwick could not abide him. To him, the child was living reminder of my abasement, my betrayal in ever leaving the farm.

The funeral was held at the house. Men from the mine saw to it Warwick was laid out in Coalton, then they brought the box to the farm on a lumber wagon. The lid was kept shut. That was the practice then; if a man died in the mines his coffin was closed for services, nailed shut, even if the man was unmarked.

The day after Warwick's funeral, all the family was leaving back to their homesteads having seen each other in a confused picnic of food and talk and sorrowful conjecture. Half the sorrow was Warwick alive and half was Warwick dead. His dying would make an end of the farm. I would leave now for Bellington, where, in a year, I would meet another man. Mam and Pa would go to live with Claude and his wife. But it was more than losing the farm that puzzled and saddened everyone; no one knew who Warwick was, really. They said it was hard to believe he was inside the coffin, with the lid nailed shut that way. Touch the box, anywhere, with the flat of your hand, I told them. They did, and stopped that talk.

The box was thick pine boards, pale white wood; I felt I could fairly look through it like water into his face, like he was lying in a piece of water on top of the parlor table. Touching the nailed lid you felt first the cool slide of new wood on your palm, and a second later the depth—a heaviness inside like the box was so deep it went clear to the center of the earth, his body contained there like a big caged wind. Something inside, palpable as the different air before flash rains, with clouds blown and air clicking before the crack of downpour.

I treated the box as though it were living, as though it had to accustom itself to the strange air of the house, of the parlor, a room kept for weddings and death. The box was simply there on the table, long and pure like some deeply asleep, dangerous animal. The stiff damask draperies at the parlor windows looked as though they were about to move, gold tassels at the hems suspended and still.

The morning before the service most of the family had been in Coalton, seeing to what is done at a death. I had been alone in the house with the coffin churning what air there was to breathe. I had dressed in best clothes as though for a serious, bleak suitor. The room was just lighted with sunrise, window shades pulled halfway, their cracked sepia lit from behind. One locust began to shrill as I took a first step across the floor; somehow one had gotten into the room. The piercing, fast vibration was very loud in the still morning: suddenly I felt myself smaller, cramped as I bent over Warwick inside his white tent of netting, his whole body afloat below me on the narrow bed, his white shape in the loose bandages seeming to glow in dusk light while beyond the row of open windows hundreds of locusts sang a ferocious pattering. I could scarcely see the parlor anymore. My vision went black for a moment, not black but dark green, like the color of the dusk those July weeks years before.

This story remains close to Jayne Anne Phillips because "I like to create stories that are monologues, but monologues that create a whole world. Not only the internal things, but details about the physical world." Thus we see a whole world beyond

Bess, including the vivid scenes of the circus and Warwick walking on a wire. Phillips adds, "I like to write stories that make connection with the past, that make the past seem present."

"Bess" was originally part of her novel, Machine Dreams, *but since the character Bess only appeared there in a lesser role and at a later age, this section was excised. Yet it provides the "secret past of a character," so she says, that often ends up only in a writer's files. More important, it deserves to be read for its own worth as a short story.*

Jayne Anne Phillips's first collection, Black Tickets, *established her as a short-story writer of distinction. Born in West Virginia, she now lives in Massachusetts with her husband and young son.*

First published in 1984 in Esquire.

JOHN E. WIDEMAN

SURFICTION

Among my notes on the first chapter of Charles Chesnutt's "Deep Sleeper" there are these remarks:

Not reality but a culturally learned code—that is, out of the infinite number of ways one might apprehend, be conscious, be aware, a certain arbitrary pattern, or finite set of indicators is sanctioned and over time becomes identical with reality. The signifier becomes the signified. For Chesnutt's contemporaries reality was "I" (eye) centered, the relationship between man and nature disjunctive rather than organic, time was chronological, linear, measured by man-made units—minutes, hours, days, months, etc. To capture this reality was then a rather mechanical procedure—a voice at the center of the story would begin to unravel reality: a catalog of sensuous detail, with the visual dominant, to indicate nature, "out there" in the form of clouds, birdsong, etc. A classical painting rendered according to the laws of perspective, the convention of the window frame through which the passive spectator observes. The voice gains its authority because it is literate, educated, perceptive, because it has aligned itself correctly with the frame, because it drops the cues, or elements of the code methodically. The voice is reductive, as any code ultimately is; an implicit reinforcement occurs as the text elaborates itself through the voice: the voice gains authority because things are in order, the order gains authority because it is established by a voice we trust. For example the opening lines of "Deep Sleeper" . . .

> It was four o'clock on Sunday afternoon, in the month of July. The air had been hot and sultry, but a light, cool breeze had sprung up; and occasional cirrus clouds overspread the sun, and for a while subdued his fierceness. We were all out on the piazza—as the coolest place we could find—my wife, my sister-in-law and I. The only sounds that broke the Sabbath

stillness were the hum of an occasional vagrant bumblebee, or the fragmentary song of a mockingbird in a neighboring elm . . .

Rereading, I realize "my remarks" are a pastiche of received opinions from Barthes, certain cultural anthropologists and linguistically oriented critics and Russian formalists, and if I am beginning a story rather than an essay the whole stew suggests the preoccupations of Borges or perhaps a footnote in Barthelme. Already I have managed to embed several texts within other texts, already a rather unstable mix of genres and disciplines and literary allusion. Perhaps for all of this, already a grim exhaustion of energy and possibility, readers fall away as if each word is a well-aimed bullet.

More Chesnutt. This time from the text of the story, a passage unremarked upon except that in the margin of the xeroxed copy of the story I am copying this passage from, several penciled comments appear. I'll reproduce the entire discussion.

Latin: secundus-tertius quartus-quintus.

"Tom's gran'daddy wuz name' Skundus," he began. "He had a brudder name' Tushus en' ernudder name' Cottus en ernudder name' Squinchus." The old man paused a moment and gave his leg another hitch.

"drawing out Negroes"—custom in old south, new north, a constant in America. Ignorance of one kind delighting ignorance of another. Mask to mask. The real joke.

My sister-in-law was shaking with laughter. "What remarkable names!" she exclaimed. "Where in the world did they get them?"

Naming: plantation owner usurps privilege of family. Logos. Word made flesh. Power. Slaves named in order of appearance. Language masks joke. Latin opaque to blacks.

Note: last laugh. Blacks (mis) pronounce secundus. *Secundus = Skundus. Black speech takes over—opaque to white—subverts original purpose of name. Language (black) makes joke. Skundus has new identity.*

"Dem names wuz gun ter 'em by ole Marse Dugal' McAdoo, w'at I use' ter b'long ter, en' dey use' ter b'long ter. Marse Dugal' named all de babies w'at wuz bawn on de plantation. Dese young un's mammy wanted ter call 'em sump'n plain en' simple, like 'Rastus' er 'Casear' er 'George Wash'n'ton'; but ole Marse say no, he want all de niggers on his place ter hab diffe'nt names, so he kin tell 'em apart. He'd done use' up all de common names, so he had ter take sump'n else. Dem names he gun Skundus en' his brudders is Hebrew names en' wuz tuk out'n de Bible."

I distinguish remarks from footnotes. Footnotes clarify specifics; they answer simple questions. You can always tell from a good footnote the question which it is answering. For instance: *The Short Fiction of Charles W. Chesnutt*, edited by Sylvia Lyons Render, Howard Univ. Press, 1974: p. 47. Clearly someone wants to know, Where did this come from? How might I find it? Tell me where to look. Okay. Whereas remarks, at least my remarks, the ones I take the trouble to write out in my journal,* which is where the first long cogitation appears/appeared, [the ambiguity here is not intentional but situational, not imposed for irony's sake but necessary because the first long cogitation—*my remark*—being referred to both *appears* in the sense that every time I open my journal, as I did a few moments ago, as I am doing

**Journal*: unpaginated. In progress. Unpublished. Many hands.

NOW to check for myself and to exemplify for you the accuracy of my statement—the remark *appears* as it does/did just now. (Now?) But the remark (original) if we switch to a different order of time, treating the text diacronically rather than paradigmatically, the remark *appeared*; which poses another paradox. How language or words are both themselves and *Others*, but not always. Because the negation implied by *appearance*, the so-called "shadow within the rock," is *disappearance.* The reader correctly anticipates such an antiphony or absence suggesting presence (shadow play) between the text as realized and the text as shadow of its act. The dark side paradoxically is the absence, the nullity, the white space on the white page between the white words not stated but implied. Forever.] are more complicated.

The story, then, having escaped the brackets can proceed. In this story, *Mine,* in which Chesnutt, replies to Chesnutt, remarks, comments, asides, allusions, footnotes, quotes from Chesnutt have so far played a disproportionate role, and if this sentence is any indication, continue to play a grotesquely unbalanced role, will roll on.

It is four o'clock on Sunday afternoon in the month of July. The air has been hot and sultry, but a light, cool breeze has sprung up; and occasional cirrus clouds (?) overspread the sun, and for a while subdue his fierceness. We were all out on the piazza (stoop?)—as the coolest place we could find—my wife, my sister-in-law and I. The only sounds that break the Sabbath stillness are the hum of an occasional bumblebee, or the fragmentary song of a mockingbird in a neighboring elm. . . .

The reader should know now by certain unmistakable signs (codes) that a story is beginning. The stillness, the quiet of the afternoon tells us something is going to happen, that an event more dramatic than birdsong will rupture the static tableau. We expect, we know a payoff is forthcoming. We know this because we are put into the passive posture of readers or listeners (consumers) by the narrative unraveling of a reality which, because it is unfolding in time, slowly begins to take up our time and thus is obliged to give us something in return; the story enacts word by word, sentence by sentence in "real" time. Its moments will pass and our moments will pass simultaneously, hand in glove if you will. The literary, storytelling convention exacts this kind of relaxation or compliance or collaboration (conspiracy). Sentences slowly fade in, substituting fictive sensations for those which normally constitute our awareness. The shift into the fictional world is made easier because the conventions by which we identify the real world are conventions shared with and often learned from our experience with fictive reality. What we are accustomed to acknowledging as awareness is actually a culturally learned, contingent condensation of many potential awarenesses. In this culture—American, Western, twentieth century—an awareness that is eye-centered, disjunctive as opposed to organic, that responds to clock time, calendar time more than biological cycles or seasons, that assumes nature is external, acting on us rather than through us, that tames space by man-made structures and with the I as center defines other people and other things by the nature of their relationship to the "I" rather than by the independent integrity of the order they may represent.

An immanent experience is being prepared for, is being framed. The experience will be real because the narrator produces his narration from the same set of conventions by which we commonly detect reality—dates, buildings, relatives, the noises of nature.

All goes swimmingly until a voice from the watermelon patch intrudes. Recall the dialect reproduced above. Recall Kilroy's phallic nose. Recall Earl and Cornbread, graffiti artists, their spray paint cans notorious from one end of the metropolis to the other—from Society Hill to the Jungle, nothing safe from them and the artists uncatchable until hubris leads them to attempt the gleaming virgin flanks of a 747 parked on runway N-16 at the Philadelphia International Airport. Recall your own reflection in the funhouse mirror and the moment of doubt when you turn away and it turns away and you lose sight of it and it naturally enough loses sight of you and you wonder where it's going and where you're going and the wrinkly reflecting plate still is laughing behind your back at someone.

The reader here pauses   Picks up in mid-

stream a totally irrelevant
conversation:

. . . by accident twenty
seven double-columned
pages by accident

I mean it started that way

started   yeah I can see
starting curiosity whatever
staring over somebodies
shoulder or a letter maybe
you think yours till you
see not meant for you at
all

I'm not trying to excuse
just understand it was not
premeditated your journal
is your journal that's not
why I mean   I didn't
forget your privacy or lose
respect on purpose

it was just there
and, well we seldom talk
and I was desperate we
haven't been going too
well for a long time

and getting worse getting
finished when shit like this
comes down

I wanted to stop but I
needed something from
you   more than you've
been giving so when I
saw it there I picked it
up you understand   not to

read but because it was
you you and holding it was
all a part of you

you're breaking my heart

please don't dismiss

dismiss dismiss what I
won't dismiss your prying
how you defiled how you
took advantage

don't try to make me a
criminal the guilt I feel
it I know right from
wrong and accept
whatever you need to lay
on me but I had to do
it I was desperate for
something, anything, even
if the cost

was rifling my personal life
searching through my guts
for ammunition and did
you get any did you learn
anything you can use on
me Shit I can't even
remember the
whole thing is a jumble
I'm blocking it all out my
own journal and I can't
remember a word because
it's not mine anymore

I'm sorry I knew I
shouldn't as soon as I
opened it I flashed on the
Bergman movie the one
where she reads his diary I
flashed on how under-
handed how evil a thing
she was doing but I
couldn't stop

A melodrama   a god
damned Swedish subtitled
melodrama you're going to
turn it around aren't
you   make it into

The reader can replay the tape at leisure. Can amplify or expand. There is plenty of blank space on the pages. A sin really given the scarcity of trees, the rapaciousness of paper companies in the forests which remain. The canny reader will not trouble him/her self trying to splice the tape to what came before or after. Although the canny reader would also be suspicious of the straightforward, absolute denial of relevance dismissing the tape.

Here is the main narrative again. In embryo. A professor of literature at a university in Wyoming (the only university in Wyoming) by coincidence is teaching two courses in which are enrolled two students (one in each of the professor's seminars) who are husband and wife. They both have red hair. The male of the couple aspires to write novels and is writing fast and furious a chapter a week his first novel in the professor's creative writing seminar. The other redhead, there are only two redheads in the two classes, is taking the professor's seminar in Afro-American literature, one of whose stars is Charlie W. Chesnutt. It has come to the professor's attention that both husband and wife are inveterate diary keepers, a trait which like their red hair distinguishes them from the professor's other eighteen students. Something old-fashioned, charming about diaries, about this pair of hip graduate students keeping them. A desire to keep up with his contemporaries (almost wrote "peers" but that gets complicated real quick) leads the professor, who is also a novelist, or as he prefers novelist who is also a professor, to occasionally assemble large piles of novels which he reads with bated breath. The novelist/professor/reader bates his breath because he has never grown out of the awful habit of feeling praise bestowed on someone else lessens the praise which may find its way to him (he was eldest of five children in a very poor family—not an excuse—perhaps an extenuation—never enough to go around breeds a fierce competitiveness and being for four years an only child breeds a selfishness and ego-centeredness that is only exacerbated by the shocking arrival of contenders, rivals, lower than dog-shit pretenders to what is by divine right his). So he reads the bait and nearly swoons when the genuinely good appears. The relevance of this to the story is that occasionally the professor reads systematically and because on this occasion he is soon to appear on a panel at a neighboring university (Colorado) discussing "Surfiction," his stack of novels was culled from the latest, most hip, most avant-garde, new *Tel Quel* chic, anti, non-novel bibliographies he could locate. He has determined at least three qualities of these novels. *One*—you can stack ten in the space required for two traditional novels. *Two*—they are *au rebours* the present concern for ecology since they sometimes include as few as no words at all on a page and often no more than seven. *Three*—without authors whose last names begin with B, surfiction might not exist. B for Beckett, Barth, Burroughs, Barthes, Borges, Brautigan, Barthelme . . . (Which list further discloses a startling coincidence or perhaps the making of a scandal—one man working both sides of the Atlantic as a writer and critic explaining and praising his fiction as he creates it: *Barth Barth*es *Barth*elme.)

The professor's reading of these thin (not necessarily a dig—thin pancakes, watches, women for instance are *à la mode*) novels suggests to him that there may be something to what they think they have their finger on. All he needs then is a local habitation and some names. Hence the red-headed couple. Hence their diaries. Hence the infinite layering of the fiction he will never write (which is the subject of the fiction which he will never write). Boy meets Prof. Prof reads boy's novel. Girl meets Prof. Prof meets girl in boy's novel. Learns her pubic hair is as fiery red as what she wears short and stylish, flouncing just above her shoulders. (Of course it's all fiction. The fiction. The encounters.)

What's real is how quickly the layers build, how like a spring snow in Laramie the drifts cover and obscure silently.

Boy keeps diary. Girl meets diary. Girl falls out of love with diary (his), retreats to hers. The suspense builds. Chesnutt is read. A conference with Prof in which she begins analyzing the multilayered short story "The Deep Sleeper" but ends in tears reading from a diary (his? hers?). The professor recognizes her sincere compassion for the downtrodden (of which in one of his fictions he is one). He also recognizes a fiction in her husband's fiction (when he undresses her) and reads her diary. Which she has done previously (read her husband's). Forever.

The plot breaks down. It was supposed to break down. The characters disintegrate. Whoever claimed they were whole in the first place. The stability of the narrative voice is displaced into a thousand distracted madmen screaming in the dim corridors of literary history. Whoever insisted it should be more ambitious. The train doesn't stop here. Mistah Kurtz he dead. Godot ain't coming. Ecce Homo. Dats all Folks. Sadness.

And so it goes.

Although this is a highly playful excursion into experimental fiction, John Wideman hastens to say that he has respect for such writing and wrote this story after a long immersion in reading and enjoying some contemporary experimental writers. "They give us a good dose of self-awareness about what fiction is," he says. He's fond of this story because he feels "it freed me to take more chances with the narrator of my novel Sent for You Yesterday," *(which won the PEN/Faulkner Award). Born in Pittsburgh, Wideman now teaches at the University of Massachusetts, Amherst, where he lives with his wife and three children. His novels include* A Glance Away, Hurry Home, *and* The Lynchers. Sent for You Yesterday *has been published with* Hiding Place *and* Damballah *(a book of stories) as "The Homewood Trilogy." He is also the author of the memoir* Brothers and Keepers.

First published in 1985 in The Southern Review.

ERNEST J. FINNEY

NIGHTS AND DAYS

What did you expect, Richard? How was I to know." His mother leaned back on her waterbed, sheet pulled up to her chin. She'd ruined his chance for a grant. On the application form he'd said he'd been independent for three years. Nobody's tax deduction. Who would have thought they'd phone? He knew just what she'd said. "Independent? He's always coming back here when he runs out of money. Takes off again if I ask him to help out around the house, take out the garbage." Twenty-two million people in the state and they had to phone her.

"Get us a cup of coffee," she said, smiling for the first time. "Unless you've given it up."

"What's that supposed to mean?"

"That girl you brought here, didn't she say she was an LDS?"

"That doesn't mean I'm one; I can drink coffee."

"You know how they convert everyone. You're so easily led. And I meant to mention before, Richard: even if she's a nurse and ought to know better, I hope you're taking precautions."

All he could think of at first to say was "I'm twenty-two years old." Then "Forget it. You're never going to see me around here again." He went through the house at a trot, slamming the screen door behind him. She was wrong about Dorothy, he thought, stepping over the R. T. he'd scratched into the sidewalk when he was in the fourth grade. He'd been going down this sidewalk his whole life. Then he realized he'd left his overdue library book on the dresser in his mother's room. He marched back through the house to her bedroom. She watched him from the bed with the same smile as he picked up the book. "Forgot this," he mumbled. He went back out through the screen door quietly.

"Pay attention, Rich; here comes the herd." Ted was at the front door in three long strides. Dozens of kids were crossing the parking lot toward the store. Rich stationed himself behind the counter, putting the girlie magazines out of sight, screwing down the lid on the jerky jar, locking the cigarette case. Without a word Ted let the first three in. The others lined up outside. Rich watched the security mirrors as the kids moved like fast fish around the store, each eventually ending up at the soft-drink cooler. He rang up the sales, the first three were let out, and three more were let in.

It was busy from then on. The dog man came in, tying his four dogs to the paper rack outside, and bought each one an Eskimo Pie. More kids. A stupid fat woman who came in every day: she seemed to buy all her food here, at twice the prices of the Safeway down the street. A guy bought three cans of motor oil, casually dropping the empties on the blacktop next to the trash can. When Ted yelled at him he threw the last empty can at the window, leaving a grease slick four feet long.

It slowed down, and Ted had come back behind the counter and was making a pot of coffee when a customer came in with a big grin on his face. He asked for a pack of Marlboroughs. Rich reached into the case with one hand and with the other picked up a book of matches. When he turned back to the counter, the man, still smiling, had a pistol pointed at Ted's stomach.

Rich took a step backward. Pointing with the pistol at the cash register, the robber said, "The money." Ted opened the cash register. Later he said he knew what was going to happen the minute the robber came in. Rich watched, frozen, mouth agape. Calmly the robber reached over and took all the bills out of the register, then slipped the money inside his shirt. He turned to go but remembered the cigarettes, put them in his shirt pocket, and walked toward the door.

He gave a casual look back before pushing one side of the glass door open. That's when Ted opened fire.

In all he shot three times, missing each time. The robber ran across the parking lot and slid into a waiting car. Ted ran out the door, his pistol at the ready, his finger on the trigger. Is this really happening, Rich thought. The only thing that had changed was that the door had three bullet holes in it. He watched Ted trying to flag down a car to give chase for a couple of minutes before he remembered to press the alarm button.

Rich got to the range early. He waited on a bench behind the shooters. He watched a woman his mother's age take aim with her pistol and fire. This was Ted's idea; he'd insisted after the robbery that he needed the practice and that Rich should learn how to shoot. This was the fifth time they'd met at the range, and, much to his own surprise, he looked forward to coming. He was getting better each time. He liked the sound best: squeezing the trigger, picking up all the slack, then the explosion. He never put on his shooting muffs unless Ted insisted that it was affecting his score.

Ted and Captain Cobb came in. The captain had been the first officer to arrive after the robbery. They were both carrying their leather gun-cases, and they didn't see him in the back. He could hear them talking between shots. "You can always tell the ones that were raised without a father around." That was Ted's voice. "All those female gestures with the hands. They walk like a woman."

"Queer?" That was Captain Cobb.

"No, not as a rule. They just need someone else to copy. Soon as I laid eyes on him, I knew. That's one reason I hired him—make a man out of him."

Rich didn't know what to do. He finally made himself stand up where Ted could see him. "Well, are you ready for some action?" Ted asked him. "We got booth one." Did Ted know he'd been there close, listening? He noticed everything. He knew what you were thinking before you said it.

Captain Cobb went first. He wore a businessman's three-piece suit, but he could never pass for a businessman. He loosened his shoulder holster by flexing his arms and at the same time he went into his perfect shooting crouch and whipped out his .44 magnum. With all the confidence in the world he fired all six shots so fast they sounded like one. Then he straightened up. "Well, it's a nice pattern anyway," he said. Every shot had missed the silhouette, and the six holes looked like a flower growing to the right of its foot. "I never miss when it counts," he added, snapping open the cylinder of his pistol and shaking out the casings.

Ted stepped up. "I'm going to give you a lesson in shooting, Cobb," he said. He took aim, left hand on his hip. "Nose," he said. A hole appeared just at the bridge. "Temple." Like magic a hole appeared in the silhouette's head. "Three in the heart." He cut loose. They were all in the circle. "One in the balls." He had called every shot.

"Come on, Rich, your turn," Ted said. "Show old Law-and-Order how to shoot." Rich grinned at the captain, pretending not to agree with Ted, hoping to ease the hurt look on his face. He looked just like a policeman ought to look: big, assertive; he spoke with authority, used phrases like *ramifications of the law,* but Ted said he was a dunce.

"I don't remember you being such a hotshot a couple of months ago when you missed at twelve feet," the captain said.

"I got buck fever that time, but that doesn't mean I can't hit them the next time. Like some people," Ted added.

"Well," Rich said, "I guess I'll take my turn." He usually liked to hear them argue. They'd argue over anything, red-faced and excited. They argued over things like who did the most in the war—the army or the navy. And Tojo—Rich could never get straight who he was: he'd never had a class in Spanish. Tonight it made him uneasy; they sounded as if they were serious. He aimed, fired; aimed, fired. It was so easy, he thought. The shoulder connected to the arm, the finger to the pistol, the eye to the target. He fired the last round. Perfect score.

The captain went home early in a huff. Ted and Rich

stopped for beer and pizza. "You can work up a thirst, listening to that guy blow a lot of smoke," Ted said. He took a long drink out of his mug. Rich wondered what subject it was going to be tonight: war, business, or women.

"I'll tell you this, Rich—if all this aggravation doesn't stop, I'm going to retire again. Who needs the headache. I just got an offer of one point two million dollars for that property of mine down on the river. I paid seventy thousand for it ten years ago. Can you beat that."

Ted had a lot of stories like that, and Rich believed them. He'd been up to his house on the north side to deliver some mail that came to the store. A maid in a uniform answered the front door. The den was half the size of his mother's whole house. His wife came in, half Ted's age, so beautiful that she looked like a movie star. She had a drink with them before leaving for an art class.

"You can't let them sit around," Ted said after she went out. "Especially if they're younger than you. It took me three marriages to realize that. It's finding the right thing for them to do. She didn't like managing a two-hundred-unit apartment building, so she went back to school. Smart, too. Probably end up a brain surgeon." He snorted.

"And what are you going to end up, Rich?" He was always asking questions like that.

And Rich was ready. "Something in computers. As soon as I save enough money I'll go back to school." He had put that in his job application. Student. But not that it had taken him almost four years to get through a community college.

Ted took another drink of beer. "Business isn't what it used to be, let me tell you. A person with a little capital could start something. Build it up to where he could make a good living. Not anymore. Nine out of ten businesses fail today. And that's with a Republican president, too. You're wondering why I keep that piddling store, aren't you. Why do you think?"

Rich took a guess. "A hobby, like you want to keep your hand in?"

"I never had a hobby in my life. How much do you think I gross in that store?"

"Including the gas pumps?"

"Right."

Rich took another guess. "A hundred thousand?"

"Would you believe two hundred and twenty thousand?"

Rich repeated the figure. "Two hundred twenty thousand: that's a lot of money."

"You bet it is, especially since I only claim half that much. It's a gold mine. Better than a gold mine. And the gas—I'm working a deal where I pay about ten cents less per gallon than everyone else." Rich was impressed.

When the pizza came they both dug in. Rich was hard-pressed to keep up with Ted, who ate so fast it didn't seem possible he chewed.

With his mouth full Ted asked him, "Tell me something. What happened to your father?" He told him. How, coming home from school in fourth grade, he found him in the bathtub, dead. The water was red. Hemorrhage, they told him. He hadn't told anyone but Dorothy before. "It's amazing how much blood the human body has" was Ted's only comment.

After Ted dropped him off, Rich stopped at Dorothy's for a minute. "My hero," she said when she opened the door. "Did you fill the larder with game?"

"I never missed the silhouette," Rich said. He had to tell her. "I overheard them talking. You know what they said?"

"What?"

"I've got feminine mannerisms. Do I?"

"I never noticed," she said. "What does it matter, anyhow."

"It matters," Rich insisted.

"Compare it with this," Dorothy said. "I put a bedpan under some old guy this afternoon and he died during his BM. That's reality. Not some knothead saying you're a homosexual."

"He didn't say I was a fruit." Rich gave up; what was the use.

He'd met her his first year at the college. His mother was wrong; they were just friends. That generation didn't understand that. While she went right through school till she got her nursing degree, he'd fiddled from program to program until, between arguing with his mother and moving in and out, he'd used up all his social-security benefits.

At one time he and Dorothy could tell each other anything. Just seeing her made him feel good. They'd sit in the back of the room in Psych 60 and make fun of the instructor and exchange traumas. It started out as a joke, but then they started telling real stories. Now it was different. Now that Dorothy was an RN, she saw so many more awful things than he did, his troubles were hardly worth mentioning. It was hard to top a dead man on a bedpan.

When he read the paper the next morning, Rich was surprised to see that another robbery and murder had occurred at a convenience store across town. Last week Captain Cobb had assured Ted they had a suspect in custody. But this one was exactly like the other murders: the clerk had been taken into the storeroom and shot in the back of the neck, and all the money, even the pennies, was taken out of the register. It was the third in six months. "We'll get him," the paper quoted Captain Cobb. "It's only a matter of time."

When he went in for work, Ted slid a new .38-caliber Smith and Wesson onto the counter. "This is yours," he told him. "You can get your own holster. Old Dead-Eye has a permit for you to carry this, legal. We have to be prepared: this business is getting hazardous."

Rich hefted the pistol. It never failed to surprise him how pleasurable a gun felt in his hands. "I'll use it if I have to," he told Ted.

After Ted left, Rich went to work stocking shelves, thinking about what kind of holster he'd buy. Maybe one for the shoulder, like Ted's; they were easy to get at. The ideal place to keep a gun would be under a person's hat; no one would think to look there. But he didn't have that kind of hat, and it'd probably give him a headache anyway. Wait until Dorothy saw the pistol: would she squawk.

"Are you crazy? You'll end up shooting yourself, or worse, some innocent person," Dorothy yelled after he'd leaped through the doorway with his pistol in a shooter's crouch.

He straightened up, grinning. "Come on, I'm going to get you the best hamburger a dollar and a quarter can buy."

"I'm not going," she said.

"Dammit, Dorothy, come on," he yelled. Her eyes narrowed, but she got her sweater. They walked arm in arm. It was like old times, like when they first met. He felt like hopping over the cracks in the sidewalk. He glanced at their reflections in a hardware-store window. She was short and chunky and walked with her feet out like a duck. He was over six feet tall and too thin and hunched his shoulders. What a pair, he thought. Was he going to end up with her? She had told him once: "I don't have to marry a Mormon. It's a religion, not a way of life." Had she meant him? He didn't want to marry her.

"What happened today?" she asked.

"Maybe we shouldn't tell each other anymore." He was having to make things up sometimes. "This is getting a little perverse."

"Last time, then," she said. "I promise."

"An old lady came in and bought five cans of dog food."

"What's wrong with that?"

"She doesn't have a dog. She lives around the corner. What's yours?"

"Doctor was examining . . . "

"Doctor! Put an article in front, *the* doctor."

"Can't I tell it my way?"

"Why make those guys out like they're God?"

"All right, *the* doctor had been examining a woman who'd passed out on the street. This was in Emergency. She was incoherent; I don't know why. Anyhow, she tried to leave, wearing nothing, walked through the waiting room like that. Would have gone outside, but the security guard stopped her."

"That's the end?" Rich asked.

"She'd had a double mastectomy. That's all," she said.

"No more," Rich said, taking a firmer grip on her arm.

"These hamburgers are made out of sawdust," Dorothy whispered happily as she chewed. She was red-cheeked from the wind and her usually carefully done hair was messy. She was almost pretty.

"Old newspapers," he whispered back, keeping his eyes on five boys in the booth next to them. They had been spitting milkshakes through their straws at each other. When they noticed Rich looking at them, they started swearing, using obscene words at random, then snickering. They looked like junior-high kids, the kind that came in the store and tried to buy cigarettes. They knew he and Dorothy could hear, and they got louder. Rich put his hamburger down and got up. He leaned over their table toward the biggest kid. "Let's go outside so I can kick your ass," he said in a loud voice. The place fell silent. "Come on."

"I'm not going with you," the kid said, trying to keep his upper lip from trembling.

The manager rushed over. "Now, now, we can't have any of that, or I'll have to ask you to leave," he told Rich.

Dorothy got up, embarrassed. "Let's go," she said.

"Lousy food anyway," Rich shouted over his shoulder as the side door swung shut behind them.

"What's got into you?" Dorothy yelled outside.

"I'm not putting up with anyone's crap, that's all."

"They were just kids; they didn't know what half those words meant."

"They didn't bother you?"

"No, they didn't."

"They bothered me. And I did something about it."

"Big deal. What a hero." Dorothy stalked off.

"The hell with you too," he said after her.

He had just sat down to clean his pistol when the phone rang. He knew it had to be his mother calling to invite him over for her birthday on the eighth. He let the phone ring five times before he picked it up.

She was using her sweetest telephone voice. "I thought you might be able to make it after all; it's my birthday. Just some of my friends from work." These occasions really meant something to her: he remembered her elaborate preparations for his own birthday parties when he was small. "You're not still sulking about that school business, Richard. I'm not going to lie for you to anyone, you know that."

"I told you, Mother; I can't make it."

"You ought to try to grow up and decide what is really important to you . . ."

"I have, Mother," he interrupted and then hung up.

He felt pleased with himself. He finished cleaning the pistol and sat spinning the cylinder with the flat of his hand while he watched a movie on TV. He thought about the store: he hadn't minded changing to the graveyard shift. Twenty cents more an hour and plenty of time to make plans. With the money he was making he could do whatever he wanted. Clothes didn't matter. A car wasn't important; the one he'd had in high school had been more trouble than it was worth. What did matter? He'd get through school first and then find out what was important.

His first night on graveyard started out quiet. Then about one-thirty two kids came in and started wandering around the store. It was so obvious. After a lot of maneuvering they tried to steal four packs of sunflower seeds and he caught them dead to rights. He called the police and the kids burst into tears simultaneously. They actually started to wail. A customer came in: Rich had the two kids sobbing behind the counter with their faces pressed against the wall. The noise didn't bother him, but the customer seemed startled, and Rich, enjoying the situation, calmly handed him his cigarettes and change as if nothing out of the ordinary were happening.

Later four bikers came in. Three shielded the fourth from view while he grabbed two six-packs. Rich knew what they were doing. He watched them, almost bemused; they never learn, he thought. He let them go outside, then followed them. He had already pressed the button under the counter. As they jumped on their motorcycles, he carefully wrote their license numbers on the cuff of his counter jacket.

One of the men got back off his bike. "You know what's going to happen to you?"

"Do you know what's going to happen to you?" Rich answered back, slowly taking out his pistol and letting it dangle at the end of his arm, enjoying the surprised look on the guy's face. Just then the cop car roared into the parking lot.

When Ted came in the next morning at seven he said, "I hear you had a little action last night."

"A little," Rich said. "Nothing I couldn't handle."

He'd worked eleven nights straight without a day off, so Ted told him to skip the next night. When he got to his apartment he was surprised to see Dorothy there, her eyes red from crying. He didn't know what to say. She ran into his arms and he hugged her. He pretended he was someone in the movies. "There, there," he said.

"It was so awful." Her face was pressed against his shoulder.

"What?"

"There's been a woman in IC for two weeks now. In a coma. Pregnant. Her baby was delivered this morning. She'll never see her baby. She'll never recover. I know we promised not to tell awful things anymore, but I had to." After a while she stopped crying and moved out of his arms and blew her nose. "How did your day go?"

"Nothing happened. Not a thing." He decided to stop pretending. Looking at her red swollen eyes and wet nose, he knew he could do a lot better.

"Something must have happened," she insisted.

"No, can't think of a thing. Nothing." He almost weakened, had to bend down and retie his shoe to avoid her eyes. "Just another day."

One night Ted came in with three enlarged photos, framed. He'd got a big write-up in the paper about shooting at the robber, and the newspaper photographer had taken several photos of Ted aiming his .38 in his right hand while reaching for his boot derringer with his left. He'd insisted Rich pose too. Captain Cobb had edged into one photo, his coat pulled back to expose his gun and holster. "Good publicity," Ted said, winking at Rich. "It'll bring in the customers. And scare hell out of anyone doing it again." He nailed the pictures up on the wall behind the cash register.

He was coming in a couple of nights a week now, when he couldn't sleep. They'd talk, Rich sitting on the counter, Ted in a chair he'd brought out from the office. About anything. Baseball. The thirties depression, which Ted was sure was happening again—now. What they would do if the killer who was robbing the all-night stores came in. Rich could get Ted to laugh by imitating Captain Cobb. "We professionals in law enforcement," he'd begin in a hare-lipped kind of garble, and Ted would roar.

When he was ready to leave, Ted paused at the door to look over the perfectly arranged store. "Keep an eye out for trouble, now. I don't want to lose my best man. Just press the button and the cops will be here fast. Cobb makes sure of that. Not only do I grease his palm; I hired his wife, too, to do some piddling job at my apartments. That cheap bastard. I gave him my Visa card for the Fourth of July. Buy drinks for the blue, I said, so they'll get here faster, and he goes and charges shoes for his whole damn family too. Five pairs of shoes at I. Magnin's. I guess he thought I wouldn't notice. That's the trouble with the public trough, especially where cops are concerned; they get to thinking everyone is as stupid as the people they can catch."

Business was good and the time went fast. The whole night was a steady stream of misfits buying cigarettes and junk food, testing him to see if he'd sell beer after two. He was too smart for that. Cobb had already tried him by sending in an undercover cop. Ted had warned him. "Just wants to keep us even. He needs to get something on me like that. He keeps score. The slime."

One morning around four a well-dressed woman half opened the door. "Twenty dollars unleaded. I'll write a check after I fill up; I want to get some other things." He fell for it. Pay first was the rule. She looked familiar. But like always he wrote down her license number. She drove off without paying. Damn. He hit the button. He was outside fast and saw her turn down J Street toward the freeway ramp. The cops were there in an instant and he gave them the number. Ten minutes later the car was back, followed by two police cars. They brought the woman in. "I forgot, that's all," she said. "I forgot; it could happen to anyone. I'll write a check."

Rich grinned. "No checks," he said.

"I don't know if I have twenty dollars."

"It's forty dollars," he said, grinning wider, showing his teeth. The two cops, in plain view, not trying to hide from him, were stuffing their jacket pockets with candy bars. The younger one filled his hat too. The woman took a roll of bills out of her purse and put two twenties on the counter, smiling back at him. "Just one of those things," Rich said, putting one twenty in his shirt pocket and the other in the drawer.

Ted laughed when he told him. "You're learning. I'll say that for you, you're learning." Rich felt so good, hearing that, he could have worked another shift. He took off the counter jacket he always wore in the store to hide his pistol and hung it on its hook. It was getting so he hated to leave the store, even after working ten hours. He was afraid he might miss something.

He'd just sat down on the bed to take off his shoes when Dorothy phoned. "Do you feel like breakfast? I stopped last night and got some country sausage."

"I don't know; I'm pretty tired."

"It's your favorite kind. I thought."

"I think I'll pass, Dorothy."

"What's wrong?"

"Nothing. I'm just tired."

"I haven't seen you for a while. Did I do something?"

"No. I'm going to say good-bye, Dorothy."

"What's wrong?"

"Quit bothering me," he yelled.

"You won't have to worry about that again," she yelled back and hung up before he could. When would she take the hint, he thought.

"Couldn't sleep," Ted said, coming in at three Tuesday morning. "Must be getting old." He sat down by the coffee machine and crossed his legs, exposing his expensive boots.

Rich lit a cigarette and blew smoke. "Well," he said, "there's nothing like keeping an eye on your investments to cure insomnia."

Ted laughed, slapping his leg. "You're getting clever, boy, mighty clever."

The front door opened and a workman came in. He was wearing a leather pouch with a lot of screwdrivers and pliers sticking out. He had on thick glasses and looked half asleep. "You got some aspirin?" he asked. "I got the damndest headache. Got called out of bed for an emergency. People never bother about shorts in the daytime; it's at night they get worried." Rich reached for the largest bottle of aspirin. When he turned back, the electrician had a pistol out. Ted had already seen it and was uncrossing his legs.

"Okay, pissant, stand back from the counter. If you press that button I'll drill you a new bellybutton." Rich took two careful steps back from the counter. "And you, dummy, stand up. Take out your pistol easy; take it out with two fingers; drop it. Now you, pissant, the same way."

Rich did it as if he were playing some game that had to be done exactly right. "Now on the floor, pissant." Rich went down as if he were shot.

"Now the one in your boot. Surprised?" the robber said. "I read." Rich was listening for the pistol to hit the floor, but when it landed it barely made a sound. "Now you get down on the floor," he said to Ted. He came around the counter and picked up the pistols from the floor. Rich could see his shoes when they came near his head. He knew what was happening by the sound. The robber shook open a bag. Pressed the No Sale, and the cash drawer slid open. His fingernails fished out the money.

"You, go open the safe," he said. Neither of them moved. He kicked Ted in the side of the head. "Who do you think I was talking to? Crawl," he yelled. Then the kicking sound again. Rich felt his arms jerked back. There was the sound of tape pulled from a spool and then the sticky feel of it wrapping around his wrists. He thought of Dorothy. He knew he wasn't going to be able to tell her about this.

He heard Ted. "Maybe we can make a deal." The killer laughed. The sound made sweat pop out on Rich's forehead and he could feel it run onto the cold floor. His whole body felt moist, like he was covered with a fine coat of oil. "Take the money. Let us go."

"And have you tell what I look like?"

"We won't tell. I promise."

"You promise, huh. What's it worth to you?"

"I'll give you a hundred thousand dollars."

"What, in a check?"

"No, no. You can take us to my bank. I'll get it."

"What about the kid?—He'll shoot off his mouth." There was a silence. "The kid's got to go. I'm tired of making peanuts, all this risk. What do you say?"

Rich felt something warm spread over his body. For a minute he couldn't think what it was. He was peeing all over himself. He thought he was going to laugh. He was peeing in his pants. He couldn't contain himself; he started to giggle. He thought of the day he'd found his father. Going through the front door, calling out "I'm home, I'm home." No one answered. His father was always home by three. He'd walked into the bathroom unzipping his fly. His father was in the tub, head resting against the back, knees up. Blood still drained from his mouth, down through the hair on his chest into the red water. He had stood still, unable to move, staring at the yellow-white of those eyes where the pupils should have been.

"Deal," Ted said.

Then there came the laugh and then the kicking sounds, Ted screaming, and then an explosion. Rich was up, diving over the counter, up again. Another explosion. Glass shattering. Running, butting open the glass door. More explosions. The darkness of the parking lot was only ten steps away. He held his breath.

Ernest J. Finney says, "I've always liked Yeats's lines 'I must lie down where all the ladders start / In the foul rag-and-bone shop of the heart.' That's where I try to begin my stories; after that they develop according to a logic of their own. I like the way 'Nights and Days' starts up the ladder."

Finney's short stories have appeared in The Sewanee Review, Kenyon Review, Three Penny, Epoch, Yankee, *and other periodicals.* Birds Landing, *his first collection of stories, was recently published. He lives in California.*

First published in 1985 in The Sewanee Review.

ROBERT TAYLOR, JR.

THE TENNESSEE WAR OF THE ROSES

1

The man who steps to the podium is short and stout, with wisps of sand-colored hair combed across his bald pate from ear to ear, a fine pointed moustache, a Vandyke.

Ladies and Gentlemen, he says. This is indeed a glorious day and a glorious occasion—

And so on. Five minutes pass, the voice drones, the birds complain, the sky is nonchalant, blue as ever, what difference can it possibly make, nobody paying it any mind. Our Bob sits to the left of the speaker, brother Alf to the right, the roses in their lapels—Bob's the white, Alf's the red—fluttering in the September breeze. Bob and Alf's moustaches are dark and thick, so much alike they might have been made in a factory, and each man has the broad high forehead common to the family, the wavy dark hair fast thinning and retreating though Alf is but thirty-eight and Bob a mere thirty-six years old. Not large men, they nonetheless convey robustness, their eyes remarkably clear, tolerably dark, appropriately penetrating, their cheeks ruddy, chins firm, noses straight and long with narrow, gently tapering nostrils.

Chattanooga is honored, the man at the podium says, Chattanooga is proud—

Will he never stop. The audience, Alf observes, begins to grow restless. A gang of ruffians out on the edge comments freely, passing a bottle amongst them, their collarless shirts ragged and sweat-stained. Oh, but who was he fooling. He'd be out there with them, yes, he would, no doubt should be, and not sitting here next to this fool, this Chattanooga simpleton in a clawhammer coat and spit-shined banker's oxfords, waving his hands in the air, talking now of tariffs, now of temperance.

What matters any of it.

Once Jennie said, Alf, I'm fond of the slant of your nose. And she took his hand and pressed it to her cheek. She was as fragrant as a flower, a fresh rose, and her skin was soft, as though she were made of lips. In the spring sunshine he walked with her, beside them the clear waters of the Chuckey and all around them a splendid entanglement of vine and branch, soft moss on the trunks of the broad sycamores, leaves giving back every bit of light they took in.

What are they clapping at. Is it time then? Look lively, Alf. No, but Bob goes first this time, don't he. This is Chattanooga. In Murfreesboro, I went first, then Bob in Shelbyville, then me in Tullahoma, and so now it is Bob's turn again, yes, that's right.

The band plays "Dixie" and he knows he's right.

Bob rises, grinning, and steps into the sunshine, his arms spread out as if to accept a hug from the air. Oh, he has a manner all right. You have to give him credit. And a voice to go with it. He has Uncle Landon's timbre, Father's lilt, and Mother's expression. A deadly combination. Whereas he, Alf—well, what does he have? Good humor, they said. A genial fellow. A winning, if somewhat workaday, sincerity. And laughs at his own jokes. Can't keep a straight face like Bob.

Now Bob begins, and, Lord, what words these!

The illustrious dreamers and creators, Bob says, in the realm of music, the Mozarts and the Beethovens, have scaled the purple steeps of the heaven of sweet sounds, unbarred the opal gates, and opened the holy of holies to the rapt ear of the world . . .

His words, that's what they are. His, Alf's, words, every last one of them. The devil! There is brother Bob delivering a speech writ by his own dear brother, and with such smoothness, the words sallying forth from that golden throat, that quick and sly tongue, as if from the heart itself. You've got to admire him. A thief, yes, but such grace. What can be done against such an opponent. Have to make up a speech from scratch. Lord, the story of my life.

2

Once those two were boys. Can you imagine it? And there was no Civil War, and they lived in a place called Happy Valley in East Tennessee. Baxter's eyes brightened just to say *Happy Valley.* Why did his grandson look so uninterested, why did he stare out the window, yawn and twitch so. These men were my uncles, the brothers of my own father. Look at their pictures there on the wall, how clear the eyes, stately the tilt of the chins.

They visited my father's house, the roses in their lapels, their boots shining in the fresh-cut grass. Baxter, they said, what a future awaits you! James, they said, now addressing my father, you're the lucky one, home on the farm, untainted by commerce with the world.

No, I was not in the war. I was born too late for that, in 1877, a good twelve years after the end of the war. The election was in '86. I saw my uncles as the very flesh and blood of greatness. You have to understand that. It was something, you see, to live up to, as if you were born mortal into a family of gods.

Baxter, Mother said, you must make your own way in the world.

I read law. I was admitted to the bar. Politics was my passion. I was an elector on the Bryan ticket. All this was good, and it was *their* way. I too would be a member of my family, no mortal, the hero of a divine romance. But soon I grew weary, hearing my prospects everywhere whispered as dependent on the glory of my uncles, and therefore with my bride I went out to the Indian Territory. I would link my fate to that of a new land, make my own name. And that is how it is that your father and then you, my grandson, were born, not in Tennessee but in Oklahoma. That is how it is.

3

Yet there was melancholy in Bob. Alf saw it and was troubled by it. He heard Bob speak of the family. It was the highest truth, the family the home of the soul, where we see our immortality in the flesh, our death every day more alive, stealthy and quick, our life a learning how to dream the dead awake. Such words. Such a man of words. As if his words were what he was made of, and, failing to believe in them, he came to doubt his existence.

Bob would not say this, not in so many words, no, not to Alf. But how could you fail to feel it when Bob came in, after an impassioned speech on the need for mercy, the compelling case for compassion, and sat down on the end of that hotel bed, his head held high, to be sure, and his great lower lip as firm as family tradition demanded, but with such a look in his eyes, a dangerous look, Alf would say, a look not meant to be seen, that you were embarrassed to have seen it and not just a little frightened for the soul it showed forth.

Alf drew back. He said nothing. He left the room.

Later Bob took him aside. Pay no mind to that, he said, his dark eyes quick and good-humored again. I was somber.

4

Alf wore the red rose, Bob the white. Nathaniel couldn't for the life of him see the logic. One family, not two. What had politics to do with blood. It would be a spectacle, such an election, his sons made the laughingstock of meanspirited journalists from Memphis to Bristol. Was he too to choose? Which son would he favor?

It was Alf that had gone out with him to Kansas, in '67 it would have been, to Medicine Lodge, when the treaties were made with the Cheyenne, the Kiowa, and the Arapaho. There was Satank and Satanta of the Kiowa tribe. Little Raven, the great Arapaho chief, who moved us all with his description of the massacre at Sand Creek. We drank whiskey with them—Emma, it is true, don't look at me that way—it was diplomacy, though some many have abused the courtesy, I will mention no names. We ate dog too, a great favorite of the Plains tribes, for the sake of diplomacy—Alf ate with restraint, Henry Stanley with relish, I found it not to my liking.

Nathaniel, your mind wanders.

No, it is home-bound, sorely domesticated. My life has been a struggle against division. I have wanted to keep things whole. It was North and South, then red and white. The nation would split itself in two, tear itself asunder one way or another. Now my sons—

Family is family, Nathaniel, and will survive us.

But how? In what condition. In what spirit.

With God's grace.

Rare in families. Unheard of among nations.

We must be strong in our faith.

And our sons and daughters? And *their* sons and daughters?

They will take care of themselves.

Lord help them. They'll take care of us too.

5

Bob's first victory was against a Major Pettibone.

Pettibone defeated me, Alf said, in the Republican primary of '78, and so the Democrats got Bob to go against him, figuring that Bob would draw the voters who had gone for me, don't you see.

Now that was a race. Bob was twenty-eight, running against a man of mature years and seasoned experience. Pettibone cut a graceful figure, and wore a wool hat to affect kinship with the rural gentry and to cover his baldspot. Our Bob took to the fiddle and the extended anecdote. Now Pettibone had the misfortune of having been born not in Tennessee but in Michigan. You can bet Our Bob made much of that. On one occasion Pettibone rose and chided

Bob severely. It was during a public debate—I believe it was in Knoxville. In his excitement Pettibone clutched his hat and waved it in the air, in itself a dramatic gesture, so few having seen his head. This man, he said, pointing his hat at Bob, is nothing but a fiddler. His talents are best expressed in doggerel:

Bob can fiddle and Bob can sing
And Bob can cut the pigeon wing!

But I ask you, what else can he do? And shall we ask him to cut the pigeon wing in the halls of the nation's capital, a representative of Tennessee!

And he sat down to silence. It was a low blow. We all felt it. Pettibone was so pleased with himself that he left his hat off and grinned like a boy about to go for an ear of corn.

Bob rose solemnly. He had dark and wavy hair in those days, though already thinning, and only a frail moustache, but make no mistake: there was nothing boyish in his manner. His cheeks had no color in them and his lips were pressed tight together. He approached the lectern, paused, looked out on the audience, took a deep breath. Then he leaned down and reached for something under the platform. His fiddle case. He lifted it up and placed it on top of the platform, the tapered end of it pointing upwards. There was no mistaking what it was. He set it there and held it firmly. Friends, he said, and his voice was low and deep and absolutely serious. Friends, he said, I ask you to choose between this that I carry with no apology—and now he made a sweeping gesture with his left hand and pointed to Major Pettibone, who was examining the sky with utmost interest—and the carpetbag so furtively carried by that one.

Well, he won that election, but Pettibone sent him home the second term—they say it was because Bob took a bride from out of the state. Sally Baird was from North Carolina.

6

The melancholy that Bob was afflicted with has run through our family from one generation to the next, weak in one member, strong in the next. Bob will defeat Alf, the white rose of Dixie prevail in Tennessee, but always there will be this sorrow. Baxter, he says to me, Baxter, the world is too much with us, the world is lush with promise, so sparse in the delivery. He had large calm eyes, dark and deep-set, such a shining pate (a boy, I asked him once did he shine it, did he polish it with a cloth the same way he rubbed the wood of his fiddle; he laughed and said he would not tell me, it was a secret, but if I lived long enough I would know the secret).

I see them taking the fiddles from their velvet-lined cases, Alf's the brighter, its belly golden spruce, Bob's a richer brown with some red in it, the grain as fine and even as ever I saw, before or since. Bob was a left-handed fiddler, a thing that you do not see much of, and because I learned from watching him I too draw the bow with my left hand, though in all else I am right-handed.

It was Alf who showed me the beauty in the wood, how sound comes through it, a gift to the ear, and how fine to be a maker of fiddles. That was when my mother died. I walked out among the trees and listened to oak, to maple, to pine, and it was as though she spoke again. Baxter, she said, there is no shame in what has become of me. You are what becomes me. In you I live. Loving, you give me life.

She was a lovely woman, said Alf.

A dedicated mother, a loving wife, said Bob.

God rest her soul, my father said, his eye already on the lovely Cora Showalter, whom he would court all the long winter and marry in the fall.

It was also during this time—the time of my mother's long dying—that Bob composed and performed his first lecture, "The Fiddle and the Bow," at Jobe's Hall in Johnson City. He had returned to Happy Valley after a year in Chattanooga in private practice, this after his two terms as governor. He had not prospered. The truth is, he had no gift for earning a living. Help me, Alf, he said, and Alf's answer was, Return to Happy Valley. You will be provided for. He did, and was.

7

It might have been in Tazewell, perhaps in Greeneville or even in Bristol, a mountain town in East Tennessee. Alf was working *for* Bob in those days, during the first, the victorious, campaign against Pettibone that issued in Bob's ascension to Congress. A long day it had been, hot and dusty, the buggy making its way from village to village along the deeply rutted and winding mountain roads, at each stop, whether before the rotting porch of a rude cabin or the flagstone steps of a whitewashed courthouse, Bob standing in the buggy and saying what came to mind, the sweat on his forehead shining in the bright sun, his hands now clenched, now open and in motion like leaves. Remember me, boys, he said. Remember me, boys. And off went the buggy with a jerk that often as not threw him back to his seat before he had finished waving good-bye. *Remember me, boys.*

He grew increasingly morose. Alf could see it coming as sure as the sweat above his brows. Bob squinted and you could see his jawbone working, as if he tried to clamp and grind his thoughts. He caught flies in his fists and tossed them to the floor of the buggy. It was the old melancholy coming on him, that was for sure.

Bob, Alf said, are you tiring of this campaign?

Tired, said Bob. Tired. Of course I'm tired. I'm tired to death of this pitiful buggy ride. Where will it lead to? To Washington, you say, yes, to Washington. At *best* to Washington. But I say, where is that? It is nowhere at all, a city of fools, a congress of ignorance, a hive of lethargy.

What kind of talk is that from a candidate!

Honest talk. Talk from the heart.

It's not the talk I'm accustomed to hearing from you, Bob.

Well, you're hearing it now.

So I am.

And since you so clearly don't like it, I'll favor you no more with it.

He shut up, sure enough, drew his lips tight together and scowled at the horses' swishing tails as if in them he saw his fate. Alf wasn't going to let it worry him. He'd seen this before and no doubt would see it again. Better to think on Jennie Anderson, her sweet little nose, eyes quick with grace and light, her small fair hands, and the very idea of her ankles. What if he was to say to her, one bright summery day when the sky hushed everything else, Jennie, I'm crazy with love for you, and let his fingertips—there, like that—just brush her wrist and come to rest in the warmth of her palm.

When the next town appeared—he could not for the life of him remember which town it was—Alf saw that a new calm had come to Bob's face. So the melancholy had gone its way, just in time. A crowd gathered around the buggy, for the most part long-faced men in overalls, with silvery stubbled chins and dark eyes set close together beneath thick, wiry brows.

Give us a tune on the fiddle, Our Bob!

Come on and dance the buck-and-wing, Our Bob!

Boys, says Bob, I reckon I am as tired of giving speeches as you are of hearing them. Alf, hand me that fiddle.

And so he played. It was "Turkey Buzzard," it was "Hole in the Kettle," it was "Shoot Ole Davy Dugger." Then he handed Alf the fiddle, said play a little "Sally Goodin" for me, Brother. I was only too glad to oblige, for I loved to see Bob dance to a fiddle tune, such a fine quickness, heel and toe in touch with all the music's mystery, and I hardly knew whether he danced to my fiddle or I fiddled to his dancing, it was that way with us, the crowd swelling, a woman or two out on the edge starting to move to the rhythm, her thick skirt swaying slowly at first, then ever which way until she took hold of it and raised it up just enough so that you could see her little feet in their black hightop boots moving like crazy. Oh, it was a fine thing. I liked it considerable better than a speech.

But that was not even the best part. The best part came

when the dancing at last stopped, this fiddler's bowing arm gone limp as a willow branch, and Bob, catching his breath while everybody clapped and cheered, took the fiddle and commenced to playing a slow, sweet air that I had never heard the likes of before nor since, so much a part of that moment was it, as if into it went all the joyous energy that had gone into the dancing, and its exhaustion too, and something else that I could not at first put my finger on, what was it, like a song within a song, a feeling inside of another feeling and still another inside of that one, and then it came to me. This was the melancholy. He was getting that blood sorrow into his music and it was damn near overpowering, everybody quietening down quick and listening hard, for they heard it too and were with him in that sobering joy as much as I was, as much as you would have been, Baxter, I know, had you been there listening.

Then he lowered the fiddle to his chest and, still drawing the bow slow and steady, began to sing:

When other lips and other hearts
Their tales of love shall tell
In language whose excess imparts
The power they feel so well,
There may perhaps in such a scene
Some recollection be
Of days that have as happy been—
Then you'll remember me,
Then you'll remember,
You'll remember me!

We'll remember you, Bobby, they all shouted as we rode away. Come Election Day, we'll remember!

In Tazewell this must have been, or Greeneville. I think not Bristol.

8

In his law office on the sixteenth floor of the Petroleum Building, Baxter looks out on all of Oklahoma City, the streets stretching toward the horizon, straight and sure, the treeless plains beyond, and he sees the hills of East Tennessee. They are out there, curving into the sun, soft as skin.

His desk is cluttered—papers and paperweights, pens, jars of ink, some dry, some full, paper clips sadly bent or rusted, envelopes with vital addresses in their corners, letters yellowing at the edges, receipts and bills, dust though a feather duster lies on its side, within easy reach, next to the tinted photograph of his wife in its gilded frame. What has he come to, who once could say, I am Our Bob's nephew, my father the brother of those that wore the roses in 1886. What now did he know, what could he know. It was 1956.

Love, he had said, we have come to Oklahoma.

Yes, Baxter. The trees are short and sparse, few and far between.

But consider, Love, the sky.

He considers it daily. It lies very close, just outside his window, vast and brilliant, the sun ranging across it as though for show, clouds now fleecy, now clumped, bursting with light. You make a pact, it seems, not with another human being but with certain landscapes, the territories you flee in youth and seek ever after, as if in the long run the soul is nothing more than the look of a place and its sound.

9

The War of the Roses. Wasn't there a beauty in that phrase? A beauty that went beyond politics? Alf meditated on it. Years after the event he thought on it. There was my brother, alive who now is dead, represented by the color of a rose. And what warfare, the triumphant dead!

Now, Alf, Bob says, it's time we sheathe our tongues and make those devil's boxes tremble.

And James's boy Baxter stands there—always was there, in the shadows, watching us as though to commit our every movement to memory. We mustn't flatter ourselves, James said. Baxter wants to have everything by heart. It's his nature.

Ain't it though.

Can you teach him, Brother, how to play the fiddle?

I can show him what I know. But the music must be his own.

Does he have the music, I wonder.

There's music in him, James. He'll grow into it in time.

Baxter stood to one side, lean and serious, in his eyes a peculiar glint. He was tall, with long arms and slender, long fingers, and wrists as narrow as a girl's. He wore cotton shirts with faded stripes, no doubt passed on to him from his older brothers Shakespeare or Pole, the sleeves so short, leaving bare his pale thin wrists. The death of his mother had had its effect on him, Alf was certain of that. She was a powerful woman, was Mary Susan, not unlike his own mother, strong in sympathy yet quick to condemn wrongdoing, the air of a prophet about her, such flashing eyes, and of a judge, such severity in the curve of her lips and the jut of her small chin.

It was when she died that Baxter, sixteen years old, took up the fiddle in earnest. Not only would he play that devil's box, but he would be a maker of fiddles. And he began to search for the best wood and to collect pieces that pleased him. Each has its own sound, he said, and of course Alf knew that. Every fiddler knew that. You brought the fiddle to rest beneath your chin and then you made the wood yield its sound and if you were only a middling good fiddler it held back and made a fool of you, leaving you with little more than you could imagine or remember. The wood resisted Baxter. A shame it was, but true. The music in him found no union with the music of the wood and therefore came forth unshapely and of shallow timbre.

But he might make fiddles. Yes. That was another proposition. Mathematics entered in, symmetry came into play. As much design as destiny, as if to repeat endlessly the very proportion of passion.

Nothing stays, James said.

Amen, said Bob.

This time they sat on the porch of their father's house. Baxter—he could not have been more than ten years old—

leapt from the steps, rolled in the new April grass, and bounded up like a light.

I'll never die, was what they thought he cried out as he ran across the lawn towards the fresh-plowed fields.

I admire that boy, said Bob. I see in him an exuberant decorum. A fine lawyer he will make. Perhaps a judge.

In a few minutes their mother—who was Emmaline Haynes, sister to Landon Carter Haynes, remember—stepped out onto the porch and said, He's gone. Boys, your father has breathed his last.

Praise God, said Bob, rising from his rocker.

His will be done, said Mother.

Baxter was out in the fields now, still running, his figure diminishing with distance, a wisp of dust trailing behind. It was the last thing Alf saw—he remembers it vividly—before he turned towards the door his mother held open for him and followed his brothers into his father's house.

10

Of the two of them, I remember Alf best. Of course he lived the longest, Bob passing away in 1912, Alf not until 1931. In 1912 I was in Oklahoma. Your father was not born yet, though his brothers were—two infants they were, your grandmother was kept plenty busy—and I had become the judge Bob foresaw in me. Bob died in Washington, near the end of his first term as senator, Alf in the Chuckey Valley, the grand old statesman of Tennessee, made governor in the last decade of his life.

Oklahoma had become my state. Already I had determined to move to its very center, its heart, hub of industry and commerce, Oklahoma City, and link my fate to its. I was not to have the success my uncles had achieved. Too easily was I used by others. But I have made my own way in this world and have learned to love the bright plains of Oklahoma as well as ever I did the shady mountains of Old Tennessee. There is wood enough—remember—wherever you go there will be wood enough to make a fiddle. That is the message I leave with you, in the hope that you will pass it on to your own children. It is what my Uncle Alf told me when I was a very young man. I listened. I hope you hear me, if not now, at least in memory. If not remembered, then imagined. Pay attention. When I talk to you, listen. Then you will have something to tell that is your own.

11

The election was over—good riddance—one son had won, Nathaniel didn't care which. Dying, he thought politics childish. It was division, and division did not signify. Nat, Johnson had said, I want you to be Indian commissioner. Let us work to make every tribe a part of this Union.

Yes, I will do what I can.

What is done does not signify. Not in this world, every campaign a loss, all treaties broken. What signifies lies secret and secure in the human heart, washed eternally in the blood, pulse and heat, grace in the making.

Nathaniel, will you come down to supper.

I'm dying.

Of course you are. So are we all.

I'm dying sooner than the rest of you.

Come eat. You'll feel better. There's sweet corn, your favorite.

I've eaten enough. At Medicine Lodge—

Nat, I'll hear no more of feasting on dogs. We have pork roast. Bob and Alf are here. Can't you come down? I'll help you.

I'd rather stay here. I'm ready to die. My heart tells me it's time.

The food is cooling, the family waiting. This is your imagination, not your heart. You know it is. A cold, Doctor Samuel said. Catarrh.

Death. I hear it. It's not one voice but many.

You hear Bob and Alf and James down on the porch, waiting for their father. You hear your grandchildren playing in the yard.

Too loud. Too many.

She left then, and he rose to dress. The Whig party, he thought, the Whig party stood for Union. That was its strength, a simple and fundamental principle worth standing for. But the Party of Division won, and then was brother against brother. Next, red against white.

He tied his tie, combed his beard, cleared his throat. This would be his last meal, by God. Hold firm a while longer, Heart. No doubt they'd ask him to say grace. He would acquit himself tolerably well. After all, they were blessed, every last one of them, blessed in spite of themselves. Just smell that sweet corn. Hear those fiddles tuning. How fortunate the living.

"The Tennessee War of the Roses" is one of a series of stories based on Robert Taylor's family—inspired by the tales he heard told and retold of the family home in Happy Valley; the patriarch Nathaniel, who went on a peace mission to the Indians; the fiddle-playing brothers Alf and Bob, who ran against each other for governor of Tennessee; their nephew Baxter, who removes to Oklahoma and is the grandfather of the young boy listening to the story (who happens to be Taylor). "The story still pleases me," he writes, "as a kind of fugue of voices, a network echoing the way family stories get told, retold, made new with each telling."

This story and others were later incorporated in his novel Fiddle and Bow, *which chronicles several generations of this family of fiddle players, their strong women and children.*

Taylor's stories have appeared in The Ohio Review, The Georgia Review, Shenandoah, Western Humanities Review, *and* Southwest Review. *He is the author of the novel* Loving

Belle Starr. *Taylor teaches at Bucknell University and co-edits the literary journal* West Branch.

First published in 1983 in The Georgia Review.

ANN BEATTIE

IN THE WHITE NIGHT

"Don't think about a cow," Matt Brinkley said. "Don't think about a river, don't think about a car, don't think about snow. . . ."

Matt was standing in the doorway, hollering after his guests. His wife, Gaye, gripped his arm and tried to tug him back into the house. The party was over. Carol and Vernon turned to wave good-bye, calling back their thanks, whispering to each other to be careful. The steps were slick with snow; an icy snow had been falling for hours, frozen granules mixed in with lighter stuff, and the instant they moved out from under the protection of the Brinkleys' porch the cold froze the smiles on their faces. The swirls of snow blowing against Carol's skin reminded her—an odd thing to remember on a night like this—of the way sand blew up at the beach, and the scratchy pain it caused.

"Don't think about an apple!" Matt hollered. Vernon turned his head, but he was left smiling at a closed door.

In the small, bright areas under the streetlights, there seemed for a second to be some logic to all the swirling snow. If time itself could only freeze, the snowflakes could become the lacy filigree of a valentine. Carol frowned. Why had Matt conjured up the image of an apple? Now she saw an apple where there was no apple, suspended in midair, transforming the scene in front of her into a silly surrealist painting.

It was going to snow all night. They had heard that on the radio, driving to the Brinkleys'. The Don't-Think-About-Whatever game had started as a joke, something long in the telling and startling to Vernon, to judge by his expression as Matt went on and on. When Carol crossed the room near midnight to tell Vernon that they should leave, Matt had quickly whispered the rest of his joke or story—whatever he was saying—into Vernon's ear, all in a rush. They looked like two children, the one whispering madly and the other with his head bent, but something about the inclination of Vernon's head let you know that if you bent low enough to see, there would be a big, wide grin on his face. Vernon and Carol's daughter, Sharon, and Matt and Gaye's daughter, Becky, had sat side by side, or kneecap to kneecap, and whispered that way when they were children—a privacy so rushed that it obliterated anything else. Carol, remembering that scene now, could not think of what passed between Sharon and Becky without thinking of sexual intimacy. Becky, it turned out, had given the Brinkleys a lot of trouble. She had run away from home when she was thirteen, and, in a family-counseling session years later, her parents found out that she had had an abortion at fifteen. More recently, she had flunked out of college. Now she was working in a bank in Boston and taking a night-school course in poetry. Poetry or pottery? The apple that reappeared as the windshield wipers slushed snow off the glass metamorphosed for Carol into a red bowl, then again became an apple, which grew rounder as the car came to a stop at the intersection.

She had been weary all day. Anxiety always made her tired. She knew the party would be small (the Brinkleys' friend Mr. Graham had just had his book accepted for publication, and of course much of the evening would be spent talking about that); she had feared that it was going to be a strain for all of them. The Brinkleys had just returned from the Midwest, where they had gone for Gaye's father's funeral. It didn't seem a time to carry through with plans for a party. Carol imagined that not canceling it had been Matt's idea, not Gaye's. She turned toward Vernon now and asked how the Brinkleys had seemed to him. Fine, he said at once. Before he spoke, she knew how he would answer. If people did not argue in front of their friends, they were not having problems; if they did not stumble into walls, they were not drunk. Vernon tried hard to think positively, but he was never impervious to real pain. His reflex was to turn aside something serious with a joke, but he was just as quick to wipe the smile off his face and suddenly put his arm around a person's shoulder. Unlike Matt, he was a warm person, but when people unexpectedly showed him affection it embarrassed him. The same counselor the Brinkleys had seen had told Carol—Vernon refused to see the man, and she found that she did not want to continue without him—that it was possible that Vernon felt uncomfortable with expressions of kindness because he blamed himself for Sharon's death: he couldn't save her, and when people were kind to him now he felt it was undeserved. But Vernon was the last person who should be punished. She remembered him in the hospital, pretending to misunderstand Sharon when she asked for her barrette, on her bedside table, and picking it up and clipping the little yellow duck into the hair above his own ear. He kept trying to tickle a smile out of her—touching some stuffed animal's button nose to the tip of her nose and then tapping it on her earlobe. At the moment when Sharon died, Vernon had been sitting on her bed (Carol was backed up against the door, for some reason), surrounded by a battlefield of pastel animals.

They passed safely through the last intersection before their house. The car didn't skid until they turned onto their street. Carol's heart thumped hard, once, in the second when she felt the car becoming light, but they came out of the skid easily. He had been driving carefully, and she said nothing, wanting to appear casual about the moment. She asked if Matt had mentioned Becky. No, Vernon said, and he hadn't wanted to bring up a sore subject.

Gaye and Matt had been married for twenty-five years; Carol and Vernon had been married twenty-two. Sometimes Vernon said, quite sincerely, that Matt and Gaye were their alter egos, who absorbed and enacted crises, saving the two of them from having to experience such chaos. It frightened Carol to think that some part of him believed that. Who could really believe that there was some way to find protection in this world—or someone who could offer it? What happened happened at random, and one horrible thing hardly precluded the possibility of others happening next. There had been that fancy internist who hospitalized Vernon later in the same spring when Sharon died, and who looked up at him while drawing blood and observed almost offhandedly that it would be an unbearable irony if Vernon also had leukemia. When the test results came back, they showed that Vernon had mononucleosis. There was the time when the Christmas tree caught fire, and she rushed toward the flames, clapping her hands like cymbals, and Vernon pulled her away just in time, before the whole tree became a torch, and she with it. When Hobo, their dog, had to be put to sleep, during their vacation in Maine, that awful woman veterinarian, with her cold green eyes, issued the casual death sentence with one manicured hand on the quivering dog's fur and called him "Bobo," as though their dog were like some circus clown.

"Are you crying?" Vernon said. They were inside their house now, in the hallway, and he had just turned toward her, holding out a pink padded coat hanger.

"No," she said. "The wind out there is fierce." She slipped her jacket onto the hanger he held out and went into the downstairs bathroom, where she buried her face in a towel. In time, she looked at herself in the mirror. She had pressed the towel hard against her eyes, and for a few seconds she had to blink herself into focus. She was reminded of the kind of camera they had had when Sharon was young. There were two images when you looked through the finder, and you had to make the adjustment yourself so that one superimposed itself upon the other and the figure suddenly leaped into clarity. She patted the towel to her eyes again and held her breath. If she couldn't stop crying, Vernon would make love to her. When she was very sad, he sensed that his instinctive optimism wouldn't work; he became tongue-tied, and when he couldn't talk he would reach for her. Through the years, he had knocked over wineglasses shooting his hand across the table to grab hers. She had found herself suddenly hugged from behind in the bathroom; he would even follow her in there if he suspected that she was going to cry—walk in to grab her without even having bothered to knock.

She opened the door now and turned toward the hall staircase, and then realized—felt it before she saw it, really—that the light was on in the living room.

Vernon lay stretched out on the sofa, with his legs crossed; one foot was planted on the floor and his top foot dangled in the air. Even when he was exhausted, he was always careful not to let his shoes touch the sofa. He was very tall, and couldn't stretch out on the sofa without resting his head on the arm. For some reason, he had not hung up her jacket. It was spread like a tent over his head and shoulders, rising and falling with his breathing. She stood still long enough to be sure that he was really asleep, and then came into the room. The sofa was too narrow to curl up on with him. She didn't want to wake him. Neither did she want to go to bed alone. She went back to the hall closet and took out his overcoat—the long, elegant camel's-hair coat he had not worn tonight because he thought it might snow. She slipped off her shoes and went quietly over to where he lay and stretched out on the floor beside the sofa, pulling the big blanket of the coat up high, until the collar touched her lips. Then she drew her legs up into the warmth.

Such odd things happened. Very few days were like the ones before. Here they were, in their own house with four bedrooms, ready to sleep in this peculiar double-decker fashion, in the largest, coldest room of all. What would anyone think?

She knew the answer to that question, of course. A person who didn't know them would mistake this for a drunken collapse, but anyone who was a friend would understand exactly. In time, each of the two of them had learned to stop passing judgment on how they coped with the inevitable sadness that set in, always unexpectedly but so real that it was met with the instant acceptance one gave to a snowfall. In the white night world outside, their daughter might be drifting past like an angel, and she would see this tableau, for the second that she hovered, as a necessary small adjustment.

Ann Beattie writes, "In "In the White Night," I started playing with visual images without first knowing consciously why they were there. I hope that language and symbol finally melded in the story—that, in a way, the closing image was complex and radiated. The party hosts' game—language—became important to me as a subject. The host was interested in what language denoted, and I was interested in what language connoted metaphorically. In retrospect, I see that he and I ended up as co-conspirators."

She was born in Baltimore and began writing at an early age. Her collections include Chilly Scenes of Winter, Falling in Place, The Burning House, *and* Where You'll Find Me. *She is also the author of the novel* Love Always.

First published in 1984 in The New Yorker.

ROBLEY WILSON, JR.

PAYMENT IN KIND

That summer she had the habit of getting up at first light, dressing quietly in the bathroom so she would not wake her husband, Paul, and going out to the kitchen to make coffee. Sometimes she used supermarket coffee, and once in a while, if the morning seemed in some indefinable way "special," she would take from the cupboard under the sink the small Braun grinder her daughter Sarah had given her and fill it with Colombian beans she bought at a specialty shop in Waterloo. The beans were small and dark and slippery; they reminded her a little of the Mexican jumping beans her father had bought for her to hold when she was a child, when she had been distressed to learn that the beans jumped because the warmth of her palms roused a tiny worm—some sort of borer—inside.

It took only seconds to turn the coffee beans to powder. She held the contraption in both hands, her right thumb pressed against its orange button until the hum of the motor rose to a higher, freer pitch. When she unscrewed the plastic top and tipped the grinder over the percolator basket, the coffee that spilled out was fine and deep brown—almost as dark as the Iowa earth—and moist, so that she had to hit the machine a couple of times against the heel of her palm to loosen it.

Then, while the coffee made in the old percolator, she went out to the front porch to assess the day. This summer, morning after morning, the days had been identical: a lip of yellow-orange along the eastern horizon, over which the light streamed into a bowl of sky that looked leaden but would turn out to be a pale, high blue; the air still, seeming, when she breathed, already to carry nearly enough of the weight of heat to smother her; ragged veils of fog hanging in the shallows of the fields that opened away from the farmhouse. And the mornings were not quite silent. The chorus of crickets was constant, there was almost always a solitary robin chirping in one of the ash trees; from the highway a mile to the north she could hear the hollow roar of trailer trucks. Somewhere she had read that in silence, absolute silence, you could hear a high-pitched sound that was your own nervous system, and a deep, boiling sound that was the circulation of your blood. Then the crickets might be her nerves, and the far-off trucks her blood. She didn't know about the robin; something of the spirit, perhaps, that the scientists always left out.

By the time Paul came into the kitchen—at six or seven, depending on what he planned to do with his day—the coffee would be half gone, and he would find her sitting at the table, cup in hand, staring idly out the screen door. He said nothing—he was a man of rare words; in all these years she still could not claim to know him—but took a mug from the drainboard and poured an inch of coffee from the percolator. If his first sip told him it was a store brand, he filled the mug and sat opposite her—not like a man making himself comfortable with his wife, but on the edge of the chair, tensed to go about some unannounced business. If the coffee was the Colombian, he would mutter something just below her hearing and empty the stuff into the sink. Either way, his next move was outside, to the weather station he had put together beyond the shed: rain and wind gauges, tools for measuring temperatures and pressures and moistures—instruments acquired as a hobby, but consulted this year with a regularity bordering on the fanatic. No rain had fallen for six weeks, the heat rose into the nineties or hundreds, day after sweltering day; humidities were high, the barometric pressure high, the winds sluggish. There were not even thunderstorms. After ten minutes with his gauges Paul would come in, scowling. "Better close up the house," he said. Never more words than those, and her heart ached for him.

This morning in mid-August she watched him come back from the ritual of reading the weather and realized, as if for the first time, how old he had gotten—or tired, or whatever it was that happened to a man in thirty years of a working life. His movements showed none of the foolish energy that used to carry him like a caprice of wind from one chore to another, one outbuilding to another, one dream to another. He walked with his head down, his shoulders slouched, one hand tucked into a pocket of his overalls and the other rubbing absently at the back of his neck. When he came up the porch steps and through the screen door, his sigh was audible, a distress signal.

"Better close up the house."

She had heard the forecast on the television news last night: no relief, no rain, highs close to a hundred. In the southern part of the state the government was letting the farmers turn livestock onto their set-aside land early, and some counties were already eligible for disaster loans. She could not recall such a summer.

Paul stood in the middle of the kitchen. He looked as if he were trying to remember something, as if he had been on his way to a place, a task, and was disturbed to find himself in an unexpected setting. Then he turned toward the sink, took a tumbler down from the cupboard and filled it with tap water. He studied the water before he drank it. Dear God, she thought, now is he fretting about the well?

"What is it?" she said.

He drained the glass before he responded, and when he did look at her he compressed his lips in what she took to be an ironic smile.

"I was thinking how my old man could have taken a look at the sky, and at the weathervane on the old barn," he said, "and known just as much about the damned weather as I do by reading all those dials."

"Oh, dear," she said. "Is this going to be the speech against progress?"

"Something like that."

"Take a few minutes and have coffee with me," she said. "You can spare me that."

He pulled out his chair and brushed the orange cat off the seat.

"I'll sit," he said, "but I'll pass on the coffee." He studied her. "What's on the docket this morning?"

"I'm going to can tomatoes—such as they are. Then I'm going into town with Nancy Riker."

Paul heard this information without reacting, his thoughts already somewhere else, his eyes reading linoleum patterns off the floor. She drank her coffee; it was lukewarm and slightly bitter.

"I think I'm going to go into that west forty," Paul said. "I walked through it yesterday. Looks to me like it might make twenty percent, but no more."

"You're going to chop it for silage?"

He nodded. "Burt Stone can feed it to his damned cattle." He hauled himself to his feet. "While you're in town, get me a six-pack of something."

Most of the morning she spent dealing with the tomatoes. The drought hadn't done them any good; there were plenty of them, but they were small and hard, not anything she would have wanted to serve in a salad. It was hot work; by ten o'clock the thermometer outside the kitchen window had reached eighty-nine—and that was in shade.

She was interrupted only once—by a woman in a gold Cadillac, who rolled into the yard in a cloud of white dust and came to the back door to talk to her about Jehovah's Witnesses. In the middle of the serious question of Salvation, Helen cut the woman short.

"It's a personal matter, isn't it?" she said. "And I've got tomatoes waiting."

The woman went away. It was only when the Cadillac turned out of the yard that Helen noticed a man slouched in the passenger seat. Perhaps the woman's husband, or father; he had an old face and wore a Panama hat. She thought how she hadn't seen a Panama hat in years and years.

A thick cloud of dust followed the car down the road. All over Iowa these gravel roads were like boundaries, defining the size and shape of the farm fields. Every mile a road to market, east-west, north-south, and heaven help the ignoramus who wanted to build a diagonal. West forty—that's where Paul was chopping down a cornfield that might have delivered 170 bushels an acre, but wouldn't touch 35 because of the weather.

Probably she ought to have said to the Jehovah's Witness lady that she didn't believe in God anyway—that she had used to believe, but in the years of living on this farm with Paul she had come to see how everything was up to her and to him, how between them each spring they made something appear from nothing just like any magic, any religious power, and how they controlled the earth and manipulated growing things and almost but not quite used the weather to best advantage. She ought to have told her that the roads and fences were what imposed order onto chaos. She ought to have said that eternity was only a succession of growing seasons, and if that were not argument enough she could have talked about Sarah and about Peter and about the third child who never got named because he was stillborn. That might have been the last glimmer of her faith; yes, probably it was. And she ought to have explained to the Jehovah's Witness lady about sweat and machinery and bank loans, and what did God know about all that?

Helen waited until after twelve-thirty to have lunch, hoping Paul would join her even while she knew he wouldn't. She sat at the table in the kitchen, a glass of iced tea and a bowl of bran flakes with milk in front of her, listening to the simmer of the tomatoes on the stove. How much she had gotten used to being alone; now that Sarah and Peter were gone, her life seemed almost reclusive, her marriage like the ritual passage of a man and woman on tracks that paralleled but rarely crossed.

Yet this was to have been the year for her and Paul to rediscover each other. When the Agriculture people announced in the spring that farmers could set aside as much as 80 percent of their land and be paid with surplus grains already stored, it had seemed to Helen that for the first time ever her husband would find time heavy on his hands. All the wives shared that belief. Helen remembered an evening in this very kitchen, in March, when Paul and Burton Stone and Jess Eriksen and Harvey Riker had sat playing a card game called Pepper and talked about PIK—Payment in Kind—while she and the wives sewed in the side parlor.

"It'll be like going back to the prairies," Stone had said. "Like the Iowa I knew when I was a kid."

"The hell," Paul said. "The Iowa you knew as a kid was leather jackets and switchblades. What's all this 'prairies' crap?"

Stone grinned. He was scarcely thirty years old, had come home from Vietnam to raise cattle on his father's land.

"You know what I mean," he said.

"Sure do," Riker said. "There won't be nothing growing on half my acres this year."

"Not going to plant cover?"

"Weeds cover." He filled his glass from a new bottle of beer; the foam spilled down the sides and puddled on the tabletop. "If I had horses, I'd plant broom or timothy—maybe alfalfa. But I don't." He lifted the glass and with the side of his palm brushed the spilled beer onto the floor.

"You could do worse than get into the horse business," Jess Eriksen said. "That pari-mutuel bill's going through. There'll be racetracks all over."

"You could raise greyhounds," Paul said. "They're legalizing dog tracks too."

"They make it legal to race Herefords," Stone said, "I'll be sitting pretty."

"Paul here ought to open a bicycle shop," Riker said. "Now the county supervisors have given the old railroad right-of-way to the bike people, there'd be lots of business real close by."

Paul made a show of looking at his cards one by one. "Play the damned game," he said, refusing to be baited.

Much later, when the Pepper was finished and the men had gone home through the crisp night, Helen lay beside Paul in bed and thought about the spring planting.

"I suppose it might be all right," she said. "Letting things go a little way back to nature."

"Don't get all romantic," Paul said. "It's just for this year; nobody's inviting the Indians back to chase buffalo."

"Maybe we could do more things together."

He raised himself on one elbow. "You think I ought to sign up for this PIK program?"

"Weren't you planning to?"

"I might." He lay back. "I might set aside that northeast corner where I need to put in tile; I'd probably have the time—and Harve might want to do the tiling on his side."

"You should talk to him about it," she said. Of course he would find a way to avoid leisure; that was Paul.

He had chuckled then. "That Kraut s.o.b.," he said, "giving me grief about that damned bicycle trail. He knows how I feel. He knows the railroad people promised to give me back the right-of-way if they ever closed down the line."

Finally, she rinsed her dishes and left them in the sink. It was time to pick up Nancy Riker; Paul could make himself a sandwich when he felt like it—if he ever decided to come back to the house before dark.

The Shed was a small, white-clapboard place on the outskirts of town. It was a man's restaurant—local farmers, truckers passing through—but the two women stopped in for coffee on the way home from the shopping mall. At the largest of the chrome-and-Formica tables, men in overalls were talking and joking. The men's conversation was not steady; long periods of silence intervened, so that what was said made a pattern of loudness and silence—a rhythm appropriate to custom and long friendships.

Neither Nancy nor Helen had bought much. Helen had rummaged through the remnants in a fabric shop until she found a length of cotton she might make into a summer shirt for Paul, and she had stopped off at Hy-Vee to buy his six-pack of Old Milwaukee. Nancy had bought nothing—had seemed to fall further and further into depression as she followed Helen past the rows of stores in the mall. She was a year or two younger, a small, solemn-eyed woman whose black hair was shot through with gray and whose skin was so pale as to seem translucent. Now she sat across from Helen, digging through her purse until she found a cigarette package with two cigarettes left. She offered one to Helen.

"No," Helen said. "Thank you." She had not smoked in nearly ten years; she didn't propose to start again.

"I don't know why that shopping mall upsets me," Nancy said. She lit the cigarette, then immediately set it to smolder in the ashtray.

"At least it was cool."

"I think it's something to do with all those children—those teeny-boppers, or whatever they call them now. How can they bear to—to just wander like that?"

"I suppose it's that they're young," Helen said.

The coffee arrived. She poured a little sugar into her spoon and stirred it into the cup.

"Do you think they look forward to anything?"

"I certainly hope so." She smiled at Nancy. Am I reassuring? she thought. "Doesn't everybody?"

"I wonder. Sometimes, evenings, I drive the highway into Waterloo, and I see those thirteen- and fourteen-year-old girls standing at the corners, leaning against the traffic-light poles. I swear—I almost know how they feel. Waiting for something. Not really knowing if they'll recognize it when it arrives."

"I think it's always a boy with a car," Helen said.

"And what scares me," Nancy said, "is maybe they're more like us than we give them credit for."

"No," Helen said. "For us it was a boy with a tractor."

"Isn't that the truth?" She stubbed out the unsmoked cigarette. "Do you ever try to imagine what life would be like if you hadn't married a farmer?"

"No. Not since the first two or three years."

"I do," Nancy said. "Dear God, I do."

Helen waited, but Nancy only looked down at the coffee cup cradled in her palms and shook her head.

"I've thought about being married to a different kind of farmer," Helen said. "I've thought, What if we kept hogs?"

She saw the shiver in Nancy's shoulders, hoping the movement meant laughter.

"Oh, Helen." Nancy raised her head. The barest trace of tears glistened at the corners of her eyes, but she was giggling. "Hogs, Helen. The smell, the dirt, the awful noises they make. And they eat people."

"Hog heaven," Helen said.

"Living high off the hogs," Nancy said. She got a handkerchief out of her purse and dabbed at her eyes. "Hog city." She subsided. "I'm sorry," she said. "You're such a funny person when you want to be."

"And sometimes I do want to be," Helen said. She glanced around the café. The men were still self-absorbed; the waitress was at the cash register, sorting through meal checks. "You have to be able to laugh at yourself—it's such a crazy way to live."

"This is the worst yet."

"I know. You can't think life is all strawberries and cream with Paul and me."

"I don't even get a civil sentence out of Harvey. I lie awake these hot nights and I think I'd rather be anywhere else, doing anything else. Anything."

"Years and years ago, when Sarah and Peter were both nutty about riding, I did use to think Paul and I could have made a good thing out of raising horses. The war in Vietnam was still on. Sarah had that wonderful quarter-horse Paul picked up at the sale barn in Waverly, and Peter talked us into buying him that huge gelding, Lopez, that was part quarter and part thoroughbred. Sixteen and a half hands. I thought we'd have to carry a stepladder so Peter could get up on him." She smiled, remembering. Why did the very though of horses make her sentimental? "Peter was ten or eleven, I can't think which."

"Sarah stayed with horses a long time," Nancy said.

"She had a year of college left when she finally decided she couldn't keep up with it, couldn't really give Cloud the care and the exercise."

"I'd forgotten what she called it."

"Red Cloud. He was a chestnut gelding." She picked up the check and looked at the numbers. "Sometimes I wish we'd gone into the horse business. The weather wouldn't affect us quite so much—I mean, it would affect feed prices, but it couldn't wipe us out."

"There's other things," Nancy said. "Like in Texas a few years back. Equine something. You recall they used to have that margarine commercial on the television, about not trying to fool Mother Nature? That's what's wrong with marrying a farmer, and it doesn't matter if you raise corn or beans or pigs or horses. You can't fool Mother Nature, but it's okay for Mother Nature to fool you."

"Why not let me buy the coffee?" Helen said.

In the pickup on the way home, they sang Girl Scout songs, and when Helen pulled into the Riker farmyard, Nancy reached out to give her a sweaty hug.

"You're always good for me," she told Helen. "You're the nicest person I know."

Just in the time since she had been at the mall, a portable sign had appeared in front of the Eriksens' produce stand:

SORRY CLOSED FOR THE SEASON

THANK YOU

GARDEN DRIED UP

The stand was shuttered tight; the fields beyond the Eriksen house and barn and tool shed were either brown or bare. She should tell Paul. He would shrug, look off into that space where he could not be followed.

She turned off the blacktop onto the county road. Inside the fences the fields of corn were brown, straggly, worthless. Only the ditches showed anything growing, and even the green weeds were faded under a thick coating of dust.

Nancy's misery was commonplace; they all felt it: What sort of life was it, that you could be fifty years old, a good mother, a patient wife, a strong worker, yet you had no more money, or leisure, or happiness than the day you chose the risk of marriage? Even the mailbox mocked her—its support made from an old plowshare painted vivid red, and the box in the shape of a barn with TOBLER printed on its sides as if her husband's name were no different than a billboard for Mail Pouch tobacco.

She stopped at the box. A pleasure-horse magazine she had never had the heart to cancel, even after Peter left home. A letter from her mother addressed in the failing hand that sent a chill of fear through her—if she let herself think about it. Paul's *Farm Journal.* She laid everything on the seat beside her.

Driving up the narrow lane to the house, she saw that the farmyard was crowded with young people on bicycles—perhaps a dozen of them, all on the flimsy "English" bikes of her childhood, fenderless, with hand brakes and skinny tires, the curious loop of chain at the rear axle, the high, pointed saddle seats that always looked too uncomfortable to be sat on. Some of the bikers wore white helmets that perched on top of their heads and strapped under their chins to make them look like hockey players or TV roller skaters. Boys or girls, they wore cutoffs that showed off their lanky, tanned legs, and sneakers without socks or colorful biking shoes with knee stockings; some of them had on T-shirts with slogans: "Scrambled Eggs and Beer—Not Just for Breakfast Anymore" or "Bikers Are Better Lovers." The girls had blond hair streaked from too much sunlight, and long, dark hair that flowed down to their narrow waists, and short, boyish cuts that caught in damp curls against their foreheads. Most of the men had moustaches or beards; they looked like brothers from an enormous family. Paul was in the midst of them, shouting, and Helen's heart sank. This had happened before, in April, when the bikers brought a petition asking support for a bike trail along the old Illinois Central right-of-way. Paul refused to sign, and long after the railroad had given the land to the county he was still furious—had tried to form a committee with other farmers, but gave up when Jess Eriksen accused him of wanting to lead "a goddamn bunch of vigilantes." Only Harvey Riker had been on Paul's side.

She parked the pickup in the shade of the barn and approached the group.

"I've got a living to make," she heard Paul say. "You think it makes me happy to see good farmland wasted?"

"It's already done," one of the bikers said. "The county's already made it a bike trail. All we're asking is for you to meet us halfway—respect our right to use it and help us protect it."

Now Helen could see they were not all young people. They were various ages—late teens to late thirties—and they were serious-faced, intent.

"A strip of land that size might make the difference between profit and loss for me someday," Paul said. "Next spring I've got to plant fence line to fence line. If this year doesn't put me in the poorhouse."

A bearded man nearby turned his front wheel toward Helen and winked. "Farmers," he said. "I've never met one yet that wasn't losing his shirt. They only keep farming because it's so much fun."

She wondered whether or not to be angry with him. "I'm his wife," she said. "You have to understand that he's telling the truth. That land was his—at least it was his grandfather's—before the railroad needed it."

"This is only about the bridge," the bearded man said, "the IC bridge over the West Fork. Some farmers out in Winthrop set fire to a bridge just like it, really wasted it. We're talking to all the farmers around here, asking them to keep an eye out for that kind of thing."

"My husband's not one of your fans," Helen said.

"We're not asking him to love us. Just live and let live."

Helen smiled at him, liking him. "That seems simple enough."

She went on to the house, put the mail on the table and

the six-pack into the refrigerator. The air in the kitchen was humid with canning heat. A solitary fly buzzed against one of the windows. "Wasted," the young man had said, and she wondered if he had been in Vietnam, one of the lucky ones who came back unhurt. She went upstairs and changed into a pair of blue shorts she would never have considered wearing outside the house and came back down to the kitchen. Paul was standing at the door, looking out. The bicyclists were just turning onto the gravel road, bent over their handlebars like jockeys, a glitter of sun dancing off their machines.

"What do you think of that?" Paul said.

"I think it was polite of them to talk to you."

"You know what's going to happen," he said. "Kids littering the place with trash from McDonald's, soda cans, candy wrappers. Wrecking the fences."

"They aren't all kids," she said. "Some of them are nearly as old as you or me."

"Second childhood," Paul said. "Then we'll have beer cans along with the soda cans, and condoms instead of candy wrappers."

He went to the refrigerator, took out one of the cans of beer she had just put in.

"That'll be warm," she said.

He opened it anyway. "What's a strip of dirt mean to somebody who can spend three, four hundred dollars on one of those fancy bicycles?" he said.

"Oh, Paul—" But words to argue with him wouldn't come—as if she couldn't betray him even when she wished to.

"I know," he said. He sat heavily and laid his cap on the table. "It isn't like me to bitch all the time."

"It's the drought," she said.

"It's everything. I chopped that field this morning and just got madder and madder. I thought, Five or six weeks from now we'll get a damned foot of rain, and it'll be too late. Just like this spring; so much rain I couldn't go into the fields to put the seed in."

He took a drink from the warm can and made a face. "What I know is, I need land one whole hell of a lot more than a bunch of overgrown babies on two-wheelers."

"You'll have the PIK money," she said.

"And that's a joke." He gave her a look that was nearly scornful. "I didn't have the brains to set aside that much, and anyway, it's the big company farms that'll rake in most of the PIK money, and the grain dealers that'll get rich, handling corn from five years ago all over again."

He set the beer can aside.

"It's the principle of the thing," he said. "President Franklin Pierce gave this land to my great-great-grandfather—the only decent thing the government ever did for the Tobler family. No one ought to ask me to give it up—not any of it."

"It's such a tiny bit."

"I don't care if it's no bigger than a postage stamp." He put on the cap and yanked its bill down over his eyes. "I'm going into town where the beer's cold," he said.

But the bike trail doesn't matter, she wanted to say, watching him climb into the cab of the pickup, hearing him grind the gears in frustration. It's the weather and the government both, and you can't beat either one of them.

For the rest of the day she tried to keep busy with odd jobs. She hauled the sealed mason jars down to the basement and shelved them alongside the green beans she had done the summer before. She thought about the young man who was probably a Vietnam veteran, and how fortunate it was that Peter had been too young for that war. She did the laundry, though she might have put it off another day or two, and got out the mending basket to do some odds and ends she had been saving for cooler weather. Once she looked up from sewing a shirt button to see that the light had changed sharply. Clouds, she imagined. In the excitement of thinking there might be rain, she went outside for a moment to look westward, but it was simply dust in the air.

It was not like Paul to solve his problems by drowning

them. To have a few drinks—that was all right, but he hated to be drunk, to feel he had given up control. What he liked—and it mostly amused her—was to clown with her, to giggle, make bad jokes, pat her buttocks. But lately—She could not say what had changed. Something that frightened her, a desperation, a willfulness. Dear heaven, if I can't put my mind on something pleasant, I'll start inventing trouble when there's already plenty to go around.

One summer, when the children were still young and at home, still interested enough in horses to feed and groom them as well as ride them, Helen took them to Kentucky, to the marvelous green expanse of the world around Lexington, to visit the horse farms. Paul had not gone—couldn't go, he said; the land needed him.

The second day she drove to Calumet Farm, still full of the pleasure of Walnut Hall the day before, where Sarah and Peter had driven a foreman crazy with questions. Walnut Hall didn't breed racehorses; the children—Peter especially—had begged Calumet, but when the three of them arrived at the Calumet gate they were stopped by a sign: NO VISITORS. Sarah took the matter calmly, acidly: "If they think they're too good for us, that's fine with me." Peter whined. Helen was disappointed. Beyond the forbidden entrance they could see white buildings trimmed in red, with red-roofed cupolas. "So near and yet so far," she said to Sarah.

In Lexington she tried to make up for the morning's failure by taking the children to a fancy restaurant, but there was no forgetting. Peter was impossible, Sarah merely petulant. After the dismal lunch she went to a public telephone and looked up the Calumet number in the book.

"I'm terribly sorry," said the woman who answered the phone, "Calumet Farm is open for persons in the horse business—not for tourists."

"I'm here with my two children," Helen said. "We drove all the way from Iowa. As it happens, we own a quarter-horse named Cloud and a part-thoroughbred named Lopez. Does that put us in the horse business?"

There had been a lovely silence.

"You all come on ahead," the woman said. "Park at the main office and I'll find a man to show you around."

Then they had been everywhere except the breeding barns—the stables, the tack rooms, the meadows surrounding. In Helen's memory the fences were an astonishing white, the trim of the buildings a dark, perfect red, the bluegrass deep and green. She and the children had reached through the rails to stroke the blazes of chestnut-colored yearlings with names engraved on brass plates riveted to their halter straps: Sunglint, Morning Sun—names she had never forgotten. And even grown up and scattered, Sarah and Peter remembered Citation, a Triple Crown winner—an enormous bay stallion, nearly twenty-five, shambling alongside his groom like a solemn old man lost in his memories. Years after, when she read of Citation's death, Helen had wanted to cry, had left the room so Paul wouldn't question her.

That wonderful summer. Traveling without Paul, coping with the two children, gaining them entry to a forbidden place. It had been the proudest and happiest event of all her married life.

She woke up in the black of night, alone in the bed. Paul's side had not been slept in; neither his warmth nor his reassuring man's smell was on the bedclothes. She imagined him sitting in the D-Town Tap, drinking beer and quarreling with the others—farmers, some of them, but laid-off factory workers too, and truckers between hauls—a small army of men whose occupations had lost their value or vanished entirely. Sensible family men getting drunk.

She looked at the alarm clock, on the nightstand on Paul's side of the bed. Its greenish-yellow hands showed nearly four o'clock. The Tap closed at two. If he'd gone off to play Pepper with his usual cronies, he would never have stayed out so late. He wasn't the sort to sit in a pickup on a back road and drink beer with a buddy—hadn't done such a thing since coming home from Korea, thirty years ago.

She got out of bed and went to the bathroom. In the harsh

glare of the overhead light she closed her eyes and touched the lids with her fingers. Her hands were hot on her cheeks; the nightgown clung to her back and sides. It used to be that you could depend on the nights to cool down. It used to be that you closed the doors so you and your husband could say silly words to each other in whispers that wouldn't alert the children—to what? To the secret that you cared more for each other than for weather and work?

She tidied herself, turned out the light, went through the hallway and gingerly down the front staircase. This year everything was weather. The sun, dry days, a crying need for rain. The dust would be far worse when the farmers in Kansas and Nebraska did their fall plowing. Then in late September and October she would notice the whole western sky dark orange—like the eerie approach of a tornado—and for days the tawny dust would be thick on everything: cars and trucks and machinery, windowsills and porch railings. When it rained—and finally it would pour, Paul was right—if you caught the rain in a bucket or pan it would be murky with Plains dirt. All those concerns lay between Paul and herself. Those and more: practical matters like credit at the Farm Fleet, credit for parts needed to overhaul the machinery in time for spring plowing and planting. And what to plant, how much to plant, what would the government do next? Helen understood without being able to tell Paul—in Paul's language—that what absorbed and frightened him likewise frightened her.

Dear Paul.

She felt her way down the front hall, unlatched the screen door and stepped onto the porch. A slight, warm breeze brushed across her face and bare arms, and sighed in the branches of the nearest ash. Too early for the robins. The night was almost black; there was no moon, but off to the east she saw the glow of light that was Waterloo, and south of that the lesser glow that must be Vinton, and due south from where she stood a throbbing of light she could not at first make sense of. It seemed to be—it was—where the old IC right-of-way met the West Fork. *Dear Paul.* She wanted the light to be—anything safe. A campfire, a bonfire tended by some of the college students having a kegger to celebrate the beginning of classes. False dawn.

She went back to bed to wait. Certainly she knew the old railroad bridge was burning, and her husband was too simple and direct not to have done it—probably with Harvey, the two of them drunk and angry after the Tap closed up. And how easy it would have been, how thorough. She had seen fence posts, kindled by spring fires set in the roadside ditches, that burned for days, slowly and to the heart, and she imagined the timbers of the bridge—black with creosote, dry with age—smoldering long after the fire-department volunteers had done all they knew to do. She could imagine the seeds of flame growing in the scars carved by axes and chisels when the bridge was built, and the charred wood steaming when the first rains touched it. Oh, the things we say we love, she told herself—dozing and waking in the stifling room—and the things we do to prove it.

She got up for good at six-thirty and made coffee from the Colombian beans, standing at the sink to watch the misty light dissipate in the fields. Paul was not home; there was no telling when he would appear, whether he would be sheepish or arrogant, whether he might have Harvey Riker with him—to soften the consequences of what he had done, the way a boy brings home a friend to shame his mother out of her anger. Yet she might be mistaken, jumping to wrong conclusions. And even if she were right, the worst of that was the way Paul would expect her to take his side, see his reasons, help him explain. He would never see that he was trying to lead her to a place where she ought not to follow. What should she do, she wondered, for this unhappy man?

When the sheriff's car came down the gravel road from the east, kicking up the dust that would add one more layer of white to the weed leaves and stems, Helen thought at first it was the Jehovah's Witness lady in the gold Cadillac. *As if I'd tell her what I really believe.* Then she saw the bubble of light on the roof and recognized the county shield on the front door. She watched the car stop near the tool shed;

watched the young deputy stride toward her in his morning-fresh khakis. *As if I'd tell anybody.*

This story was inspired by the burning of a bridge near Wilson's home in Iowa. To fill in the background of the story "I collected details from my students from farm families. That's how I found the game of Pepper; it's played around here." By creating a fully realized woman, who stands at the center of his story, Wilson accomplishes something that is often difficult for male writers. Why did he choose to write from a woman's viewpoint? "I felt a woman would provide a more sensitive filtering of the experience than the man." And did he know how the story would come out? "Yes, farmers' wives are always loyal."

Born in Maine, Robley Wilson, Jr., has lived for the past twenty-three years in Iowa, where he is editor of the North American Review *and* Iowa Woman, *quarterlies of fiction and poetry. His stories can be found in three works of short fiction:* The Pleasures of Manhood, Living Alone, *and* Dancing for Men, *which won the 1982 Drue Heinz Award.*

He teaches at the University of Northern Iowa.

First published in 1985 in The Sewanee Review.

ALICE ADAMS

SINTRA

In Lisbon, Portugal, on a brilliant October Sunday morning, an American woman, a tourist, experiences a sudden rush of happiness, as clear and pure as the sunshine that warms the small flowers near her feet. She is standing in the garden of the Castel San Jorgio, and the view before her includes a great spread of the city: the river and its estuary, the shining new bridge; she can see for miles!

Her name is Arden Kinnell, and she is a journalist, a political-literary critic, sometimes writing on films; she survives somewhat precariously, although recently she has begun to enjoy a small success. Tall and thin, Arden is a little awkward, shy, and her short blond hair is flimsy, rather childlike. Her face is odd, but striking in its oddity: such wide-spaced, staring, yellow-green eyes, such a wide, clearly sensual mouth. And now she is smiling, out of sheer pleasure at this moment.

Arden and her lover-companion—Gregor, the slightly rumpled young man at her side—arrived the night before from Paris, and they slept long and well, after only a little too much wine at their hotel. Healthy Californians, they both liked the long, rather steep walk up those winding, cobbled streets, through the picturesquely crumbling, red-tile roofed old quarter, the Alfama, up to this castle, this view of everything. Arden is especially struck by the sight of the distant, lovely bridge, which she has read was dedicated to the revolution of April 1974, the so-called Generals' Revolution that ended fascism in Portugal.

The air is so good, so fresh and clear! Breathing in, Arden thinks, Ah, Lisbon, how beautiful it is. She thinks, I must tell Luiz how much I like his city.

Madness: in that demented instant she has forgotten that at a recent party in San Francisco a woman told her that Luiz was dying (was "terminal," as she put it). Here in Lisbon. Now.

And even stranger than that friendly thought of Luiz, whom she once loved wildly, desperately, entirely—dear God, friends is the last thing they were; theirs was an adversary passion, almost fatal—stranger than the friendly impulse is the fact that it persists, in Arden, generally a most disciplined woman; her mind is—usually—strong and clear, her habits of work exemplary. However, *insanely*, there in Lisbon, that morning, as she continues to admire and to enjoy the marvelous sweep of city roofs, the graceful bridge above the shining water, she even feels the presence of Luiz, and happily; that is the incredible part. Luiz, with whom she experienced the wildest reaches of joy, but never the daily, sunny warmth of happiness.

Can Luiz possibly just that day have died? Can this lively blue Portuguese air be giving her that message, and thus causing her to rejoice? Quickly she decides against this: Luiz is not dead, he cannot be—although a long time ago she surely wished him dead, believing as she then did that only his death could release her from the brutal pain of his absence in her life.

Or, could the woman at the San Francisco party (a woman whom she did not like at all, Arden now remembers—so small and tautly chic), could that woman have been mistaken? Some other Luiz V. was dying in Lisbon? But that was unlikely; the woman clearly meant the person that Arden knew, or had known—the rich and well-connected, good but not very famous painter. The portraitist.

Then, possibly Luiz was ill but has recovered? A remission, or possibly a misdiagnosis in the first place? Everyone knows that doctors make such mistakes; they are often wrong.

Arden decides that Luiz indeed is well; he is well and somewhere relatively nearby, in some house or apartment that she can at least distantly see from where she is standing, near the crenellated battlements of the castle, on the sun-warmed yellow gravel. She looks back down into the Alfama, where Luiz might be.

Gregor, the young lover—only five years younger than Arden, actually—Gregor, a photographer, "knows" about Luiz. Friends before they became lovers (a change in status that more than once has struck Arden as an error), in those days Arden and Gregor exchanged life stories, finding that they shared a propensity for romantic disaster—along with their similarly precarious free-lance professions. (And surely there is some connection? Both she and Gregor take romantic as well as economic risks?)

"Can you imagine a woman dumb enough to believe that a Portuguese Catholic would leave his wife and children just for her?" Arden asked, in the wry mode that had become a useful second nature to her. "Oh, how stupid I was!" she lamentingly laughed. And Gregor countered with his own sad love adventure; she was a model, Lisa. "Well, can you imagine a photographer who wouldn't know not to take up with a model?" This was when Gregor, just out of art school, was trying to get a start in New York; Lisa, though younger than he, was already doing quite well. But Lisa's enchanting liveliness, and her wit, as well as her lovely thin body, turned out to be coke-maintained. "No one then was doing anything but plain old dope and a little acid," was Gregor's comment. "I have to hand it to her, she was really ahead of her time. But *crazy*."

Gregor too can be wry, or does he imitate Arden? She sometimes has an alarmed sense that he sounds like her, or tries to. But he is fun to talk to, still, and often funny. And he is smart, and sexy. Tall and light-haired, he is not handsome but very attractive, with his huge pale Russian eyes, his big confident body. A good photographer; in fact, he is excellent.

At moments, though, Arden feels a cold enmity from Gregor, which is when she wishes that they were still "just friends." And is he an alcoholic, really? He drinks too much, too often. And does he love her?

Oh, *love*, Arden thinks. How can I even use that word.

Gregor and Arden do not in fact live together, and although she sometimes tells friends that she considers this an ideal arrangement, often she actually does not. Her own house in Larkspur is small, but hardly too small for two, and it is pleasantly situated on a wooded knoll, no other houses in sight. There is a pool, and what Arden considers her recreational garden, an eccentric plot all crowded with squash and nasturtiums and various lettuces. Gregor spends much of his time there with her—he likes to swim, although gardening does not interest him—but he also keeps a small place of his own on a rather bleak street near Twin Peaks, in San Francisco, high up in the fog and winds. And his apartment itself is bleak: three small rooms, monastically clean and plain and white. There is also a darkroom, of course, where he often works late at night. No personal traces anywhere, no comfortable mess. Forbidding. Arden has been there only twice. Even when they are in the city it always seems better to drive on back to Larkspur, after the movie or concert, whatever. But Arden thinks of him there, in those rooms, on the nights that he stays in town, and her thoughts are uneasy. Not only the existence of that apartment, an alternative to her house, as well as to herself, but its character is threatening to Arden, reminding her of aspects of Gregor himself: a sensed interior coldness, an implacable emptiness. When she thinks of Gregor's house she could be imagining an enemy.

She has never seen any food around, for instance: does he only drink there, alone, in his white, white rooms? She does not imagine that he sees other women, but certainly he could. He could go out to bars, bring women home. This, though, seems less likely, and therefore possibly less threatening than just drinking alone, so grimly.

At the end of Arden's love affair with Luiz there were hints in local gossip columns that he had a "somewhat less than professional relationship" with a few of the subjects of his portraits, and the pain of this information (explaining so much! so plausible!) was a further unbearable thrust to Arden.

In any case, since Gregor knows about Luiz, including the fact of Lisbon, home of Luiz (but not the possible mortal illness; Arden has not been able or perhaps not seen fit to mention this), does Gregor think it strange that so far in Lisbon Arden has not mentioned Luiz, whom she used sometimes to talk about? Here she has not once said his name, in any context. She herself does not quite know why she has not.

Still, just now she is happy, looking down to small balconies of flowers, of vines that climb up on intricate iron grillwork. She wonders: Possibly, is that where Luiz lives, that especially handsome, long-windowed apartment? With the dark gray drapery?

Arden is happy and well and suddenly very hungry. She says to Gregor, "Isn't that a restaurant over there? Shouldn't we try it? It looks nice, and I can't bear to leave this view."

"Well, sure." Gregor's look in Arden's direction is slightly puzzled—as well it might be, Arden thinks. She too is puzzled, very. She loves Lisbon, though, and her blood races dizzily.

They go into the restaurant; they are quickly seated at a white-clothed table, with the glorious Lisbon view.

"Had you ever, uh, heard about this place before?" asks Gregor, once their wine has come. This is his closest—if oblique—reference to Luiz, who surely might have mentioned to Arden a favorite restaurant, with its marvelous view. But as though realizing what he has done Gregor then covers up. "Or did you read about it somewhere? a restaurant guide?"

"No, actually not. It just looked good. The doors—" The front door is of heavy glass, crossed with pitted, old-looking iron bars. "An interesting use of glass, don't you think?"

"Yes," says Gregor.

They regard one another suspiciously.

Remembering Luiz, Arden sees flat smooth black hair, that shines, in bedside lamplight. She watches him as he dresses, while she lies there spent and languid; she watches everything shining, his hair and his bright black eyes, their dark glitter. He comes over to kiss her good-bye, for that day, and then he cannot, does not leave.

"This is an illness, this endless craving that I have for you. A mania—" Luiz more than once remarked, with an accuracy that Arden could not then admit to herself. She did not feel ill, only that all her nerves had been touched, involved.

Luiz is (or was) an excellent portraitist. His paintings were both elegant and penetrating, often less than flattering; on the other hand, on occasion, very flattering indeed. He was at his best with women (well, of course he was, Arden has thought). Once she went to an exhibit of his paintings at a Sutter Street gallery—though not, naturally, to the opening, a social event much reported in the papers.

In fact they first met at a gallery opening. From across the room Luiz found Arden (that is how he put it, "I *found* you there"), coming over to talk to her intently for a while (about what? later she could never remember). He called the next day; he called and called, he would not be put off.

This was in the early sixties. Arden, then much involved in the peace movement, saw his assault on her life as an incursion, an invasion. He attacked with superior weapons, and with the violence of his passion for her. And he won. "I think that you have fallen in love with my love for you," he once (again accurately) remarked.

Out of her depth, and dismayed by everything about Luiz—the wife and family at home in Portugal, a Fascist country—Arden found some small comfort in the fact that all his favorite writers seemed to be of the left: Silone, Camus—and that his favorite movie director was Pasolini.

She pointed this out, rather shyly—the shyness of an essentially defeated person.

"My darling, I have a horror of the right, of *fascisme.*" (But in much the same tone he also said, "I have a horror of *fat,*" as he stroked her thin thigh, then cupped the sharp crest with his wise and skillful hand.)

You could simply look at his eyes, or his mouth, Arden thinks now, and know that Luiz was remarkable.

She remembers his walk. The marvelous confidence in that stride. During all the weeks of suffering so acutely from his absence in her life (classically, Luiz did not get the promised divorce, nor did he defect from the Fascist government he railed against; he went back to Lisbon, to his wife, to that regime)—during all that time of suffering, it was the thought of his walk that caused Arden the most piercing pain: that singular, energetic motion of his body, its course through the world, without her.

After lunch, much more slowly than earlier they had climbed the streets, Arden and Gregor start down. The day is still glorious; at one point they stop at a small terrace where there are rounded cypresses, very small, and a lovely wall of soft blue tiles, in an intricate, fanciful design—and a large and most beautiful view of sky and majestic, glossy white clouds, above the shimmering water of the sea. From this distance the commemorative suspension bridge is a graceful sculpture; catching the sunlight, it shines.

Arden is experiencing some exceptional, acute alertness; as though layers of skin had peeled away, all her senses are opened wide. She sees, in a way that she never has before. She feels all the gorgeous day, the air, and the city spread below her.

She hardly thinks of Gregor, at her side, and this is something of a relief; too often he is a worrying preoccupation for her.

Their plan for the afternoon has been to go back to their hotel, where they have left a rental car, and to drive north to Cascais, Estoril, and Sintra. And that is what they now proceed to do, not bothering to go into the hotel but just taking their car, a small white Ford Escort, and heading north.

As they reach the outskirts of the city, a strange area of new condominiums, old shacks, and some lovely, untouched woods—just then, more quickly than seemed possible, the billowing clouds turn black, a strong wind comes up, and in another minute a violent rainstorm has begun, rains lashing at the windshield, water sweeping across the highway.

Arden and Gregor exchange excited grins: an adventure. She thinks, Oh, good, we are getting along, after all.

"Maybe we should just go to Sintra, though," he says, a little later. "Not too much point in looking at beach resorts?"

Yielding to wisdom, Arden still feels a certain regret. *Cascais.* She can hear Luiz saying the word, and *Estoril*, with the sibilant Portuguese *s*'s. But she can also hear him saying *Sintra*, and she says it over to herself, in his voice.

A little later, looking over at her, Gregor asks, "Are you okay? You look sort of funny."

"How, funny?"

"*Odd.* You look odd. And your nose. It's so, uh, pink."

Surprising them both, and especially herself, Arden laughs. "Noses are supposed to be pink," she tells him.

Normally, what Arden thinks of as Gregor's lenslike observations make her nervous; they make her feel unattractive, and unloved. But today—here in Portugal!—her strange happiness separates her like a wall, or a moat, from possible slights, and she thinks, How queer that Gregor should even notice the color of my nose, in a driving rainstorm—here, north of Lisbon, near Sintra. As, in her mind, she hears the deep, familiar, never-forgotten voice of Luiz saying, "I adore your face! Do you *know* how I adore it? How lovely you are?" She hears Luiz, she sees him.

Then quite suddenly, as suddenly as it began the storm is over. The sky is brilliantly blue again, and the clouds are white, as Arden thinks, No wonder Luiz is more than a little erratic—it's the weather. And she smiles to herself.

Suppose she sent him a postcard from Lisbon? *Ego absolvo te.* Love, Arden.

Would he laugh and think fondly of her, for a moment?

Is he dying?

In Sintra they drive past a small town square, with a huge, rather forbidding municipal building, some small stores. The wet stone pavement is strewn with fallen wet yellow leaves. They start up a narrow road, past gates and driveways that lead to just-not-visible mansions, small towered castles. (The sort of places that Luiz might visit, or own, for weekends, elegant parties.) As they climb up and up in the small white car, on either side of the road the woods become thicker, wilder, more densely and violently green—everything green, every shape and shade of green, all rain-wet, all urgently growing. And giant rocks, great dead trees lying beside them. Ferns, enormously sprouting. Arden is holding her breath, forgetting to breathe. It is crazy with green, she thinks, crazy growth, so old and strong, ancient, endless and wild, ferocious. Like Luiz. Like Portugal, dying.

Gregor is making some odd maneuver with the car; is he turning around, midroad? Trying to park, among so many giant rocks, heavy trees, and brilliant, dripping leaves?

In any case he has stopped the car. On a near hill Arden can see the broken ruins of a castle, jagged black fragments of stone, and in the sky big clouds are blackening again.

Willing calm (though still having trouble with her breath), Arden says, "I think it's going to rain again."

Huge-eyed, pale, Gregor is staring across at her. He says, "You cut me out—all the way! You might as well be here alone!"

He is right, of course; she is doing just that, pretending he is not there. So unfair—but his staring eyes are so light, so *blue.* Arden says, "I'm sorry, really—" but she can feel her voice getting away from her, can feel tears.

Gregor shouts, "I don't know why we came here! Why Portugal? What did you expect? You could have just come by yourself!"

But Arden can hardly hear him. The rain has indeed begun again; it is pelting like bullets against the glass, and wind is bending down all the trees, flattening leaves.

And suddenly in those moments Arden has understood that Luiz is dead—and that she will never again feel for anyone what she felt for him. Which, even though she does not want to—she would never choose to feel so much again—still, it seems a considerable loss.

In fact, though, at that particular time, the hour of that passionate October storm (while Arden quarreled with Gregor), Luiz is still alive, although probably "terminal." And she learns of his death only the following spring, and then more or less by accident: she is in Washington, D.C., for some meetings having to do with grants for small magazines and presses, and in a hasty scanning of the *Post* she happens to glance at a column headed "Deaths Elsewhere."

Luiz— —V. (There were two intervening names that Arden has not known about.) Luiz V. had died a few days earlier in Lisbon, the cause of death not reported. Famous portraitist, known for satire, and also (this is quite as surprising to Arden as the unfamiliar names)—"one of the leading intellectuals in Lisbon to voice strong public support for the armed forces coup in April 1974 that ended half a century of right-wing dictatorship."

Curiously—years back she would not have believed this possible, ever—that day Arden is too busy with her meetings to think about this fact: Luiz dead. No longer someone she might possibly see again, by accident in an airport, or somewhere. No longer someone possibly to send a postcard to.

That day she is simply too busy, too harried, really, with so many people to see, and with getting back and forth from her hotel to her meetings, through the strange, unseasonable snow that has just begun, relentlessly, to fall. She thinks of the death of Luiz, but she does not absorb it.

That quarrel with Gregor in Sintra, which prolonged itself over the stormy drive back to Lisbon, and arose, refueled, over dinner and too much wine—that quarrel was not final between them, although Arden has sometimes thought that it should have been. They continue to see each other, Arden and Gregor, in California, but considerably less often than they used to. They do not quarrel; it is as though they were no longer sufficiently intimate to fight, as though they both knew that any altercation would indeed be final.

Arden rather thinks, or suspects, that Gregor sees other women, during some of their increasing times apart. She imagines that he is more or less actively looking for her replacement. Which, curiously, she is content to let him do.

She herself has not been looking. In fact lately Arden has been uncharacteristically wary in her dealings with men. In her work she is closely allied with a lot of men, who often become good friends, her colleagues and companions. However, recently she has rather forcibly discouraged any shifts in these connections; she has chosen to ignore or to put down any possible romantic overtones. She spends time with women friends, goes out to dinner with women, takes small trips. She is quite good at friendship, has been Arden's conclusion, or one of them. Her judgment as to lovers seems rather poor. And come to think of it her own behavior in that area is not always very good. Certainly her strangeness, her removal in Lisbon, in Sintra, was quite enough to provoke a sensitive man, which Gregor undoubtedly is.

On that night, the night of reading the news item (Deaths Elsewhere) containing the death of Luiz—that night Arden is supposed to meet a group of friends in a Georgetown restaurant. At eight. In character, she gets there a little early, and is told that she will be seated as soon as her friends arrive; would she like to wait in the bar?

She would not, especially, but she does so anyway, going into a dark, paneled room, of surpassing anonymity, and seating herself in a shadowed corner from which new arrivals in the restaurant are visible. She orders a Scotch, and then wonders why; it is not her usual drink, she has not drunk Scotch for years.

By eight-ten she has begun to wonder if perhaps she confused the name of the restaurant. It was she who made the reservation, and her friends could have gone to some other place, with a similar French name. These friends like herself are always reliably on time, even in snow, strange weather.

The problem of what to do next seems almost intolerable, suddenly—and ridiculously: Arden has surely coped with more serious emergencies. But: should she try to get a cab, which at this crowded dinner hour, in the snow, would be difficult? And if she did where would she go?

In the meantime, at eight-twenty, she orders another drink, and she begins to think about the item in the paper. About Luiz.

Odd, she casually thinks, at first, that she should have "adored" a man—have planned to marry a man whose full name she did not know. And much more odd, she thinks, that he should have publicly favored the '74 revolution, the end of dictatorship. Opportunism, possibly, Arden first thinks. On the other hand, is she being unfair, unnecessarily harsh? He did always describe himself as anti-Fascist. And perhaps that was true?

Perhaps everything he said to her was true?

Arden has finished her second drink. It is clear that her friends will not come; they have gone somewhere else by mistake, and she must decide what to do. But still she sits there, as though transfixed, and she is transfixed, by a sudden nameless pain. Nameless, but linked to loss: loss of Luiz, even, imminently, of Gregor. Perhaps of love itself.

Understanding some of this, in a hurried, determined way Arden gets to her feet and summons the bill from her waiter. She has decided that she will go back to her hotel and order a sandwich in her room. Strange that she didn't think of that before. Of course she will eventually get a cab, even in the steadily falling, unpredicted snow.

This story, Alice Adams says, is a particular favorite because "it was torn from my heart." It's a story also that has evoked an unusual number of responses from readers telling her "that's my *story." Asked if time and its abyss is a theme that interests her in fiction, she answers, "That's what I try to show in all my stories. Because I don't believe that any of us ever really gets over anything."*

Adams was born in Fredericksburg, Virginia, and graduated from Radcliffe College. Her stories have appeared in the O. Henry Prize Stories *many times, and her collections of short fiction include* Beautiful Girl, To See You Again, *and* Return Trips. *Her novels include* Careless Love, Families and Survivors, Listening to Billie, Rich Rewards, *and* Superior Women. *She now lives in San Francisco.*

First published in 1985 in Grand Street.

GAIL GOODWIN

OVER THE MOUNTAIN

If you have grown to love your life, it seems ungrateful to belabor old injustices, especially those that happened in childhood, that place of sheltered perspectives where you were likely to wake up and go to bed without anyone ever disabusing you of your certainty that all days were planned around you. After all, isn't it possible that the very betrayal that flags your memory and constricts your heart led to a development in character that enabled you to forge your present life?

This is not a belaboring. I know by now that behind every story that begins "When I was a child" there exists another story in which adults are fighting for their lives. It is because I accept this that I am ready to go back and fill in some of the blank spaces in the world of a ten-year-old girl whose mother takes her on an overnight train journey. The train carries them out of their sheltered mountains to a town some thousand feet below. The mother and daughter walk around this town, whose main attraction is that the mother spent her happy girlhood years there. The mother and her little girl stay the night in a respectable boardinghouse. The next day, they get on the northbound version of yesterday's train and go back to the mountains.

Why do I remember nothing particular about that journey? I, with my usually prodigious memory for details? Except for a quality of light and atmosphere—the lowland town throbbed with a sociable, golden-yellow heat that made people seem closer, whereas our mountain town had a cool, separating blue air that magnified distances—I have no personal images of this important twenty-four hours. I say important because it was a landmark in my life: it was the first time I had gone away alone with my mother.

Despite the fact that I believe I now know why that excursion lies blank among my memory cells, there is something worth exploring here. The feeling attached to that event, even today, signals the kind of buried affect that shapes a life.

We were not, our little unit of three, your ordinary "nuclear" family, but, as I had known nothing else, we seemed normal enough to me. Our living arrangements were somewhat strange for a trio of females with high conceptions of their privileges in society, but, as my grandmother hastened to tell people, it was because of the war. And when the war ended, and all the military personnel who had preempted the desirable dwellings had departed from town, and we continued to stay where we were, I accepted my mother's and grandmother's continual reminders that "it was only a matter of time now until the right place could be found."

The three of us slept in one gigantic room, vast enough to swallow the two full-sized Persian carpets that had once covered my grandmother's former living room and dining room and still reproach us with its lonely space, even when we filled it with all the furniture from the two bedrooms of her previous home. The rest of her furniture crowded our tiny living room and dark, windowless kitchen and then spilled out into the shabby public entrance hall of our building, euphemistically called "the lobby" by our landlord and my grandmother. My grandmother spent a lot of time trying to pounce on a tenant in the act of sitting on "our" sofa in the lobby, or winding up "our" old Victrola. She would rush out of our apartment like a fury and explain haughtily that this furniture did not belong to the lobby, it was our furniture, only biding its time in this limbo until it could be resettled into the sort of room to which it was accustomed. She actually told one woman, whom she caught smoking while sitting on "our" sofa, to please "consider this furniture invisible in the future." The woman ground out her cigarette on the floor, told my grandmother she was crazy, and went upstairs.

Our building was still known in town by its old name: The Piping Hot. During the twenties, when Asheville overflowed with land-boom speculators and relatives visiting TB patients, this brown-shingled monstrosity had been thrown up on a lot much too small for it. It had come into existence as a commercial establishment whose purpose was to make money on not-too-elegant people willing to settle for a so-so room and a hot "home-cooked" meal. Therefore, it had none of those quaint redeeming features of former private residences fallen on hard times. The reason our bedroom was so huge was simple: it had been the dining room.

It was a pure and simple eyesore, our building: coarse, square, and mud-colored, it hulked miserably on its half acre with the truculent insecurity of a social interloper. It was a building you might feel sorry for if you were not so busy feeling sorrier for yourself for living in it. Probably the reason its construction had been tolerated at all on that leafy, genteel block was because its lot faced the unsightly physical plant of the proud and stately Manor Hotel, which rambled atop its generous acreage on the hill across the street; moreover, the guests at the Manor were prevented by their elevation from seeing even the roof of the lowlier establishment. Our landlord had bought Piping Hot when it went out of business just before the war, chopped it up into as many "apartments" as he could get away with legally, and now collected the rents. Whenever he was forced to drop by, breathless and red-faced, a wet cigar clamped in one corner of his mouth, he would assure my grandmother he had every intention of sowing grass in the bare front yard, of having someone come and wash the filthy windows of the lobby, of cutting down the thorny bushes with their suspicious red berries that grew on either side of the squatty, brown-shingled "shelter" at the sidewalk's edge, where Negro maids often sat down to rest on their way to the bus stop from the big houses at the upper end of the street.

The most "respectable" tenants lived on the ground floor,

which must have been some consolation to my grandmother. The Catholic widow, Mrs. Gannon, and her two marriageable daughters lived behind us in a rear apartment which had been made over from pantries and half of the old kitchen. (Our kitchen had been carved out of the other half.) When my grandmother or Mrs. Gannon felt like chatting, either had only to tap lightly on the painted-over window above her sink; they would gossip about the upstairs tenants while snapping beans or peeling potatoes at their facing sinks. The apartment across the lobby was inhabited by another widow, the cheerful Mrs. Rhinehart, who went limping off to work in a china shop every day; her numerous windowsills (her apartment was the Piping Hot's ex-sunporch) were crowded with delicate painted figurines. She suffered from a disease that made one leg twice the width of the other. Among the three widows existed a forbearing camaraderie. Mrs. Rhinehart did not like to gossip, but she always stopped and listened pleasantly if my grandmother waylaid her in the lobby; and, though both my grandmother and Mrs. Gannon thought Mrs. Rhinehart had too many little objects in her windows for good taste, they always amended that, at any rate, she was a brave lady for standing in a shop all day on that leg; and when sailors trekked regularly past our side windows on the way to call on the Gannon girls, my grandmother did not allow her imagination to run as wild as she would have if those same sailors had been on their way to one of the apartments upstairs.

Except for the policeman and his wife, whose stormy marital life thudded and crashed directly above our bedroom, the other upstairs apartments were filled with people my grandmother referred to simply as "the transients." They didn't stay long. You would have to be pretty desperate to stay long in those rear upstairs apartments, which were weird amalgams of former guest rooms, opening into hallways or one another in inconvenient, embarrassing ways, their afterthought bathrooms and kitchens rammed into ex-closets and storage rooms. We didn't even bother to learn their names, those constantly changing combinations of women, of women and children and the occasional rare man, who occupied those awkward upper quarters. They were identified merely by their affronts: the two working girls who clopped around most of the night in their high heels; the woman with the little boy who had written the dirty word in chalk on the sidewalk shelter; the woman who sat down on "our" sofa and stomped out her cigarette on the floor.

Those were the politics of our building. There were also, within our family unit, the politics of my mother's job, the politics of my school, and the subtler triangular dynamics that underpinned life in our apartment.

"Today has been too much for my nerves," my grandmother would say as we huddled over her supper at one end of our giant mahogany dining table which, even with its center leaf removed, took up most of the kitchen. "I was out in the lobby trying to wipe some of the layers of dust off those windows when I happened to look out and there was that little boy about to eat some of the berries on those poison bushes. I rushed out to warn him, only to have his mother tell me she didn't want him frightened. Would she rather have him frightened or dead? Then, not five minutes later, the LaFarges' Negro maid came along and sat down in our shelter and I happened to see her hike her dress up and her stockings were crammed with eggs. I had to debate with myself whether I shouldn't let the LaFarges know. . . ."

"I hope you didn't," said my mother, rolling her eyes at me in that special way which my grandmother was not meant to see.

"No. You have to let them get away with murder if you're going to keep them. I remembered that. Do you remember Willy Mae, when we lived in Greenville?"

My mother laughed. Her voice was suddenly younger and she looked less tired. Greenville was the town on the other side of the mountain where, in a former incarnation, she had lived as a happy, protected young girl. But then a thought pinched her forehead, crimping the smoothness between her deep blue eyes. "I do wish that ass Dr. Busey could see through that snake Lu Ann Leach," she said.

"Kathleen. Lower your voice."

My mother gave an exasperated sigh and sent me a signal: We've got to get out of here. After supper we'll go to the drugstore.

"He hasn't said anything about her staying on at the college, has he?" asked my grandmother *sotto voce,* casting her eyes balefully towards the painted-over window above our sink behind which even a good friend like Mrs. Gannon might be straining to hear how other people's daughters were faring in this uncertain world without a man.

"No, but he hasn't said anything about her leaving, and now she's taken over the literary magazine. She was only supposed to fill in for Miss Pennell's operation and Miss Pennell has been back three weeks. The college can't afford to keep all three of us. There aren't that many students taking English. All the GIs want their math and science so they can go out and make *money.*"

"Well, they have to keep you," declared my grandmother, drawing herself up regally.

"They don't have to do anything, Mother." My mother was losing her temper.

"What I mean is," murmured my grandmother in a conciliatory manner to ward off a "scene" which might be overheard, "they will naturally want to keep you, because you're the only one with your M.A. I'm so thankful that Poppy lived long enough so we could see you through your good education."

"You should see the way she plays up to him," my mother went on, as if she hadn't heard. "She has that plummy, little-girl way of talking, and she asks his *advice* before she'll even go to the bathroom. If she weren't a Leach, people couldn't possibly take her seriously; she couldn't get a job in a kindergarten."

"If only Poppy had lived," moaned my grandmother, "you would never have had to work."

"My work is all I've *got,*" blurted my mother passionately. "I mean, besides you two, of course."

"Of course," agreed my grandmother. "I only meant if he had lived. Then we could have had a nice house, and you could have worked if you wanted."

My mother's eyes got round, the way they did when someone had overlooked an important fact. She was on the verge of saying more, but then with an effort of her shoulders harnessed her outburst. She sat with her eyes still rounded, but cast down, breathing rapidly through her nostrils. I thought she looked lovely at such times.

"Can we walk to the drugstore and look at the magazines?" I asked.

"If you like," she said neutrally. But, as soon as my grandmother rose to clear the dishes, she sneaked me a smile.

"The thing is, no matter how much I wipe at those lobby windows from the inside," my grandmother said, as much to herself as to us, "they can never be clean. They need to be washed from the outside by a man. Until they are, we will be forced to look through dirt."

"It was on the tip of my tongue to say, 'If you stay *out* of the lobby you won't have to worry about the dirt,' " my mother told me as we walked to the drugstore a block away.

"That would have been perfect!" I cried, swinging her hand. "Oh, why *didn't* you?" I was a little overexcited, as I always was when the two of us finally made it off by ourselves. Here we were, escaped together at last, like two sisters from an overprotective mother. Yet even as the spring dusk purpled about our retreating figures, we both knew she was watching us from the window: she would be kneeling in the armchair, her left hand balancing her on the windowsill, her right hand discreetly parting the white curtains; she could watch us all the way to our destination. She had left the lights off in the apartment, to follow us better.

"It would have been cruel," my mother said. "That lobby is her outside world."

Though complaining about my grandmother often drew us closer, I could see my mother's point. It was not that we didn't love her; it was that the heaviness of her love confined us. She worried constantly that something would happen to us. She thought up things, described them aloud in detail, which sometimes ended up scaring us all. (The mother of the little boy about to eat the berry had been right.)

We had reached the corner of our block. As we waited for a turning car to go by, we looked up and saw the dining-room lights of the Manor Hotel twinkling at us. The handful of early spring guests would just be sitting down to eat.

I looked up at one of the timbered gables. "There's nobody in Naomi Benjamin's room yet," I said.

"The season will be starting soon. All the rooms will be filled. But never again will I ever write *anybody's* autobiography. Unless I write my own someday."

My mother and grandmother had been so excited last summer when Naomi Benjamin, an older woman from New York who had come to our mountains for her health, offered my mother five hundred dollars to "work with her on her autobiography." Someone at the Manor had told Naomi that my mother was a published writer, and she had come down from the hill to call on us at The Piping Hot and make her offer. We were impressed by her stylish clothes and her slow, gloomy way of expressing herself, as if the weight of the world lay behind her carefully chosen words. But, before the end of the summer, my mother was in a rage. Sometimes, after having "worked with" Naomi Benjamin all afternoon, and after typing up the results at night, my mother would lie back and rant while my grandmother applied a cold washcloth to her head and told her she was not too young to get a stroke. "A stroke would be something *happening*," snarled my mother, "whereas not a damn thing has happened to that woman; how dare she aspire to autobiography!" "Well, she is Jewish," reflected my grandmother. "They never have an easy time." "Ha!" spat my mother. "That's what I thought. I thought I'd learn something interesting about other ways of suffering, but there's not even that. I'd like to tell her to take her five hundred dollars and buy herself some excitement. That's what she really needs." "Kathleen, tension can burst a blood vessel. . . . " "I wish to God I could make it up," my mother ranted on, growing more excited, "at least I wouldn't be dying of boredom!" "I'm going to phone her right now," announced my grandmother, taking a new tack; "I'm going to tell her you're too sick to go on." "No, no, no!" My mother sprang up, waving the cold cloth aside. "It's all right. I'm almost finished. Just let me go walk up and down the street for a while and clear my head."

We had reached the drugstore in the middle of the next block, our oasis of freedom. We passed into its brightly lit interior, safe for a time behind brick walls that even my grandmother's ardent vision could not penetrate. Barbara, the pharmacist, was doing double duty behind the soda fountain, but when she looked up and saw it was us she went on wiping the counter; she knew that, despite her sign (THESE MAGAZINES ARE FOR *BUYING*, NOT FOR BROWSING), we would first go and look through the pulp magazines to see if there was any new story by Charlotte Ashe. But we always conducted our business as quickly and unobtrusively as possible, so as not to set a bad example for other customers; we knew it pained Barbara to see her merchandise sinking in value with each browser's fingerprints, even though she admired my mother and was in on the secret that Charlotte Ashe's name had been created from the name of this street and the first half of the name of our town.

There was no new story by Charlotte Ashe. It was quite possible all of them had appeared by now, but my mother did not want to spoil our game. It had been a while since Charlotte Ashe had mailed off a story. During the war, when my mother worked on the newspaper, it had been easier to slip a paragraph or two of fiction into the typewriter on a slow-breaking news day. But now the men had come home, to reclaim their jobs at the newspaper, and fill up the seats in the classroom where my mother taught; there was less time and opportunity to find an hour alone with a typewriter and let one's romantic imagination soar—within the bounds of propriety, of course.

We sat down at the counter. It would not do to make Barbara wait on us in a booth. She was, for all her gruff tones, the way she pounced on children who tried to read the comic books, the pharmacist. As if to emphasize this to customers who might confuse her with a mere female employee, Barbara wore trousers and neckties and took deep, swinging strides around her store; she even wore men's shoes.

"Kathleen, what'll you have?"

"A Coke, please, Barbara, for each of us. Oh, and would you put a tiny squirt of ammonia in mine? I've got a headache coming on."

"How tiny?" Barbara's large hand with its close-clipped nails hovered over the counter pump that discharged ammonia.

"Well, not too tiny."

Both women laughed. Barbara made our Cokes, giving my mother an indulgent look as she squirted the pump twice over one of the paper cups. All the other customers got glasses if they drank their beverages in the store, but my grandmother had made us promise never to drink from a drugstore glass after she saw an ex-patient of the TB sanatorium drink from one. "Your cups, ladies," said Barbara ironically, setting them ceremoniously before us. She and my mother rolled their eyes at each other. Barbara knew all about the promise; my mother had been forced to tell her after Barbara had once demanded gruffly, "Why can't you all drink out of glasses like everybody else?" But Barbara did not charge us the extra penny for the cups.

We excused ourselves and took our Cokes and adjourned to a booth, where we could have privacy. As there were no other customers, Barbara loped happily back into her rear sanctum of bottles and pills.

At last I had my mother all to myself.

"How was school today?"

"We had field-day practice," I said. "Mother Donovan was showing us how to run the three-legged race and she pulled up her habit and she has really nice legs."

"That doesn't surprise me, somehow. She must have had a real vocation, because she's certainly pretty enough to have gotten married. How are you and Lisa getting along?"

"We're friends, but I hate her. I hate her and she fascinates me at the same time. What has she *got* that makes everybody do what she wants?"

"I've told you what she's got, but you always forget."

"Tell me again. I won't forget."

My mother swung her smooth pageboy forward until it half curtained her face. She peered into the syrupy depths of her spiked Coke and rattled its crushed ice, as if summoning the noisy fragments to speak the secret of Lisa Gudger's popularity. Then, slowly, she raised her face and her beautiful dark blue eyes met mine. I waited, transfixed by our powerful intimacy.

"You are smarter than Lisa Gudger," she began, saying her words slowly. "You have more imagination than Lisa Gudger. And, feature by feature, you are prettier than Lisa Gudger. . . . "

I drank in this litany, which I did remember from before.

"But Lisa likes herself better than you like yourself. Whatever Lisa has, she thinks it's best. And this communicates itself to others, and they follow her."

This was the part I always forgot. I was forgetting it again already. I stared hard at my mother's face. I could see myself reflected in the small pupils, contracted from the bright drugstore lights; I watched the movement of her lips, the way one front tooth crossed slightly over the other. The syllables trying to contain the truth about a girl named Lisa Gudger broke into smaller and smaller particles and escaped into the air as I focused on my mother, trying to show her how well I was listening.

I partially covered up by asking, after it was over, "Do you hate Lu Ann Leach the way I hate Lisa?"

"Now that's an interesting question. Now, Lisa Gudger

would not have had the imagination to ask that question. I do hate Lu Ann, because she's a real threat; she can steal my job. I hate her because she's safe and smug and has a rich father to take care of her if everything else falls through. But Lu Ann Leach does not fascinate me. If I could afford it, I would feel pity for her. See, I've figured her out. When you've figured someone out, they don't fascinate you anymore. Or at least they don't when you've figured out the kind of thing I figured out about her."

"Oh, what? What have you figured out?"

"Shh." My mother looked around towards Barbara's whereabouts. She leaned forward across our table. "Lu Ann hates men, but she knows how to use them. Her hatred gives her a power over them, because she just doesn't care. But I'd rather be myself, without that power, if it means the only way I can have it is to become like Lu Ann Leach. She's thirty, for God's sake, and she still lives with her parents."

"But you live with your mother."

"That's different."

"How is it different?"

My mother got her evasive look. This dialogue had strayed into channels where she hadn't meant it to. "It's a matter of choice versus necessity," she said, going abstract on me.

"You don't hate men, then?" I could swear I'd heard her say she had: the day she got fired from the newspaper, for instance.

"Of course I don't. They're the other half of the world. *You* don't hate men, do you?" She gave me a concerned look.

I thought of Men. There was the priest at school, Father Lilley, whose black skirts whispered upon the gravel; there was Jovan, our black bus driver; there was Hal the handyman who lived in a basement apartment under the fifth-grade classroom with his old father, who drove the bus on Jovan's day off. There was Don Olson, the sailor I had selected as my favorite out of all those who passed our window on their way to see the Gannon girls; I would lie in wait for him at our middle-bedroom window, by the sewing machine, and he would look in and say, "Hi there, beautiful. I might as well just stop here." Which always made me laugh. One day my grandmother caught me in the act of giving him a long list of things I wanted him to buy me in town. "She's just playing, she doesn't mean it," she cried, rushing forward to the window. But he brought me back every item on the list. And there was my father, who had paid us one surprise visit from Florida. His body shook the floor as he strode through our bedroom to wash his hands in the bathroom. He closed the bathroom door behind him and locked it. My mother made me tell everybody he was my uncle, because she had already told people he had been killed in the war: a lie she justified because, long ago, he had stopped sending money, and because people would hire a war widow before they would a divorced woman. Still, I was rather sorry not to be able to claim him; with his good-looking face and sunburnt ankles (he wore no socks, even with his suit), he was much more glamorous than my friends' dull business fathers.

"Sure. I like men," I told my mother in the booth. I was thinking particularly of Don Olson. The Gannon girls were fools to let him get away.

"Well, good," said my mother wryly, shaking her ice in the paper cup. "I wouldn't want *that* on my conscience. That I'd brought you up to hate men."

As if we had conjured him up by our tolerant allowance of his species, a Man materialized in front of our booth.

"Well looky here what I found," he said, his dark brown eyes dancing familiarly at us.

My mother's face went through an interesting series of changes. "Why, what are *you* doing home?" she asked him.

It was Frank, one of her GI students from the year before, who was always coming by our apartment to get extra help on a term paper, or asking her to read a poem aloud so he could understand it better. Once last year, out of politeness, I had asked him to sign my autograph book; but whereas her other GIs had signed things like "Best of luck from your friend Charles," or "To a sweet girl," Frank had written in a feisty slant: "To the best daughter of my best teacher." His page troubled me, with its insinuating inclusion of himself between my mother and me; also, his handwriting made "daughter" look like "daughtlet." It was like glimpsing myself from a sudden unflattering angle: a "daughtlet." And what did he mean *best* daughter? I was my mother's only daughter. At the end of last spring, when I knew he would be transferring to Georgia Tech, I took a razor and carefully excised his page.

"I can't stay out of these mountains," said Frank, reaching for a chair from a nearby table and fitting it backwards between his legs. Barbara looked out from the window of her pharmacy, but when she saw who it was did not bother to come out.

"I should think it would be nice to get out of them for a change," said my mother.

"Well, what's stopping you?" asked Frank, teetering forward dangerously on two legs of his chair. He rested his chin on the dainty wrought-iron back of the chair and assessed us, like a playful animal looking over a fence.

My mother rolled her eyes, gave her crushed ice a fierce shake, and emptied the last shards into her mouth. They talked on for a few more minutes, my mother asking him neutral questions about his engineering courses, and then she stood up. "We've got to be getting back or Mother will start worrying that we've been kidnapped."

He stood up, too, and walked us to the door with his hands in his pockets. "Want a ride?"

"One block? Don't be silly," said my mother.

He got into a little gray coupe and raced the motor unnecessarily, I thought, and then spoiled half of our walk home by driving slowly along beside us with his lights on.

"I wish we could go off sometime, just by ourselves," I said in the few remaining steps of cool darkness. My grandmother had pulled down the shades and turned on the lamp, and we could see the shadow of the top of her head as she sat listening to the radio in her wing chair.

"Well, maybe we can," said my mother. "Let me think about it some."

We went inside and the three of us scrubbed for bed and the women creamed their faces. I got in bed with my mother, and, across the room, my grandmother put on her chin strap and got into her bed. We heard the policeman coming home; his heavy shoes shook the whole house as he took the stairs two at a time. "He has no consideration," came my grandmother's reproachful voice from the dark. There soon followed their colorful exchange of abuses, the wife's shrieks and the policeman's blows. "It's going too far this time," said my grandmother, "he's going to kill her, I'm going to call the police." "You can't call the police on the police, Mother. Just wait, it'll soon be over." And my mother was right: about this time the sound effects subsided into the steady, accelerated knocking against our ceiling which would soon lead to silence. "If Poppy had lived, we would not be subjected to this," moaned my grandmother. "Even he couldn't keep life out," sighed my mother, and turned her back to me for sleep.

Our trip alone together came to pass. I don't know how my mother talked my grandmother out of going with us. She was a respectful daughter, if often impatient, and would not have hurt my grandmother's feelings for the world. And it would have been so natural for my grandmother to come: she was the only one of us who could ride free. The widow of a railroad man, she could go anywhere she wanted on Southern Railways until the end of her life.

But, at any rate, after what I am sure were exhaustive preparations sprinkled with my grandmother's imaginative warnings of all the mishaps that might befall us, we embarked—my mother and I—from Biltmore Train Station south of Asheville. My grandmother surely drove us there in our ten-year-old Oldsmobile, our last relic of prosperity from the days when Poppy lived. I am sure we arrived at the station much too early, and that my grandmother probably cried. Poppy had been working at Biltmore Station when my grandmother met him. His promotions had taken them out of her girlhood mountains to a series of dusty piedmont towns which she had never liked; and now here she was back in the home mountains, in the altitude she loved—but old and without him. My mother and I were going to the first of the towns to which he had been transferred when my mother had been about the age I was now.

I do not remember our leaving from Biltmore Station or our returning to it the next afternoon. That is the strange thing about those twenty-four hours. I have no mental pictures that I can truly claim I inhabited during that time span. Except for that palpable recollection of the golden heat which I have already described, there are no details. No vivid scenes. No dialogues. I know we stayed in a boardinghouse, which my grandmother, I am sure, checked out in advance. It is possible that the owner might have been an old acquaintance, some lady fallen on harder times, like ourselves. Was this boardinghouse in the same neighborhood as the house where my mother had lived? I'm sure we must have walked by that house. After all, wasn't the purpose of our trip—other than going somewhere by ourselves—to pay a pilgrimage to the scene of my mother's happy youth? Did we, then, also walk past her school? It seems likely, but I don't remember. I do have a vague remembrance of "downtown," where, I am sure, we must have walked up and down streets, in and out of stores, perhaps buying something, some small thing that I wanted; I am sure we must have stopped in some drugstore and bought two Cokes in paper cups.

Did the town still have streetcars running on tracks, jangling their bells; or was it that my mother described them so well, the streetcars that she used to ride when she lived there as a girl?

I do not know.

We must have eaten at least three meals, perhaps four, but I don't remember eating them.

We must have slept in the same bed. Even if there had

been two beds in the room, I would, sooner or later, have crawled in with my mother. I always slept with her.

My amnesia comes to a stunning halt the moment the trip is over. My grandmother has picked us up from Biltmore Station and there I am, on Charlotte Street again, in the bedroom *née* dining room of the old Piping Hot.

It is late afternoon. The sun is still shining, but the blue atmosphere of our mountains has begun to gather. The predominant color of this memory is blue. I am alone in the bedroom, lying catty-cornered across the bed with my head at the foot; I am looking out the window next to the one where I always used to lie in wait for the sailor, Don Olson, on his way to call on the Gannon girls. The bedspread on which I am lying is blue, a light blue, with a raised circular pattern in white; it smells clean. Everything in this room, in this apartment, smells clean and womanly. There is the smell of linen which has lain in lavender-scented drawers; the smell of my mother's Tweed perfume, which she dabs on lightly before going to teach at the college; the acerbic, medicinal smell of my grandmother's spirits of ammonia, which she keeps in a small green cut-glass bottle and sniffs whenever she feels faint; the smell of a furniture polish, oil-based, which my grandmother rubs, twice a week, into our numerous pieces of furniture.

Where are they? Perhaps my grandmother is already in the kitchen, starting our early supper, hardly able to contain her relief that our trip without her is over. Perhaps my mother is out by herself in the late sunshine, taking one of her walks to clear her head; or maybe she is only in the next room, reading the Sunday paper, grading student themes for the following day, or simply gazing out at the same view I was gazing at, thinking her own thoughts.

I looked out at the end of that afternoon. The cars were turning from Charlotte Street into Kimberly, making a whishing sound. I could see the corner wall of the drugstore. But there was no chance of going there after supper, because we had already been away for more time than ever before.

An irremediable sadness gathered about me. *This time yesterday, we were there,* I thought; *and now we are here and it's all over.* How could that be? For the first time, I hovered, outside my own body, in that ghostly synapse between the anticipated event and its aftermath. I knew what all adults know: that "this time yesterday" and "this time tomorrow" are often more real than the protracted now.

It's over, I thought; and perhaps, at the blue hour, I abandoned childhood for the vaguely perceived kingdom of my future. But the knot in my chest that I felt then—its exact location and shape—I feel now, whenever I dredge up that memory.

A lot of things were over, a lot of things did come to an end that spring. My mother announced that she would not be going back to teach at the college. (Lu Ann Leach took her place, staying on into old age—until the college was incorporated into the state university.) And then, on an evening in which my grandmother rivaled the policeman's wife in her abandoned cries of protest, my mother went out for a walk and reappeared with Frank, and they announced to us that they were married. The three of us left that night, but now we are talking about a different three: my mother, Frank, and me. All that summer we lived high on a mountain—a mountain that, ironically, overlooked the red-tiled roofs of the Manor Hotel. Our mountain was called Beaucatcher, and our address was the most romantic I've ever had: 1000 Sunset Drive. Again we were in a house with others, but these others were a far cry from the panicked widows and lonely mothers of Charlotte Street. Downstairs lived a nightclub owner and his wife and her son (my age) from an earlier marriage; upstairs lived a gregarious woman of questionable virtue. One night, a man on the way upstairs blundered by accident into my room—I now had a room, almost as large as the one we three had shared in the life below—and Frank was so incensed that he rigged up a complicated buzzer system: if my door opened during the night, the buzzer-alarm would go off, even if it was I who opened it. That summer I made friends with the nightclub owner's stepson, learned to shoot out streetlights with my own homemade slingshot, and, after seeing a stray dog dripping blood, was told about the realities of sex. First by the boy, the stepson, in his own words; then, in a cleaned-up version, by my mother. I invited Lisa Gudger up to play with me; we got into Frank's bottle of Kentucky Tavern and became roaring drunk; and I beat her up. My mother called Mrs. Gudger to come and get Lisa, and then hurriedly sewed onto Lisa's ripped blouse all the buttons I had torn off.

My grandmother, who had screamed she would die if we left her, lived on through the long summer. And through another summer, during which we were reconciled. Frank had quit Georgia Tech to marry my mother, and worked as a trainee in Kress's. Within a year, my mother and Frank had moved back to the old Piping Hot. They now had the former apartment of the policeman and his wife. My grandmother slept on in her bed downstairs, and I divided my time between them.

A few years later, we left my grandmother again. Frank was being transferred to a town on the other side of the mountain. One of those hot little towns a thousand feet below. After we had been away for some months, my grandmother shocked us all by getting her first job at the age most people were thinking about retiring. At the time most people were coming home from work, my grandmother pinned on her hat and put on her gloves and hid all of Poppy's gold pieces and his ring and his watch in a secret fold of her purse, and took the empty bus downtown to her job. She worked as night housemother at the YWCA residence for working girls. It was a job made in heaven for her: she sat up waiting for the girls. If they came in after midnight, they had to ring and she let them in with an admonition. After three admonitions she reported them to the directress, a woman she despised. We heard all about the posturings and deceptions of this directress, a Mrs. Malt, whenever we visited. My grandmother's politics had gone beyond the lobby into the working world; she was able to draw Social Security because of it.

When our brand-new "nuclear family" arrived in the little lowland town where Frank was to be the assistant manager of Kress's, we moved into a housing development. Our yard had no grass, only an ugly red clay slope that bled into the walkway every time it rained. "I guess I'll never know what it's like to have grass in the front yard," I said, in the sorrowful, affronted, doom-laden voice of my grandmother. "Hell, honey," replied Frank with his mountain twang, "if you want grass in this world, you've got to plant it." I forgive him for his treachery now, as I recall the thrill of those first tiny green spikes, poking up out of that raw, red soil.

Years and years passed. I was home on a visit to my mother and Frank and their little daughter and their two baby sons. "You know, it's awful," I told Mother, "but I can't remember a single thing about that trip you and I took that time on the train. You know, to Greenville. Do you remember it?"

"Of course I do," she said, her eyes going that distant blue. "Mother took us to the station and we had a lovely lunch in the dining car, and then we went to all my old haunts, and we stayed the night at Mrs. ———'s, and then we got back on the train and came home. It was a lovely time."

"Well, I wish I could remember more about it."

"What else would you like to know?" asked Frank, who had been listening, his eyes as warm and eager to communicate as my mother's were cool and elegiac.

But she suddenly got an odd look on her face. "Frank," she said warningly.

"Well hell, Kathleen." He hunched his shoulders like a rebuked child.

"Frank, please," my mother said.

"Well, I was there, too," he flared up.

"You were not! That was another time we met in

Greenville." But her eyes were sending desperate signals and her mouth had twisted into a guilty smirk.

"The hell it was. The second time we went, it was to get married."

Then he looked at me, those brown eyes swimming with their eager truths. She had turned away, and I didn't want to hear. Fat chance. "I drove down," he said. "I followed your train. You were sick on the train and you had to have a nap when you got there. I waited till your mother met me on the corner after you fell asleep. And then after you fell asleep that night. Well, dammit, Kathleen," he said to the cool profile turned away from him, "it's the truth. Did the truth ever hurt anybody?"

He went on to me, almost pleading for me to see his side. "I don't know what we would have done without you," he said. "You were our little chaperon, in a way. Don't you *know* how impossible it was, in those days, ever to get her alone?"

Gail Godwin describes how this story began:

"I was in a "resting phase," having recently finished a novel I had been working on for three years, and it was a winter afternoon in February, just getting dark. I was reading a story by Mark Helprin, "A Vermont Tale," and when I came to the last scene between the boy and his grandmother and read the words, "For reasons I could not discern, I began to cry," something started hurting me but in an interesting way. I sat very still in the chair and kept repeating to myself 'For reasons I could not discern . . . For reasons I could not discern . . . " *Something from my own experience lay just beneath the surface of that phrase, but I couldn't get to it.*

I didn't know why, but the story made me want to write a matching story. An echoing story. But an echo of what? Of some kind of . . . betrayal, that was what.

A betrayal that wouldn't be recognized as such until years later, by which time the narrator, the "betrayed," would somehow have incorporated the betrayal into her destiny. Would even have come to love *the betrayal, painful as it was to acknowledge it, because it had become recognizable to her as an important part of her personal myth.*

In such a gingerly fashion, as a timid person climbs backward down a ladder, clinging tightly to the sides, taking one rung at a time and trying not to think of the distance to the bottom, I descended into the repressed memory of the train trip. Once that *was recalled, and I allowed myself to feel the exact quality of sorrow I had felt as a child when the trip was over, I could begin to construct, in an almost joyous mood, the events that must have led up to it and to its fateful aftermath. And I could compress and exaggerate and invent, wherever the truth of the story—always more important than the literal truth—demanded it.*

I suppose I love this story most among my recent ones because of the companionable way it suggested itself to me through the work of another writer. I like the idea of freemasonry among writers. I also like the thought that somebody will be reading a story of mine some dark winter afternoon and suddenly receive from it the gift of a lost memory—or the spark for a new story. Which, in turn, will inspire another reader on another dark winter afternoon, etc."

Gail Godwin's short fiction has been collected in Dream Children *and* Mr. Bedford and the Muses. *She grew up in Asheville, North Carolina, and has taught English and creative writing at the University of Illinois at Urbana, the Iowa Writers' Workshop, Vassar College, and Columbia University. Her novels include* The Perfectionists, Glass People, The Odd Woman, Violet Clay, A Mother and Two Daughters, *and* The Finishing School. *She lives in Woodstock, New York.*

First published in 1984 in Antaeus.

to order use coupon on next page.